KILLINGLY

ALSO BY THE AUTHOR

Alcestis

KILLINGLY

—

Katharine Beutner

Published by
Soho Press, Inc.
227 W 17th Street
New York, NY 10011

Library of Congress Cataloging-in-Publication Data

Names: Beutner, Katharine, author.
Title: Killingly / Katharine Beutner.
Description: New York, NY : Soho Crime 2023.
Identifiers: LCCN 2022041935 |

ISBN 978-1-64129-571-0
eISBN 978-1-64129-438-6

Classification: LCC PS3602.E828 K55 2023 | DDC 813'.6—dc23
LC record available at https://lccn.loc.gov/2022041935

Interior and endpaper design by Janine Agro

Printed in the United States of America

10 9 8 7 6 5 4 3 2 1

For my mother, the artist

—

*. . . the science of life . . . is a superb and dazzlingly
lighted hall which may be reached only by passing through
a long and ghastly kitchen.*

—Claude Bernard, *An Introduction to the Study of
Experimental Medicine* (transl. by H. C. Greene), 1865

—

Vivisection is an unmanly crime.

—Alan Mott-Ring, MD, Arlington Heights, MA, in
*The Report of the American Humane Association on Vivisection in
America, Adopted at Minneapolis, Minn., Sept. 26, 1895*

—

All classes have some little lamb / Who loves to go to school

—Written on a notecard found in the 1897 scrapbook of
Katharine Shearer, Mount Holyoke College student

KILLINGLY

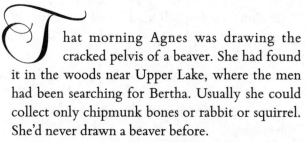

That morning Agnes was drawing the cracked pelvis of a beaver. She had found it in the woods near Upper Lake, where the men had been searching for Bertha. Usually she could collect only chipmunk bones or rabbit or squirrel. She'd never drawn a beaver before.

The men were still searching for Bertha. Agnes had wondered, briefly, what else they might find in the ponds. Perhaps there were other girls who had vanished in the College woods, other bones tangled in the roots of the pines along the grassy edges of the water. The bow of the clavicle, the bowl of the pelvis. She had wanted to see. But it was habit now to keep to herself, to appear as unobjectionable as possible. Mute as the white cross hung upon her wall and banal as the cross-stitched hymns beside it. She'd been spared freckles and red or black hair; hers was dark brown like soaked wood and lay flatter against her head than was fashionable. She and Bertha simply scraped their damp hair back after a washing—because dowdiness was permissible, even godly. Dowdiness had been a shield for them both.

Agnes had a narrow room on the third floor of Porter Hall, a slim little desk and chair designed for the ministers' daughters who thronged the College. Bertha had fit these chairs well. Agnes herself was not narrow. She was a broad spare girl of twenty, trim but tall and square-shouldered and square-hipped. She never drew self-portraits, though she was a fine draughtswoman in the anatomical mode. She did not wish to look at herself long enough to see the truth of her body, how its overlapping rectangles would sit like bare fenced pastures on the page: Agnes Sullivan, all enclosure.

The girls on her hall usually left her alone, as they had left Bertha alone, because they disliked her almost as much as they had disliked Bertha. They still disliked Bertha, in the midst of their fluttering about her mysterious fate. Their dull antipathy did not bother Agnes. Being alone meant that she could concentrate on her work. But Agnes could not trust, any longer, that she would be left alone. Not after what she had done.

There were certain things Bertha had told Agnes that she might still need to do.

Bertha had said: *You must lie. No one knows anything, no one can prove anything. Just us. So you can't—you can't give in. You must go on. Be strong.*

Bertha said, as she kissed Agnes's hand: *I don't want you to leave college. But you might have to.*

And Agnes said: *No. I won't.*

Bertha had been missing for one full day. Agnes bent closer to her sketch. Her pencil feathered in a shadow on the page: the fissure in the beaver's bone, where its strength had failed.

WHILE AGNES DREW, the Reverend John Hyrcanus Mellish and his older daughter, Florence, stood outside the president's office in a dark anteroom with thick red carpets that made the place feel muffled, like a silent cavern of some massive body. The building, Mary Lyon Hall, was massive, too—another collegiate Gothic cathedral of rough red stone with a grand clock tower that pierced the gray sky. Florence found herself struggling to breathe inside its bulk. She had been struggling to breathe since the telegram arrived.

Florence and her father had taken the train up from Killingly through Worcester shortly after dawn. The Reverend had dozed against the window while Florence sat straight beside him in miserable anticipation, her stockinged knees thick lumps under her skirt, and drummed her heels against one another to keep blood moving in her feet. They'd changed trains again in Springfield, in a station astringent with the smell of urine even in the chilly weather. A filthy boy had tried to lift Florence's purse and cried when she shoved him back, and Florence had thought, *Nobody is getting what he wants today.*

Despite the cold she had taken off her gloves and spent the last hour of the journey picking at the base of her left thumbnail until it bled—an old, bad habit to keep panic at bay. Even in the dim light of the anteroom, now, she could see a brown dapple on the green fabric of her glove.

Mrs. Mead opened the office door herself: a sturdy older woman in a black gabardine dress and a starched blouse with a fringed lace collar that nearly touched her prominent ears. Her gaze was clear and cold. She couldn't have been more different from delicate Mrs. Ward, who had been the College's president in Florence's time. Florence remembered waiting outside Mrs. Ward's office on a sunny May morning, preparing to make her apologies for her departure from Mount Holyoke after only one year. She had blamed her mother's poor health, and Mrs. Ward, a trusting soul, had been most understanding.

"Miss Mellish, Reverend Mellish, come in," Mrs. Mead said, shortly, and waited for Florence to settle her father in a chair. "I am very sorry for your distress. I will tell you all I know."

There wasn't much to tell and Mrs. Mead made short work of it. She described the dragging of the lakes and the teams of searchers in the woods: men were walking the banks of the Connecticut River in case Bertha had gone out on one of her long hikes alone and tumbled in; the police were finding a Parrott gun to fire over the water, to raise the corpse with the force of its concussion. Mrs. Mead said "the corpse" quite calmly, with no gulping or quavering. "Of course," she added, and here she seemed to warm, the way an iron warms in fire, "there is still reason to hope that she has not drowned—that we will find her alive, soon."

As they exited the building, the crisp air forced a gasp from Florence's lungs. It was not a sob. She would not allow that.

Her father tugged at her elbow.

"I want to look over the campus," the Reverend said, his gaze tracking up Prospect Hill, the promontory that stretched along the College's eastern border. From there, you could command a view toward both Upper and Lower Lake, surveying the manicured trees and impressive structures of the freshly expanded campus. She knew what he wanted. He was hungry to discern Bertha camouflaged like a dryad among those trees and buildings. Desperate to search her out, drag her away from the College, just as Florence had once been dragged away.

"She's not here," she whispered, knowing he wouldn't hear.

But it was easier to obey than to argue, most of the time. They made their slow way to the bridge across the brook at Lower Lake, and with each step Florence heard Mrs. Mead's voice. *The corpse*, she thought, *the corpse*.

Even in her time at the school they'd told the story of the Lady of Lower Lake, a senior so distraught over her failing grades that she'd flung herself to a hanging death from this bridge while stabbing a dagger into her own heart. As a young woman Florence had thought this tale comically baroque, especially its coda—the voice of the dead girl echoing from beneath the bridge when a classmate crossed it. *Help me*, the girl had cried, *I'm down here*, while her body cooled in the pond water.

As they crossed the bridge now Florence felt as if her whole body had opened wide like the bell of an ear trumpet, attuned to every sound. A kind of listening that stalled the breath. Once Florence had been practiced at this kind of listening. She had imagined, more than once, how Bertha would sound when pleading for help and what she would do to rescue Bertha. She'd spent the train ride from Killingly rehearsing those visions in new detail. Over and over she'd enfolded that conjured-up Bertha in her arms, smelled the grassy tang of sweat along her hairline, squeezed her fierce little body—and in every fantasy Bertha would finally struggle free of Florence's arms and pat Florence's cheek and smile, just as she had as a baby.

But no sounds came from below the bridge. Just absence, Bertha's absence, echoing.

Florence's father was a husk beside her. He clung to her round arm and puffed weak steam into the air as they ascended the slope. Once he had been an imposing man, though he had never been the sort of minister who thundered from the pulpit. Instead he'd merely looked at you with those flat brown eyes, looked and put his hand on your shoulder, and pressed a firm thumb into the divot below your collar-bone. He had been compelling.

On this campus he drew eyes only because he was a man and Bertha's father. In the hours since they'd learned that Bertha was gone, the young women of Mount Holyoke had begun creeping around the cold campus with books clasped to quivering bosoms. The girls directed polite smiles at the Mellishes, but their eyes showed wide and white as Florence and the Reverend passed by. She could almost hear their silent prayers: for Bertha's safety, of course, but really to ward off loss and threat. That Sunday's mandatory prayer meeting would have an unusual fervency and more clutching of hands than was common. At church, Bible study, their YWCA sessions—all day the girls would pass tremors from palm to clammy palm.

Florence and her father limped up the walk to the grand gazebo at the top of the hill, another addition. Empty now, but big enough for ten girls to picnic under its shingled roof, or twenty if they were cozy. Florence had heard a girl call it the Pepper Box. The Reverend leaned against the gazebo's steps to catch his breath, and Florence turned away to look out over the campus. The morning sun softened the harsh shapes of the new buildings. If she had not been compressing an endless shriek in her belly all would have appeared tranquil and safe. The boathouse, the two tree-lined avenues and winding gravel paths, the wrought iron lampposts, the few streets of South Hadley past the College gates—and then the woods rolling endlessly into the distance, and Bertha lost somewhere within them.

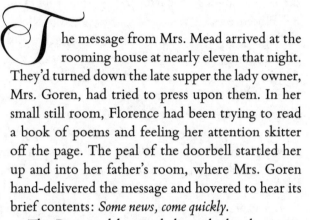

2

The message from Mrs. Mead arrived at the rooming house at nearly eleven that night. They'd turned down the late supper the lady owner, Mrs. Goren, had tried to press upon them. In her small still room, Florence had been trying to read a book of poems and feeling her attention skitter off the page. The peal of the doorbell startled her up and into her father's room, where Mrs. Goren hand-delivered the message and hovered to hear its brief contents: *Some news, come quickly.*

The Reverend lectured through the short carriage ride back to campus. He was trying to tell Florence that she should not worry overmuch. Bertha's disappearance was a matter of faith, like any trial. "Florence," he said, "if God wills that she be found, she will be found. We must not fail in our duties because our afflictions increase. God blesses the open-hearted."

Florence was no defiant agnostic, as Bertha was. Bertha liked to flash her eyes covertly at Florence during John's tirades about the Satanic malignancy he saw in modern society and the duties of a faithful congregation. Bertha liked to question her father endlessly on what she called "dogma"; Florence preferred to think of God as a light so powerful not even the Reverend's sins could blot it out. But to hear her father make himself a martyr, to cast Bertha as a sacrifice in service of his piety—

"We are not living in a parable, Father. She's in

danger. She could be sick. Someone might have taken her. I won't fold my hands in prayer when I could be searching—"

"Bertha," John said out of shocked habit, used to rebuking the other daughter for irreverence, then caught himself. "That is—Florence—"

"Don't speak to me," she said, quietly, and tucked her gloved hands away when he fumbled to take one in his own.

The anteroom was empty, their footfalls deadened by its thick carpet. Mrs. Mead looked up as they entered her shadowy office. She was alone; she was frowning. "Reverend, Miss Mellish. I won't waste your time with pleasantries. A report has just come in of a girl in Boston, at the City Hospital, calling herself Bertha Miller. I have no other information. If you can travel to Boston now, the police there will take you to her."

Dread and relief thrashed around in Florence's chest like a pair of stunned fish. "Of course," she said, "we'll leave—"

"No." John looked to Mrs. Mead. "I will go alone. Dr. Hammond will be here soon. He will direct you."

Henry Hammond, their family doctor, was the first person her father had contacted when the telegram arrived from the College about Bertha's disappearance. The Reverend had ordered the bewildered delivery boy to go next to Hammond's house, to deputize the doctor to seek out the South Hadley sheriff while they went straight to campus. Florence had been left to pack furiously while John sat reading his Bible, seeking what guidance it could offer in the case of a lost child. Now she was to stay here under Hammond's direction while her father went to rescue Bertha?

Florence's feelings were scattered and terrible, like the mess of little foul creatures that scuttle out from an overturned log on the forest floor. She *had* to go to Boston. She had to.

"You'll need me to help." Her throat clotted. "Bertha will need me."

"Florence," the Reverend Mellish said. "No."

"I must know if—"

"Florence."

She looked to Mrs. Mead for support, but the woman's expression was opaque—no motherly comfort to be found. Florence wanted to howl. But instead she stood with eyes downcast beside her father as he made arrangements with Mrs. Mead to travel alone.

Florence accompanied the Reverend to the tiny Holyoke station to catch the three A.M. Boston & Maine and half lifted him up the rail coach's narrow steel steps with the help of the timid young policeman who'd driven them. The skies were black as tar and the platform dim and quiet, lantern-lit.

She returned to the rooming house and tried to rest. In her rattled dreams circled specters of Bertha's face: A Bertha with bared teeth and wildcat eyes, like her uncle David in the asylum just before his death. A Bertha, anguished, with some criminal's hands on her dear body. A white-faced Bertha whose closed lids were sluiced with stream water and hair thickened with a coronet of muddy leaves.

AGNES DID NOT DREAM that night—or if she did, we cannot see it. Her mind was segmented as the chambers of a shell and similarly armored. Unless we mean to pry her open, oyster-like, there are things we cannot know about Agnes Sullivan until we have traversed those chambers.

There were many things no one at Mount Holyoke College knew about Agnes.

That she was born in a skip behind the factory where her mother Nora wove cloth. As a baby Agnes had been unrewarding, silent and stiff in Nora's arms.

That her sister, Adelaide, was born in Agnes's own small bed, not the one Nora sometimes shared with her sot of a husband. The sisters would share the bed until Agnes left for college. Slowly, she would grow accustomed to Adelaide's body alongside hers, the only embrace she'd ever welcomed besides Bertha's. When Agnes was alone in the room—which was rare—she would sometimes

strip back the thin sheet and curl herself into the bloodstain
Adelaide's birth had left on the mattress ticking, like the print of
a massive spread-winged bird, and spread her fingers out upon it.

That their father had died of his habitual drunkenness when
Agnes was seven and Adelaide four, with two babies born dead
between them. Her mother didn't have the money to bury him,
so Agnes had to help carry him down the tenement stairs from
their third-floor room and roll him into the gutter, where the
early morning patrol would haul him away for burial on the city's
charity. Two days later Agnes overheard the neighbor women
murmuring about how long the city kept bodies waiting to be
claimed. She had despised her father, but for four months she
had nightmares about his round white belly puffing in some city
morgue basement, his fingers swelling, his red beard inching out
into tangles. Then the nightmares stopped and she hardly spared
him a thought again, asleep or awake.

That Agnes learned on charity, just as her father was buried on
it. She had been the best student in her grade in the local public
school and won small scholarships for her recitations: nothing
extravagant, but enough to pay for Sunday beef dinners during
one cold winter and to buy her and her sister new boots in another.

That Miss Kelly, a once-Catholic Congregationalist who lived
up the lane in the nicer part of their neighborhood, had read the
tiny item about those scholarships in the *Herald* and had looked
up Agnes's mother to offer her guidance. Miss Kelly was plain
and small and terribly freckled, but to Agnes she also seemed
bright against the drab walls of their apartment, lit up by her
calm certainty in her own talents, her earnest desire to better
Agnes, to school her. It was Miss Kelly who thought of sending
her to Mount Holyoke, her own alma mater. Miss Kelly taught
her to scour the Irish from her speech and warned her that she'd
have to hide her faith at the College. She didn't know that what
Agnes really worshipped was the earthly body, its strung tendons
and ligaments, its stony structures. "It will be worth it, Agnes

dear, I promise you," she said, clasping Agnes's broad hand with her tiny fingers. "It is the best education you could receive. It will do everything for you."

That her sister Adelaide fell pregnant while working as a housemaid for the Allens in the fall of Agnes's freshman year and tried to hang herself from the coat hook in their apartment after Mrs. Allen threw her out. When Nora found her she was half-strangled, her heart hardly beating. She lost the baby—poor lamb, said all Nora's friends, though they were grateful, too. Nora wouldn't have to choose whether to feed herself or her grandchild, whether or not to abandon the little thing to Saint Mary's Asylum, which was as good as killing it with her own hands. But Adelaide was, as a result, not quite herself. She could no longer manage anything more complicated than piece-work done at their kitchen table; she limped, she forgot how to read. Miss Kelly no longer talked of recommending Adelaide for admission to Mount Holyoke as she had Agnes. So Agnes resolved to do everything for Adelaide herself, if the College could not.

That Nora still worked in the same factory to support herself and Adelaide, though she was forty-six and not hearty and surrounded by girls a third her age doing the same work faster and better.

That Agnes rarely had money to send home and prided herself on never asking for any.

That she worked tirelessly on her drawings not only because she sought perfection for its own sake but because she thought she might be able to work as a medical draughtsman if she could train her hand to be precise enough. Already, the other girls paid her to correct their lab sketches. Her dream was to be a surgeon; she would apply to medical school, and she thought she might even earn a spot. But she had learned to be practical; she had learned always to have two routes of escape.

That she had only been kissed once, by a boy from her school who trapped her in an alley when she was walking home late from Miss Kelly's and pressed her into the wall and put his dirty hand up her skirt and thrust his dirty fingers into her as if she were a glove. As if she were water, all give and no resistance. As if she were nothing. His mouth tasted of blood and rot. She cut the back of her head on the brick getting away from him—but she cut his cheek with her knife.

That she was still prepared to marry, if she had to, to provide for her mother and Adelaide.

But that she was determined it would not be necessary.

BERTHA KNEW ALL THESE things. But Bertha was not at the College—not anymore.

3

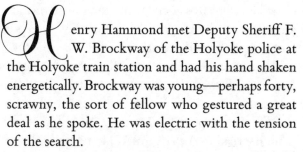enry Hammond met Deputy Sheriff F. W. Brockway of the Holyoke police at the Holyoke train station and had his hand shaken energetically. Brockway was young—perhaps forty, scrawny, the sort of fellow who gestured a great deal as he spoke. He was electric with the tension of the search.

Hammond had not known if the local police would welcome his presence, given that he was not a member of the family, but Brockway seemed relieved to deal with him rather than the distraught sister or aged father. "Not what you want to discuss with the family, the sort of trials that might lead a respectable girl to commit a desperate act," Brockway said as they hurried to the police cart, and Hammond suppressed a flicker of rage.

They rolled through browning fields as Brockway blathered about how they'd found the Parrott gun, which had been sheltering in the barn of a Northampton reservist tasked with maintaining it. They were going to meet his convoy of men and artillery and horses at the Connecticut River near Smith's Ferry, where a brook entered the river and pooled under a small bridge. It was Brockway's opinion that if Bertha Mellish had gone into the water, whether willingly or not, she was most likely to have done so near this bridge and this pool. If her body was trapped in the pool's silty hollow or bogged down somewhere nearby in the curls of the river's course, the cannonball's force might dislodge it.

"Yes, of course," Hammond said, only half listening. He was certain Bertha had not gone into any water, in this river or elsewhere, but it was clear that the police meant to focus their attention on the Connecticut until they were satisfied of that fact as well. "Are there other leads in the case?"

"A man came to the station right after we put the word out." Brockway flicked the reins once more against the backs of the two cart horses. "Said he saw her on the road to Mount Holyoke the day she disappeared. My men found some boot prints going from the road to the riverbank. No tracks back. Little feet, like a child's, almost."

Her sweet small feet. Hammond felt a frisson of dread and suppressed that, too. "How do you know the prints weren't old?"

Brockway shrugged. "Difficult to tell with the freeze and thaw. It's been bright this month. Unusual."

As they arrived at the river Hammond took a moment to set himself right—smoothing his hair under his hat, polishing his glasses. "You must tell me how I can help," he said to the deputy sheriff as they climbed down from the cart. Brockway might've been callow but he was in charge of this search, and Hammond had no standing to question the police's methods. He was only John Mellish's representative, as far as they knew.

Brockway gave him an unseemly grin. He was too young to have been in the War, so of course he found the cannon-firing exciting. "Just stand back, Doctor."

The gun was manned by an elderly ex-sergeant from the Tenth Massachusetts Battery, who talked to the horses as softly as he must have at Ream's Station, and by four old cannoneers, one still a coal deliveryman, one a retired fireman, one a druggist, and one too shambling from years of drink to show any evidence of his profession. Hammond spoke with them all as they readied themselves. There was comfort in talking with fellow veterans, and he had the greatest respect for artillerymen; in battle, they might have been based behind the lines, but their work made them targets for every galloping bravo on the field. The ex-sergeant, he discovered, had been an insurance man. Hammond watched him survey his comrades and linger on the last man with a regard that suggested a blunt professional pity toward someone he would not, under any inducement, have sold a life policy.

"You knew the girl," the ex-sergeant said to Hammond as they watched two of the other men worm out the bore and swab it, set the range, and aim.

"Yes," he said, suddenly stricken, "yes," and stepped back to let them fire.

The ex-sergeant pulled the lanyard and sent the round crashing into the underbrush on the opposite side of the river. It wasn't just a boom; the gun had a shrill top note, a ripping shriek and whistle, and a cavernous depth to its report that settled in the men's bellies. They'd grown used to it during the war and they did not flinch. But they sympathized with the shying horses and the terrified crows scattering from the woods on the near riverbank, and Hammond, standing with the deputy sheriff's searchers, wondered how many old men in the valley had just lifted their heads from their work and looked toward a window or the horizon, seeking out the danger that matched that sound.

He couldn't escape the feeling that the men had just sounded Bertha's death knell. A tremendous echoing call along the floor of the valley, bigger in the ears than any church bell. Everyone at the College must have heard it. Florence Mellish must have heard it.

The sergeant watched the policemen pick their way along the brown banks of the river and peer into its murk. The cannoneers weren't needed any longer—one shot would have to be sufficient, as there were farms nearby and more blasts might upset the livestock—but they stood around the rifle for a while, talking to each other and the horses, until it was clear that no bodies were going to rise up from the river's depths. Then they packed up all the rifle's gear, the sight and the swab and the wire, the lanyard and the firing table, and turned their backs on the river.

Nearby, the police dragged chains up Batchelder Brook for several hours before being thwarted by ice and came up with nothing useful—some trash and a mess of branches and leaves, a deer's half-consumed carcass. Later they dragged the river with grappling hooks, too, and stretched a net across it miles downstream. They drew down the lakes on campus and found a number of glinting hairpins, a smashed hat that might once have been blue, a belt buckle, a cluster of old bricks, half a teacup, the nickel-plated clasp from a handbag, and the sodden remains of several textbooks still bound together with a leather strap, probably thrown in jubilantly by a Holyoke girl at the end of term.

There was no hint of Bertha among the wet weeds.

4

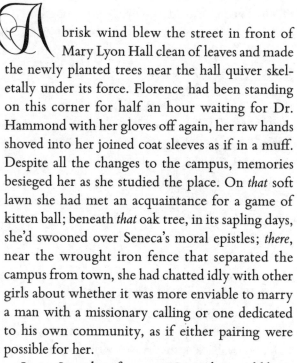brisk wind blew the street in front of Mary Lyon Hall clean of leaves and made the newly planted trees near the hall quiver skeletally under its force. Florence had been standing on this corner for half an hour waiting for Dr. Hammond with her gloves off again, her raw hands shoved into her joined coat sleeves as if in a muff. Despite all the changes to the campus, memories besieged her as she studied the place. On *that* soft lawn she had met an acquaintance for a game of kitten ball; beneath *that* oak tree, in its sapling days, she'd swooned over Seneca's moral epistles; *there*, near the wrought iron fence that separated the campus from town, she had chatted idly with other girls about whether it was more enviable to marry a man with a missionary calling or one dedicated to his own community, as if either pairing were possible for her.

It was Saturday afternoon. Soon she would have to return to work, whether they had found Bertha or not. A substitute would cover her classes this week, but the principal's indulgence was limited even in cases of emergency. Florence had left an unread pile of essays on the desk in her bedroom at home, with a note imploring her mother, Sarah, not to touch them.

If Florence was lucky, their neighbor Mrs. Christopher, whom she'd begged to stay with her mother, would tire Sarah out with talk of fine-work and thread and the inconsequential town gossip they both delighted in. If Florence proved unlucky, her mother might not be satisfied with dull Mrs. Christopher, might go wandering about the house, since the Reverend was away, and injure herself. She had been unsteady on her feet for decades, but the last year had been the worst: six spills, with the bruises from the last still pale iodine yellow on her papery skin. Sometimes Sarah seemed to fall on purpose, to force the Reverend's attention or Florence's. Sometimes she seemed to have no more intention than a moth fluttering about in a bare closet.

They had not informed Sarah of Bertha's disappearance yet. "When we return," her father had said, "if we must, we'll tell her then," and Florence found herself in rare agreement with him.

Students passed while Florence waited, twenty or thirty of them. Those in groups fell silent as they approached her, and all the girls bent their heads to avoid meeting her eyes. They were so lovely, so healthy and fine in their variety that her heart stung to see them. She studied a pair of elegant cheekbones; a broad hand clamped around the spine of a textbook; a tendril of hair caught in a girl's blinking eyelashes; a nervous little mouth not yet thinned, as it would thin, with age.

In a fortnight, Florence would turn forty-one. She'd be back in Killingly, back at the school with her students, back in the dull dreadful house in the evenings with her mother and father. These girls would still be here, still growing, like vines tacked to a trellis. And where would Bertha be?

There had been no news from her father, nothing about the girl in the city who called herself Bertha, though he ought to have arrived in the city hours ago. She told herself that he must not have seen the girl yet. The police were busy, and he would want to be sure before he sent word.

The wheels of Dr. Hammond's carriage rattled in the dust as it drew near. He must have seen her standing there, but the carriage stopped a good twenty feet away. She tried to control the icy surge of disgust she felt at the sight of his genial face and neat whiskers and at the alacrity with which he swung down from the carriage. She had expected a somber expression in these circumstances, but instead he looked almost cheerily determined, as if his presence would be all that was required to sort out the horrible mess of Bertha's absence. If only God had not taken Justin Hammond, this Dr. Hammond's father, in '73—if he had lived just four years longer—she would not find herself beholden to this particular condescending man, who'd taken such a possessive interest in Bertha and kept himself so close to the family that Florence could not see how he would ever be extricated from their lives.

"Miss Mellish," Dr. Hammond said as he approached. Cordial, as if they were meeting at a dinner party and about to have a pleasant chat. "I am so sorry. I've come as quickly as I could. Your father is in Boston, I understand? At the hospital?"

"Dr. Hammond," she answered, shifting back from the billow of his cologne. "There was a girl admitted as Bertha Miller, so the Boston police notified the College. But he has not sent any word since he arrived this morning. I doubt that it is her."

He grasped her forearm and she jerked unhappily. She always aimed to avoid his touch. "You mustn't worry. I'm here now to help you find her. I've just come from Brockway, the deputy sheriff. They've been searching the river. No sign, of course."

She imagined her arm heating until it scorched his palm through the sleeve of her coat. Still he did not release her, and she did not wrest her arm from his grasp, because he was right. His presence mattered here as it mattered everywhere. He was a respected widower in his mid-fifties, and she was the spinster sister—and she would do anything for Bertha, even let this man think himself her keeper and look at her with his pitying eyes.

"We should talk to the girls," she said when he finally did let go. "There's one, Agnes, who seems to be closest with her. And a girl named Mabel, Mrs. Mead says, that Bertha asked to go walking on Thursday. What did my father tell you?"

"Very little. His letter was . . ."

She waited.

"Confusing," Dr. Hammond said, after a moment. "It concerned me. As his physician. Are you sure it was wise for him to go to Boston alone?"

A disbelieving laugh caught in her throat. "Hardly. But it was not my choice. He would not let me go with him."

"I see." Of course he didn't see. He thought her too harsh and unloving to her father. He was hypothesizing, as Bertha would've said haughtily, based on incomplete information. "Brockway told me the police found footprints at the river, but the gun—There was nothing."

He looked toward the river—almost involuntarily, it seemed— as he spoke. Florence said nothing. She had heard the cannon fire. She knew what it was meant to do. But what good could come of thinking of Bertha's body floating up from the river's depths?

Hammond turned back. "Why don't you tell me what you know, Miss Mellish."

"She's been gone since Thursday afternoon, but nobody knew it until Friday, yesterday, first thing. There were men out walking the woods yesterday. There are people saying they saw her on the roads by the river." He was frowning. She had to agree with his dismissal; people wanted to see Bertha, to be the ones to find the missing girl, so they thought they had. "And then there's the rumor of the girl at the hospital. But—"

"Yes." Dr. Hammond cut her off, rather gently. "You think it's not her."

"No." As she said it she knew it was true. "It's not."

Dr. Hammond looked up at Mary Lyon Hall. A woman was waving to them from the arched doors below the clock tower. "Come. We'll speak to the girls. Perhaps you're wrong."

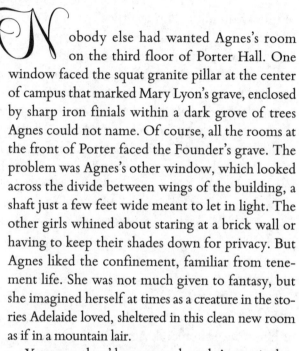

5

Nobody else had wanted Agnes's room on the third floor of Porter Hall. One window faced the squat granite pillar at the center of campus that marked Mary Lyon's grave, enclosed by sharp iron finials within a dark grove of trees Agnes could not name. Of course, all the rooms at the front of Porter faced the Founder's grave. The problem was Agnes's other window, which looked across the divide between wings of the building, a shaft just a few feet wide meant to let in light. The other girls whined about staring at a brick wall or having to keep their shades down for privacy. But Agnes liked the confinement, familiar from tenement life. She was not much given to fantasy, but she imagined herself at times as a creature in the stories Adelaide loved, sheltered in this clean new room as if in a mountain lair.

Yet now they'd come to beard Agnes in her den: Florence Mellish, Bertha's older sister, and an older man whom she clearly did not like much. Florence offered Agnes her hand to shake. Bertha's sister had coarse skin and calloused fingers, and she looked older than Agnes had expected but strong, a workhorse of a woman. Agnes saw Bertha in the soft under-curve of her jaw and the pert angle of her nose. Otherwise, they barely resembled each other. Florence's bones were broad and heavy, and Bertha's had been so finely made that she seemed bird-light and fluttery until you saw the metal in her eyes and the tight crank of her determined smile.

Florence kept the gentleman accompanying her at heel. At the sight of him Agnes was struck by an unfamiliar sensation of queasy timidity. This was the fearsome Dr. Hammond, who had delivered Bertha and treated her for years for what he called "nervous complaints," what Agnes would have described as stubbornness and singularity. She'd never seen him in person before, but she knew a great deal about him from Bertha, who'd shown her all the letters he'd sent, letters now stored in her own trunk along with Bertha's other correspondence. The letters had begun as encomia to Bertha's many virtues, but since the beginning of the year they had swerved decidedly toward chivalric romance. Bertha had told Agnes about Hammond's letters because she knew Agnes would never push her to accept or deny him. She'd known that Agnes was perfectly indifferent to the men who pursued her, as long as they did not actually threaten to take her away from her studies.

But Agnes could not afford to be indifferent to Hammond now.

"This is Dr. Hammond, our family physician," said Florence, and Agnes extended her hand to the man as if she knew nothing of him. "Dr. Hammond, Agnes Sullivan, Bertha's dearest friend at the College."

Agnes supposed that Hammond was always dapper and finelooking, but today he seemed to have dressed with special care in a pin-striped suit and waistcoat. His collar stood up boldly, his watch chain gleamed, his gray-brown mustache had been trimmed with mathematical precision, his salmon-colored pocket square rose to a tender little point. A handsome enough man, for his age, but soft-looking somehow. He was tucking a pair of spectacles away inside his coat as he reached out to shake her hand. He even smelled expensive, like lemon and talcum and spice. Next to his polish, Florence's simple crown of braids, brown dress, and checked shawl looked shabby rather than neat.

"Dr. Hammond is sure that Bertha must still live," said Florence.

Agnes looked at him with sharper eyes. "I should hope so," she said and wondered at his composure. He didn't seem concerned in the least that she might tell Florence she had seen him on campus before. Did he think that Bertha had kept his letters secret? Or that the Reverend Mellish would endorse his suit?

"The police are doing all they can," he said, looking upon Agnes gravely, "and if their efforts prove insufficient there are other means of investigation. You must not lose hope, Miss Sullivan. We will seek out Miss Mellish and return her to her loved ones."

Hammond was a speechmaker by nature, Agnes could tell, and considered himself a leader of men. He edged past Florence's elbow, deeper into Agnes's room. She had no photograph-studded fishnet dangling from the walls, no gleaming Gibson Girls smirking down from posters. Only books, her paltry personal effects spread on the dresser's top, the cross-stitched Protestant hymns and the plain cross left by the room's previous tenant, and the sole indulgence of her true interests—a few lists of Latin names tacked to the plaster as *aide-mémoire*. Agnes found herself exchanging a speaking glance with Florence Mellish. She felt reassured by Florence's obvious distaste for the man. Bertha had told Agnes little about her sister, in that protective way she had, afraid of saying too much about the things she really loved. It was one of the first things Agnes had recognized in her when they were freshmen. She knew that Florence was a teacher; honorable work, especially for a woman who'd been too unwell to finish her own education.

"Did she appear upset to you? Before?" Florence asked. "About her studies, perhaps, or some other affair? Has she told you of anything that's been worrying her?"

"No," said Agnes. "She's been anxious about the debate, but she was excited, not upset." She had told herself to answer only what she was asked when they came to speak with her, but

Florence's face was so awfully open, so eager for more knowledge of Bertha that Agnes did not stop. Nor did she lie, when she could avoid it. She told them which recitations Bertha had liked best, how her preparations for the debate on vivisection had been proceeding, what she had eaten and what she had only picked at, how often she retired to her single room and put up the *Engaged* sign to keep the other girls out. Agnes had her own *Engaged* sign. It was hanging from her room's doorknob at that moment, and even now, even after Bertha's disappearance, none of the Porter girls were likely to brave Agnes's room. They thought all she did inside was study and pray.

"There were no disputes with any of the other girls? Perhaps over a young man." Hammond turned back to the two of them. Agnes kept her face blank.

Florence's eyelids tightened. "She's said nothing to me about—"

"You are not her bosom friend any longer, Miss Mellish," Hammond said in a poisonously gentle tone, and Agnes saw a shudder go through Florence's body. Bertha's sister was twisting her hands together in front of her stomach: an unconscious expression of anxiety, or a desire to throttle the doctor. Or perhaps both.

"Nothing of that sort," Agnes said. "Bertha is too busy with her studies to bother with the other girls much. And certainly she has no interest in their parties or their young men. She doesn't loll around cooking fudge in a dish when she could be doing real chemistry."

"What does she do on a Friday evening, then?" Hammond picked up one of Agnes's books from the dresser top and thumbed through it, and Agnes felt the same shudder, as if his hands were on her own skin. She thought of the last happy Friday evening she'd spent with Bertha—side by side in the library, heads bent at the same angle, pens scratching in rhythm. Bertha had drilled her on anatomical terms and read Greek lyrics aloud as she translated them, bright-eyed as Athena, strange vowels in the wine-darkness of her mouth.

She said shortly, "We study together. We always study together."

"Do you," said Florence in a softer voice. "I'm glad to know that. She is always cheerful in her letters, but it is hard with Bertha to know—if she's happy. Truly happy."

Agnes didn't know what to say. It had been hard to know if Bertha was happy, it was true. She watched as Hammond put the book down atop the dresser a good foot away from where it had been before.

After a moment Florence cleared her throat. "Do you think—could she have had some reason to avoid the Founder's Day ceremony?"

"I don't believe so. It's tiresome but not very long. I left early myself. Nobody minds, if you have to. But Bertha didn't—" Agnes drew a deep breath, thinking of her lungs filling, her heart slowing. "Bertha didn't plan to go in the first place. She was working on her arguments for the debate, doing more research. She said there was always more to do if she wanted to be the best prepared."

That made Florence exhale a little laugh. "Our Bertha," she said, looking into Agnes's eyes so that Hammond was neatly excluded.

Yes, Agnes thought. *Our Bertha.*

"The girls say that no one saw her at the ceremony at all, but Mrs. Mead tells us that one girl did claim to have seen her elsewhere on the campus, walking to the west. Carrying books—She used to do that as a child, you know," Florence said, clearly arrested by memory. Her hands fell to her sides and her eyes glazed. "Go for a long walk with a book and get so lost in it I would have to go out in search of her for supper. We joked about calling out the sheriff to look for her." She breathed out heavily. "My God."

Dr. Hammond crowded close to put a meaty hand on Florence's shoulder. "Take heart," he murmured, then looked to

Agnes. "Miss Sullivan, you never saw anything or heard Miss Mellish say anything that seemed extraordinary, in the last few days?"

"Bertha is always extraordinary," said Agnes. Florence shook off Hammond's touch by reaching out to grasp Agnes's fingers in what seemed to be a gesture of thanks for that statement. Agnes did not like to be touched, either, but forced herself to remain still and to ignore Hammond's gaze upon the two of them. She recited the tendons of the hand to quiet her mind—first dorsal interosseous, abductor pollicis, extensor pollicis longus, extensor digitorum communis—and soon enough Florence pulled her hand back. Often when Agnes recited silently to herself that way people thought she was praying. She could not tell what Florence thought. Reading others' emotions was always difficult, and on Florence's face, with its echoes of Bertha, all Agnes could see was misery.

Guilt stabbed at her viscera. They were both staring at her now, Hammond hovering behind Florence's left shoulder like a haunt. Agnes said, "She might have spoken to Mabel about these matters."

Florence's eyes narrowed. "Mabel?"

"Mabel Cunningham, I mean, Bertha's senior—"

"Her senior?" Hammond interrupted.

"There's a system," Florence said impatiently. "For matching up the upperclassmen with girls the year below, so everybody has a particular friend to look up to."

Agnes nodded. "Bertha asked Mabel to go out walking—that day. Thursday. Before she disappeared. But beyond that—there is nothing else. I am sorry."

"She sent us a letter on Sunday," Florence said. "Full of news about the debate and her other projects. It was all enthusiasm. Nothing that showed any distress. It's in the papers this morning, that she was troubled. But you know her, Agnes, you know she is not. Not like that."

Not like that.

"Bertha is not troubled. She is the smartest girl I know," said Agnes. "The most loyal, and the best."

She saw knowledge bloom in Florence's face, then surprise—that Agnes loved Bertha. That anyone loved Bertha. This made Agnes fume in silence. So Bertha was a quiet and peculiar girl. It was what all the girls were babbling to one another, what they would write to their shocked mothers and tell the newspapermen. Queer and strange, not known to make girl friends easily, never once accompanied to a party by a young man, not even a classmate from Danielson High School. All of that was true, but Florence must know all the other truths about Bertha. The glories of her.

Agnes called Bertha to mind. She had been resisting this because thinking of Bertha now caused her tremendous pain, though not like the pain of a bruise or a fracture. Like a deep incision. She'd cut herself twice with her scalpel in freshman year so that she would know what it felt like: carved two cold-burning slices into the soft skin over her inner biceps. Bertha had bandaged them, her little fingers nimbler and her eyes knowing but kind.

Bertha's very presence was a salve for the foolishness of the all-around girls, their pranks and songs and tawdry camaraderie. She offered Agnes the inexpressible relief of being understood. Bertha would declare herself an agnostic to any YWCA girl unfortunate enough to ask why she never went to the Congregational church next to the College to hear the new minister sermonize, but she never said a word to anyone else about Agnes's Catholic childhood. She knew that history alone put Agnes at risk of expulsion from Mount Holyoke, only three years into its new life as a college rather than a seminary school and still dedicated to educating its girls to resist the blandishments of Catholic Europe. Bertha was accomplice and protector.

Florence was giving her a measuring stare, and Agnes looked down in distress. She was used to turning that look on others, not to suffering it. She could see now why it made the other girls flinch.

They stood in silence. Agnes kept studying the plain floor-boards. Hammond, his back to the two of them, gazed out her window toward Mary Lyon's grave. Florence drew in a slow breath.

Agnes wanted them to leave; she wanted Florence to take her terrible sadness away.

She had her work to focus on, her French and Latin and German to study and the last round of research for her zoology dissection project to begin. Before Florence and Hammond arrived she had been drilling conjugations. After they left she would return to it for thirty minutes, and then, after a five-minute break, would read one of the short pamphlets she had found in the library on the cat fancy. She believed in honoring the creatures she had to sacrifice for her own education by learning about them—learning everything she possibly could.

Work was all Agnes could do now. Work was what she had promised Bertha she would do.

"Please," she said to Florence and Hammond, her voice raw. "I am sorry. I have so much to do before Bible study."

6

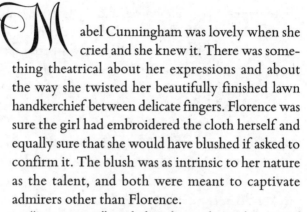abel Cunningham was lovely when she cried and she knew it. There was something theatrical about her expressions and about the way she twisted her beautifully finished lawn handkerchief between delicate fingers. Florence was sure the girl had embroidered the cloth herself and equally sure that she would have blushed if asked to confirm it. The blush was as intrinsic to her nature as the talent, and both were meant to captivate admirers other than Florence.

"I am sorry," Mabel said, touching the tips of those elegant fingers to the shell-pink coverlet beside her, as if to steady herself. She'd led them from the drawing room back to this haven of femininity on the third floor and had sunk down upon the edge of her bed at Dr. Hammond's first question. "It's just that we are all so worried about her."

Florence studied Mabel as she wiped at her eyes, then looked to Dr. Hammond, who was frowning at the girl in a way that would have chilled a less ebullient spirit. But even in anguish, auburn-haired Mabel glowed demurely. She was a different model from the girls who had reigned during Florence's year at the College, but no less winning. Florence had envied their easy success, their freedom. But she had no patience for the girl's performance today. She wanted to dig her fingers into the puffs of Mabel's sleeves and shake her.

"I feel terrible about having refused her," Mabel

said without prompting. She reached for one of the jade-flowered pillows propped at the head of the bed and pressed it against her middle. Her fingers twined in its ivory ruffles. The whole room had a feeling of abundance. The bookshelves held as many framed photographs as they did books, and the bedside lamp and mirror were garlanded with ribbons and other mementos. The stoppered glass perfume bottles on the dresser whispered of lilac, violet, musk. It was everything Bertha's room was not.

Dr. Hammond nodded at Mabel, curtly, as if to say: *You should*.

"I was studying—I had a Latin exam the next day, and of course I had to attend Founder's Day. I thought of going with her just for a little while, but it was clear that she wanted a long walk, and I just hadn't the time. And she was quite nice about it really—or nice for Bertha. I mean, not that she wasn't usually nice, just that she could be a bit short sometimes, if you understand?" The girl gave a graceful shrug, sounding both fond and critical. "When she was really involved with her schoolwork. But she always did treat me awfully well, and she never expected too much of me."

"Expected too much?" Dr. Hammond narrowed his eyes. "What do you mean by that, Miss Cunningham?"

"I'm her senior," Mabel said. "A sort of—elder sister." She darted an opaque look at Florence. "Everybody said—Well, there were some girls who didn't want to take Bertha on because she was so quiet. You know the type, maybe. The all-arounders who think a week is incomplete without a fête of some sort, a dance with a young man or at least a gathering in someone's room with a really fine spread to take everybody's mind off studying. That kind of girl. They weren't much for Bertha, and I can't say she was much for them, either. But I liked her." She caught herself. "I like her."

"What did she expect of you, then?" Florence asked.

Mabel's brow tensed. "Why, just an ear, on occasion, I suppose. More often than not we talked about the debates. We're to argue the affirmative together, and she's really very promising—everybody says so. Classics students are such good rhetoricians. I don't know what we'll do without her. I suppose it may be put off—"

Dr. Hammond interrupted her. "But she has not told you anything private, anything you think could help the police as they search for her?"

Mabel went wide-eyed. "Oh, no, of course not. I'd have said at once if I thought there was anything. It's just that—I haven't seen her as much this year. I saw her more before I was her senior, honestly, because of debate. She's always so busy preparing this project or that, or writing up her little lectures. And of course my schoolwork keeps me busy, too, and so does basketball. And William," she said, with a flare of dimples, "my fiancé. He's finishing his medical degree at Dartmouth this year." Florence closed her eyes for just a moment. Against her eyelids came flashes of the dreams she'd silently cherished: Bertha wed to a man worthy of her. Bertha in white lace, embracing Florence in front of the congregation. "But—I'm sorry, you must forgive me; it's like a disorder, I simply can't stop talking about him. What I meant to say was that I haven't seen Bertha as much since the fire."

"The fire," said Hammond, looking bewildered by the rush of Mabel's speech.

"Last year the seminary building burnt—you must remember. The fire was enormous, everything was destroyed, and nearly all of us lost our belongings. They put us up in town, mostly. I lived in the Boyds' hotel with a few other girls from the class of '98. And Bertha and Agnes, they lived in Mrs. Drew's house, out on the ferry road. Everybody thought it rather fitting," she added shyly, "the two odd birds nesting together."

Florence thought she discerned the slightest sidelong look at the end of that sentence, as if Mabel were evaluating her for inclusion in the category of "odd bird." It would be impossible to control the rumors of madness in the family, that was certain— how stupid she'd been to hope that the girls would emulate Mrs.

Mead's restraint. Behind his polite expression she could see that Hammond was furious. Her father would be, too.

Mabel continued, "Even though we all live in Porter now, I only really see them at meals and classes. So even if Bertha had anything secret to share, which I rather doubt, I don't know that she would have thought to share it with me."

"Well, regardless, if you recall anything that seems relevant—even the smallest item of information may be crucial—I hope you will tell Mrs. Mead directly. Or tell me." Dr. Hammond passed her one of his cards and stood. "I will be staying in town until we know more, to assist the family."

Mabel turned the force of her blue eyes squarely on Florence. "Miss Mellish," she said warmly, "I will be thinking of you."

"My thanks," Florence managed to say. How strange it was to imagine Bertha exchanging a single sentence with this glossy paragon of a girl.

Outside Mabel's room, Florence stopped and put one hand to her mouth. She closed her eyes. A few rooms down the hall a girl chattered about a biology assignment. Farther away, another girl practiced scales. Her voice wobbled up and down like a cat's cry.

Hammond fussed with one of his cuffs, then looked at the wall as if its paper fascinated him. Its pattern contained the same colors as Mabel's room, Florence noticed, the pale pink of the ground, the soft green figures. Probably he was trying to decide what condescending thing would be best to say to her. How precisely to encourage her not to lose heart or to remain strong or to think of her sister. As if she had ever stopped thinking of Bertha—or ever would.

AS FLORENCE AND HAMMOND left her room, Mabel settled uneasily back against her pillows, sorting through her recent memories of Bertha. She hadn't exactly lied—she did like the girl, admired her gift for argumentation, her tenacious mind.

But Bertha also unsettled her. That little smirk on her clever lips that said without speaking: *I don't need you and I don't care a whit what you think of me.*

Whatever inner strength was required to stand apart from the other girls, Mabel did not possess it. She drew sustenance from their adoration, and she'd campaigned subtly to secure it from the moment she arrived on campus as a freshman. It wasn't so difficult: a girl obtained popularity at the College the same way she did anywhere else, just with rather more kissing in addition to displays of generosity and well-placed compliments. Mabel was careful to show herself as passably, likably talented at most pursuits and stellar at a few. She joined the right clubs, captained the basketball team, climbed trees with her skirts bound above the knee, picked out tunes on a friend's banjo, knew how best to arrange pretty china plates of salted peanuts and tea biscuits, and shone in the campus's many performances. In June all the girls had swooned when she'd played the Fairest of the Flowers and wedded the six-foot-tall sophomore cast as the Prince of Bumblebees. Her engagement to William had cemented her authority. People want to love a girl who is seen to be loved by others.

No one on campus could rival Mabel. Prettier than bulldoggish Nan Miller, sweeter than bossy Mollie Marks. Nothing connected her to Bertha except their shared love of debate. Mabel could have ignored Bertha outside of that activity, if she'd wanted to. But it wasn't only a sense of obligation that had driven her to take up Bertha as a minor project even before she officially became the girl's senior this year. She didn't like that the other Porter girls treated Bertha so dismissively—it spoke poorly of their dormitory. What harm did it do the other girls if Bertha and Agnes Sullivan were determined to be grinds? Why should Mollie Marks pull faces behind their backs because Agnes looked threadbare as an old widow and Bertha worked in a woolen mill in the summers? It was like William said—everybody had their level and there was no shame in that.

She'd tried to stand up for them publicly once, last year, when they were all slogging to campus from their respective houses in town after the fire. One of Mollie's dull sycophants had nearly winged Agnes with a snowball during the annual match as the tall silent girl hurried by. Mabel had dropped the handful of snow she'd been preparing to shove down Daisy's collar and started lecturing the offender, only to see Bertha come around the corner of Mary Lyon Hall to meet Agnes. Bertha had surveyed the scene with a derisive shake of her head—and that smirk, a smirk that Mabel would never forget. Words of defense had died in Mabel's mouth. And after that she had seen less of Bertha, as she'd told the girl's sister. She had even stopped frowning regally at the other Porter girls when they rolled their eyes at one of Bertha's declamations about agnosticism or Agnes's conversational stumbles.

They were so separate, Bertha and Agnes. Sufficient unto themselves. Creatures who disdained the common way. Mabel could not admit to herself how powerfully she wished for the freedom she assumed they must feel. They did not suffocate under others' expectations; they behaved as they wished. If Bertha wanted something, she pursued it, even at the risk of public shame.

Bertha had been a poor junior to her, truth be told, dutiful but perfunctory. It had fallen to Mabel to keep their connection alive in a small way, through debate and those occasional walks, even though she was supposed to be the one courted. Certainly she'd resented it, at times, watching Mollie and the other seniors be presented with carefully prepared platters and sweet little bouquets by their adoring juniors. "I simply don't know why I put up with her," she'd sigh to Gail and Ruthie, to hear them coo about how many other girls would be keen to acquire Bertha's crush if Mabel had tired of the match.

But she hadn't tired of Bertha at all. The girl's hauteur was enticing. Mabel wanted to puzzle out what enabled her boldness. What would it be like, she wondered, to feel free to stand and declare, "I will win this debate, and I defy any girl to prevent me," as Bertha had during one otherwise-quiet lunch hour? Or to let one's face simply reflect one's thoughts—without bothering to shape a pleasing expression? She watched Bertha carefully when they were together. When they weren't together, too.

How many weeks since she and Bertha had traipsed around Lower Lake while Mabel talked idly of her nuptial plans—three? Four? She had chosen that direction to walk, wanting to see if Bertha would betray her secret by looking off into the woods or blush if Mabel did. But instead Bertha's eyes had been on the lake or the ground before them. To keep talk flowing Mabel had been describing the house William's family meant to let for them in Washington Square, and she'd said slyly to Bertha, meaning to provoke, "Of course, you'll be in Boston, living with Sullivan in monkish harmony"—and instead of the quick sharp answer she'd anticipated, gotten only a strange silence.

Just for a moment, then Bertha had recovered. "Of course," she'd replied, in something like her normal tone, and quickened her steps to pull away a little, her hands clasped behind her back, leaving Mabel to follow helplessly after.

7

In the dormitory drawing room Dr. Hammond shifted on the ugly green velveteen sofa as they waited for the next Porter girl to come down. Florence sat with eyes downcast. The room's furnishings were all still painfully new, the upholstery unrubbed, the dark shining tables unscratched. For months the girls had been stepping over buckets of paint and piles of rags and boards bristling with nails. Bertha had written of the construction noise and the mess in her letters to Florence. Now the new dormitory building was finished, but she could tell that Bertha's disappearance had spoilt it in some subtle and ineradicable way. As lively as the girls' halls felt, all paper hearts tacked to doors and scrawled mash notes, the shared spaces of the house sat echoing and cold.

Florence felt as if she could sense Agnes upstairs, marble-still, just as Bertha was when she studied. She'd trained herself not to interrupt too often when Bertha was at her books, but sometimes she would allow herself to bend down and fold her arms around Bertha's shoulders and kiss the ridged hair just above her bun. Bertha would sigh and mark her place in whatever she was reading, and then she would turn her stubborn, adoring face to Florence and smile.

It seemed likely that no one would ever look at Florence with such love again.

She'd learnt nothing from questioning these

girls that she did not already know. Bertha's classmates were bemused by her scholarly dedication and disliked her outspoken religious questioning; private doubts were expected among New Englanders, but they thought Agnes a saint for tolerating her public declamations. The girls were carefully polite, nonetheless. They complimented Bertha's performance in rhetoric and her French pronunciation and admired the thoroughness with which she'd been preparing for her debate. Most had expected her team to win it handily. "I think she must have read *every* pamphlet that's *ever* been printed on vivisection," said one girl, sounding honestly dazzled. Florence could not bring herself to ask how many the girl thought that might total.

The front door of Porter clanked open and shut. "Oh, Mabel, Mabel!" trilled a girl from the entry hall, her skirts whisking past the open French doors of the drawing room. "I lost my best pen somewhere, the one from my brother. Have you seen it, darling girl?"

Hammond pushed up from the sofa, clearly irritated. He didn't seem to like what he'd been hearing from the girls. "My apologies. I need a breath of fresh air. Call me in when the next one bothers to appear."

Florence frowned after him. But only a few moments later, a slight curly haired girl they'd spoken to earlier—Eva?—peered into the room, having apparently followed the warbler and slipped past Hammond.

"Miss Mellish?" She held a sheaf of papers bound in twine before her like a shield. "I'm sorry—Dr. Neilson asked me to bring this to you. Bertha has rhetoric with her."

Florence took the papers from the girl and looked toward the door, thinking of calling Hammond. But the girl stepped closer, her gray eyes insistent.

"She said—bring it to *you*."

The bundle was a manuscript, with a folded note stuck between the twine and what looked like a title page. Florence pushed the note down the page and saw Bertha's large spidery print: *La Petite: A Story of Mattawaugan Mill.*

When she looked up, the girl was gone.

FLORENCE DID NOT FETCH Hammond from the dormitory porch. She locked herself in the little bathroom on the first floor of Porter, beside an embroidered hand towel and little carven soaps, and pulled the twine from Bertha's manuscript. First she read Dr. Neilson's note.

Dear Miss Florence Mellish,

I understand that you and your father are visiting the campus in search of your sister, Bertha, my student. I feel I must send you an assignment she recently completed in my rhetoric class, as it may have some bearing on her disappearance.

The students were to craft a moral argument. Most of them wrote essays, but Bertha chose to write a tale. After I returned it, she came to see me, unhappy with my comments on the piece. She asked me to read it again. Forgive me for not offering a précis here; you will judge its contents for yourself.

Bertha told me that I had misinterpreted the story's moral. Frankly, it seems only too evident: be virtuous and responsible, don't marry too young, et cetera. If she meant something else, I couldn't discern it. I offered to reconsider the mark, but she said she didn't care about that, which was unusual. She does take pride in her high grades. When she gave the story back to me, she would offer only the following in explanation: "The most abhorrent thing of all is to be stuck."

I would not have thought it possible, but I am afraid that Bertha may have done herself harm. I hope to God that I am wrong. If I can assist you in any way, please call on me.

Sincerely yours,
Dr. R. Neilson

Florence's fingers trembled as she flipped over the title page. *I am afraid that Bertha may have done herself harm—*

The manuscript was Bertha's handwriting, sure enough. Florence knew it as intimately as her own. But as she read, she felt as though she were trying to parse a badly translated text.

As far as she could make out, it was the story of a sweet French-Canadian mill girl named Marie, romanced by a young mill worker with no prospects and doomed to share his destitution after she lost her own position. She bore his children but was terribly unhappy. The girl telling the story, her friend, went to visit Marie and found her fleeing into the woods—and they raced up Mount Holly, the narrator giving chase, before Marie threw herself to her death. They tumbled down together, broken by the fall, but the friend lived to tell the tale, lived to raise Marie's daughter.

"What on Earth," Florence murmured. Her ears were ringing as she read and read again.

> *Those were happy days for me that summer, when Marie made the work no longer hard. The sunshine preceded us in the morning and waited upon us home at night . . . The girl beside me sang softly at her work, and the mill was even a cheerful place . . . I linger over those bright days. Darkness and sorrow came too soon—*

Someone rapped on the bathroom door.

Florence shoved the manuscript into her satchel, crumpling its edges in haste. Her face in the dull bathroom mirror was white and set.

Dr. Hammond, waiting in the hallway, didn't notice. "We're needed at Mary Lyon Hall," he said and shepherded her to the front door of Porter. His pace was uncommonly fast, and she struggled to match it, her breath grating in her throat.

"Is there news? Is it her?"

"I don't know," Hammond said grimly.

When they entered her office minutes later, Mrs. Mead looked up with a visage so serious that Florence instantly feared a hundred things, a thousand.

But before she could speak, Mrs. Mead said, "Miss Mellish, it's your father," and Florence was shocked to find herself swaying on her feet. Dr. Hammond grabbed her elbow and eased her into a chair, and she wrapped her hands around its arms and dug her fingers into the gaps between the domed metal tacks at the leather's edge. Mrs. Mead was still talking. She said, "No, Florence, he's well enough. But he has collapsed, likely from exhaustion. The girl there was not your sister, unfortunately, and the shock—They've got him a room in Boston for now. He'll return tomorrow so that you can take him home."

"It wasn't her?" Florence repeated. "It's not her?"

"No," said Mrs. Mead. Her gaze rested on Florence, her thick gray eyebrows taut.

"Surely the Reverend won't travel by himself," Dr. Hammond said. "I could—"

"Of course not. There's a private detective the Boston police suggested, an expert in matters of missing persons, and he'll accompany your father on the coach." Mrs. Mead was still speaking to Florence rather than Hammond.

"Why do we need—What do they think has happened to her?" A shameful quaver in her voice.

The softening of Mrs. Mead's lined face told Florence she had been right to fear.

THEY SAT IN THE dining room of one of the other new dormitory halls—not Porter, thank goodness, where Florence would've had to picture Bertha sitting distracted beside her, reading and spooning porridge into her mouth. The room was warm and wood-paneled, with large windows that faced an open lawn framed by bright pale-yellow curtains, and it held six round tables with chairs tucked up expectant around their edges. The place smelled like onions frying in butter, like soapy dishwater and heat, those gladdening scents of community Florence remembered with aching precision from her own work circle shifts.

Through the kitchen doorway pots clanked and girls talked as they peeled potatoes, several high voices puzzling over where one might have left her favorite checked scarf. Otherwise the house was quiet and the dining room empty, since places had already been laid for dinner and pitchers of cool water set out on carts by the kitchen door, where Florence watched their dull metal sides bead up and drip.

Florence had exhausted her handkerchief and the doctor's and had borrowed a napkin from the setting in front of her. "I'm sorry," she said as she wiped hard at her eyes. "I'm sorry."

Dr. Hammond shook his head, and for once he didn't speak.

In front of her was a half-drunk mug of coffee and a plate with one piece of toast scraped with jam, brought to her by a silent student when she and Dr. Hammond had arrived at the dining room—Florence sobbing under his arm like a child. Mrs. Mead had suggested this respite, as unflustered by Florence's tears as she seemed by every duty of her position. "Have you eaten today, Miss Mellish?" she'd asked, her hand on Florence's shoulder, and Florence admitted she had not.

"Try to finish the toast at least," Dr. Hammond said now. "It will settle your stomach with that coffee."

The jam was strawberry and so startlingly sweet that it felt illicit. Was Bertha hungry where she was? Florence wondered. As a child she'd licked her fingertips and stuck them in the sugar jar and sucked the crystalline caps off her fingers, no matter how many times Florence had scolded her for it.

"What should we do?" Florence asked. "What can we possibly do?"

"I will speak with Sheriff Brockway again. They may search the river again today. Then we'll see to your father when he arrives."

She had to show him the manuscript. The thought made her flush with a reluctance on the edge of revulsion. He had seen so much already; he treated Bertha in such a proprietary manner. She hated to open for him this window into Bertha's thoughts. But then she felt a surge of guilt. He might see something in the writing that she didn't, loath as she was to admit it. Something that could lead them to Bertha.

"Dr. Neilson—she teaches rhetoric—she had a girl bring me a manuscript of Bertha's."

Dr. Hammond looked directly at her in his surprise. "A manuscript? Of what sort? What do you mean?"

"A story that she wrote for class, an assignment, to write a moral argument," Florence said. "Bertha wasn't happy with the mark. She went back to discuss it with Neilson." Though as she spoke, she remembered—Neilson had said Bertha didn't care about the grade. How strange that was.

"Miss Mellish, I'm afraid I don't understand."

"It's the story of a mill girl. She got to know some of the French-Canadian girls at the mill in the summer." She tried to explain the story's plot, and when she described the death of the mill girl's friend, Marie Racine, the doctor tipped back in his chair as if she'd shoved at his breastbone. His eyes never left her face.

"It's narrated by a friend who tries to rescue the girl and raises her daughter when Marie Racine dies," Florence continued, desperately. If she stopped talking she would have to think about what the story's ending meant. Bertha would never have killed herself or allowed herself to be ruined like the girl in her story. And what a romantic frippery of a name for Bertha to give her supposed double! If anything, Bertha was far more like the noble narrator—stubborn and loyal, even when society disapproved. But Marie Racine—

Marie Racine had left her work far too young, moved into isolation, and had a baby girl, who was raised without true knowledge of her parentage.

Dr. Hammond was staring at her, concerned. Florence forced

her breathing to quiet and let her eyes close for just a moment. Bertha on the insides of her eyelids. Bertha in her heart.

She could hardly bear to draw the manuscript out of her bag and pass it to Hammond, but she forced herself to do that, too.

He pushed back the plate set out before him to lay the papers on the table. As he bent to read he traced the edge of the paper delicately, perhaps unconsciously, straightening the sheets. His fingers ghosted over the title and Bertha's name.

Of course he'd want to read it immediately. He would want to know what the manuscript contained of Bertha, just as Florence had. But Bertha was everything to Florence. She was not supposed to be everything to Henry Hammond.

Florence watched as he read, her breath shallow. She tried to drink her cooled coffee. A burst of laughter came from the kitchen and was quickly smothered. Around them the dormitory house thrummed with the life of its charges, hungry girls racing back from class to meet their friends at these tables, to tease and commiserate and complain just as her friends had when this college had still been a seminary school. When she had been safe.

Beside her, Dr. Hammond let loose a long exhale that ruffled Bertha's manuscript and sat back from the table.

"Thank goodness the woman had the sense to deliver this to you directly," he said. "If she'd given it to the police or, God forbid, to a reporter—"

"Dr. Neilson?"

"Yes, of course. We must control access to this very carefully. I'll speak to Mrs. Mead about it. The police must know of its existence, I suppose, but the thing itself, that cannot be disseminated. Brockway's judgment—I wouldn't trust him with such a document."

Florence took a deep, slow breath at the casual ownership of Bertha's writing Hammond's words implied. "What danger do you think this story represents, Dr. Hammond?"

He blinked and leaned closer, his hands laced together atop the manuscript. "It depicts a young woman's ruin and suicide, Miss Mellish. We must keep its content private. Surely, the implications for Bertha's reputation are clear to you!"

"You cannot believe that Bertha had some mysterious secret lover," she said and hated herself for blushing as she spoke. "Nor that she ran mad and flung herself off a cliff. It's a piece of fiction."

"I said nothing about her own life," Hammond said gently. "I think Miss Mellish was caught up in someone else's trouble, and it affected her sufficiently that she wrote about it. I think the story shows a well-developed moral sense. The uprightness I would expect. But you must see that the public might not look upon this story so kindly. A prurient reader might treat it as evidence of her own conduct."

"It was a school assignment, not a diary."

"Yes. But she chose to write what she did. Unless the instructor suggested that all the class write about the ruin of young women or about their deaths."

Florence stared down at her plate. "No."

"Miss Mellish selected the topic, and the moral, herself."

Intolerable, the teacherly way he spoke to her. She raised her head. "It wasn't some—private fantasy. But it was important to her. Something in it was important."

They stared at each other sidelong across the table. Hammond was tracing the edges of the manuscript again.

"I don't yet know," he said, "how the manuscript might help us find her. We must consider all possibilities, since it is one of the only clues we possess. But if the public wants to see scandal in it, I doubt they will be dissuaded by the fact that she produced it for a college assignment. The morality expressed in the story is perfect and the sentiments just. But it does cause me to fear for her, nonetheless. We must keep this manuscript secret."

He was good at keeping secrets, she knew.

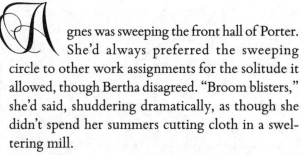

gnes was sweeping the front hall of Porter. She'd always preferred the sweeping circle to other work assignments for the solitude it allowed, though Bertha disagreed. "Broom blisters," she'd said, shuddering dramatically, as though she didn't spend her summers cutting cloth in a sweltering mill.

The solitary nature of the work did not soothe Agnes now. After she finished the front hall, she would have to descend to the basement, where she no longer liked to go, to sweep the laundry and the furnace room. She'd been forced to visit the furnace room again just days ago, after Bertha was gone, burning the letters Bertha had sent her that summer. After lights out, she'd removed the neat twine-tied stacks of paper from her trunk and crept down to the furnace room and shoved the letters into its great belching hot drum almost without looking at what she did. She meant to rid herself of evidence— earlier, she had slipped into the woods and hidden the knife she had taken from Bertha in the knotty hollow of one fallen oak tree and hidden the small gun she had acquired from a Boston acquaintance in another—but in doing so she had to rid herself of Bertha, and it hurt.

Bertha's letters were not "dear baby" letters, the nonsense missives the Porter girls pinned to each other's doors as much to display their connections as to maintain them. Instead, from the first letter Bertha had sent two weeks after they'd gone home at the end of freshman year, they were serious, thoughtful essays on her reading. Sometimes she described a Killingly scene or a family moment, but more commonly she wrote in a grand philosophical style. On paper that style was a little harder to take than in person, since the pretensions of her thought were not softened by her bright eyes and flying hands, but Agnes could imagine her excitement. Agnes loved her excitement. Bertha could make anything interesting. In July she'd sent an entire letter about the phenomenon of applause, digressing from Roman gladiatorial competitions to the development of theatre to the mechanics of the act of clapping; she'd been reading on the subject, during lunch breaks at the mill, as a possible focus for the long Philosophy paper she'd have to write in the fall. *I tend to progress very slowly through my lunch books*, she wrote. *There are always people wanting to talk, at the mill. I confess I don't understand why, but I don't dare seem unfriendly, or they will all snub me terribly, and that grows tiresome, as we both know.*

Now it stung Agnes bitterly, to realize how much the letters had left out.

One she still could not bear to part with, the letter that recalled the fire that had destroyed the old seminary building the September before. When Agnes burned the other letters, she sewed that envelope into the lining of her one small leather suitcase. She saved it not because it was the letter of Bertha's she loved best but because it was the only one she had yet to fully figure out, because the paper seemed to hum under her fingertips like a tuning fork whenever she touched it.

The letter, dated August 20, 1897, was the last Bertha had sent before they both returned to the College. Bertha had smudged the date while writing, which was unusual; she was ordinarily fastidious about her correspondence. Yet the first part of the letter was unremarkable. It contained Bertha's commentary on the philosophy book she'd just read, given in her usual style, and a mention of Florence's recovery from a recent touch of the 'flu, with a proud note that Bertha's nursing had surely helped to shorten its duration.

Then the letter careened to a fierce height of emotion Bertha rarely expressed. It began gently enough:

> It seems strange to be returning to school and to think of living on campus again, in a new dormitory house. Do you remember hearing Mrs. Mead as we all stood there and watched the fire— how she said "I think we can go on!" while the hall crashed into rubble in front of us? How sure and brave she sounded. I recall you standing behind me as we observed the flames. They slipped across the building like a white-orange sheet dragged over its frame—do you remember that? The smell of it, too, I remember. The sharp thickness of the smoke, and the heat, almost its own scent, like the mill workings all going at once.
>
> The next morning, when we were all in church in the village, I think was the only time I have ever felt what most people feel in a vestry during prayer. Just to hear Mead telling us all that the glory of the latter house shall be greater than the former. "Be strong and work, for I am with you," was part of the reading, I believe, from Haggai. Well, we must continue to be strong, Agnes, and we must work in our new house as we did in the old. You will be with me, won't you, to do our work?

That was all. When Agnes had received the letter she had not known what had prompted Bertha's odd spasm of nostalgia. Agnes had puzzled over it for the week before they returned to the campus and Bertha appeared at her door, as small and brown and serious as ever. All had seemed well. Agnes had not known then—she still did not know—everything that had made Bertha so anxious to return to work, return to the College.

The letter vexed Agnes, awake and asleep. On many nights after the seminary fire, in their little bedroom at Mrs. Drew's house, she had watched the tame glow of the fireplace shift Bertha's features about and spark her dark eyes. Now she had nonsensical dreams. Her mind took up those and other memories and reshaped them. Half a dozen times since Bertha vanished she'd gasped awake in the dreadful certainty of guilt, thinking that they had burnt the building together, she and Bertha, that the furious firelight on Bertha's face had shown a great unsatisfied longing, black hollows where her eyes and mouth should be.

No one knew what had first set the seminary building alight. Rags in a bucket, left out by a workman painting a sill? A girl smoking where she oughtn't? But in these dreams they were alone in the old laundry and they were the fire's mothers. Agnes cupped a votive candle, wax threading between her fingers, and Bertha held a torch that roared with light—and then she let it fall.

Agnes swept on, thinking of Bertha in the flames.

9

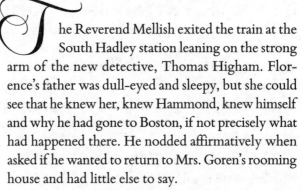

he Reverend Mellish exited the train at the South Hadley station leaning on the strong arm of the new detective, Thomas Higham. Florence's father was dull-eyed and sleepy, but she could see that he knew her, knew Hammond, knew himself and why he had gone to Boston, if not precisely what had happened there. He nodded affirmatively when asked if he wanted to return to Mrs. Goren's rooming house and had little else to say.

Florence took his weight onto her own arm while they all waited for a carriage outside the station; Higham was to accompany them to the rooming house, to discuss the investigation, before securing his own lodging.

The detective was nearly of an age with Dr. Hammond, she thought, but his thick black eyebrows and neat goatee showed only a few white strands. He had a rather menacing way of rolling his heavy shoulders beneath his coat that recalled boxing match posters, as if his hands wanted to hover, ready, between him and the world. His face did not shift when he spoke. He turned to her now with a smile, and while it stretched his lips and creased his eyelids, it was unnervingly as if someone inside the man tugged on strings to make the gesture.

"Miss Mellish, at your service," he said in greeting, with little evident Boston accent. Hammond had shown her the note the Boston chief of police had written to recommend Higham's services; he was retired from the force and apparently famous for having discovered the whereabouts of a missing bride who'd meant to run west with a girlhood friend. "Tracked her down so quickly that the family concealed the entire affair," Dr. Hammond had told her with a significant look.

Now Florence pictured the rough man in front of her dragging a tearstained girl from some flophouse and stiffened in discomfort. "Mr. Higham."

"I will want to speak with you about your sister." His irises were the color of thick coffee. In the shadow of his hat's brim, they held no luster.

"Of course," she said. "At the rooming house."

Hammond nearly elbowed her aside and leaned in to talk to Higham of the searches, their shoulders meeting like a wall. Florence tried to listen for details he hadn't shared directly with her, but after a moment a hand slipped into her own—her father's fingers squeezing hard despite his weakness.

"Florence." She bent closer to John to hear. "Florence, it wasn't her."

Florence said, "I know, Father."

An awkward carriage ride delivered them to Mrs. Goren's on Mosier Street, between the train station and the College, close to the brook that flowed from the two lakes on campus. Florence could hear it burbling through the dense woods behind the stable. Once the building might have been a farmhouse, but the land around it had grown wild, ivy creeping toward the edges of the gravel yard and paint flaking from the white windowsills.

With the men's help she settled John in her own rented bed, not the other room he'd stayed in when they first arrived in South Hadley. She would sleep on the spider-webbed cot the owner's boy had hauled down from the attic and cranked open lengthwise along the bed's footboard. Twenty years ago, or even ten, the prospect of sharing a room with her father would have terrified her. Now it was merely another discomfort to be endured.

Her father seemed to be drowsily watching the curtains shift in the late afternoon shade. Did he remember that it was Sunday? Florence had joined the congregation next to the College grounds for that morning's eleven o'clock service. She'd watched the girls from the College, including Agnes Sullivan and Mabel Cunningham, lifting their pale faces to the young pastor for guidance, and she'd thought about her stricken father, whom she would never be free of, even when he died. She'd thought: *If Bertha will only come back to me, I will tell her everything.*

A snatch of conversation rising from the front hall of the rooming house broke into those thoughts and froze her in place.

Higham's voice, deep: "—that you want to ask, Doctor?"

Hammond said something she couldn't quite hear. Florence edged through the half-open bedroom door into the upper hall until she could just see the tops of their heads through the banister rails: Hammond's gray, Higham's salt-and-pepper. Their hats were hanging on the coatrack just behind the doctor. If she shifted, she could glimpse a bit of Higham's face, impassive. Unimpressed.

"You're not satisfied," the detective said. "You think I can't find the girl. So ask what you must to reassure yourself—because I've been paid for the job and I mean to do it."

"I don't . . ." said Hammond, and stopped.

Florence shifted, trying to see better. The air in the hallway smelled of the dish of dusty potpourri Mrs. Goren had set out on a side table between the bedrooms: desiccated rose petals, shriveled lavender blossoms.

The men had seemed collegial enough at the train station— Hammond had been eager to meet Higham, hopeful that his expertise would energize the local police. She'd only been upstairs with her father for a few minutes. If she could just see their expressions, she felt that she'd know how the tension she heard now had built up so quickly. Had the detective said something about Bertha? Something about Bertha—and Hammond?

"Or you don't want me to find her," Higham continued in an equable tone. "In which case I can't reassure you much."

"Sir, you are on dangerous ground—"

"Am I? I thought I was in a boardinghouse, at your invitation."

Hammond spun away and knocked against the coatrack, jostling the hats from their hooks and fumbling to catch the thing before it collided with the wall. Florence shrank back. She could hear Hammond breathing hard, but from the detective, nothing. She worried at a fingernail until she felt a little barb of pain.

Finally she heard the floor creak and the shifting of clothing—what she thought must have been Hammond turning back to the detective. Giving in, most uncharacteristically.

"So you want her found. All right." Higham paused. "I won't ask your reasons unless I have to. But I need to know her reasons."

No answer from Hammond.

"The usual troubles among young women," the detective said, "are deceit and petty thievery. Rumors. Nastiness of that sort. Rivalry over men."

Hammond said, tautly, "We've learnt nothing to suggest that Miss Mellish had a rivalry with anyone at the College. The rest is simply beneath her."

Higham went on as if he hadn't heard. "But it's your other cases, your queerer ones, that the chief used to send my way."

"You think the chief of police brought you in because he saw something queer in Miss Mellish's disappearance."

"The queerness is right on the surface. Gone in the middle of the day, not a word to anyone, not a sign of her since. An unlikely girl to make trouble, I understand. Quiet. Studious. Responsible. Isn't she?"

"Yes."

"The easy ones to find, they do it for attention. To be at the center of things."

"Not Miss Mellish." Low and certain.

Higham's voice warmed slightly. "Seeing as how you know her well, Doctor Hammond, seeing as how you're a long-time friend of the family, I'll ask this only once. You didn't cause her to flee?"

"I did not, sir. Bertha would not flee from me."

"That's quite an answer. You didn't hurt her?"

"I would never hurt her." Almost grunted, wrenched from Hammond's gut. "I will find her. I must."

Florence ducked back into the room, her breath coming fast—she'd been holding it, straining to listen. John, eyes closed, didn't seem to have noticed her absence or to have heard the heated exchange below.

Dr. Hammond was coming up the stairs. She composed herself to meet him, her insides still alight with what she had heard. *I will find her.* Her father stirred under the coverlet, and she rushed to help him sit, keeping her hot face turned away from Hammond as much as she could while she rearranged blankets and pillows. *I must.*

"How is he?" He sounded calm, as if he hadn't been locking horns with Higham a moment before.

"Weary," she said tightly.

"I must examine him, Miss Mellish. I'll need you to leave."

She wheeled on him, a pillow in her hands. His cheeks were ruddier than usual beneath his gray beard. "But I must know what you find. How to care for him, if we are to go back to Killingly while you remain here."

Hammond tried to argue that their neighbor Dr. Darling's visits would be sufficient in his absence, but Florence disagreed.

Finally Hammond gave in, though he required her to observe from behind the nearly closed door, where she could see only her father's white head and a slice of his shoulder. Spying, for the second time in an hour.

The floor creaked under the doctor's feet as he crossed the room, then the clasp of his bag clicked open. She heard the soft thwap of the stethoscope settling around his neck.

Hammond said to her father, "All right, Reverend, we'll start with mobility. Follow this. And here. And—here. Can you"—a pause—"touch, good." Another. "All right. Flex your fingers for me, this hand. Other hand. Put your arms out straight. I'll push—good. Good."

That was the soft, abrupt professional voice Florence knew from her own experience as his patient. Dr. Hammond usually employed it when speaking to women—and, for that matter, when speaking to his cats. Florence was stunned to hear him talk to her father that way, as if they were no longer equals. "A little cold, my apologies," he said, bending down with the stethoscope, and his hand moved under the cloth between her father's shoulder blades like a blind, seeking creature.

The sight, familiar somehow, made Florence's innards convulse. She turned away and startled to find Higham just a few feet away from her, watching her with undisguised curiosity. She'd heard no footfalls.

"My apologies," he said. "Didn't mean to scare you."

"We can speak in the parlor," Florence said, flustered, and led him down the stairs, leaning heavily on the smooth-worn banister. Behind her, the detective made the amount of noise she would expect from a man of his bulk, which unsettled her further—that he could choose to be so covert, or not.

Thank God Mrs. Goren was out somewhere, not hovering with her bottomless coffee pot and plates of stale cookies. Florence sat on the dusty sofa; Higham stood, his weight on the balls of his feet as though he were ready to give chase if she fled. At first he asked her the questions she expected. When had she last heard from Bertha; had she seen any indication of distress in Bertha's letters or behavior; did she know of conflict between Bertha and the other girls at the College or of romances or any other reasons Bertha might flee; how was the family bearing the worry of her absence? Yet as she answered she felt that he was only half listening to her words. He had that look a hound gets when it hears a distant whistle above the range of human perception.

When she stopped speaking, Higham cocked his head, dark eyes intent. He said, "Tell me about your sister. What is she like?"

Florence stared at him. The enormity of the question.

He smiled at her, a small true smile, kinder than the mannequin fakery of the train station. "Tell me anything you like. I need to have a sense of who she is if I'm to find her. And you know her well, Miss Mellish. You know what she loves."

"What she loves," Florence echoed. "She loves—"

A cough. Hammond stood in the wide doorway to the parlor, stethoscope still around his neck, the picture of a modern medical man. He looked discontented with the direction of their conversation. "I've examined the Reverend. He should rest here tonight before you travel home, Miss Mellish, but I don't believe there's any immediate danger."

—*truth*, Florence finished silently. She nodded to Hammond. "All right. Thank you, Doctor."

"A diagnosis?" Higham asked.

"It could've been a small stroke. There may be slight weakness on the left side—difficult to tell without seeing him engage in more activity. I'm taking his temperature now, but I don't expect a fever. His breathing and heart sound relatively normal. I think it's exhaustion, mental as much as physical."

Florence nodded again. Was it disappointment she felt upon hearing that her father might recover some strength? Quash the

sensation; don't examine it. An old habit, to pulverize sentiment and press its fragments into any breach in her defenses,
like mud daubed where the wind whistles. But Hammond was
looking sidelong between her and Higham, as if he had more
to say. "What is it?"

"Agnes Sullivan," he said slowly, then to the detective,
"Bertha's—Miss Mellish's friend."

"What about her?" Higham said.

"There's a manuscript of Miss Mellish's—I'll give you my
copy, Higham—that may be important in the case. What I
want to know is, if this story was so important to Miss Mellish,
why did Miss Sullivan not mention it? She said they studied
together."

"Well, I'm sure they did," said Florence, startled by his
suspicion. "I doubt they talked over every single assignment."

"Has Miss Sullivan even spoken to the police?" Hammond
asked. Across the room, Higham raised an eyebrow, sharp as a
stage villain, and that gesture alone seemed to amplify the simmering tension between the men. Hammond's chest inflated
under his fine waistcoat.

Florence, glancing between them, said, "Of course she has.
Mrs. Mead said so this morning."

Dr. Hammond acknowledged that with a curt nod. "All right,
yes, I'd forgotten. But I don't like her involvement in this."

"There's no question that she is Bertha's friend," Florence
said, frustrated. "Bertha never wrote much about her friends,
but she's mentioned Agnes many times. All the girls say they
were constantly together. I don't see—"

"That's as may be—"

"I'll speak with her." Detective Higham stepped forward.
"I'll speak with everyone in the case."

Hammond nodded jerkily, red-faced again. "We cannot let
these girls conceal anything," he said. "Every day is more per-
ilous for Miss Mellish. We cannot be timid in our pursuit."

Florence's eyes stung. "Your thermometer must be ready," she said and turned her back on them both, walking down the hall past the coatrack and out the front door, into the dull, cold sunlight of the yard, where the brook whispered through the dark trees and leaves flaked to dust under her feet.

10

On Monday there was still no news. That morning, the Holyoke police had taken a grappling hook to the Connecticut River and again they'd found nothing. Florence had amassed a growing list of sightings of Bertha on this road or that, but most were only glimpses and half got Bertha's appearance wrong. On Friday, on Saturday, on Sunday, she'd clung to the hope that they would discover Bertha nearby. Something had detained her—a twisted ankle in the woods, a misstep on a slippery rock—but Bertha would come limping home with an arm slung over some policeman's shoulder and her expression half-apologetic and half-mutinous, the way she looked whenever she knew she'd caused Florence worry.

But sunk under Florence's hope was a creeping, clawing, nauseating, quaking fear more profound than any she'd ever felt. She'd never shared Hammond's certainty that Bertha was alive. Never. As soon as the Reverend had opened the first telegram from Mrs. Mead and looked up at her with an unusual silent attention, a part of her had rung with the knowledge of her loss. Now her whole body resounded with it. She walked the wintery campus paths, desolate.

Apparitions of her younger days surrounded her. Girls swinging their joined, mittened hands; girls deep in serious talk or gentle chatter; girls averting their mournful eyes when they felt her gaze. They adjusted their steps to slip past her—all but Agnes, whose abstracted look, so much like Bertha's, stung Florence's heart. Agnes seemed always to be striding between the buildings of the College, skirts a-swirl, in that lightweight, ill-fitting gray flannel coat that made her look like a laborer, her grubby collar yanked up to cover her throat and several books trapped against her chest. As she walked she raised her eyes on occasion to look unseeing on her passing classmates. Behind her eyes were—what? The diagrams and lists of names Florence had seen pinned to her walls, flipping like lantern slides? A scribbled onionskin of labels laid over the world.

Florence wanted to clench her fingers into the gray flannel over Agnes's shoulders and shake her, force her attention, rattle loose some fact that would set everything right. She didn't share Hammond's dislike of the girl, but she, too, was frustrated by Agnes's inability to explain Bertha's disappearance. How could Agnes have known Bertha so well and yet not have known what Bertha would do? But that raised the bitter question of how Florence had not known, herself.

She stopped at the wide stone steps of Mary Lyon Hall, where she was to meet Dr. Hammond. The paired windows of the clock tower looked down upon her like rows of accusing eyes. Detective Higham was still with the police in Holyoke, reviewing the case. She wanted to ask Hammond if she could speak to the police as well. But when he came barreling out of the building, he was looking past her, his mouth open. Always ready to speak.

"Miss Sullivan!" he called, and Florence twisted to look across the lawn.

Agnes stopped on the path, perhaps thirty feet away. She looked genuinely startled to be addressed, and for a moment Florence thought she might drop her books and bolt with those long legs. But she came toward them instead and followed when the doctor ushered them both into the empty vestibule inside the dark arched doorway. Her mouth was a thin line.

"Miss Mellish, Doctor," Agnes said. "There is no—"

"No," Florence said quickly. "No news."

"Miss Sullivan, I wonder if I could ask your opinion of Miss Mellish's manuscript," Hammond cut in. "The story about mill workers she wrote for—what class was it again, Miss Mellish?"

"Rhetoric, with Dr. Neilson," Florence said hesitantly. How like Hammond to make her his accomplice in ambushing the girl.

"Her manuscript?" Agnes echoed, blinking. Her eyes were bright, but as she stood before the white plaster wall, Florence saw marks of exhaustion on her face: purple smudges beneath those eyes, as if somebody had pressed thumbs there. Lips chapped and raw in a way the weather could not explain. "I don't—What does that have to do with anything?"

"Have you read this story?" Hammond pressed, stepping closer to Agnes.

"I—I suppose so." She shifted the books she held against her chest as if the *Elementary Text-Book of Zoology* would serve as a shield.

"You have or you have not, I'd say—"

Florence interrupted. "Agnes, child, did Bertha tell you anything about the story she wrote? Dr. Neilson sent it to me, you see, and she thought it might be connected to—wherever Bertha has gone."

Agnes was shaking her head before Florence finished her first sentence. "She just told me she hated the assignment. It was taking time away from her debate work. She likes Neilson, but she was trying to write her opening remarks and she had to stop to write that story instead. So I only read a bit of it, when she was stuck."

"Stuck?" Florence repeated involuntarily.

"On a word. She couldn't think of the right way to end it."

"But it ends—" Florence stopped. "That is, in the end, one of the mill girls dies." Agnes's sharp hazel eyes flickered wider for a moment, then narrowed. She looked about to ask a question Florence was quite sure she would not want to answer.

Hammond thrust himself back into the conversation. "I am most concerned with determining who are the persons involved. This Joe—in the story, there is a Frenchman who corrupts the mill worker Marie—do you know if he is drawn from life?"

"What do you mean?" Agnes's jaw tightened—her entire body seemed to tighten, as if she might spring at Hammond. Her eyes were level with his. "Are you asking if a Frenchman corrupted Bertha? I can assure you that no one could."

Hammond raised his hands between them, placating. "Miss Sullivan, of course not. I don't mean to suggest impropriety on Miss Mellish's part. But that doesn't mean that she mightn't have been plagued by a persistent admirer. One who might, perhaps, have grown angry with her after repeated rebuffs?" He spoke lightly, but Florence heard a tart undertone to his words.

"Is that in the story? We never talked about anything like that, I told you," Agnes said. "And I'm sure I would have noticed if anyone had been hanging around her, Frenchman or not." She glanced from Hammond's face to his fine boots.

"You're certain she has no suitors," Florence said, half-reassured.

Agnes's eyes flickered toward Florence. "I'm certain."

Hammond tilted his head. "I must ask you this, Miss Sullivan: If Miss Mellish were abandoned—if a man had gained her trust and then betrayed her—do you think she would ever do an outrage to herself for that reason?"

"Never," said Agnes, her voice grown fierce. "Not for that."

"No, I agree." Hammond nodded sharply. "*She* never would."

"Is there nothing else you can tell us about the manuscript, Agnes? Or of her private life?" Florence asked.

"No," said Agnes simply and ducked out the door. Cold air shoved between Florence and the doctor, and they both fell back a half step in the tall girl's wake.

Hammond huffed and shook his head. "A prickly creature."

Florence felt prickly herself. She felt spiny as a porcupine. But she turned a calm face up to him. "What have you been discussing with Mrs. Mead?"

"Next steps," he said, raising his chin. "The College will offer a fifty-dollar reward. Tomorrow Higham and I will meet with the town treasurer to determine how best to continue the search. I will want to speak to you about that."

"Yes, of course," she said again.

"But someone else requires our attention now," he said, and Florence blinked in surprise.

"Who?"

"Your father, Miss Mellish," Hammond said. "Who else? He must be taken home."

Of course: her father, whose needs kept her tethered, as they always had.

IT WAS A LONG night for Florence on the cot at the foot of the bed, hearing her father's murmurs and exhalations. She woke chilled several times and tried to burrow deeper under the blankets, though it wasn't that sort of chill. In the end she had to put her head beneath the pillow before she could sleep, and even then she twitched into awareness twice more before daybreak, her hands thrusting free of the bedclothes to push at the empty air.

Yet when morning came, she woke her father and helped him to dress with a hospital matron's calm, constructed through long practice of smothering her feelings as a soaked blanket might smother flames.

She counted the beats of his pulse and looked into his haggard face. When Dr. Hammond arrived, she let him into the room and waited uncomplaining in the hall.

Over more toast and jam and coffee in the boardinghouse's cramped dining room—as if they were traveling companions breakfasting before a tour—they had a perfunctory conversation about the continuing search. Dr. Hammond felt Higham's presence to be beneficial; the detective had helped persuade the treasurer to agree to another three days of manpower despite the upcoming Thanksgiving holiday and to press the Northampton chief of police to lead the next search.

"A useful tool, that fellow," Hammond said, inspecting Florence's face for approval. He didn't want her opinion; he wanted her to agree that more searching would lead them to Bertha. She could not, so she busied herself with her coffee spoon.

Soon he was gone in a bustle of cloth, napkin to his mustache, thick fingers fussing with his collar and the lapels of his coat. Off to meet with the other important men in the case.

Their train would not leave for several hours. There would be sufficient time to pack their things and measure more fully the effects of the last few days on her father's strength. There was also, therefore, sufficient time to sob into her handkerchief in the narrow bathroom while the toilet chain clanked and water gurgled in the pipes to cover her crying. Time to pat at her cheeks with some of Mrs. Goren's Pond's Healing Cream in the bathroom mirror until she no longer looked as dreadful.

In the parlor she had seen a poetry miscellany on the sideboard. *The Best Poems for Young Ladies*, it was called; the sort of publication she half despised and was half desperate to see her own writing printed in. She took it upstairs with two buttered rolls and read to her father while he ate, skipping through the pages to find all the devotional poems, the ones she knew he would like. He didn't thank her but smiled as she read.

AGNES WAS NOT AMONG the wet-eyed girls who clustered by the college gates to bid the Reverend and Florence farewell when they left the campus to return to Killingly. Mabel Cunningham was. She stood tall in the center of the group of girls like a chieftain's daughter.

Mrs. Mead walked Florence out to the carriage on College Street, where her father waited clearer-eyed but still exceptionally quiet. There was not much to say—they had already discussed when Florence might be able to return to South Hadley—just a sympathetic nod exchanged between them as Mrs. Mead went to stand by her students.

The girls didn't wave. They lifted their hands as if they could beam goodwill directly from their palms. Mrs. Mead kept her hands tucked inside her thick maroon cape. Florence's hands were shaking. Everything seemed to be collapsing upon her at once: the reality of leaving without Bertha, without any knowledge of Bertha, without any hope.

"Never come back," said the Reverend as the carriage pulled into College Street—a plea or a command, Florence wasn't sure. She choked on the unexpected force of those words. How deeply she wanted to defend the College, even if it had swallowed Bertha alive, even if it had failed to protect them both. Florence had almost forgotten what this world of women was like, how it made everything seem possible when you were young, and how it did not, after all, fix the troubles of the world or even your own troubles as a woman. How, though it was beautiful, and though she and Bertha had both loved it above all else, it was just a place. Just a school for girls. Just a noble experiment.

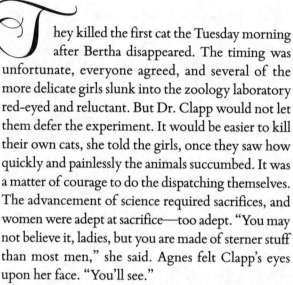

They killed the first cat the Tuesday morning after Bertha disappeared. The timing was unfortunate, everyone agreed, and several of the more delicate girls slunk into the zoology laboratory red-eyed and reluctant. But Dr. Clapp would not let them defer the experiment. It would be easier to kill their own cats, she told the girls, once they saw how quickly and painlessly the animals succumbed. It was a matter of courage to do the dispatching themselves. The advancement of science required sacrifices, and women were adept at sacrifice—too adept. "You may not believe it, ladies, but you are made of sterner stuff than most men," she said. Agnes felt Clapp's eyes upon her face. "You'll see."

Clapp had brought the cat in with her just before the bell rang for class. None of the girls knew where it had been kept the night before: in Clapp's office, in her room? The rumor was that the professor fed the animals well for a few days before the dissection so that her students would be able to properly observe the digestive processes. Some girls, feeling sentimental, imagined her sitting up half the night with the cat curled on her blanket-covered lap, allowing it a last few hours of comfort and care. Every year, Clapp had told them, it was a struggle to find cats for dissection. They seemed to know their days were numbered and would, as she said, "simply light out." This year she had gotten a postcard from Moody's

Corners, a suburb of South Hadley, inviting her to come and take all the cats she wanted. The girls had laughed a little when she showed them the postcard; between the three zoology classes, Clapp would need over a hundred of the creatures so each girl could clean and articulate her own feline skeleton.

Inside the cage the cat hunched silently, unseen. It had not made a sound since Clapp brought the basket in. A sense of anticipation swelled in the room. Death was coming; that alone would have agitated some of the girls on any regular Tuesday. But Agnes's presence added an extra frisson of apprehension. They were waiting to see how she would react in the moment. Would she crumple and cry, releasing her concealed grief over Bertha's absence? Would she blurt out a grim untold story of Bertha's end? Or would she remain as impassive and alien as they usually thought her to be?

Agnes felt their interest, but she was so accustomed to ignoring stares, to evading attention that she did not quite recognize how intently her classmates were observing her. Her mind was bent on the procedure—how quickly the chloroform would take effect, what instrument Clapp would use to make her first incision.

Beside her stood Amy Roberts, the only other girl Agnes considered serious about medicine. Amy was indeed serious— she would write to her parents, later, that this dissection assignment was "the most interesting work I've ever taken." But even she was distracted by Agnes's proximity. Amy, like many of the other girls, had been writing impassioned letters home about Bertha's disappearance: . . . *a dark cloud has appeared in our clear sky and is hanging heavily over us. One of the girls, a Junior, has disappeared. No trace can be found; it seems as if she had absolutely dropped out of existence . . . The general theory is that she is in the river. But, O, this uncertainty is terrible.* She didn't pretend to closeness with Bertha, who *was very reserved and didn't care to mingle with the girls or have them take any notice of her . . . and always kept her Engaged sign out so the girls wouldn't come in*, but she still worried about the damage the Mellish family would suffer. *I'm sorry it must be in the papers*, she wrote, *for of course it will be misinterpreted in every way imaginable.*

Other girls in the classroom had written similar reports home. Helen Calder, hovering in the back, had characterized Bertha as "the most peculiar, quiet, reserved girl at the College." She recounted to her parents the searches underway, the presence of detectives on campus, and the gossip inexorably spreading. *There is insanity in the family on her father's side, and two members of her family were taken with sudden fits of insanity, so that, as she was so very queer, it is possible that she was taken with one of these fits and threw herself in the river, but we do not __know__ anything at all.* She felt "a great gloom resting over the College, and a great strain on us all."

If she'd read them, Agnes would have been appalled by these letters. A great strain on the girls who barely knew Bertha? She would've wanted to strike out their words like a military censor. But she would have been equally appalled by what remained in the letters—the cheerful all-arounder chatter about honor society elections campaigning, the new pastor's wife, and how several feathers and three-quarters of a yard of green ribbon could revivify last year's hat. Bertha's absence as one bit of news among many, framed with nonsense and reduced to rumor.

A few girls were not thinking of Agnes or Bertha at all. A brown-haired sophomore named Grace, who had so far escaped Agnes's notice, found herself wondering how she'd managed to misplace the packet of tea her aunt had sent from London. Others, focused on the cat, clenched their teeth against nausea or dread. Ruthie from Porter wished furiously that her sweetheart Nan were in the class so she could hide her face against Nan's broad shoulder, and had to make do with clutching her friend Ida's hand.

The round bamboo cage swung a little as Clapp lifted it to

the demonstration table at the front of the room. The cage was about two feet tall, sized for a parrot rather than a cat, but Clapp was tall as well. She ignored the murmur that squirmed around the classroom, ignored the cage beside her. From a drawer in the desk she withdrew a pair of sturdy leather gloves that would encase her wrists and half her forearms, like a falconer's gear or a soldier's gauntlets. The girls who hoped that she had cared sweetly for the cat the previous night felt a heaviness in their stomachs at the sight of Clapp in the gloves, Clapp calm and steady, Clapp ready to dispatch an animal for them. For them!

"Come up here, all of you," the doctor said. "No squeamishness, if you please."

The girls rose and moved toward her desk, those who would be nearest the cat shying back so that Agnes stood before them in a row of her own. Clapp gave them an exasperated nod. On one end of the table sat arrayed the bottle of chloroform, Clapp's shining surgical instruments, and the silver tray upon which the dissection would be conducted.

Clapp undid the fastenings on each side of the round cage top and lifted off the lid slowly, as if she were prying open a jar. She reached in and a long high wail rose from the basket.

"That's enough," Clapp said gently and bent lower. She lifted the crying cat out with one hand wrapped around its thin chest. It was a long, skinny animal and its hipbones pressed out like thumbs beneath its fur. Mostly black, but its front paws were white, still dirtied by South Hadley alleyway grime. Down its belly ran a long white stripe that faded into sprinkled tufts. It scrabbled for the edges of the cage, but its claws glanced off the lacquered bamboo and milled helplessly in the air.

Clapp forked her other hand above its hips and stretched the animal out for the girls to see. "Female," she said. "Probably had at least one litter. Young. Less than a year."

The cat hung panting in her grip. Most likely it had been

some farm girl's loved kitten once, before it wandered. It had survived by hunting, and surely it smelled the old blood in the zoology classroom, the traces of vomit in the cracks between the floor tiles. Surely it knew its fate.

Clapp gathered up its hind feet in her other gloved hand. "Agnes, the chloroform," she said.

Agnes reached for the bottle and a cloth and twisted off the cap, then covered the mouth of the bottle with the folded cloth as she tipped it upside down. She felt the cool brush of the liquid against her skin as it evaporated from the cloth. All the girls smelled its sweet antiseptic tang, and so did the cat. Perhaps it had not known before the sort of danger it was in, but when the scent of the chloroform reached the animal it reared and bucked in Clapp's grip and tried to bite.

Clapp tucked the frantic animal against her body and took the chloroform-soaked cloth from Agnes. She held the cloth over the cat's nose as it struggled, and after a moment the cat sagged and its head lolled in Clapp's grip so that she had to follow it with the cloth, bending the cat's neck in a sick curve, to be sure the chloroform had done its job. Then the cat was dead and a few of the girls were gasping and urine had puddled on the table beneath where Clapp held the dead cat aloft.

She stepped sideways and laid the cat down. On the black examining counter it looked like a silken rag. Its mouth was softly open and its pink tongue peeked out.

The girls' eyes flickered between its body and Agnes, whose fingers were still chilled by the chloroform's evaporation. This they would not recount for their mothers and fathers. This they did not know how to describe.

12

ix Porter girls remained at college over the holiday—Nan Miller, Ida Burney, Mollie Marks, Evangeline Bissell, Daisy McFarlane, and Agnes. Mollie and Ida had gone to Mrs. Mead and begged to be moved anywhere else on campus, "just not in here all alone with Bertha gone; it's too horrible." They shuddered about the icy emptiness of the lawns, the echoing quiet of the dormitory cottage hallways, the desolate feel of Bertha's vacant room.

If Bertha had been with her still, Agnes would have thought the holiday heavenly: a silent room in a silent college, with hot coffee when she wanted it and plenty of work to do. Even without Bertha, she wanted to stay in Porter. But the whining girls got their way.

Early on Thanksgiving Day, Agnes stacked together the books she was using. She pried the tacks from the corners of her study cards and peeled them from the sticky wall and put them in her small trunk—smaller even than Bertha's—with the books, two dresses, her underthings, her pencils, and her best pen. She draped two shawls around her neck and shrugged into her jacket. She hardly intended to go outside much, not when there was so much quiet to be found inside.

She followed the other girls uncomplainingly next door to Rockefeller Hall and was pleased to find, when they emerged on the second floor, that while the others had doubled and tripled up in rooms together, she had been given a single at the opposite end of the long shadowed hall. It was hung about with delicate dangling things and cluttered with photographs of insipid-looking people, but it would do. She pinned up her study cards on the room's one bare strip of wall, dragged the desk chair over to face them, and went to work.

MRS. MEAD READ THEM the President's Thanksgiving Day address at ten in the morning after a quick service by the new minister. The girls gathered in the chapel, perhaps thirty of them total, most hovering near the center aisle to trade embraces and sorrowful looks and gossip about the holiday affairs of their luckier absent friends, which functioned as a kind of pathetic currency among them.

"Well, you know Mabel takes dinner to a poor family downstreet before she and her family sit down for their own," Eugenie was saying as Agnes found a seat. "She says it was William's idea, but really it was hers."

Mrs. Mead cleared her throat. She read out President McKinley's words: "In remembrance of God's goodness to us during the past year, which has been so abundant. 'Let us offer Him our thanksgiving and pay our vows unto the Most High.'" They were to be thankful that industry had prospered, labor conditions improved, "the rewards of the husbandman" increased. All safety and comfort was due to God's watchful providence; thanks to his care, all Americans shared "closer bonds of fraternal regard and generous cooperation," the War safely decades behind them.

As Mrs. Mead read, Agnes saw Bertha's laughing face quite clearly in her mind. She had been delighted by the new, self-congratulatory Protestant fad for the Thanksgiving pageant and the pilgrim story. "No more history, only *pie*," Bertha had said their first year together, thrusting her spoon into a gelatinous mess of apples and cinnamon. "What a spectacle."

Each year Bertha disdained the rest of the meal while Agnes

mechanically consumed the dry turkey and stuffing and dense potatoes and thickish cranberry preserves, too practical to let so much food go to waste even though the heft of it in her stomach made her dull afterward. At Mrs. Drew's, where they'd lived after the fire, she'd drowsed in bed beside Bertha, reading with crisp sheets under her cheek, while Bertha nudged her with her toes each time her eyes closed.

"Glutton," Bertha had said. "Rather frowned upon among your sort, I thought."

"Potatoes are not frowned upon," Agnes had muttered.

"Shove over, then, potato eater. I'm half off the mattress."

Would Bertha's voice always be in her ears, saying inconsequential things like that? And saying harder things, too, that Agnes could not think about. It was not surprising that pain lingered, after what had happened. But for once knowing the cause of her distress did not remove it.

At the podium in the nave, Mrs. Mead was still talking, her gray head bent. ". . . let our prayers ascend to the Giver of every good and perfect gift, for the continuance of His love and favor to us, that our hearts may be filled with charity and goodwill, and that we may be ever worthy of His beneficent concern."

Agnes didn't pray, even though the chapel felt like a cathedral with its great stone pillars and arches and stained-glass rose window. She thought of the Mellishes at home in Killingly, of the old man nodding off over his dish and of the blankness that was Bertha's mother, Sarah, about whom Bertha had always been silent. She imagined Florence sitting miserable across from Bertha's empty seat and the pie, the damned pie, growing cold and sticky on the table. Bertha had pretended that she stayed at college for the short holidays because of the cost of going home, but really she had been afraid, Agnes knew, that if she went home too often she would one day be trapped there just like Florence. Killingly was like tar paper under her feet, and Boston the same for Agnes. They had felt easier at the College, safer, as if proximity to books and professors could ward off the dangers of poverty and marriage.

Mrs. Mead was speaking now about the many blessings bestowed upon the College. She hadn't yet mentioned Bertha, but she would. Bertha hovered over the day, over the chapel, like an astringent pagan fog. Her absence crisped the edges of the hymnals and chilled the glow of the pendant lights.

Agnes had a pew to herself, but the room felt dreadfully close. Heat rushed up her throat even as a draft from the door slipped around her ankles. Someone had come in late. Not a College girl. She craned around to look—and there was Hammond settling into a pew in the middle of the chapel. In the high filtering light from the long windows lining the room he looked remote and dignified, little like his usual self.

He saw her at once. If he'd had a ruff or a fanning tail, he would have deployed it in unconscious challenge.

Agnes knew she ought to turn away, but she couldn't. Mrs. Mead had begun talking about Bertha, and it was as if Agnes's diaphragm and the muscles of her trunk had turned crystalline and brittle. She would shatter if she moved. Shatter and wail. She heard another girl get up and hurry from the room, crying, but she couldn't look away from the doctor.

She had tried to proceed with her work as Bertha wanted, to distance herself from any inquiries as cleanly as she could. But she could see that Hammond would not leave until he had discovered Bertha or satisfied himself that she was dead.

Beside Hammond sat another man with sharp-focused eyes, someone Agnes did not know. Hammond leaned to whisper something in his ear, looking at Agnes as he spoke, and those eyes settled on her. Dark eyes, like Bertha's, capable of seeing too much.

13

arly on the morning of Saturday, November twenty-seventh, someone delivered a letter to the rooming house as Hammond slept in the room adjacent to Florence's former bedchamber. He had dined with Higham and the South Hadley chief of police the night before, and his sleep was as heavy as the beer he'd drunk. In the morning he was sore in the shoulders as he stretched and scratched in the animal moments of waking. His eyes felt like hot marbles under puffy lids, and he was rubbing at them roughly when he saw the letter resting on the carpet.

To Dr. H. L. Hammond, said the envelope in a small looping script. *Regarding Miss Bertha Mellish.*

Hammond tore into the envelope and yanked the letter free.

> *Dear Dr. Hammond,*
> *I cannot tell you who I am or how I have come to write this letter. Merely by writing it I deliver myself almost to your hands. I trust, I must trust, that you won't endanger me by searching me out. It is very hard for me to get away even to leave this letter. I am always watched. But I must tell you what I know of Miss Mellish, for I believe that you are the only one who still has faith in her. I believe that you can save her.*
> *My dear sir—Miss Mellish is alive. She is in*

hiding as I write. I do not know where she is. I only know [here a long phrase, scratched out to incomprehensibility] *that she felt she must escape her college. She intended to find a place to "hole up" and insisted that she could not return to her family. I tried to impress upon her the dangers of a woman traveling alone, but she was immovable. I fear that her plans have miscarried terribly and left her without assistance.*

I write to you now so that you will do what I cannot. You must find her and rescue her.

I cannot say why she had to leave South Hadley—her reasons for fleeing are her own. Indeed, I can tell you no more now. Please forgive me. I will write again as soon as I am free to do so. I beg you, do not give up hope! Say that you will search for her and deliver her to safety!

Yours in hope,
A Friend

For a moment after he finished reading he stood and clenched the edges of the paper damply in his fists and breathed in the dust and lavender of the quiet house. Then he thundered down the stairs and out through the front hall, where he nearly knocked over the landlady in his haste.

There was no one outside the house. No clear footprints in the yard. Not a solitary soul visible on the stretch of road, not a cart or a horse.

"Dr. Hammond," Mrs. Goren called in a fluster from the doorway, "whatever is the matter?"

He spun and brandished the creased letter at her. "When did this come? Who brought it?"

"My Matthew, of course."

"No. Not to my room. To the house, this morning. Someone must have come in the night to deliver this." He had crossed the yard somehow as he spoke. His hands were on the lady's shoulders, and her small dark eyes blinked up at him. He saw that his urgency had startled her and knew he ought to desist at once, brush at her thin blue shawl and apologize for his impatience.

"Well, yes, it was by the front door when I came out this morning for the milk. It must have been left overnight. I'd have seen it in the evening," she said. "I always light the lamp after supper in case a guest comes back late, every night. I'd have seen it when I lit the lamp."

"No one saw her, then?" He felt both desolation and excitement. To have lain in drunken sleep while someone with knowledge of Bertha moved secretly in the darkness! And now to hold this letter in his hand, like a key.

"Saw who?"

"The lady who delivered it."

"Surely it wasn't a lady," said Mrs. Goren mildly, regaining some composure. "Not running around in the middle of the night leaving letters on doorsteps. Not here in South Hadley. Not alone."

Hammond looked down at the letter and at once he, too, felt more composed. Not alone, he mused. That was certainly intriguing. But—had the writer ever stated clearly that she was a woman? Upon rereading the letter, he saw no unambiguous evidence of the author's sex, simply declarations of helplessness and fear that he had read as feminine.

Mrs. Goren's eyes brightened at the prospect of gossip. She stood waiting as he read, her hands folded in front of her belly as if she were preventing herself from reaching for a sweet. "Is it—is it something important? About the missing young lady from the College?"

"I don't know," Hammond said and tucked the letter inside his jacket. He wanted to protect it from the grubbiness of gossips like the landlady, as if he could protect Bertha herself by folding the letter against his heart. "It may be nothing. There have been so many false communications. People want to help. They think they are helping, by writing these letters." He had sent the other letters addressed to him to Deputy Sheriff Brockway at first, then handed over the later ones to Higham. The police reaped their own paper harvest. Most concerned sightings of a girl who looked like Bertha—difficult to trace, harder still to verify. Of the pile, just a few had warranted investigation. But this letter felt different.

"—course they want to help," Mrs. Goren was saying. "We all just do what we can, you know. It's no surprise that anybody who might have seen the poor girl would write in to tell you about it."

"No, no surprise at all," he answered, not thinking of what he said.

"There's no name to it, then?" she asked. Her little nose lifted.

"None," said Hammond, thinking of the signature: *Yours in hope.*

14

On Saturday Bertha's ghost was sighted near Pearl City Pond, straight north of the College and a short walk from where Batchelder Brook met the river. It was reasonable, in the minds of South Hadley's more susceptible inhabitants, to think a spirit might have drifted through the woods to hover about its marshy edges. Who knew where Bertha's long walks might have taken her or where she might appear now, dead and vengeful? They could not think of a reason why she would not be skimming down Pearl Street like a woman out of Wilkie Collins, trailing a white wrapper and lifting a doleful hand to her forehead.

Two days later, back in her room in Porter, Agnes read about the Pearl City sighting in the Northampton paper. She read all the papers from the surrounding towns and catalogued the stories about Bertha that appeared next to ads for stomach tonic and fine shoes. Afterward, she folded them into neat packets and burnt them in the furnace. She had grown adept at quietly prizing open the furnace door, though the wash of heat still made her blink and waver.

The newspapers told her that the people of South Hadley and Willimantic and Providence—the people of Boston and New York—the people of Killingly—were eager for more of Bertha, eager enough to see her everywhere. That they, like

Hammond, like Florence, like Agnes herself, were not ready to let Bertha go.

There were other living ghosts. These girls in dark dresses appeared in train depots from Springfield to Baltimore and in public houses in Williamstown and Bedford. A black man from Boston called the police there from his rooming house's hand-crank telephone to say that he'd seen the girl from the newspapers on a New York train as he traveled to the city and back looking for work. He wouldn't give his name; he didn't tell the police about the long tearing moment when he'd wanted to scramble after the odd brown-haired girl when she left the train in Hartford, to catch up to her and see if she was all right, and had instead swallowed the impossibility of it like bile, knowing that he could never run after a white girl, not even to save her life.

Mostly the ghostly girls haunted the towns near the College. One stood on the Amherst road, looking uncertain. One walked dejected along a path through the forest near Mount Holyoke; a hunter almost shot her, thinking her a doe, but by the time he scrambled down to the path she had vanished. In downtown Northampton, a third girl was seen stepping into the druggist's, though when the druggist was questioned later he could not remember having served a girl who matched Bertha's description. "And I'd have recalled that," he told the police. "I fired that Parrott gun last week, down by the river. I'd far rather see her in my shop than in the water, I tell you."

It was as if the world had hidden in its belly a machine capable of stamping out copies of Bertha like a row of tin figures made flesh; she was everywhere and nowhere. Specters of her drifted in street and station. Each time someone claimed to have seen her, the news wound its way by telegraph line and letter and sympathetic word to the people who were searching for her, who loved her, as they struggled through the new rhythm of their days.

Florence lingered in her empty classroom at the day's close

to avoid the cold walk home—and home itself—as long as she could. John slumped at a desk on the upper floor of that home while spilled ink bloomed on the page of the letter before him, obscuring the opening lines of his strangely altered handwriting. Agnes read her papers and books and pamphlets in a carrel at the library, annoyed by the Porter girls in the stacks behind her who traded furious whispers about missing silver dollars. Higham grappled pleasantly with a fey new acquaintance named Ernest in the cellar of Ernest's general store in Amherst; even amid the demands of a new case, he found that time spent on recreation lubricated his investigative process. Hammond sat in the ante-room outside the Northampton treasurer's office and waited to be seen. He was unused to waiting and found himself made meek by the quiet of the room and the tired sighs of the man's secretary as she slit open envelopes one by one. Mrs. Mead gazed out the window of her office in that firm-chinned and resolute pose leaders strike unknowingly. Bertha hovered miasmic over her thoughts of the budget, of final improvements to the chapel building, of the ordering of gravel and salt for the campus walks.

Two of those Bertha had left behind had more irregular habits and were not where others might have expected to find them. These two did not miss Bertha at all.

The first was a man named Joseph, though he went by other names at times to conceal past trouble with the law. He had worked in the woolen mill that summer, then tried to find work in Massachusetts, near the College. When that fell apart, he'd moved on with customary good cheer. There were so many more lovely creatures in the world to meet and know. Joseph moved through the world with a swing in his step, in his heart, in his hips—parallel to the world that Bertha inhabited, with its respectable credentials and uptight expectations, its pressures and punishments.

No one in that world knew about Joseph yet.

The second person who did not miss Bertha was Sarah Mellish. It would be kinder to ascribe this to her ignorance and madness;

John and Florence still hadn't told her of Bertha's disappearance. But the secret of Sarah's life, the shame that had undone her, was that she had wished Bertha gone more times than she could count. Not dead, not missing—but elsewhere. Removed. Trimmed from their lives like excess cloth. She loved the way a scissors closed on fabric. Loved the thin song of the blades, even the dull pair she had for quilting now. And she had always loved patterns, even when she'd been Sarah Lane, an innocent schoolgirl with notebooks full of sketched finery. Not ball gowns: she was never so impractical. Pretty shirtwaists and skirts and jackets, hats with swooping brims and veils. Gloves, parasols. All impeccable.

She'd thought to cut a pattern for her own life. But Florence was lumpen and sickly, a stoic child with a reproachful stare. John alone could make Florence laugh; John alone brought her joy. It hurt, being refused by her own daughter. The closer John and Florence became the quieter Sarah's heart grew. She was glad of John's travels to other congregations, as he often took Florence with him. She didn't wish him beside her in bed or hope for a deeper communion with him. She was dully delighted to be left alone. She skimmed upon the surface of her life like a leaf on water.

Sometimes the water frothed into turbulence and she thrashed and shouted and fell on the stairs. When Florence came home from college, sick. When the new baby was born. When John gave Sarah's father's name to the new baby—Bertha Lane Mellish—and made Sarah care for it while Florence worked. When Bertha was old enough to speak and wouldn't, then wouldn't stop. When she heard John's voice soft in Florence's room or Bertha's. When Bertha read to her from a pamphlet on vivisection about a bitch that had its puppies cut living from its belly and roused itself to lick them and whimper, though it snapped at any other creature, and Bertha's eyes left Sarah scorched and gasping in her attic bed.

She wasn't in the attic room now. It was midnight and the whole house slept, but Sarah was in the kitchen watching a beeswax candle burn. They thought they'd hidden the matches, but she'd seen Maggie take them down from the cabinet by the sink to light the stove. *Let someone else do it, Sarah,* they'd say, *no need to trouble yourself. You must be tired.* She was always tired. But she had had enough of letting someone else do for her. So she would light her own candle and carry it to her room, she would watch her body's shadow dance and twist up the stairwell, she would not fall, she would not pause by her husband's door or her daughter's, and when she had wearied of the candle she would snuff it in the pitcher of water by her bed to hear it hiss.

And she did. Florence never knew her mother had stirred from her attic bed. Sarah dropped no candles, lit no fires. Usually Florence was alert to every creaking board—a habit once practiced in self-defense and now a duty of care, to ward off accidental falls or nighttime wandering. She'd been trying for years to convince her mother to sleep in the parlor instead of up two flights of narrow stairs. But the Lane women were stubborn and ungovernable, as her father used to say.

Florence's parents were her burden, her responsibility, whatever they had been and done before. She hated to think it, but she was obliged to them both, as Sarah was obliged to John. He might have cast either of them off—the infirm wife, the disgraced daughter—but he hadn't. And now she kept them both safe and fed, practicing a kindness she didn't truly feel. Indeed, she felt a power she could not help enjoying in being the one charged with ensuring her parents' safety—the caretaker who must keep *them* confined.

When she was young Florence had hated John for not sending Sarah away. She'd dreamed that a Sarah who left Killingly might miraculously grow well, forget her hatred of Bertha, and return in a fury to fetch both girls. But every dream had concluded with that triumphant rescue. She'd never been able to imagine a life outside John Mellish's house.

That night, after news of more sightings that had evaporated to nothing, Florence came home late to the dark house. Just one lamp burned in the kitchen. Every shadowed corner of the place seemed haunted—by Bertha, by the girls who weren't Bertha. Maggie had made up a plate for her, covered in a tea towel, but Florence left it cold on the counter and went directly to Bertha's bedroom, where she curled on her side atop the quilt and heaved dry sobs into the lacy edge of Bertha's pillowcase. She heard nothing but her own grief.

15

Someone was pinching things from Porter—that was what the girls in the library had been blathering about, Agnes discovered, now that everyone had returned from the holiday and they were back in their usual dormitory houses. The whispers surged through the dining room and down the halls. Girls who should have been studying for examinations lingered in the open doorways of their rooms, ticking off missing items on their gloved fingers, saying, *It was from my father, he sent it for my birthday*—

Some of their outrage was sincere, Agnes thought, and some manufactured. The thief gave the girls of Porter something to talk about that was not Bertha.

Then Agnes began to hear Bertha's name interwoven with chatter about the thief. The two stories folded together in a way she did not like at all.

The thief had begun in Brigham Hall with a scarf and a pair of fine lavender kid gloves. That was the first week in November, before Bertha disappeared, so the girls who had lost their belongings had soon been distracted. Nothing else had been taken from Brigham. But immediately after the holiday the Porter girls began to realize that they were also missing nickels and quarters, a dollar bill or coin or two. Never enough to be really obvious, never more than a girl might have misplaced through carelessness or absent-minded worry.

A few other material goods vanished, too, but nothing as large or identifiable as a scarf. Hairpins, an ink bottle, a packet of tea, a candle. Practical things that might be subsumed into the thief's daily routine unnoticed. How could a girl triumphantly identify her very own hairpin? Agnes half admired the thieving girl, whoever she was, for the forethought employed in the campaign. She did not admire the girl's timing.

Then Mollie Marks, an officious girl with a long equine face who was nominally Agnes's "senior" but seemed satisfied with their policy of mutual avoidance, missed her pearl-handled knife, a pretty little thing she cherished and always carried with her on picnics and apple-picking excursions. Mollie thought it must be evidence that the thief had grown bolder and went around telling everyone so.

In fact, the knife's absence had nothing to do with the Porter thief. Bertha had stolen it from Mollie's room in the depths of her distraction, and Agnes had taken it from Bertha in turn. But only Agnes knew that, and she couldn't—wouldn't—tell.

At once the house was astir. The girls of Porter were certain that the culprit must be one of their own. There were a few full-time maids and workmen at the College, but they were loved, trusted, and condescended to, and any girl who dared to accuse one of them of theft would face the entire College's severe disapproval.

So they began to turn on one another, as Agnes watched.

Mollie Marks marched up and down the halls after morning classes, knocking on doors and noting down from each girl what she thought she was missing. When Mollie rapped stiffly at her closed door Agnes told her she was missing a black ribbon and a dollar in quarters. She thanked Mollie gravely for collecting their information.

As Agnes was closing her door, one of Mollie's followers murmured, "A black ribbon, sad drab thing," and Mollie did not even try to hush her.

Half an hour later, at dinner, Mollie was still railing about the thief. Agnes had brought a book as she often did, but she could not help overhearing. Mollie and her group usually sat at the table closest to the kitchen door in hopes of begging extra cookies at the meal's end. They paid Agnes no mind. She put down her book and picked up her spoon. Dinner that day was ham and creamed onions and brown bread. She was not hungry. She forced herself to eat the ham anyway as she listened to Mollie tell Nan Miller that she thought Mrs. Mead and the staff ought to search all the rooms in Porter and the trunks, too.

"They ought to do it at night," Mollie said, eager. "With lanterns. And dogs, to sniff out our things."

"That'll scare the freshmen silly," said someone else at their table. "What with B—"

A general shushing. Agnes scooped up some creamed onion.

"You think whoever's stealing the money is just going to keep it all in one tidy little pile, like a dragon hoard, Mollie?" That was brash, ruddy-cheeked Nan. "Are you St. George in this scenario? You'd look fine in armor. I bet we've got some from the last theatrical that would suit you perfectly."

"Of course not," Mollie barked. "I'm not stupid. But a good scare might be helpful. Isn't that the whole principle behind having police in the first place?"

"The police?" said the second voice, disbelieving, and Nan chimed in:

"Really, Mollie, it's a little early for that, don't you think? Especially given what's been going on lately?"

Mollie said, with a clever air, "Well, how do we know there's no connection between the events?"

The table fell silent. Agnes ate two more bland velvety spoonfuls of onion.

"Whatever do you mean?" Nan asked finally.

Someone said in a deep sepulchral tone, "The ghost of—"

"Stop!" More than one voice, in reproach.

Mollie gave an affected laugh. "How dreadful! No, but we still haven't any idea what's happened to the poor girl, do we? Or if anyone at the College was involved?"

"They'd know by now," said Nan.

"Be that as it may," said Mollie, "I still think our rooms ought to be searched. I've got nothing in mine that I'm afraid to show. And it really is not right for Mrs. Mead to sit by and let a thief roam the school. There must be some way to figure out who's been doing this, and I don't see how we can start if we don't muster a bit of organization among ourselves."

"In other words," said Nan, "you will tell us all what to do."

Mollie stood with a huffed exhale. "I don't believe anybody could tell you what to do, Nan Miller. But no matter what you say, I am going to talk to Mrs. Mead. And Mabel's going with me."

Agnes set her dish down on the table harder than she meant to. A general search of the house intended to find stolen money or other girls' belongings was unlikely to endanger her, she reasoned. She'd burned or hidden nearly all of Bertha's letters and tucked the few she'd saved into the lining of her trunk or suitcase, along with several from Hammond. The pearl-handled knife Bertha had stolen and the gun Agnes kept were still safe in their knotholes. She'd returned the supplies she'd taken from Clapp's lab. And she truly was missing the black ribbon and quarters she had told Mollie about.

Yet she remembered how Detective Higham's sharp dark eyes had marked and measured her in the chapel. In the newspapers they wrote of him frequently now: the man on the scene, here to loom over the rural police with his old Boston badge and his threatening manner. She'd thought herself prepared to speak to him, but he had not come to interview her, and she didn't know why.

She wanted Bertha's opinion of the man. Bertha would tell her if she was misjudging the detective; Bertha would know whether she should let the girls search her room or not.

"You think everyone should make decisions the way you do,"

Bertha had teased her once while they were living at Mrs. Drew's, during one of their spirited debates about how their governance would improve the world. "Just calculate the likely outcomes and choose sensibly. But some people are driven by emotions, Agnes, not probabilities."

"I know that," Agnes had said, mildly affronted. "But their emotions are idiotic. I don't see why I ought to have to think about them."

"Of course they are. And I suppose you don't have to. But then how can you predict what they will do?" Bertha had leaned up to sink her fingers into Agnes's hair and touch the knot of scar tissue hidden just under her bun. Agnes had let her. Bertha's eyes had looked strange, her pupils wide. Then the moment had broken. "When you are queen, Agnes," she'd said lightly, "you shall ban all feeling. But you know what happens to papist queens," and her fingers had raked across Agnes's throat and set them both to laughing.

Then another memory: the feel of Bertha's hair clammy with sweat under her hand, Bertha's cheeks hectic red and white.

Agnes became aware that she was sitting with her spoon suspended over an empty bowl and that the dining room had gone quiet. Her breath came fast and whispery. These memories of Bertha were like membrane-covered vats of viscous liquid. She could move across their taut surfaces, seemingly secure, until the membrane split and deposited her gasping in the past.

She pushed away the bowl and looked around the dining room. Mollie's table had emptied. Normally, at this time, the girls of the house would retreat upstairs to flop onto their beds and call to each other down the halls with complaints about afternoon classes, then rouse themselves, neaten their hair, and proceed to those classes as cheerfully as ever. Agnes usually went to her Latin class directly from her meal, but now she stood and buttered her remaining slice of bread and wrapped it in her handkerchief.

She kept her head down as she walked up the stairs to her room. The hall was quiet and most of the girls' doors were three-quarters closed, a position that seemed to signal *I am here and I invite your curiosity, but I won't beg you to enter.* Agnes went to her room, put down her book and her packet of bread, and raised her face to the mirror propped upon her dresser. She thought she might see some hint of the yearning for Bertha that swamped her insides, but it was invisible; she looked as she always did.

As she left the room with her Latin books she heard Evangeline Bissell's voice across the hall, rising high with emotion. But Eva was not crying, which was unusual. Eva's weepiness was her sole noticeable trait. Agnes had heard her crying about Bertha when they were in Rockefeller for the holiday, and for once the girl's frailty had stirred her heart.

Eva and Daisy McFarlane's door was also slightly open. Agnes crept closer.

Eva sounded angry. Agnes would not have believed it possible. "Little Eva," the Porter girls called her because there had been another, senior Eva, when she'd been a freshman, and because she was so small and pale and delicate. She was Daisy and Nan and Ida and Ruthie's pet, always being coddled and kissed by the other girls in her group like a kind of babyish mascot—though Bertha would not have thought that description fair. Bertha had liked Eva well enough. "So soft-hearted it's a wonder she has a pulse," she'd said, and Agnes had told her that the heart was not a metaphor.

"—hate it," Eva was saying now, presumably to Daisy. They sounded as if they were on the opposite side of the room, probably near the windows, Agnes guessed—she had never been invited inside. "All this suspicion, and Mollie's stupid list, everything. I wish it would all just go away. Even if they find the girl who's taking things it'll still be terrible because it's one of us. And what if—what if the girl has a good reason?"

"What do you mean, a good reason?" asked Daisy, a hint of scorn in her voice. "Eva, you're too much, pudding. What good reason could there possibly be for stealing from your own house?"

"Oh, I don't know, I'm sure there isn't one." Just like Eva to give way at once. "But so many girls have such money troubles. Or—like with Bertha Mellish. What if a girl got in some awful scrape and couldn't tell about it? We'd *want* her to have the money, wouldn't we, then? If it would help?"

Agnes found herself clutching the edges of her book so hard her fingers ached. What if Bertha had instead gone to Eva with her terrible story? If she had gone to someone, anyone, earlier—if she hadn't been so afraid of disappointing Agnes and her sister—would she be down the hall now in her single room, drilling Greek declensions until the last minute before class, perhaps chastened but present, wonderful, herself?

There was a short silence. "Have you heard something? About Bertha?" Daisy whispered.

"No!" A pause, then Eva said again, more softly, "No."

"*You've* lost money to this thief," Daisy said. "And you can't afford it any better than your hypothetical girl could, so I don't see how you can excuse that kind of meanness."

"I'm not excusing it," Eva said. "I wish it weren't happening, that's all, and I don't like seeing everyone get all heated up to catch the girl. They're not thinking of what it will be like if they do catch her."

"And you are thinking of it, of course, little one," said Daisy tenderly, and then there was a soft sound, some kiss or caress. "All right, all right. I'm convinced. Mollie Marks can suck an egg, and I'll tell her so if you like, thief or no thief. Come on, get your books and let's go to Nan's for a minute."

Agnes darted clumsily back into her room. She left her door open just a crack, and after a moment she saw Daisy and Eva sweep past, Daisy's arm slung comfortably around Eva's thin shoulders. Pure melancholy pinched her gut. How much love these girls had—how capacious their understanding of one another. They could speak to Eva like a child, ignore her like a child, and still recognize it when she said a wise thing and ought to be listened to. Eva could tolerate their cosseting and their "little ones," she could cry in public and yet say what she believed with no fear of being cast out of her small circle.

Agnes stood in the corner behind her door with her Latin books dangling by her side. She wasn't thinking about the thief or about having her room searched. She was pitying herself in her loneliness, lost in the dark hollows of memory, thinking of how much more she ought to have sacrificed for Bertha's sake.

THE NEXT DAY, AGNES walked out of Wilmot's elocution class to find Detective Higham waiting, as if her worry had summoned him. He'd taken off his hat but was still wearing his spotless black coat, and he stood like the former cop he was: hulking, hands clasped behind his back. "Miss Sullivan," he said. "Some questions."

"Yes," she said.

"Not in the hallway."

Higham asked Dr. Wilmot if the classroom was free and she nodded, but her eyes stayed on Agnes and her mouth tightened with worry. "Girls," Wilmot said sharply to the stragglers—Nan and Ruthie, the lovebirds, who'd spent half the class cooing about the locket Nan had bought Ruthie to "keep me close to your heart"—and hustled them out. As they passed Agnes they pretended not to stare, but even she could sense the messages being traded through the squeezing of their joined hands.

Higham held the door open for her and pointed at a chair. Agnes deposited her books there and sat in the next one.

"You were expecting me, I gather," Higham said as he stripped off his coat and folded it upon the heavy desk at the front of the classroom, perhaps ten feet away. He leaned back against the desk and a glint of a smile showed under his black mustache. Down the hallway, echoing from the stairwell, a coruscation of feminine laughter punctuated his words. Other classes letting out, other girls trying to cheer each other. He didn't look away from Agnes.

"Yes," Agnes said again.

"Are you English or Irish, Miss Sullivan?" He leaned unsubtly on her name.

"I have Irish heritage."

"Converted when?"

"As a child," she said. "In the public schools. I was lucky."

"Lucky, you say."

Agnes's hands curled together in her lap. She never knew what to do with her hands when she was nervous, and Higham made her profoundly nervous. He was a hunter, that much she could discern. Akin somehow to the large wild cats she'd read about: the loping run that let them tire a smaller creature, the final sweep of a paw and crunch of incisors on the vertebrae of the cervical spine.

"To have left the Church young, so that I could come to college. There was a woman on our street, a Congregationalist. She helped me find a place here."

"Where did you come from?" Higham asked.

"Boston." She dared to shoot him a skeptical look. "Just like you."

Higham nodded acknowledgment. "What do you know about Miss Mellish's manuscript?"

"Very little," she said.

"As you told her sister and the doctor," Higham said. His broad hands curved around the front edge of the desk and two fingers on his right hand tapped almost soundlessly against the wood as he spoke. She wanted to seize his hand and force his fingers quiet. They were all asking the same questions, over and over, and she had to recite the same answers, because they would seize instantly upon any mistake. She couldn't think with his fingers drumming like that.

"Yes."

"But you read it," he said.

"I read a paragraph or so. About running in the woods. Bertha had a question about vocabulary," said Agnes, watching his fingers.

"So you didn't know the story ended with a suicide."

"What? No. Not then. Miss Florence said—she said the girl dies at the end."

"Would you have worried, do you think, if you'd known about the ending of the story?"

Would she have worried. It wasn't the ending of the story that had shaken her, as Bertha whispered it to her later. It was the story's middle, when the mill girl Marie lost her job through carelessness and subsided into motherhood. That was what led to the ruinous ending. That was where it all went wrong.

Higham was staring at her, his fingers still. Agnes forced herself to shake her head. "It's a story," she said.

"Yet you know about her family history, do you not? The congressman uncle who ran mad in his prime? And Bertha's mother, rather frailer than her years would suggest."

"Yes. Bertha told me." Agnes met the detective's eyes. "Nobody in the family has killed himself, I don't believe. Her uncle died before she was born."

After that he asked more anodyne questions. Had she noticed any change in Bertha recently, what had it been like when they lived together off campus after the fire—that one she hated to answer. It felt like a lie to pretend that time had been no different from sharing a dormitory hallway with Bertha. But she couldn't explain how protected she had felt as they lay in the darkness of their shared bed at Mrs. Drew's, whispering secrets like children, Bertha spooling out how their lives would proceed once they graduated. "You'll cut and I'll write," she'd whispered, breath feathering Agnes's hair. "You'll keep me and I'll fortify you."

The room had fallen silent. Higham looked down at a cold bar of light edging across the floor, and she followed his gaze. It was late morning, and the windless world outside was made distant by the window glass, as if they were trapped together in a strange terrarium. No sounds from the students on the gravel paths, walking together to their next classes. No one in the hall coming to interrupt this questioning. "What do you think of Dr. Hammond?"

Agnes engaged in a moment of furious silent calculation.

What did she think of Dr. Hammond? She thought of the last time Bertha had read out a letter from Hammond, back in early September, when she was still in fine fettle—an amused look in her eyes, voice flat as an automaton's, stripping away sentiment from the doctor's fine missive to render it a mechanical offer of marriage.

Hammond wrote in a tiny hand that Agnes had admired for its neatness, but Bertha, whose script sprawled over the page, derided it. "It shows a decided lack of character and confidence," she'd said. "Why write in such minute hieroglyphics unless you're convinced that what you're writing is worthless?" *Con-vinced*, Bertha had said. But though Bertha was willing to mock Hammond in private, she'd never refused his visits. She'd met him for walks away from the dormitory house—by the ponds or in the nearby village, where Agnes could not observe their interactions. Agnes understood that the connection between their families made it difficult for Bertha to reject him directly. But she'd never understood the change that seemed to come over Bertha as she prepared for those walks, how muted and meek she became.

"Why, what do you think of him?" she asked Higham.

Another partial smile, a nimble turn. "What does Miss Mellish think of him?"

"I don't know." Her voice sounded strained. She hoped he wouldn't sense the fierce regret she felt for the truth of those words. "Why do you ask?"

Higham lifted a shoulder, let it drop. "Someone should," he said, and she felt blood rise in her cheeks. She'd thought of the detective as second in command and Hammond his master. But Hammond was no whip hand to tame this man's fierceness. And Higham, undomesticated, might abandon the orderly investigation, the rote questions. He might select his own prey.

16

Hammond, fresh from another useless meeting with the local police, met Higham for the daily meeting with Mrs. Mead—a ritual emptied of meaning, where they reported to one another that they had nothing to report. The girls were going on unhappily with their last weeks of term. Soon they'd leave campus for the winter break, and any information they possessed would be submerged under a flood of eggnog and swept away by holly branches. And Hammond would have to return to John Mellish in Killingly and tell him that his daughter had truly vanished, that he had failed to find her, that she had gone beyond their protection and been surrendered to God's.

Mrs. Mead was careful to address them both equally, but she favored Higham's proposals for what to do next. Of course, Higham offered more suggestions, casually supported by his experience. All those missing girls; all those crying families. Years and years of them, while he, Hammond, had been palpating businessmen and wiping the crusted French-Canadian noses of poor Killingly children. Hammond felt himself at a loss in a way he rarely did.

Higham said nothing to Mrs. Mead about the letter delivered to the rooming house; when Hammond had showed it to the detective, he'd said it seemed no different from the flood of other fruitless tips they'd received. But just before they left, she

told them one surprising thing: that someone, probably a student, had been stealing trinkets and small amounts of money from the girls' rooms in Porter Hall—Bertha's dormitory cottage. "They're quite upset by it, as you can imagine," she told Higham. "Some of them are worried that it might be related to Miss Mellish, though I can't see how. Do you think that possibility ought to be explored?"

"Unlikely," said Higham. "Thieves generally stick to thieving, I've found. We've seen no evidence that anyone from the College was involved with Miss Mellish's disappearance. And if a person were involved, that person would have to be extremely reckless or extremely stupid to risk exposure for petty theft. I doubt any of your students fit that description, ma'am."

Mrs. Mead did not smile. "Quite."

"Is there much theft at the College?" Hammond asked.

"It happens on occasion. They're still children, you know, some of them, even at twenty."

"Of course," said Hammond soothingly.

Mrs. Mead lifted her head and pressed her shoulders back. "I'll speak to the Porter girls tonight. Some of the girls are turning a bit mean, trying to sort out who might be doing the stealing, and that won't do at all. Shall I keep you informed about the thief?"

"Why not." Higham bowed a little in farewell, raising his hat to his chest.

"What of Agnes Sullivan?" Hammond asked as they walked down the stone stairs of Mary Lyon Hall.

"What of her?"

"You don't find her—rather odd?"

That smirk again. He had never before noticed the special brand of knowingness policemen had; it was most distasteful. "Yes, I find her rather odd," Higham said, "but not particularly interesting. She gave her account of Miss Mellish's behavior preceding her disappearance. They don't seem to have talked much of frivolities, and I expect they both thought most everyday matters frivolous."

"But she—"

Higham looked at him sidelong. "You think she's the thief, then?"

"No," said Hammond and found that it was true. "It's only—she is different. There's something about her behavior that is not like the other girls'."

"Would you not have said the same of Miss Mellish?"

"No," he snapped, surprising himself. "That is—yes. She's different, too, but not like that, not so strange as Miss Sullivan. The other girls who live in Porter, when we've spoken to them, they've been nervous. She doesn't seem nervous. She doesn't seem scared. Her best friend in the world disappears, and she's not scared?"

Higham tilted his head consideringly. "Perhaps she doesn't get scared. Some don't, you know. And she herself is not in any danger, not unless Miss Mellish's disappearance has far deeper roots than we've yet discovered."

"What do you mean, deeper roots?"

"There is the matter of the family's political history."

"I thought her uncle was to be left out of it," Hammond said. In fact, he had been waiting for Higham to raise this. In 1874, Bertha's uncle David Mellish had been a brilliant young politician, serving his first term in the House of Representatives—working in support of a bill Hammond himself had been eager to see pass, one that aimed to "get the civil rights of black and white citizens settled on a basis of equality." He'd succumbed to mania while giving a speech on the House floor and been committed to an asylum, where he died less than two weeks later. The Mellishes never spoke of him. The story was that he had simply worked himself to death, though Hammond suspected some deeper physiological disorder.

"What in the world would David Mellish's death have to do with Agnes Sullivan?"

Higham shrugged. "Surprising what people will do sometimes to keep family business private. If Miss Sullivan really did know Miss Mellish so well, she might have seen signs of madness that could embarrass the family, if—"

"She said nothing about signs of madness! She said Bertha was well and happy—"

"If there were any to see," Higham went on. "The uncle's decline was certainly an embarrassment. A public breakdown of that sort. The family might doubt Agnes Sullivan's discretion."

"The family?" Hammond knew he was spluttering. "You make it sound as if Miss Mellish came from some powerful dynasty. Whom do you suspect? Sarah Mellish? She's not all there, sure enough." He saw Higham raise an eyebrow and knew what the detective was thinking—madness on both sides of the family, then. He barreled forward anyway. "I examined the Reverend Mellish myself, and he's weak as a kitten. It's half killed him, Bertha disappearing. You think he'd be hiding in the bushes here to ambush Agnes Sullivan, is that it?"

"Or perhaps he intervened earlier, to silence Bertha himself," Higham said. "Guilt can destroy a man as handily as grief."

Hammond stared. He was thinking of John Mellish's tenderness with Bertha, how he doted on his ailing wife—how he'd forgiven Florence her sin. The stern pastor softened by love.

"Dr. Hammond," Higham said, holding up his hands, "I'm not suggesting that John Mellish would harm a girl—or his own daughter—to prevent a scandal—"

"You certainly are."

"All right," said Higham. "Maybe I am. But that's why I'm here, isn't it. To make suggestions. To ask these questions, if it finds the girl."

Hammond's chin went up. "Miss Mellish."

"Miss Mellish," Higham allowed. "You know I'll need to go to Killingly next."

17

Mrs. Mead filled the captain's chair she'd had placed below the steps up to the nave of the chapel, so the rose window hovered behind her like a foreboding halo. The place was echoing quiet, all the girls of Porter packed into the front pews. Rows of bowed heads, hands folded in their skirts. Agnes bent her head, too. She'd hung back as the girls filed into the chapel, so she was sitting in the last occupied pew, near a second-floor girl whose name she had forgotten. Even with her eyes cast down, Agnes could see Mabel Cunningham's beautifully dressed auburn head swiveling to take stock of the room.

"Girls, this is simply no good," Mrs. Mead began. Agnes lifted her head. "I am very disturbed to learn the extent of the problem in Porter Hall. We will do all we can to get to the bottom of these thefts. I assure you, they will stop and we will track down the culprit. But the limericks, girls, and the teasing. I won't tolerate it. There is a difference between spirit and cruelty. I should not have to tell you this—you, especially. Porter has been shaping up to be such a congenial house."

Agnes had seen one of the limericks, evidently written by Mollie and her crew, that compared Nan Miller to a Holstein, illustrated by an accomplished drawing of that sort of cow. What cows had to do with theft Agnes did not comprehend, though the size of the animal's hindquarters made the insult to Nan quite clear.

A murmuring spread among the girls, and Mrs. Mead tilted her head in inquiry. "Is there something else?"

Mollie Marks raised her hand, and Mrs. Mead nodded. "Yes, Mollie."

"Mrs. Mead, it's the College's responsibility to get back our property, isn't it? Who's going to repay the money that's been taken?"

"Your personal effects are your own responsibility," Mrs. Mead admonished, looking out over the assembled girls. "Don't let these losses make you forget what you owe to one another. Thievery is always upsetting, but it should not make us betray each other in suspicion. Sometimes things are lost through no fault of our own."

"It's not suspicion," Agnes heard Nan Miller mutter to Ida Burney. "I hate that nosy shrew, that's all."

The nosy shrew in question spoke again without raising her hand. "Mrs. Mead, what if it's Bertha Mellish? What if she's been hiding somewhere in the house and stealing our—"

"You blithering fool, Mollie," rasped Nan. "Stop scaring—"

"That is enough," Mrs. Mead said. "Both of you. The best detectives and policemen are searching for Miss Mellish, but they are no closer to finding her. Now, that is not because she is hiding in your house, Mollie. It is clear that she is not on this campus. If she remains alive, she may be in grave danger." Her gray eyes were grim and her voice increasingly firm. "I will not have you using the poor girl's name idly. I want no talk of ghosts or mysterious happenings, and no nonsense about a connection between Miss Mellish and this petty thievery, do you understand?"

The chapel filled with the shuffling silence of embarrassed bodies. Agnes imagined Bertha rolling her eyes in derision. Bertha, she thought with a bittersweet pang, would have loved to be a ghost. She would have tested the most efficient methods of rustling curtains and flinging hairbrushes—the highest yield of swoons and screams.

"Do you understand, girls?" Mrs. Mead repeated, and they chorused obediently that they did. "That's all, then. If you have any concerns, you will come speak to me directly. Mollie, Nan, I'll speak with you both now. Good night, girls."

A subdued "Good night, Mrs. Mead" rose from the assembly as the girls stood and Nan and Mollie pushed down the aisle to attend Mrs. Mead. Agnes tried to get out of the pew quickly, but the girl in front of her dawdled, gesturing to a friend farther back. She turned to glance down the long empty pew, but no—too conspicuous to escape that way while everyone else filtered out through the center door.

She turned back to wait. The Porter girls were watching her as they came up the aisle in their little groups, not with outright hostility but with curious, distressed looks. Only Eva, tucked under Daisy McFarlane's arm, smiled tremulously as she passed Agnes's pew. But then Mabel stumbled against someone's heel and the girls' attention shifted, their voices rising.

Agnes watched them clutch at each other, and emotions she did not wish to feel battered powerfully against her interior armor.

DETECTIVE HIGHAM WANTED TO speak to Florence's mother. "No need to disturb the Reverend," he said, and nodded gravely when she told him that John was resting and that Sarah did not know of Bertha's disappearance. He gave no sign that he thought it strange for Florence to have withheld that information.

"You can't tell her yet," Florence whispered, even though Sarah was two floors away from the parlor, too far to hear. "Not until we know more. She would not understand."

"Of course." A neutral tone. "I leave such decisions to the family."

Florence had been surprised by his appearance at their door, sans Hammond. She couldn't remember the last time she'd stood in the parlor alone with a strange man and felt embarrassingly aware of her body, her movements. The space she took up. But the detective was surveying the room, not her. It was late afternoon and warm in the front room from the day's sun, and the plain furnishings sat austere in the twilight. How provincial it all must look to his city eyes—an environment Bertha could have been eager to escape.

"Shall I fetch her, then? Please, take a seat."

Florence entered the attic tentatively. Sarah was not asleep in her armchair, though at first Florence thought so, as her mother's eyes were closed and her messy, half-done embroidery hoop slipping from her lap. She was simply wherever she went in her mind. When Sarah heard the door hinge squeal, her blue eyes fluttered open: expectant, slightly wary, big in her bony withered face.

"Are we late for school?" Her voice was reedy. "I don't want to go today."

"No, Sarah," Florence said, forcing cheer. "No school today. We have a visitor. Let's get you sorted." She helped her mother up and tucked mussed strands of white hair back into Sarah's coif. Her mother hummed a little in pleasure.

Higham watched, smiling, as Florence helped Sarah down the stairs, tucked her into the opposite armchair, and hovered near the doorway. She was desperate to flee, but she wouldn't leave Sarah to speak with the man alone—God only knew what she might say. Or what he might say.

"Do sit, Miss Mellish," prompted Higham, "and introduce me to your charming mother."

Maggie had brought tea. The detective drained the china cup and set it in his saucer, then reclined against the armchair across the parlor from Florence. The Mellishes did not own chairs designed for lounging, and he seemed almost to take that as a provocation.

He was smiling at Sarah again, his keen edge disguised under pleasantry. Florence stumbled through an explanation of his presence—he was a friend of Dr. Hammond's, broadening his acquaintance in the town. Higham played his part amiably. Yes, he was from Boston, though his accent was not very strong. Yes, the trains had improved a great deal of late with the new electric lines, as Sarah had heard. It was an easy journey now from the city and one he was happy to make to assist his friend the doctor. Florence, praying all the while that John would not wake and hear their voices, thought he gave a droll twist to that last phrase.

He didn't ask about Bertha at all. At first Florence was glad—anything to steer Sarah's thoughts elsewhere—but the longer he avoided Bertha's name the more surreal the conversation felt, as if they were all players acting out a shared scene from wildly different scripts.

"Are you new to town, Mr. Higham?" Sarah asked, sipping at her cooled tea. She'd made the same polite inquiry twice before, but barring that repetition she bore little resemblance to the hazily silent figure who had joined Florence for breakfast. The exceptional manifestation of a guest in her parlor had activated her social training; brief conversations Sarah could often manage well enough to fool most people into thinking her functional. She was not fooling Higham.

"Just visiting, ma'am," Higham repeated. His eyes met Florence's, a dark jolt. Did she see sympathy alloying the scrutiny?

After a few minutes of bright, empty talk about the town's churches, Higham stood and bowed his head to her mother. "Well, I won't take up too much of your time. I'm told I can be fatiguing."

Sarah's laugh had never aged. She gave the detective her thin hand to kiss.

Florence saw him out and followed him onto the stoop, pulling the front door shut. Her stomach was tight with relief. John had stayed safely confined in his room. Higham had asked no questions that suggested he knew about Bertha's history or her own. She'd been certain that if her father had come downstairs to join them in the parlor, if Higham had observed her with both the Reverend and his wife, he would glean truth from their tense exchanges. Her life was built on concealment, shored up by the willingness of others to avoid inspecting it closely, and Higham's sharp attention felt like a tunnel undermining a castle wall. Breached and under siege.

"Detective Higham. Why are you here?" She kept her voice low, thinking of the neighbors.

He turned back at the bottom of the steps. "In Killingly?"

"To see my mother."

"The home, the family, is central to many cases of this sort," he said. "I need to know where your sister comes from in order to find her."

Florence stared. What if that were true? What if he couldn't find Bertha because Florence couldn't bear to admit to the devastation that had framed her life?

She had to tell him.

"My mother barely knows what day it is," she said faintly.

She couldn't. She couldn't.

He peered at her as if she'd said something surprising. "Yes, I see," he said after a minute.

On the stoop, she stood a little taller than he did and could see that his shirt collar needed starching. That helped her to marshal herself. "If you're investigating in Killingly, I should come along with you. I know these people. I teach their children."

He shook his head. "I'm afraid that isn't possible. You must understand—an outside eye is needed here."

"You hardly know the town. Surely—"

"I appreciate the offer, but you must leave me to my work, Miss Mellish, and keep on at your own."

The set of his mouth troubled Florence. She'd been thinking

only of what he might sense in her home. But his compressed lips said, silently, that he knew something he would not share.

She looked to the graying horizon, trying to compose herself. He and Hammond would notify her when they felt it necessary and proper, of course. Perhaps it was nothing—that's what they would say to one another. *No need to worry the poor woman until we know more.*

"Hammond won't be accompanying me, either," Higham said, as if that ought to satisfy her. He settled his hat atop his dark head and tilted the brim at her.

Florence wondered if he expected her to offer her hand in limp farewell, as Sarah had. She swallowed a wash of rage and turned back to open the door. "Thank you for the visit, Detective," she said over her shoulder. "I trust you'll keep me informed."

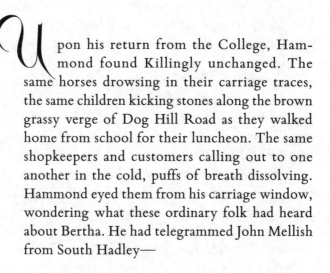

pon his return from the College, Hammond found Killingly unchanged. The same horses drowsing in their carriage traces, the same children kicking stones along the brown grassy verge of Dog Hill Road as they walked home from school for their luncheon. The same shopkeepers and customers calling out to one another in the cold, puffs of breath dissolving. Hammond eyed them from his carriage window, wondering what these ordinary folk had heard about Bertha. He had telegrammed John Mellish from South Hadley—

WILL RETURN TOMORROW WITH DET HIGHAM STOP I PROPOSE TO RAISE REWARD AND WILL FUND STOP

—and a grateful, positive answer came so quickly that he wondered if the operator had conveyed the message to the Mellishes or simply answered directly.

His house on Pleasant Street looked so well that it lifted his mood at once; there were candles in the downstairs windows and a rosemary wreath above the door-knocker. He opened the door with a surge of relief. The cats looked hale and happy, thank God. Columbia and Tricksey were elsewhere, but Carmilla and Gerry came trotting to greet him, both scolding like squirrels and circling across his path as he tried to walk toward the kitchen.

"Hello, darlings, hello, yes," he said, "I'm home, I'm home. I know. Where's your mama gotten to, Gerry?" Gerry was the one who held conversations; Carmilla simply made demands. At this moment she was demanding that he carry her, so he put down his case and opened his arms and she leapt delicately into the cradle of his elbow, then leaned up to butt at his chin. "Hello, sweet Carrie doll. Hello, good girl," he whispered as he stroked her narrow striped shoulders. She purred and dug her claws into his coat.

Mrs. McDowell came out of the kitchen, wiping her hands on her apron. Her gray-blond hair frizzed about her round face, and tendrils of it waved gently when she walked as if she were underwater. He had a flash of her as a younger woman, cheeks thinner and eyes clearer, before her husband died. Her husband—Joseph, like the Frenchman in Bertha's tale—had suffered a heart attack, sprawled facedown in the back garden with one hand still tangled in a tomato cage. Then his Emma had died, and now Bertha was gone. And here they were, the widowed housekeeper and the widower doctor.

"Welcome home, Doctor Hammond. Are you back for good, then? Any news of the poor girl?"

"No, no news, I'm sorry to say. The detective wanted to speak more to the family, so I've come back as well to make sure I haven't lost my entire livelihood in my absence. And to see these unruly creatures, of course," he added as Gerry trilled and jumped up onto the sideboard. "They've been good for you, I hope."

"Lively as ever, Doctor," she said and let Gerry arch and rub against the back of her hand. "That Carrie's been taking wild every afternoon at four on the dot. Goes racing up and down the stairs and along the front hall, and nearly flattens herself every time."

"The freedom of youth," said Hammond, and he had to press his face to Carrie's soft ear for a moment. Dr. Darling had left some files in his study, Mrs. McDowell told him, and wanted to see him later to catch him up on John Mellish's treatment and the progress of Hammond's other patients. He went up to find the papers and to seek out Columbia.

She was in her bed atop the cabinet by his desk, curled like a nautilus with her pointed tail around her back legs and the vee of her upturned white chin vulnerable. He deposited Carrie onto his desk and bent to kiss the soft mottled fur of Columbia's middle. She grumbled a little and tightened all over with a noise of pleasure, a spring of a cat, a perfect machine for sleeping and hunting and adoration. Next to Bertha, she was the most beautiful thing he'd ever seen.

AFTER HIS CONFERENCE WITH Darling, Hammond walked a ways down Hartford Pike to clear his head, into a wind that numbed his legs and neck. He returned to find Higham waiting outside his house, cheeks striped with color, smoking and staring down the poplar tree out front as if it might challenge him to a duel. The detective said nothing in greeting, just tossed down the butt and turned in behind Hammond on a neat rotation of his heel. Hammond wondered, not for the first time, if he'd been a military man.

"You could've waited inside," Hammond said, irritated with himself for considering what the neighbors must have thought to have seen Higham standing in the yard like a servant. "Mrs. McDowell!"

She leaned out into the dining room. "Sir?"

"Tea," he said and blew his nose again. Higham was still on his heels. They went into the front sitting room and warmed their hands above the fireplace grate.

"I see what you meant, about Mrs. Mellish," Higham said. "She's quite delicate."

"It's more than that, isn't it, though? She doesn't know that Bertha is missing." Higham brushed an errant cat hair from his sleeve, then looked over at Hammond. "Didn't say a word about her."

Hammond kept his eyes on the flames. "Oh?"

"Got the impression Florence Mellish thinks of nothing else. *She's* rather fierce. Wanted to help with the investigation."

Hammond exhaled a laugh. "I assume you told her that would be inadvisable."

"Quite," said Higham, though he didn't sound amused. "I'll stay a few days, have a look around the mill. See what they remember about Bertha from the summer. Any strange behavior. And I'll ask around for a mill worker named Joseph, just in case."

A log in the fireplace popped, and for a moment they were silent.

"You must stay here; there's plenty of room," Hammond said then, without enthusiasm.

Higham shook his head and cut a look at him. In the firelight his eyes were molten. "I'm at the Attawaugan Hotel in Danielson. It's better, if anyone has information. They won't come to your house with their secrets."

Hammond felt affronted and relieved. The people of Killingly came to his house with everything else: with their sores and their sorrows, their gassy bellies and their swollen feet. They came to hurry him back to their dirty kitchens, where he'd have to sweep weeks of greasy crumbs off a table before laying a child out for an examination. But he had to admit that Higham was correct—his patients didn't confide in him. They treated him, especially the Catholics, as a kind of saint who might intercede with a distant god of health.

The detective said he'd come back tomorrow. Hammond followed him and waved him off and stood there in the frigid doorway for a long moment, the tang of rosemary surrounding him.

A brush against his leg. He'd forgotten!—and he reached down just in time to wrap his hand around Tricksey's belly and haul her back over the threshold. "*No*," he said, stricken, "don't ever, Tricks," and lifted her up and muttered against her squirming side. She, alone among the cats, hated to be held. He held her anyway.

EARLY THE NEXT MORNING he hung up the wooden sign that announced he was home, and by afternoon he'd gone to see three patients: a fever, a broken ankle, and a swelling behind the left ear. Just as he'd returned home from the last visit, he heard a tentative rap at the front door and found an unfamiliar young man, brown-haired and wide-faced. "Doctor?"

The man's wife had fainted at her work that afternoon, so Hammond sent Mrs. McDowell upstairs for his medical bag and followed the young fellow on foot toward the other, shadow Killingly, where French-Canadian immigrant families lived packed into tract houses built by the mills. At four-thirty the mill was mid-shift—the whistle wouldn't blow until seven—and Hammond wondered if a kind foreman had let the husband off for the day or if he were risking his job. Mostly the mill families called for doctoring at night. Though it was near enough to night now, in the growing darkness. The man led him to a little row house, dimly lamplit.

The thin wife sat in a rocking chair by the fire, arms loosely encircling a toddler on her lap. She had two thin dirty-blond braids and a purpled bruise on her cheek. Hammond put his bag upon the kitchen table. Clean, this time.

"Mrs."—he looked to the husband for prompting—"Fortin, I hear you felt a bit faint earlier today."

"It was nothing," she said. "He worries over nothing. I can do my work."

"Yes, of course," Hammond said with as much cheer as he could. She barely looked capable of standing, much less picking thread all day. "Here, give the little one up to your husband, if you would, and let's have a look at you."

The husband took the child on his hip and went through to the other room. Hammond listened to the woman's breath, strong enough; felt her cool forehead; helped her to stand; and prodded gently at her belly to be sure it wasn't the appendix.

"You fell at work?" he said, nodding at her bruised cheek, and she agreed. Never easy to tell if a woman was telling the truth about her bruises, but the husband seemed earnestly solicitous. She would likely be all right.

"How did it come on? Were you hot first? No fever now."

"No, not hot. Just sick to my stomach, like. Then I was out."

Hammond gave her a look.

"No. No, I can't be," she whispered. Her gray eyes flooded. "I'd know. And I'm still giving suck." There was a baby, she said, asleep upstairs.

But she was pregnant, Hammond was nearly certain. He helped her sit. "Look, it must be quite early—"

She raised hopeful eyes. "You think I could bring on my courses again?"

Hammond hated this discussion. Had all the pills and powders available to women for reinstating the menses been safe, he would've had no qualms about the process: far better an early resolution, before the fetus quickened, than a late and bloody intervention. But many of the potions were ineffective at best and poisonous at worst. "Perhaps. I can't guarantee it. And you must be careful, Mrs. Fortin. If a dose does not work, you mustn't take more, do you understand?"

She understood.

"There's a fellow in downtown Killingly whose medicine is supposed to be reliable. Do you know who I mean—Boucher?" Then another thought struck him. "Tell me, did you know Miss Bertha Mellish? She works in the mill in the summers."

Mrs. Fortin blinked up at him. "Oh, the preacher's daughter?"

"The Reverend's daughter, yes."

"He means Paul's girl," the husband said in a loud whisper from the doorway, bouncing the sleepy toddler in his arms. "You know her, chérie."

"What did you say? Whose girl?" He'd dropped his stethoscope on the table. He snatched it up and tucked it blindly into his bag while his heart thundered so loudly in his chest that no man would need a stethoscope to hear it. It felt as if it might leap between his ribs onto the kitchen floor.

Mr. Fortin looked taken aback. "Paul, that is—he works at the mill, too."

"I see." Hammond made himself speak calmly. "Is he French, this Paul?"

"Yes, of course," said Mr. Fortin. "French like us."

19

He told Higham at once: went directly to the Attawaugan Hotel and paced around the man's room while he recounted what little the Fortins had said. They'd gone quiet once they realized how closely he was connected to Bertha's family. All they would say was that this Paul—they did not call him Joseph—had seemed close with the Reverend's daughter or perhaps just friendly with her. Both had seen the two conversing during lunches at the mill.

Higham received the news in his usual unruffled manner. "Clammed up, did they? All right." Then he put on his coat, his pistol a bulge beneath it, and herded Hammond out of his hotel room. He didn't want to talk about what it might mean that a Frenchman's name had been connected to Bertha's, he didn't want to tell the sheriff, and he certainly didn't want Hammond tagging along on his mysterious excursion. Hammond stalked home and slammed his front door so thoroughly that one of Emma's decorated porcelain plates sprang from the wall and shattered, and Mrs. McDowell and the cats skirted him nervously for the rest of the night.

Then, after ten, a knock came. The Darlings' lights were out already, Mrs. McDowell in her apartment. Hammond went to the door in his dressing gown, his stomach tense beneath it.

The Higham he found was not the Higham he'd seen earlier that evening. This man's eyes had an unsettling spark, like Tricksey with a bird in her sights—slinking, eager, wild. In the light of the foyer Higham's face looked wind-chapped about the jaw and chin, and when he removed his hat Hammond saw an angry scrape along the side and heel of his right hand, the sort produced by gravel.

"Are you quite all right, Detective?"

"Never better," said Higham, stepping past him. His voice even sounded deeper.

"Have you found this Paul?"

"No. I've found evidence of his connection with Miss Mellish. Somebody saw him with a letter addressed to a Joseph." He saw Hammond's confusion. "Plenty of reasons an itinerant fellow might call himself by different names with different sorts. He fits the story. Twenty-one and handsome, it seems. An accent—wasn't born here. Popular with women."

Hammond braced himself against the back of Tricksey's favorite armchair. He had to think. Think what could have possessed Bertha—"Where is he? Where does he work?"

"The old Sayles mill, same as Miss Mellish," Higham said. "He's not there any longer. They let him go a few months ago for lateness."

"So he's not still in town," Hammond said. *Or you would have brought him to my door tonight as well, in a sad state.*

"No. Looking for work somewhere south." Higham tilted his head a little, drolly. "So they say."

"Where did he live?"

"Down by Gendreau. You know it."

"Yes." Countless times Hammond had been there. Still he found himself trying to tally them: How many times might he have walked past this man, this seducer? How many lectures on the dangers of drinking to excess had he delivered while this man passed smirking by outside the window? He couldn't bear it.

Higham was eyeing him. "This friend who saw the letter, he swears he never saw Paul with Bertha Mellish at the mill. Your sad couple might be the only ones who would cop to it, after it's been in the papers so long." He shrugged. "Or not. Give me some time, I can find out."

An unsavory, blunt threat in the detective's voice. But Hammond was only half listening, turning over a terrible new possibility.

"What if she lied," he said. "What if—she could have gone with him. What if he went to her at college and convinced her to go with him?"

"No evidence of that," said Higham. "She took nothing with her. She was close with her sister; she would've written by now."

"Closer than you think," Hammond said and instantly longed to take back the words.

Higham stepped closer. "What do you know?" he asked, almost a growl.

Hammond moved away, as if greater distance would help. "What I know, I know as a physician," he said. "It's private to the family."

"Nothing is private until I find her."

"It's an old story, nothing to do with Bertha being gone."

"About twenty years old?" Higham paused, clearly phrasing his words with care. "When you were called to help Florence Mellish deliver a girl child in secret? A child she named Bertha?"

Hammond didn't turn back to Higham to confirm it. He didn't have to.

"And you don't . . . know the father?"

How could the fellow make a hesitation between words sound so defamatory? "I do not," Hammond said curtly, rounding on him.

Higham's eyes weren't like a cat's eyes. More reptilian, flat and shining black, shadowed by his brow. The firelight picked out the line of his chin, his nose. He said, "We won't get another word from the mill workers here. They'll stay loyal to him. It's how these people are. I'll take down a description from the owner and send it out to the police in other states. To Quebec as well. And I'll take it back to South Hadley, to see what I can see there."

"What should I do?"

"Continue as you are," Higham said—and that was feline, that hint of disdain. "That's all we can do, is it not?"

"What shall I tell Miss Mellish's sister—her family?" Hammond whispered.

Higham shrugged again.

"I don't—I can't tell them she had a lover."

"No," Higham agreed. "I can, if you wish. I think Florence Mellish would want to know."

"No, not yet," Hammond said. "Nobody can know yet. Not the police. No one. You can send the description, but don't say why."

Higham observed him for a moment, then nodded.

"If we can find her safe," Hammond said, "if she's safe, none of it matters. Do you understand? Do you understand me, Higham?"

"Yes," said Higham. Then he said, almost gently, "Good night, now."

"FLORENCE. FLORENCE. DAUGHTER."

She came awake in terror, webbed in memory, and flailed out at the familiar shape looming over her in the darkness. A squawk, then the unmistakable hard thump of a body meeting the floor.

Florence sat up, her chest heaving. Moonlight through the curtains showed her father prone where he'd fallen back against her desk chair. His eyes were white and black in the gloom, and he was breathing heavily through an open mouth. She went to him and felt under the wiry hair at the back of his head but found no lumps, no blood on her fingers. A strong whiff of urine.

"Are you all right?"

"I can't—I need to wash," John said in a boy's small, shamed voice.

When pressed he said he wasn't hurt. Florence got him to his knees, his hands on the spindles of her chair, then to his feet. She'd done this with Sarah many times, her mother's bird-lightness easier to maneuver than her father's bigger frame, though he, too, was thin now—different in her arms.

He insisted on walking down the hallway unsupported. Florence kept close behind him in case he toppled. In the bathroom she turned away to light the gas lamp and run the water till it warmed, and behind her she heard the rustlings of John disrobing and the damp weight of his nightshirt as it collapsed against the floorboards. She stared down at the water rising.

This was the first time she'd had to bathe her father. She'd wondered how he was managing to wash these days, stepping into and out of the tub without help, but as he hadn't complained she'd simply chosen not to anticipate the moment when his balance would betray him. It didn't bear thinking about. But many things that didn't bear thinking about had come to pass. This, her father naked and urine-stained, leaning on her shoulder as he swung one skinny leg into the tub and then the other, was just one more.

Florence helped him settle back against the tin wall of the tub. Before Bertha disappeared she'd been saving to buy one of the new ceramics—for comfort, and for the relief of discarding this vessel and what it held. The whole house contained memories of hurt and joy layered endlessly over one another, like wallpaper pressed continually over older patterns. In pieces she'd tried to remediate those memories—dedicated the money from several years of poetry sales to purchase a new mattress, for example, a decade before. But that expenditure struck her now as a sad attempt at self-persuasion. It would be no better to sluice water between her father's shoulder blades in a ceramic tub than in the old tin. And she'd borne Bertha in this very bathroom. They'd had to throw away the rug.

Her father's words were weakening, along with his body. He was silent in the bath and scrubbed himself hard, punitively, until Florence had to tell him to stop. Finally she helped him to his feet again.

He stood dripping in the towel she wrapped around him. "I'm sorry," he whispered.

How awful it was to feel gratitude where one hated, like pigments intermixed to mud.

John had forced himself upon Florence for the first time when she was twelve years old.

For dreadful years he had done it. In her adolescence he'd run off the man she'd fleetingly hoped to marry—Charles Cutcheon, a lawyer and War veteran with legs withered thin as a greyhound's who'd smiled gently up at Florence from his wheeled chair after meetings of her father's congregation. Florence hadn't known if she could carry a child at all, then—would God allow it? Yet she thought Cutcheon might accept her even if she were barren, as long as he didn't know how she had been polluted.

But their rapport had been enough to ignite John's jealousy. When Florence went away to college he had not been able to bear her freedom. He'd demanded that she return home from Mount Holyoke, and during the next year the frequency of his attentions had increased—her father had barred her in her room as if it were the top chamber of a tower and he the dragon at its base. He'd wronged her terribly; yet he'd given her Bertha and the only experience of being a mother she would ever have.

Cutcheon did not come to save her. Nor had she saved herself, as she once thought she might. But she'd tried to save Bertha.

Florence didn't respond to her father. She dropped the towel's hem and stepped back to make room for him to climb out of the tub. Her hand shook as he clasped it, but she bore up under his weight.

20

Before leaving Killingly Higham had warned Hammond, told him all the usual true things. *The colder the trail the less likely it is that I'll find her, and if I find her, I may find her dead.* The words bounced right off. Higham had learned to recognize men who would commit themselves to a lost woman, whether she was daughter or wife or mother or nothing nameable in law. Hammond would not stop searching. Never mind that her bones were probably whitening in a ditch somewhere already; never mind that she might have run on her own.

Men like that would generally keep paying you until they bled themselves dry, which was convenient. But they'd dog you, too. Slow you down. Today Hammond was still in Killingly seeing patients, which would keep him off Higham's heels while he sifted the dirt of Holyoke and South Hadley and Northampton for Bertha's Frenchman. Perhaps he'd soon have something solid to bring to Florence Mellish.

In Holyoke the men hung out drunk and stupid by the ferry docks. He tripped one, broke the nose of another. No Joe or Paul with a Québécois accent, not there, they swore it. They were river boys and didn't hold with mill boys anyway. They'd tell no tales for a French weaver.

In a stone arch under the train tracks in Northampton men squatted in ragged tents. They were less drunk but more desperate for work. Here he had better luck and so did they—no one's bones were broken and a few ended up with coins in their pockets. One had talked to a French-sounding Paul back a few weeks ago. The man was dark-haired, blue-eyed, and handsome-faced, as the mill owner had said. Better kept than some tramps, polite and friendly, but with one particular anxiety.

"Always lookin' out for the cops," said Higham's best informant, a balding copper-bearded wreck named Thomas who'd been charmed by their shared name. Higham had chosen to be charmed, too, and they were all getting on quite nicely. Jokes circulated about how Frenchwomen liked it, how their hair down there was straight and wiry like a moustache.

My-Name's-Thomas-Too said, "They like to come down here and roust us every so often, and this fella couldn't handle that, y'see? Said he couldn't sleep a wink 'cause of it. He was here, what, two days?" A few nods. "Itchy to move on. Asking about how to find work northward. Told him if I knew where to go I'd be up north myself."

"Did he say where he'd come from?"

The man shook his head. "Some closed-up mill. Enough of those around here."

"Hey, why you lookin' for him?" one of the other men, this one maybe part negro, called. "He kill a man or something?"

Higham stared the man down. He looked around at their dirty faces, now uncertain, open. Finally he said, "I'm looking because it's my job. Somebody wants to talk to this Paul. You see him again, you tell the police and they'll tell me. They might ease up on you boys for a bit. Might even be money in it for you. You understand?"

It was pleasant, being understood.

HIGHAM'S INTEREST IN WOMEN was exclusively professional. If he'd known Bertha Mellish before she vanished, he might have liked her in a general way; he liked unusual things. But iconoclastic as the Porter girls thought her, Bertha wasn't so original. She was a grind, a freethinker, a constant student. The sort of girl deplored in editorial essays by men who believed that higher education deformed the female mind and unsuited women for their wifely duties. Higham didn't have a wife and didn't care about wifely duties except as they influenced the behavior of others. Bertha's absence would likely earn him a respectable sum, given the uncertainty of the case—but best of all it had brought him a puzzle. He loved nothing better. In fact, he loved nothing else, except books.

Higham was a reader. He kept up with the New York papers as well as Boston's—mostly the *Journal*, with its mix of gruesome city gossip and breathless war dispatches. He especially liked the stories by their woman reporter, Annie Green; she had an eye for the human reasoning underneath everything. Nothing made more sense than what the papers called "senseless crime," if you bothered to look into it.

When he wasn't working a case, and sometimes when he was, he read novels. He'd started when he was still police, in breaks between shifts when calisthenics were not enough to calm the tension thrumming through his body. The house he'd lived in then, split into single rooms for single men like himself, had kept a tattered library in its front parlor. He had soon discovered that novels, especially those by women, were explorations of mankind's behavior, and sometimes explanations of it. His preferred writers were Thomas Hardy and Jane Austen. Austen in particular helped him to understand women—what they wanted and what they would do for it. He'd once thought he wanted some of the same things, but the novels taught him that women didn't generally want men the way he did. They liked strength but they wanted kindness and fine words with it; they also liked a man to kneel before them, but hardly ever for the same reasons as he did, and in a well-appointed drawing room rather than an alley, if you please.

It was harder to tell what Bertha Mellish had wanted. If she'd yearned for a college degree so badly, why slut around with a no-good mill boy? Why keep him secret from her few friends, then write him up as a character in a school assignment? She might as well have taken out an advertisement in the paper.

He didn't think well of Bertha's manuscript. He'd read it thoroughly before Hammond reclaimed it to form the centerpiece of his growing shrine to Bertha, and Higham agreed with Florence Mellish that it seemed uncommonly moralizing for a girl so loudly skeptical of her society's beliefs. But he saw no obvious meaning in the writing, either.

From everything her classmates and professors had said, she wasn't a subtle girl or a tortured one. Coded messages didn't seem her style. Unless she'd gone mad; there was no discounting the possibility, not in this family.

When a case became confusing, he took notes.

Bertha Mellish's story
"French Joe": Joseph/Paul, Killingly mill worker, whereabouts unknown.
Marie Racine: mill worker, bears Joe's children, jumps from "Mt. Holly."
Narrated by a female friend who is injured trying to save MR.
Written for rhetoric class (Prof. Neilson).
Showed some of it to Agnes Sullivan while writing.

On a separate sheet he listed relationships and familial ties.

David Mellish: insane. Died 1874, in asylum.
Sarah Mellish: insane. Confined to Mellish house.
Florence Mellish: Bertha Mellish's mother. Bertha's father unknown. Left Mt. Holyoke after 1 yr.
Hammond delivered Bertha Mellish of Florence. Therefore, Florence Mellish distrusts Hammond.

John Mellish: ill after Bertha's absence discovered. Conscience or sorrow?

Hammond distrusts Agnes Sullivan. Reason unknown—jealousy likely.

The only name on both pages was Agnes Sullivan. Back to college he would go.

HE CAUGHT AGNES IN the darkness outside the library doors. He'd waited there for nearly an hour, after another girl said Agnes was always at the library at night or in the zoology lab with her ghastly skeleton. It was a real hindrance, how difficult it could be to speak to a college girl alone.

Agnes Sullivan was carrying a book, *The Report of the American Humane* something, a long title half-concealed by her shabby coat-sleeve. Her brown dress hung short of her ankles and her boots needed polishing; a few strands of hair had fallen from her coif and been tucked haphazardly behind her prominent ears; her cheeks and lips were pale, her eyelashes fine. The overall effect was of threadbare neatness far removed from fashion. An unworldly, ungainly soul.

"Detective," Agnes said, not distressed by his arrival as she had been before. Curious. "Is there news?"

Higham shrugged. "In a manner of speaking. There's been some report that the French Joe in the story was a real man." *See what she thinks of that.*

She pushed past him. She smelled of lye soap and a tang of bleach. "I don't believe it."

"Somebody Miss Mellish knew in Killingly, when she worked at the mill. He may have gone by the name of Paul." Hammond would be furious to learn that he had shared this information with Agnes, which made the telling sweeter.

She stopped and turned back. He could see half her long face, cut up by shadow. "At the Sayles mill?"

"What do you know of the mill?"

He had her. She'd been holding her arms bent near her middle, and now her hands fell to her sides—she nearly dropped the book. Her eyes were gray in the darkness, narrow.

"She didn't like to speak much of it. She didn't like the work or the people," she said. "Or that is what she told me, anyway."

"You said she never told you of men."

"She didn't. We only talked of interesting things."

"Like your work," Higham said.

"And her work." Her nose was running in the cold. She swiped at it irritably with a gloved hand.

He was surprised to find himself liking the girl. She was ugly in a quiet way, mannish and stern, and her poverty was of an utterly familiar sort, though he didn't hear the Paternoster or the parish in her tongue. Her prickly reserve reminded him of himself and other police he'd known, and of chilly, tough old Irish maids who would *oh-Jaysus* you one minute and crack you over the head with a bottle the next. In motion she was long-limbed and awkward, like an ostrich. Almost prim—he had the sense that she had taught herself primness and had suppressed some other style of behavior in the process. People who learned new mannerisms were always interesting. It meant that they wanted to escape something.

Agnes Sullivan lifted her head toward the lit windows of the library, but she wasn't really looking at the building. She was looking at the Bertha Mellish inside her head. Higham had a feeling that her Bertha was a fair approximation of the real thing, and he wished he could extract that essence of Bertha, the way you squeeze juice from an orange. On the force no one would have blinked if he'd squeezed an Irish girl a bit too hard. Without a badge, you had to be more careful; you had to make the walls close in.

"It was in the papers that you and Dr. Hammond had gone to Killingly."

"Yes," Higham said.

"Did you go there to look for a Frenchman?" He couldn't read the look in her eyes, but her tone was contemptuous.

"Not exactly. But that's what we found. A real mess your girl has left behind. And a real man, it seems."

"This Joseph, if he is real. Do you think he killed her?" Most women would have whispered that question. Agnes asked it calmly.

"I don't know," Higham said again. He found himself leaning toward her. "I don't know, Miss Sullivan."

Agnes nodded. In the light, he remembered, her eyes were close to the greenish gold of the water in the campus's carefully picturesque ponds, the ones they'd drained to search for Bertha.

There was a point early in every case when he felt as though he were slogging through a muddy swamp himself, mistaking each submerged branch for a waving arm. He was approaching it now, he could feel it. "What do you know about this rash of thefts in Porter Hall?" he asked, jabbing at her now as much out of habit as any hope of a new revelation. "Have you lost anything yourself to the thief?"

Another brisk nod. "A dollar in quarters. A ribbon. Everyone in the house is upset about it."

"Yes, so Mrs. Mead reported," Higham said. "Did you need that money?"

"Of course I did." Agnes looked at him as if she were concerned for his intelligence.

"Are you saving for anything in particular?"

She was still giving him the same look. "My family."

"Planning to support them once you're done here, is that it? How will you do that?"

"I'll be a surgeon. I will go to medical school."

"Will you now," said Higham, eyeing her. He could believe it. And then he remembered something he had meant to ask her the first time they spoke—something that had bothered him as he wrote his lists. "You were not the first to realize Miss Mellish was missing."

Agnes shook her head. "No. I would never have bothered her. I thought she was writing."

"Writing?"

"Her debate speech. Supporting the practice of vivisection."

"You'd wait for her to come to you, then," he said, and Agnes nodded slowly.

"Yes. I'd wait."

BACK IN HIS ROOM in the little village hotel Higham reclined on the uncomfortable bed to read the debate notes Bertha had prepared. After their little exchange, Agnes Sullivan had handed them over with less reluctance than he'd expected, though she'd expressed her doubt that the notes would do him any good.

It was possible she was right. Higham was not a philosopher, nor had he ever reflected much on the morality of experimental surgery. He began reading with some trepidation but quickly found himself absorbed in the neatly written notes. Bertha had been assigned to argue the affirmative: *Resolved, That vivisection for scientific purposes is justifiable*, and she did so persuasively, with a passionate lucidity that made him think of Florence. The speech began by defining terms, to *get this debate down fine right off*. Bertha argued that the old meaning of "vivisection" hardly applied to modern medical experimentation on living beings, which could be performed painlessly and with aseptic cleanliness. The terrible scenes summoned by opponents of vivisection—gutted unfortunates writhing under the gaze of pitiless doctors, whimpering pups licking the hands that held them down—recalled old horrors now universally condemned. And, she wrote, it was foolish to assume equivalency of sensation between man and beast:

> *The question is not—does the prick of a needle make an animal start as quickly as a man would? But—what impression does this needle-prick make on an animal's consciousness? Furthermore, if the animal in question can be prevented from feeling pain, we must*

*ask whose suffering truly concerns the opponents of vivisection.
Could we not reasonably suggest that they aim to spare themselves
suffering as well? If we attempt to transplant ourselves into the lives
of the lower animals, it is always we who are there: we, with our
own susceptibilities, not theirs, and our intellects working up the
raw material of their experiences.*

Bertha's real concern, Higham saw, was with the grander
ethical questions the debate suggested. *What does it mean to consider
an act undertaken for the advancement of scientific knowledge "justifiable"?*
she asked. *To whom must we justify our actions and beliefs?* Philosopher
or not, Higham had wrestled personally with that question—
wrestled with suspects, wrestled with lovers, wondering how the
world would judge him and how much he cared.

What is cruelty? Bertha Mellish wrote. *The wanton or excessive
infliction of pain. The wanton infliction of pain is that for which there
is no justification; the excessive that for which there is justification in
fact, but not in degree. Here we must examine our own actions in life.
Do we never consider it justifiable to inflict pain on others?* Even those
who would label all physiological experimentation cruel and
unnecessary, she suggested, would grant that a mother might
make a painful choice for her child and remain morally upright
or that a doctor could ethically complete a painful operation in
order to heal a patient. The study of living animals, conducted
with voluntary regulation and inflicting no wanton or excessive
harm, promised great benefits for all of humanity through work
few could bear to do. Yet opponents of vivisection considered
physicians immoral and inhumane—while they enjoyed their
own steaks and mink muffs.

The entire speech was an impassioned defense of experimental
surgeons against what Bertha saw as hypocritical condemnation.
It was a defense of Agnes Sullivan and her chosen profession. And
Agnes had handed it to him almost blithely, as if she did not realize
it. She hadn't even asked for the papers back when he was done.

Higham felt a rueful new kinship with the girl in that moment. She was like him. Some kinds of passion were inaccessible to them both.

He had a feeling that Joseph was less vital to the case than Sullivan. But he'd be damned if he'd let Hammond know that—at least not yet.

21

nstead of slamming the door to Bertha's room, Florence pressed it shut until the latch sprung into place. That was a discipline women perfected with age: transforming fury into precision.

Her father had been quizzing her all day. Had she heard anything else from Dr. Hammond? Why hadn't the newspaper come? There were no new telegrams, no news from the College? He'd asked the last question in front of Sarah at dinner, and Florence, overwrought, had shoved back from the table, snatched up her mostly untouched plate of boiled beef and potatoes, and fled.

She set the food down on Bertha's desk and stood in the center of the little room with her pulse skittering in her ears. No matter how many times she visited this room, no matter which objects she gazed at with longing or touched to feel her fingerprints overlapping with her daughter's, it could not substitute for being in the world, actively searching. The room yielded nothing but vacancy and sorrow.

But she couldn't stop. For now, it was all she had.

Most of the drawers in Bertha's dresser were empty—her clothes still sat in her room at the College, awaiting her return. She'd left only a few things at home. A shirtwaist, torn by the laundry mangle, that Florence had been meaning for months to repair; a brown corduroy jacket Bertha said bound her shoulders too tightly; the blue cotton

dress she'd worn into the ashes of the old College building to look for her trunk, its hem blackened with soot.

Florence lifted the dress free and laid it out on Bertha's quilt. She'd scolded Bertha so seriously for these stains and rips, for her absentminded dismissal of feminine practicalities. In general Bertha maintained herself neatly, out of obligation rather than interest, but when she'd been quartered off campus the year before, she'd been rather less diligent. At the time Florence had felt torn between frustration at the cost of new clothing and an envious approval of Bertha's unconcern.

"I had to try to find my trunk," Bertha had said when she brought the dress home at Christmas last year—she'd been wearing it happily all fall. "It was exciting, you know, poking around in the ruins like an antiquarian. And besides, Agnes doesn't give a hoot if my hems are dirty."

Florence had been so happy when Bertha first wrote home that she'd been paired with Agnes at the home of a welcoming lady named Mrs. Drew. The Old Main fire would sadden those who looked back at their seminary years with unsullied joy, certainly, but if the new living arrangement secured a close friendship for Bertha—the sort of passionate bond Florence had yearned for herself as a freshman—that gave Florence real relief. Agnes's was just about the only name that had ever recurred in Bertha's letters, and it seemed things had been harmonious at Mrs. Drew's. Bertha had even liked the woman well enough to participate without complaint in prayers before each meal.

Her eyes stung. She rubbed at the charcoal dust on the cotton skirt and noticed for the first time that the very edge of the cloth felt crisp and flaky, as if it had actually burnt. The remains of the building must still have been smoldering when Bertha ventured through.

"Make something for yourself from it," Bertha had told her at Christmas, airily unaware that the fabric of one of her dresses would by no means suffice to cover Florence. "Chop it all up, I don't care."

Had something been changing for Bertha, even then? That was what Florence found herself turning over in her mind. Bertha's letters from Mrs. Drew's house had been sparkling and bold, full of ideas for her classwork and stories, boasts about how she and Agnes would become the finest philologist and surgeon Boston had ever seen. She hadn't noticed much difference in the Bertha of summer and fall, or if she had, she'd attributed it to lassitude from Bertha's work at the mill. Some girls were just livelier at College than anywhere else. Bertha had still been talkative, though less extensively descriptive of her future dreams. Florence had even waved her off, at times, when she went on for too long about her latest reading. But she wondered now whether those speeches had masked an alteration still not intelligible to her, if the prattle had shielded an injury that had left Bertha fragile—crumbling, almost invisibly, like the cloth in her hand.

HAMMOND WAS BACK IN South Hadley, in Higham's overheated rented room, arguing against the detective's foolish proposal to publicize their search for the Frenchman. He had taken an early train up expecting new information: instead, this blockheaded plan. "It will ruin her," he said, unbuttoning his jacket irritably. "You must see that."

The radiator beside him clanked and gurgled. Hammond threw his jacket on Higham's chair and thought of Bertha in the cold. She hadn't even been wearing a coat when she disappeared, near as they could tell.

Higham said he'd found only rumors—in Northampton, the Frenchman had claimed to be heading north. "Makes me think he likely went a different way entirely. If we don't put out a sketch, offer a reward for him, too, there's precious little to go on, Doctor."

"Then we go on with precious little," Hammond said. "If her name appears in the papers, if she's linked with this Paul-Joseph, everyone who reads it will assume she's run away with him. They'll assume she's lost her virtue."

"If she dies because we haven't found him, preserving her honor matters somewhat less."

"It matters more than you know," Hammond snapped. "She doesn't deserve it. We have no certainty—she may only have been friendly to the man, for goodness's sake. We cannot sacrifice her, not knowing if he was her lover at all."

He could picture their disapproving faces: the men of his lodges in Killingly, the church congregation, all arrayed in judgment. The college girls who had anguished over her disappearance would never welcome her back among them. Mrs. Mead would incline her head in sadness as she refused Bertha readmission to the College. He saw Bertha sitting crumpled in his bedroom, their bedroom, like a ghost of her withered mother. He could imagine her ruination printed up in the papers: MISSING COLLEGE GIRL IN MYSTERIOUS LOVE PLOT. MISS MELLISH'S SECRET REVEALED. A CASE OF LOOSE MORALS.

"Even if she's dead already."

Hammond wheeled on him. Rationally he knew the man was correct. Bertha had been missing for weeks; it was folly to be sure she lived. But he *was* sure. And the way Higham said it—the casual tone of his voice, the quirk of his mouth! "Even then."

Higham shrugged.

"I don't think you understand what's best for Miss Mellish," Hammond said around his anger.

"And I'm sure you do. I just know what I'm paid to know. I will be paid, won't I? The Mellishes have been a bit behindhand."

"Just keep Bertha's name out of it," said Hammond, ignoring the question.

"I'll say he owes money, then, shall I? And that he may be traveling with a woman. A mill girl, with some education."

He would have hit the detective in that moment if he hadn't been utterly certain that any punch thrown would have ended with a knife at his throat or a gun at his temple. Higham knew it, and Hammond could see the triumphant knowledge in those feral eyes.

"West seems more likely to me than north or south. I'll go through Pennsylvania. See yourself out, won't you." Higham turned to wipe clear a swath of the fogged window and look out through it, as if he were already imagining Hammond's back receding down the street outside.

HIGHAM WAS TO LEAVE the next morning. It was stupid to be glad of this, but Hammond could not help it. He sat at the small desk in his now-familiar room at Mrs. Goren's rooming house with the quilt wrapped around his shoulders as if he were a little boy. It was not yet dark, and the red glass lamp on the desk cast circles of light on the dusty ceiling and an unsettling glow on the paper before him.

He was trying to write a letter to John Mellish that would explain the circumstances of Higham's departure. But the words were blocked by other words, things he could not say to Bertha's father—the man Bertha knew as her father—or even to Florence, who might be the one reading the letter after all. He scratched out sentences again and again. *My dear Reverend Mellish, I am terribly sorry to tell you of a discovery we have made—*

I am terribly sorry to tell you that Detective Higham is now searching for a man he believes may have dishonored Miss Mellish—

As if Higham alone thought it; as if Higham alone were responsible. No, he couldn't write that.

And who was this man, this Joseph or Paul? How had Bertha come to love him? Had he followed her to the College after the summer ended? Had he, like Hammond, waited outside her dormitory house to walk with her, only to be told in her firm voice that she could spare but thirty minutes before she had to return to her work and that they had better walk about Upper Lake for it would be quieter there?

Sometimes she had walked a little ahead of Hammond and he had let her. When she walked before him, after all, he could not see her abstracted gaze; he could enjoy the unconscious sway of her hips and allow himself to think that he might someday rest his hands on the little curves of her waist under that plain jacket. He could imagine that her body and her sweetness were for him, held in reserve as she grew. He'd never begrudged Bertha her time at the College; indeed he felt the same sadness for her that he felt for all clever young women who were granted sips from the Pierian spring. But he had always been confident that she would be happy as his wife and would learn to enjoy managing his household and assisting him with his work and with the cats, as Emma had done. He had felt certain that, under his tutelage, she would become the woman she was meant to be: bright and dedicated and kind. She would transcend her parentage, all unknowing, and rest contentedly in the place he had made for her in the world.

How could he tell John Mellish—tell Florence—that he might have been wrong? That, instead, Bertha might have slipped from the path of goodness on the same treacherous slope that had downed her sister? That her sweetness was not, as he had sometimes feared, doomed to be ground to powder by the turning gears of her mind but had been given to another, even as Hammond had declared himself and patiently awaited her? He had accepted her gentle distance, even considered it right given the closeness of their families, and all the while she had been loving some wreck of the mills, tearing herself away from her studies for *him*, no doubt. Letting this Joseph kiss her pen-callused fingers and her serious mouth.

He had never known, when she walked with him, if she would turn back with her curious little smile or with a face gone blank and pure in thought. That uncertainty had captivated him. He had labored untiringly for her love. Even now, even as he wrote, he yearned for her presence and attention—yearned to be once again the object of her incisive looks, to feel the restrained force of her mind.

> *I am terribly sorry to tell you that I have often met with your daughter at her College, on the most chaste and proper terms, and that I had intended to ask you for her hand in marriage upon her graduation, but that I now fear she may be lost to me forever, either at her own hand or at the hand of a faithless lover, and I cannot say which would be worse.*

He had read and reread Bertha's manuscript, looking for clues in the neat round vowels and scratched-out words. He knew he ought to give it back to Florence Mellish and told himself he would—but not until he had wrenched every bit of meaning from it.

On his last long day in Killingly, while Higham was writing his own notes in South Hadley, Hammond had drawn up a key to the manuscript as well. The similarity of their annotations would have horrified him.

Bertha is Marie Racine—"*La Petite,*" he wrote. *Joseph remains Joseph. Mt. Holly is Mt. Holyoke. The Narrator*—

Was the narrator, the friend who tried to rescue Marie when she fled Joseph's home to her death—was it the mysterious letter-writing woman? Why would she lie? And why would Bertha write her own story from the perspective of a devoted friend?

He'd tried to force a space for himself in the story as that devoted friend, racing through the woods after Bertha as she escaped Joseph's miserable house. He could still save her, virgin or no. But every time he read the manuscript it shifted: evidence of her ruin, evidence of her virtue. Only the ending remained the same.

Hammond looked down at the scribbled paper.

My dear Reverend Mellish, he wrote:

I write to tell you that Detective Higham will leave town tomorrow, to follow a lead from his investigations in Killingly. There is a mill worker, a friend of Miss Mellish's, who may know something of her disappearance. Detective Higham will look for this individual. While I hope that he will succeed, the trail, as he says, has gone cold. I must confess that I do not feel the same confidence in Detective Higham's abilities that I once did. I am sorry to say there is no other news to report. I will stay in South Hadley for now and meet again with the police. If you have other instructions, please relay them to me.

I remain your sincere friend,
Henry L. Hammond

Once he had written that letter to the Reverend, Hammond sent an announcement to the Willimantic paper, the South Hadley police, and Mrs. Mead. The Springfield paper ran a story about it that very evening, December first:

MAY STIMULATE EFFORT

Increase In Reward Offered For Recovery Of Body Or Finding Miss Bertha Mellish Alive

---

SPRINGFIELD Dec. 1—The failure to find any trace of Bertha Mellish, who disappeared from Mount Holyoke College, South Hadley, two weeks ago, has aroused a lingering hope that she may still be alive.

Dr. Henry L. Hammond of Killingly, Conn., the Mellish family physician, on behalf of Miss Mellish's relatives, announced today that a reward of $200 would be paid for the recovery of the body and that $500 would be paid if Miss Mellish should be found alive.

The reward offered by the College was only $50, and the increased inducements are expected to renew activity in the search, which has of late lagged.

On December 4, a Saturday, the Mount Holyoke *Daily Transcript* required only a few lines of print—tucked in the South Hadley news section below a longer paragraph about the "pretty general" belief "that the body of Miss Mellish . . . lies at the bottom of the Connecticut"—to slip past suggestion and straight on to libel. The family remained "haunted," panted the paper, "by the more terrible fear that she met with foul play." Then the anonymous reporter let fall a final *on-dit*: "It is said that Mrs. Mellish, mother of the strange girl now missing, was subject to fits of insanity before the birth of their daughter. So it might have been an inheritance."

This had been one of the things Hammond feared most, that Bertha and the Mellishes might find their private matters exposed in the press. Now it seemed almost a relief. The newspapermen knew nothing of Joseph, or Paul, or whatever the vile creature called himself. They knew nothing of Bertha's real parentage. The reporter had even gotten the period of Sarah's worst illness wrong; it had been after Florence gave birth to Bertha, not before.

Five hundred dollars of his own money "on behalf of Miss Mellish's relatives." Hammond worried—was it enough money? Would it ever be enough?

But his fears were misdirected.

22

The telegram arrived on the afternoon of Florence's forty-first birthday: December fifth, a Sunday, when Bertha had been gone for seventeen days. When the telegram delivery boy raced up on his wheel, Florence was standing by one of the windows in the dining room, breathing steam from a cup of brandy-splashed tea Maggie had handed to her with a nod. Her birthday present, this tiny numbing.

She watched, stunned, as the boy tossed down his bicycle and flung open the front gate. He looked like a little hawk with his chin jutting out and a wool cap peaked on his head.

They found her, she thought hazily as she put down the mug, not sure whom she meant—some group of men, police or Hammond and the private detective. Then, incredulous: *On my birthday?*

The boy nipped a nickel from her trembling hand. Freezing air rushed into the hall as Florence tore open the telegram envelope.

It was from her father's brother, George.

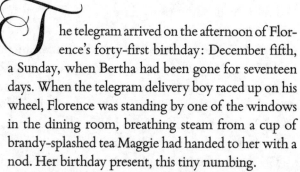

BODY FOUND IN AUBURN POND TODAY STOP YOU MUST GO TO SEE IF IT IS BERTHA STOP CONSTABLE WILL AWAIT YOU AT STATION STOP BRING THE DOCTOR STOP

Florence fell to her knees. Maggie, drawn by her wail, found her doubled over there in the hallway and knelt beside her, murmuring, "Oh, Miss Florence, Miss Florence," not asking her what had happened, not prizing the telegram slip from her fingers, not pressing. Sitting with her under the weight of the blow that crushed so many, the blow Maggie herself had felt: the death of one's child.

GEORGE MELLISH AND HIS wife, Emeline, had lived in Auburn, Massachusetts, for some years—a town over from Oxford, where John and George and their siblings had been raised. Auburn was right on the train line from Killingly to Worcester. Florence had watched its ponds skim by hundreds of times en route to the College or to Boston.

George worked in Manhattan in some financial position Florence had never cared to decipher. He and Emeline had moved to the city just before Florence began her first and only year at Mount Holyoke; for his career, Florence had thought then. But now the cause seemed so clear. Their last baby, the boy, had died the year before they moved, and there had been two little girls' funerals just before the War, which Florence had attended as a callous, bored adolescent. Every failure of compassion she'd committed was redounding upon her tenfold.

She was on a train with Hammond. They were going to examine a body. A body pulled from a pond.

Hammond was watching her with pity; he did not believe the body to be Bertha but he knew that she feared it. She could feel that he was trying to be kind. Beyond that she felt very little. Her body seemed inflated with anxiety, a balloon that might detach from the earth at any moment and float into the deepening black blur of the early winter evening outside the train windows.

"She barely knows the town, isn't that right?" he said now. "There were not frequent visits to your uncle's house."

Through her trembling, she nodded. "Not since she was small. We saw them in New York once. They came to Killingly. But we have been to Oxford to see the family plot there. And she has been on this train, I don't know how many times. She knows the stops. She knows—"

Where the waters are.

Her hands twisted in her lap, and Hammond reached out, hesitated, then took one of her hands in his own. Startled, she allowed him to. His hand was hot through their gloves.

"It may be—difficult. Viewing the body of this unfortunate. We do not know how death occurred. Drownings can be quite— and the effects of the water on—"

Nausea washed up her throat. Florence pulled her hand away as delicately as she could. "Please, can we speak of something else."

"Of course. Of course."

But he did not, not for a long moment. Beneath his mustache his mouth contorted. Then he said, "There was a story, in the South Hadley *Transcript*, the day before yesterday. It specifically mentioned your mother's troubles and suggested that perhaps Bertha's absence was due to . . . an inheritance. Forgive me, that's the word they used."

At least he had not said it—that, as Bertha was in fact Sarah's granddaughter, the inheritance was more distant than any reporter knew.

"If she has drowned herself—I think it very unlikely, but if she has—we must burn that manuscript," he said. "Don't you see, Miss Mellish, how it could give credence to that theory. Or lead to even worse speculation. We can't have that sort of public noise about her or about your family."

"If she has drowned," she got out, and then her stomach seized and she had to shove to her feet and push past him to the train lavatory to heave and gulp air above the foul toilet. She spent some minutes leaning against the wall of the compartment in the particular misery of public sickness. Waiting it out, still floating, and remembering, again—how she had been sick in the church bathroom once, all those years ago, before she knew what was wrong, and a few women of her father's congregation had looked at her with sharp certainty in their eyes, certainty she'd only understood when she felt Bertha quicken.

The weakness subsided. Florence straightened her hair and her collar and opened the flimsy door and returned to her seat across from Hammond, who took her measure with a sympathetic eye and did not try to speak to her again.

ALL THREE OF THE Auburn constables met the train. They stood on the platform looking cold and serious in their overcoats, two tall men in middle age and a shorter one with a babyish face and shaggy black sideburns.

Florence did not listen to all their names, but the lead man, Nye, shook Hammond's hand and gave her a quick bow. "At your service, Dr. Hammond, Mrs. Mellish. We've called up to Boston, but their man won't be down until tomorrow. We aren't none of us investigators."

The man kept talking, in the cold, over the noise of the train departing. George Mellish had notified them of his missing niece repeatedly, by mail and telegram, and the combination of that pressure and the shock of the body's discovery had rendered them grim and urgent. Auburn did not regularly produce the bodies of young women floating grotesquely in ponds. They were unprepared, uncertain of procedure. Nye spoke of "the case" but did not seem eager to speak of the body itself or to take her to see it.

"Please, where is she?" Florence interrupted.

The men exchanged looks she did not like. "Now, we don't know that this girl is your sister, Mrs. Mellish," Nye began, "so if we could ask a few questions, perhaps we can figure—"

Hammond cut him off. "It's Miss. Miss Mellish."

Florence stepped forward, vibrating. "Can we please go to see the body now? I will not be any trouble. I know it may be gruesome. You must—you must understand. If it's her, I have to know."

Nye looked to Hammond, and finally, finally! he nodded and gestured to the younger man. "It's in—we'll go to the cemetery."

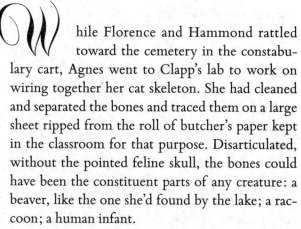

hile Florence and Hammond rattled toward the cemetery in the constabulary cart, Agnes went to Clapp's lab to work on wiring together her cat skeleton. She had cleaned and separated the bones and traced them on a large sheet ripped from the roll of butcher's paper kept in the classroom for that purpose. Disarticulated, without the pointed feline skull, the bones could have been the constituent parts of any creature: a beaver, like the one she'd found by the lake; a raccoon; a human infant.

The lab was usually empty on a Sunday night. Agnes turned off all but a few of the smaller lamps at one of the examination tables and pulled out her instruments and materials. Paper-lined tray of bones; clamps and tweezers and pliers and spools of wire; nails barely thicker than a sewing needle that could be pounded into the bone with a small hammer; tiny screws and bolts. She would reassemble the animal in a crouch, as if preparing to leap on a hapless mouse. It had been a brown-striped tabby, in life. A miniature tiger.

She had been working amid the shadows for twenty minutes or so when someone called her name.

"So you *are* in here," said Mabel Cunningham, closing the door to the hall. There was an expression Agnes had read once: *wreathed in smiles*. It had stuck with her because it made so little sense; it suited Mabel beautifully. The whisking of her skirts when she walked sounded as if a mob of lilac-scented women were converging upon Agnes's desk. "I've been looking for you, Agnes."

"I'm sorry," Agnes said, returning to the pin she was trying to insert in one of the smallest vertebrae.

Mabel gave a little laugh. "You haven't got to apologize for being a hard worker! My, we'd have to trade apologies all year long if that were true. I only meant you aren't easy to find. It's a lucky thing I saw the laboratory light from outside."

Agnes hummed noncommittally and grasped the pin with a pair of pliers to bend it around the bone. She would loop the wire there as an extra anchor, then circle it back—

Mabel's hand landed on her wrist and pushed her hand gently to the black tabletop. From where Agnes sat on the high stool, Mabel had to look up at her, and the angled lamplight hollowed her cheeks like a skull. Against her flushed cheeks her blue eyes seemed to glow. She had long chestnut-brown eyelashes. Familiar, somehow. That plaintive look.

"Agnes, how are you? You must be so horribly worried, and here we are, fussing about our final examination papers and our missing trinkets."

"It's kind of you to ask," Agnes said. "It is hard without Bertha. I admit that I try not to think of it." Even saying that much made her feel as if she were the one pinned open for examination. Under the loose bracelet of Mabel's covered fingers, the pulse in Agnes's wrist beat faster.

"Of course," Mabel said. "I am sorry for not having spoken up sooner. I'm ashamed that it took Mrs. Mead's concern to bring me to my senses. It's just that I know you prefer quiet, and I guess none of us have known if you wanted our sympathy or if you'd rather be left alone. I know you and Mollie never really got along—"

Agnes tugged her hand back slightly and Mabel let her go at once, showing her exquisite white teeth in a smile.

"Well, Mollie takes some things too seriously and other things not seriously enough, don't you agree? So I thought I could be your senior, too, if you need one. I thought it might be nice to have someone to talk to. I don't mean to reminisce about Bertha," Mabel added in a rush, "because I'm sure they'll find her somewhere safe and happy. But to unburden yourself a little. If you ever need to."

Mabel's eyes were on hers. She'd laid a strange emphasis on the word *unburden*, and the air of the laboratory suddenly seemed heavy with her perfume.

Agnes looked down at her glinting tools, the scattered bones. "Thank you," she said, low.

She heard Mabel sigh and looked up to see the girl smiling again, features cleared like wiping steam from a mirror. "No wonder you're hiding out down here. All this silliness about the thief!" Mabel stepped back from the lab table, skirts flouncing around her ankles, and began to wander around the room as she talked, trailing her gloved fingers along the lines of countertops and drawers, as if she were conducting a slow, graceful inventory of the place.

"I feel rather bad for having helped Mollie at all. I didn't think she'd make it such a crusade. Such a degeneration from our usual tone in Porter, don't you think? I was telling William about it—my intended—and he was shocked to know that girls wrote those sorts of silly things about each other, too. He thought juvenile pranks were the sole province of college men. Not the sort of argument for womanly talents one wants to make, is it?" Mabel said, over her shoulder, as she ran a finger down the labels affixed to a set of metal drawers. Agnes knew exactly what was in each of those drawers, and what could be borrowed, used, cleaned, and returned without Clapp noticing; she hadn't realized that Mabel might know, too.

"Mrs. Mead is right," the girl went on after she realized Agnes would not answer. "It does reflect poorly on us to have stirred up such a tempest about a few stolen dollars when Bertha is missing. Not you, Agnes—we all know you'd never be involved in that sort of muck-raking. But Mollie and Nan and those girls. Now that it's over it seems quite ridiculous."

"Is it over?" Agnes asked.

Mabel turned back. "Well, I expect so," she said, slowly. "Nothing else has gone missing since Mrs. Mead scolded us all. Not that I've heard of, anyway."

"I'm sure you would have heard."

She didn't mean to be comforting, but Mabel seemed to interpret her words that way. "Yes, I'm sure," Mabel echoed, and again the smile that seemed to brighten the entire room, the eyelashes dipping to her cheeks. "Well, I'll leave you. It's spooky in here after dark. But don't forget what I said, Agnes—promise me you won't?"

"I promise," Agnes said, and Mabel nodded.

"I'll see you in Porter!" She tugged her sleeves down over her gloved wrists and looped her scarf gracefully over the shining knot of her hair and gave Agnes a cheerful wave as she left, as if she'd simply completed a social call: duty done, noblesse obliged, solitary Agnes reminded of her connections to her classmates and Mabel's own primacy. But whatever Mabel wanted didn't feel so simple to Agnes. A breath of lilac hung in the air, overlaying the sharper smells of formaldehyde and surgical spirits.

Agnes sat for a long moment on the wobbly stool, looking down at the tray of bones. Then, suffused with an unfamiliar anger, she stood and crossed the room to the enamel sink. The bones were clean, and Mabel hadn't touched her skin, but she found herself scrubbing at her wrist under the cold water. She just wanted to work, with purpose and without interruption, as she'd trained herself to do. Why wouldn't they let her work?

Why did Mabel's eyelashes make her think of Bertha crying?

Why these breaches in the walls within?

24

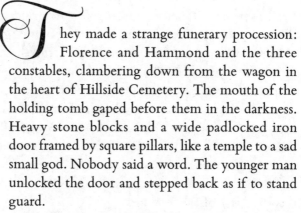hey made a strange funerary procession: Florence and Hammond and the three constables, clambering down from the wagon in the heart of Hillside Cemetery. The mouth of the holding tomb gaped before them in the darkness. Heavy stone blocks and a wide padlocked iron door framed by square pillars, like a temple to a sad small god. Nobody said a word. The younger man unlocked the door and stepped back as if to stand guard.

The hinges shrieked as the door swung open. Nye, the head constable, went ahead of Florence and Hammond, ducking into the dark tunnel of the stairs. The stone wall sucked heat through her glove as she braced herself against it. They came down into a chill and musty space, warmer than the freezing air above and silent the way caves are silent, mazed by the light of the constable's lantern. At the end of the tall central hall several plain pine coffins stood upright like lockers. Two stonework bays opened off the hall, each with just an arm's length of space on each side of the central biers. Room for attendants or mourners. Both biers held the unmistakable shapes of bodies under covering shrouds. Florence realized she had been thinking of Bertha laid out serenely on a stone slab: Juliet at her funeral, the Lady of Shalott reposing picturesquely in her little boat. Velvet and candles and camphor. This was not a resting place. This was storage.

"Which one?" she asked the constable. "Which one?"

Nye pointed to the right and said the body had been in the water for some while, as if that would dissuade her.

Florence went to the body on the wicker bier. It did not have Bertha's shape—its belly rounded like a pregnant woman's—but she knew that meant nothing, that the body might have been changed by its time submerged. Under the shroud the body appeared to be naked. The dark hair showing at the edge of the draping gray cloth looked felted. She turned down the shroud tenderly to reveal the face, holding her breath, holding on to the long moment in which the cloth was moving but the face not yet revealed, in case it was Bertha, in case this would be her last moment alive without having seen her daughter dead.

"Bring the lantern closer," she told Nye, and light fell upon the bared face of the dead girl.

The skin of the girl's face was white and thick, with a strange flat sheen like candle wax. Her eyebrows were wrong, thick bars rather than delicate curves. No little scar where she'd hit her forehead on the corner of the stove. The bridge of her nose—a mole under the left eye—none of it was right. None of it was Bertha. It wasn't Bertha.

Florence looked to Hammond, who had come to stand beside her. At that moment they were thinking the same thing, though neither knew it: *It's not her. I see it, I saw it at once, because I know her. Do you see it?*

Florence shook her head.

Hammond shook his head.

Air seemed to flood into the tomb, like a vacuum experiment reversed. Nye gave a little ragged laugh of relief, and Florence drew a deep breath through her nose, hardly registering the body's stink of pondwater and rot. The floating sensation that had carried her from Killingly to Auburn had dissipated in a moment, leaving her heart rabbiting in her chest and her ears ringing as if from a blow. It wasn't Bertha. It wasn't Bertha.

"You're sure it's not Miss Mellish," Nye said.

"I'm certain." Florence looked down at the dead girl again, at her swollen cheeks and teeth just bared by slightly drawn-back lips. Even so distorted, she was some mother's baby. Some other woman would stand here and fold down the shroud, and instead of the reprieve that Florence felt all through her body she would scream in recognition. Or worse: No one would come. No one would ever know this girl again except as an object to be studied.

"Do you know if she died before entering the water or after?" Hammond asked Nye. "There are signs, to tell." She could hear in his voice that he had researched the features of drowning. When they first boarded the train, while she sat across from him in silent agony, he had been reading a thick text with interest, in apparent calm. She had thought at the time that he must have been trying to distract himself from worry.

"We don't know, sir." Nye lowered the lantern, shifting the shadows it cast. "We've got one surgeon in the town, and he's ill. I imagine she'll go by train to Boston if they care to perform a full examination."

Hammond leaned close to Florence to peer at the girl's face, and Nye obligingly raised the lantern again. Over the whiff of decay came the powdery scent of Hammond's cologne, familiar enough now that it was almost comforting. "No froth around the nostrils. That's one indication. There are no clear wounds on the body?" He reached as if to pull the shroud down farther.

"Henry," Florence said in rebuke, and he pulled back. She lifted the cloth to re-cover the girl's face. "Leave her in peace. The constables will see to it."

"Some damage, maybe from animals. Hard to tell when," Nye answered, as if she hadn't spoken.

"What will it cost?" Florence asked. "To bury her when the investigation is complete. She will be buried here?"

Both men turned to her in surprise.

"I suppose so, ma'am," Nye said slowly. "Be around fifteen dollars, for the casket and a spot on the hill here."

It was more than she'd expected, certainly more than she had with her. "If she is not identified—if you will write to me in Killingly—I will pay."

"Florence," Hammond said, and though she had not noticed when she spoke his first name a minute before, she startled at the sound of hers in his mouth.

Nye was nodding, smiling carefully in a way she did not trust, as if he were playing out a conversation with her uncle George in his head. "Of course, ma'am. If nobody claims her." He gestured to the stairs. "If you please."

She touched the frame of the bier once more in silent benediction and followed Nye up the stairs, Hammond at her heels. Outside the two other constables broke away from the wagon when they saw Nye, who went at once to tell them that the girl was not George Mellish's niece. Florence looked out over the rows of tombstones glinting in the darkness, the low boughs of the trees along the gravel path. She felt all the exhaustion her nerves had kept at bay.

Nye turned back to them. His movements had a new looseness; if no one came to claim the girl, there would be no family to handle, no wealthy pillar of the town to disappoint. "You can't stand around the station till the five-thirty comes. Let me take you to your uncle's house."

On the way to George Mellish's house, the men stopped the wagon to drop off the younger constable, Pickering, at the home of the town telegrapher so he could send to Killingly the message Florence scribbled on a scrap of paper from Hammond's coat pocket:

NOT HER. COMING HOME IN MORNING.

HER UNCLE'S HOME WAS smaller than Florence had remembered it, hunched beside the looming town hall, a newly finished white building that looked as if a large house had swallowed a church. In his absence, her uncle's house had been used as the town's library. Stacks of books rose from floors and tables like ancient tree stumps or the towers of a miniature city.

"We're moving it all next door," Nye said apologetically as he led them to a shut-up room in the back of the chilly house, where two rocking chairs sat in front of a bare mantel. "You'll have to sit up, I'm afraid. Unless you'd rather come to my house for a spell? We could move the children."

Hammond made a noise of interest, but Florence shook her head. She could not face a family now—and she'd had the sudden wild thought that she would find Bertha *here*—not floating in some pond but among these piles of words in her uncle's house, asleep in a cobwebbed corner with a volume open in her lap. Where better to hide, if she needed respite? But the dream curdled in a moment. The house felt like a husk, animated only by the sounds of the constable shoving wood into the fireplace and Hammond breathing heavily, rubbing his hands together for warmth. No matter where she went to look for Bertha she found only men.

Tears pricked at Florence's eyelids but she forced them back.

Soon Nye had built a fire and piled dusty quilts on the chairs. He left with a promise to return at five-fifteen, and then the house was quiet but for the popping of the burning wood.

Hammond settled into the chair on the left. "Quite an evening," he said placidly.

"It's morning." Florence sat and arranged her own quilt. Despite her grainy eyes, she could not imagine trying to sleep sitting next to Hammond in a pair of rocking chairs like an old married couple.

"Indeed." He shifted, looking at the fire. "Your offer to Nye, for the burial costs—it was generous of you, but that is costly sympathy. Should you not save that money to put toward finding your daughter?"

Her whole body jerked under the quilt. No one, not even

Hammond in his role as physician at the birth, had ever called Bertha her daughter before. The word was like a tiny bomb, ricocheting debris inside her head. "Don't say that," she said, dazed, as if swallowing the word would suppress its meaning. As if he hadn't known for twenty years.

"I beg your pardon," Hammond said. "You've had a shock, I know, even if the girl was not Miss Mellish. But you cannot afford to fling your money at charity cases."

Florence turned to study him. Firelight glinted off silvery stubble below his neat beard. "How were you so sure it would not be her, Dr. Hammond?"

"I do not know, really," he said slowly. "I simply knew it could not be. I fear many things for Miss Mellish, but when I read that telegram I felt quite certain suddenly that it would not be George Mellish who led us to her. I can't explain it."

He wanted to be the one to find Bertha, the one to save her. That was why he'd been so sure.

Florence remembered Hammond's wife, Emma, holding Bertha on her lap after Hammond had treated Bertha's fevers. Bertha in her third year then, a serious dark-eyed toddler, all frowning concentration as she stuck her fingers through the holes in Emma's lace collar. And Hammond smiling genially in the corner, like a father. Like Bertha's father.

"I want Bertha's story printed," Florence said, each word like a coal in her mouth.

He frowned. "Would it not be better to destroy it?" She was shaking her head even as he spoke, but he kept talking. "The public will think, here is a girl who admitted to her mistakes in her own hand! Why should they keep looking for her, then?"

"It's a story, not a confession. And it will make people remember Bertha—keep her in their minds."

"As a ruined woman," Hammond said with forced patience.

"So that's what you object to, really. It's not just the suicide, is it. It's the lover, Marie Racine's lover."

"Miss Mellish," he said, clearly shocked by that word on her lips.

"Bertha is not your charge," she said around the pure thick rage rising in her throat. "And I am not, either. I will pay to bury that girl if I wish to. I will reread Bertha's story and decide what is best. You'll need to give me the manuscript."

That provoked a flare in his eyes—not the anger she anticipated but shame, as if she'd caught him doing something untoward. "Of course," he said, in the falsely hearty voice she hated, and looked toward the hearth.

She leaned into the space between their chairs, dislodging the quilt from around her shoulders as the chair rocked forward. She no longer felt the room's chill. "I told you from the first, I don't care what she wrote. I can't believe Bertha would risk her schooling for a lover."

He looked at her again. "Florence." Gentler now. "I'm not saying I believe it all to be true. But I'm not sure you know everything. There may be—there are things she didn't tell you."

He said this apologetically, as if he wished to spare her pain. All Florence heard was that he had withheld knowledge of Bertha—kept it locked away as he would have locked away Bertha herself.

"What is it?" she demanded. "What?"

"There was—a letter."

Her hands tightened on her knees. "What did this letter say? Who wrote it?"

"The writer claims that Bertha is alive. That she left the College of her own free will. It's not signed. It came to the boarding-house."

"Never," Florence said. "I don't believe it. She would've come to me."

"The letter writer says she was afraid to," he said haltingly, "to tell her family."

Florence took a shallow breath and then another.

"You see, it was nothing to bother you with. It may still turn out to be all misdirection. Higham should know soon."

"That's why you and Higham came to Killingly," she said. "So he could observe us. Make a study."

Hammond said nothing. His eyes reflected the firelight.

"Did the letter say where she is?"

He shook his head.

"Then where is Higham now?"

"Florence—"

"Tell me. He found something, didn't he? Tell me!"

Hammond drew in a long breath and let it out. "At the Sayles mill, there was a man called Paul, a French-Canadian. He fits the description of Joseph in the story. He left the mill a short while before Bertha disappeared. Nobody would—" He faltered, reached out, but she twisted back against her chair. "This man Paul was in Northampton. He told different stories about where he might go to find work. Higham has gone to look for him."

She stared.

"So you see why Bertha's writing cannot be published, then. If anyone found that it was true, that she really did have a lover—"

"I don't see," Florence said through clenched teeth. "Because it's not true. She would have told me. I won't believe it. She knows better. She would never listen to a man's lies."

Hammond leaned back, his chair rocking. "Did she know—about you?"

It was not exactly nausea that Florence felt when he asked but a sensation of sudden impalement, as if a cold metal rod seared solid where her spine had been. Everything that had been subdued in her for decades felt frozen and freed in the same moment. Her guts seethed and her eyes locked on his. "You know nothing about me."

"I—"

"I protected her," she said. The quietest howl. "I stayed to protect her."

"What—" He fell silent. "You can't mean—" and again he stopped.

Understanding came into Hammond's face like poison diffusing in water: that the Reverend John Mellish had gotten a child on his plain elder daughter. That his Bertha, the girl he wanted to marry, was a child of incest.

Hammond must have encountered many unspeakable things in his life, Florence thought coldly. A doctor, a medical man, would meet horrors; before that, the War. Yet despite all his worldliness, he looked now like a man who had survived an explosion, left standing in a crater as clods of earth finished falling to the ground, and scrabbled in the deafened silence to feel for his limbs—to determine what he had lost.

She watched him collect himself and find that he was still whole. That he could remain whole, if he denied this knowledge.

She watched him decide to disbelieve her.

25

The day they returned from Auburn, Hammond paid to have notices printed with Bertha's face and *$500 reward* bold across the top of the page. The notices said: *Bertha Lane Mellish, a student at Mt. Holyoke College, South Hadley, Mass., disappeared from the College on the 18th of November, 1897, and no trace of her has been found since that time.* The notices described her appearance, her dress, down to the label sewn into her skirt. The notices said: *The above reward will be paid for the girl alive.*

He did not consult Florence about this. Nor did he consult her on December ninth, when he raised the reward to seven hundred fifty dollars. On December tenth, this broadside, now outdated, was printed and distributed anyway—in South Hadley, in Killingly, in Providence and Hartford and Boston and New York.

$500 REWARD

BERTHA LANE MELLISH.

Bertha Lane Mellish, a student at Mt. Holyoke College, South Hadley, Mass., disappeared from the College on the 18th of November, 1897, and no trace of her has been found since that time

The following is a description : She is 20 years old, about 5 feet 5 inches in height, medium build, dark auburn hair, fair complexion, brown eyes. round face, full lips. Sometimes wore her hair parted and sometimes combed straight back. Very small faint scar in the center of forehead.

When last seen wore a black dress, shaggy black jacket, black cloth Tam 'o Shanter. Underclothing was marked "Mellish." She wore a gray flannel skirt.

The above reward will be paid for the girl alive, by Rev. John H. Mellish, at Dayville, Connecticut. In addition to the $50 offered by the Mt. Holyoke College, the family will pay $50 additional for the recovery of the body.

Dayville, Conn., December 10th, 1897.

Around three-thirty the next morning, when Porter was quiet and the other girls all slept, Agnes lit a stub of beeswax candle, the sort she had used as a makeshift votive when she was a child. She couldn't sleep. She had read the report of "Miss Mellish's sister and Dr. Henry Hammond" traveling to Auburn to examine a corpse, and the knowledge of the journey was eating like sulphur at her innards.

Agnes had seen the broadside, too, with its description of Bertha's "full lips," and known it to be Hammond's doing. Yet the disgust she expected to feel at his presumption did not come. She could not help but gaze at that photograph of Bertha visibly thinking, as if the texture of her mind were trapped in the photographic medium, reproducible. A copy of the broadside had been pinned to the board in the Porter front hall. Agnes had taken it down, fingered the pinholes in its corners, pressed its edges flat.

So many pale copies of Bertha had appeared in the world since she disappeared from the College. These printed facsimiles of her face; the sightings; this girl in the lake in Auburn whose body Florence Mellish had been summoned to identify—Florence Mellish and Hammond both. Agnes forced herself to include the doctor in her perseverating. Much as she disliked the man, she did feel sorry for him, in some small recess of her being. There was so much Hammond did not know about Bertha.

Perhaps she ought to envy Hammond, Agnes thought, for what he wouldn't know. He could prepare this broadside with the hope of obtaining some new information. He could fill himself with the righteous energy of the searcher. He could believe in a rescue to come.

But her mind kept returning to Florence Mellish, called to examine a body that might have been Bertha's. The train, the waiting. The horror Florence must have felt before the corpse was revealed and the pitiful relief at its unfamiliarity. Florence knew nothing before she saw the body and she knew nothing more afterward. She was never going to know.

Bertha had forbidden Agnes to tell anyone, even Florence, what had happened to her. But if Agnes had been able to speak, if she had been willing to break that vow, she could have saved Florence that misery.

She could have told Florence—that body could never be Bertha's.

That knowledge was what howled under Agnes's skin. That was why she felt any sympathy for Henry Hammond at all. Like Agnes herself, like Florence Mellish, he would never see his Bertha again. And it was Agnes's fault.

THE GUILT SHE CARRIED was its own danger. The next night, when she went to Clapp's lab to work on her skeleton, Agnes found Mrs. Mead, Dr. Clapp, and the Porter Hall mistress, Mrs. Abbott, clustered around one of the lab tables with their heads together. She knocked on the doorframe, and Mrs. Mead lifted her head, frowning.

"I came to work on my skeleton," said Agnes, looking to Clapp for permission. "I can come back later."

Clapp beckoned her in. Between their bodies she glimpsed a brown paper packet splayed open on the table, and she caught the occasional word of their whispers: *concerned, students, Porter*. Enough to make it clear that the packet contained something related to the thief.

She'd barely settled her materials at the second-best table when they approached. Squat Mrs. Mead and Mrs. Abbott framed tall, thin Dr. Clapp, one of them—probably Abbott, to cover her gin stink—smelling strongly of lily-of-the-valley. Agnes put down her pliers.

The questions Clapp asked in her grand, nasal voice were anodyne enough—how often had she come to work in the lab that week, what other girls had she seen and when. But Agnes could sense their suspicion, and they were not wrong to suspect her. That knowledge made her stumble over her answers.

Mrs. Mead bore the paper packet toward Agnes like a gift and set it down heavily upon the table. It contained a handful of coins and folded paper bills.

"The money from Porter," Agnes said, and Mead nodded.

"Except for one dollar," said fluttery Mrs. Abbott. "We counted it twice."

"It was here?" Agnes asked.

"In the back of one of the specimen drawers," Clapp said.

Mrs. Mead studied Agnes's face. "It's only the money, none of the trinkets. I'm afraid we have a nonsensical thief who steals money only to hoard it."

Mrs. Mead, tough as she was, had always seemed to like her. Agnes had known she would spend her final year and a half here fretful, miserable, always on her guard—that was her penance. Still it stung, to be suspected of this trivial thing.

"Except for the dollar," Mrs. Abbott said again.

"That's what I'm missing," Agnes said, trying to keep her voice even, for she saw that Mrs. Mead was about to say the same. The president nodded. "It wasn't me, if that's what you're asking."

"No one's saying anything of the sort, Agnes," Clapp said, with a sharp look at Mrs. Mead. "The lab is open for hours every day without a supervisor. Any student who has taken zoology or biology would know where those drawers are and could have hidden this."

"Agnes," said Mrs. Mead, gently. Her face was set. "I mean no insult. But grief can cause a person to do unusual things—uncharacteristic things."

"Not me," said Agnes, lying.

26

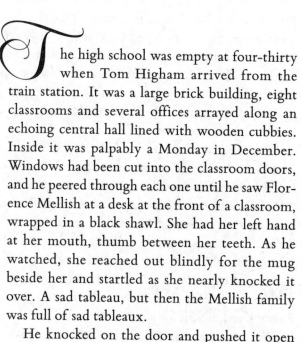

he high school was empty at four-thirty when Tom Higham arrived from the train station. It was a large brick building, eight classrooms and several offices arrayed along an echoing central hall lined with wooden cubbies. Inside it was palpably a Monday in December. Windows had been cut into the classroom doors, and he peered through each one until he saw Florence Mellish at a desk at the front of a classroom, wrapped in a black shawl. She had her left hand at her mouth, thumb between her teeth. As he watched, she reached out blindly for the mug beside her and startled as she nearly knocked it over. A sad tableau, but then the Mellish family was full of sad tableaux.

He knocked on the door and pushed it open without waiting for a response.

"Miss Mellish," he said, and Florence saw him and bolted from her seat. That terrified scramble families of the missing learned.

"Detective—is there—"

"No, I'm sorry, no new information. A routine visit."

She sank back to her seat. Beneath the shawl she was wearing a high-collared maroon jacket and a gray plaid skirt, neither fashionable. It took her only a moment to calm herself.

"Please come in. Have a—" She gestured at the desks lined up between them.

"I'll stand, thank you," said Higham, who had never liked sitting at a desk in school or in the police. He didn't plan to stay long. First they went over the business of the floating body, another Mellish uncle, Florence's uncertainty about what to do next. She was getting to the worst of it now. The horrible thoughts, impulses unimaginable to anyone who still dwelt in the daylight world of safe and living children: *If it had been her, at least I would have known.*

"I'll tell you what to do next," Higham said. "This manuscript of Miss Mellish's—"

"Dr. Hammond says it shouldn't be published," Florence said heavily. "I don't feel I can go against him. I'm sure you know how much he is supporting the search."

"He will have a shock, then." Her eyes flashed up to his face. "I've been to see your father today, when I got into town. He's decided to sell the right to publish the story to the *Willimantic Weekly Journal.* I believe it's to appear this evening. They were quite eager to run it."

"My father? To the *Journal?*" One of her hands covered her downturned mouth for a moment. As before, she wore no rings at all—no adornment. Her nails were bitten down, raw. "But he didn't have it—Hammond did. He's not—"

"The Reverend borrowed the copy I made of the manuscript," Higham said. "I can't agree with your Dr. Hammond. I know his objections to publishing the material. He fears for her reputation, and so on. But I think you see it as I do, that the story will stir up interest in the case again. Maybe draw the eye of someone who has seen her. There are already stories circulating. At least her own story might make people pity her. Leave it in the hands of the newspapermen, they'll spin whatever they like. Whatever will sell."

"He is never my Dr. Hammond," said Florence.

"Indeed. My apologies."

"He will be angry."

"Send him after me."

"I certainly will," she said. Her hands tightened on the edge of her desk, the coffee and papers in front of her forgotten. "We have little money. You know that. He's put up most of the reward."

"You have a little more now. From the *Journal*."

He watched her struggle for a moment before she asked, reluctantly, "How much?"

"Fifty dollars."

She gave a short, humorless laugh. "I promised to bury the girl in Auburn if her relations are not found. I suppose that will be easier now."

Higham clasped his hands behind his back and looked around the classroom. He had swept over it when he first came in, checking the windows, looking for other doors. An old habit. But now he studied the calligraphed poems tacked to the wall. Whittier and Dickinson, other nonsense of the children's-magazine sort. A few awful watercolor paintings on warped card stock, proudly signed. Quotations done in a different hand, probably Florence's. He walked over to look at one. It was not written in the same script as the mysterious letter Hammond had received.

"I suppose it's too late to stop the story being printed," Florence said, and Higham turned back to her in curiosity. Her expression had grown bleak.

"Why?"

"Dr. Hammond told me about the French-Canadian mill man. He told me why you were in Pennsylvania."

"That surprises me."

"Yes, it was a surprise for me as well," Florence said, her anger flaring. "It was a surprise to know that Bertha might have had a lover, that the two of you were trying to find this lover, and that no one saw fit to tell me about it. I understand choosing not to tell my father. But I don't understand the rest. Help me understand this, Detective Higham."

"Under orders from Hammond." He shrugged. That was

another skill you learned in the police, the range of noncommittal replies the body could communicate. No idea where your wife is, sir. No idea where that bruise came from, where that knife came from, where that block of dope could've gotten to. He'd never exactly been dirty himself, but he knew about dirt and he knew about orders. "As you said, he pays. He told you about the letter as well as the mill worker?"

"He did," said Florence evenly.

"Between you and me, Miss Mellish, the good doctor doesn't know what to fear more—finding your sister dead or the public discovering that she wrote about a man. I've been tracking this Paul, or Joseph, or whatever he may be. I didn't find him in Pennsylvania. I believe he went through there, then kept going west."

The evidence of that was scanty enough, and Higham didn't think it worth explaining how he'd obtained it. He'd put Hammond's money to good use, pulped a few noses, bitten a few soft lower lips. And for that he'd learned that his instinct to go west had likely been correct: Paul-Joseph had almost certainly stopped in Philadelphia, might have touched down in Reading. The man hadn't been arrested and hadn't frequented any of the establishments where the mill workers drank. They were hot with union fever down there, hardly eager to talk much to police, current or former. But from the bits of information he'd gleaned, Higham had begun to wonder whether he'd been wrong to think the mill man less important than Agnes Sullivan.

"Do you think he hurt Bertha?" A rough croak of a question.

Higham turned back to the poems on the wall so she would not have to feel his eyes. "I don't rightly know, Miss Mellish. I'm not sure we will know. But I do not think she's gone with him, wherever he is. I didn't hear anything about a young woman accompanying him. He may have had nothing to do with this at all. Perhaps Hammond's precious letter is correct and she left alone. But I have a feeling about this mill man, I'll admit it. I have a feeling."

Silence. He looked back to see her nodding. "All right," she said. Then after a moment: "Could we put out notices? To find him?"

"You could," Higham told her. "But that'll cost. You'll need Hammond's help."

Florence Mellish gave an unladylike snort, the liveliest thing he'd heard from her yet.

"I'd wait a day or so," he said, and she looked up and smiled and thanked him, and after they had parted, as he rode back to the hotel in the nostril-prickling cold, he thought about that smile, the thinness of it, the bravery, the surprising charm it showed in her round face. It was unfortunate that the future seemed likely to offer her so little to smile about.

"LA PETITE: A STORY of Mattawaugan Mill" appeared in the *Willimantic Weekly Journal* that night. Numerous copies sent to South Hadley—hardly the usual distribution pattern for a Connecticut town paper—sold briskly.

The story's publication inspired quite a range of reactions. The girls of the College traded copies and whispers; the townspeople of South Hadley and Killingly frowned in concentration, trying to determine how best to interpret its words. Reporters up and down the East Coast read descriptions of the story in the larger Connecticut papers and wrote their own provocative and often inaccurate summaries.

Those who knew the story's contents practically by heart—Florence, Higham, and Hammond—tried to resist reading it again in print and could not. Frustrating as they found the manuscript, they kept circling back to it. Bertha's story, in Bertha's words.[1]

---

1 The text of Bertha's actual story, as published in the *Willimantic Weekly Journal* in 1897, is included as an appendix on page 332.

And there was one thing Florence found especially shocking, that kept her squinting at the newsprint long into the night. The suicide they had all been so horrified to read about now seemed to her almost secondary. The story was all mothers and abandoned daughters: Marie Racine, who had never known her mother and whose father wasn't "steady"; Marie Racine, who killed herself and left a daughter for her best friend to raise.

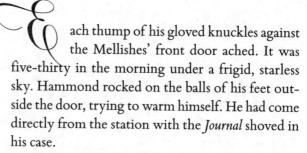ach thump of his gloved knuckles against the Mellishes' front door ached. It was five-thirty in the morning under a frigid, starless sky. Hammond rocked on the balls of his feet outside the door, trying to warm himself. He had come directly from the station with the *Journal* shoved in his case.

Florence opened the door in a brown wrapper, her mousy hair loose around her shoulders. The resigned look on her face roused a swell of pure hatred in him. He'd told her not to do this—he had told her why—and now she had ruined Bertha just as she'd ruined herself. She was the root of it all.

"What is this?" he demanded, yanking the paper from his case and brandishing it at her. "What did you do?"

"Come in, Dr. Hammond. And for God's sake keep your voice down."

He pushed past her into the entryway. "Blast my voice. How dare you do this without telling me? Did you sell it to them? Why would you do it? You know I will pay whatever is necessary—"

"Henry Hammond!" A shout from the upper realm of the house.

"Marvelous," Florence murmured and stepped away from him with a shake of her head.

John Mellish appeared at the top of the staircase in a nightshirt and stocking cap. He had that insectile look men sometimes develop in their dotage, and his shirt draped awkwardly over his bundled limbs as he levered himself from stair to stair. At the bottom of the steps, Florence lifted her arm for her father to take, her face expressionless.

Perhaps it was best that Emma had lost the babies, Hammond thought savagely. *He* would never find himself at the mercy of a traitorous daughter like Florence.

"Reverend Mellish," he said as the old man approached. "I am sorry to have awakened you."

Mellish jabbed him in the chest with a finger. "Why are you here, Hammond? We've no need of your services. No illness in this house."

"No, of course," Hammond said, taken aback. "I'm here to speak to Florence, about the investigation. I didn't mean to trouble you."

"What?" the Reverend snapped. "What of it?" The stocking cap had slipped to a rakish-looking angle on his white head, calling to mind boys Hammond had known in the Army who liked to wear their caps tilted and lost both cap and courage when a cannonball hit.

He told the Reverend: the *Journal* had published Bertha's manuscript "expressly against my wishes," he added, jerking his head toward Florence, "because *she* cannot bear to let me have any say in how this investigation is managed!"

Mellish grabbed at him again, this time snagging the sleeve of his coat and shaking it ineffectually. "You keep a civil tongue in your head when you speak to my Florence." Florence tried to push between them and Mellish shook her off, as if he didn't recognize the daughter he was defending.

"My apologies, Reverend. I don't think you understand the problem. This manuscript—it could ruin Bertha's reputation. She writes of suicide and common-law marriage. And I told Florence, I told her it would be terrible if that story was published, and she—"

The Reverend puffed air like a bull. He grabbed at the hem of his nightshirt to wrestle it over his head, but it stuck, mercifully, around his shoulders, leaving Hammond with a dizzy impression of the man's genitals slapping against his withered thighs. "You don't say a word about my daughter—" Mellish babbled, fingers scrabbling under the cloth, and twisted his body to shove between Hammond and Florence.

Hammond had the distinct, dismaying sense that the Reverend intended to fight him bareskinned to protect Florence's illusory honor. He and Florence both struggled to yank the nightshirt back down, and their hands collided. "Sorry, sorry," Hammond found himself saying, and finally they succeeded in pulling the nightshirt out of her father's grip. The old man slumped back against Florence's arm, still muttering and glaring at Hammond, but blessedly did not try to strip off his shift again.

For a moment they all stood and panted. Hammond could hear air whistling through Florence's nostrils, her gritted teeth. He found that he wanted to see her eyes, but she would not look at him. Instead he turned back to Mellish. "For the love of—Reverend, I'm here to protect your daughter. This story she wrote—"

"He sold that story." Florence, quiet in her breathlessness. Her cheeks were mottled red.

"What?" Hammond stared at her. Now she stared right back.

"Your man Higham. He came to speak with the Reverend and helped him to sell it."

Mellish stirred against her, a bit clearer-eyed. "More information," he said. "Said it would help." His eyes were on Florence's face, not on Hammond's. Hammond did not want to think about why.

"Did you know about this?" Hammond demanded.

Florence shook her head. "Not till last evening. Higham came to warn me. But it was already done."

"And you didn't think to warn me?"

"I thought he'd done the same for you," she said.

"Higham's done nothing," he said. "He wrote me from

Pennsylvania. He couldn't find that mill worker. Lord knows if the man even exists."

Mellish drew himself away from Florence's arm and leaned in close to Hammond. "It's just a story!" His breath smelled like rotten fruit. "Keep her in the news. To bring her home. Keep up interest."

It was like hearing Higham's voice piped through the Reverend's mouth. Hammond stood amazed for a moment and his silence seemed to convince the other man that he agreed.

Mellish nodded. "Florence," he said. "Show the doctor out."

"I will, Father."

Florence and Hammond both watched anxiously as the Reverend climbed the stairs. Florence's hands hovered in anticipation of the need to catch him. Ever the dutiful helpmeet.

If what she claimed was true, how could she possibly have borne that role for so many years? The heroic will, the extreme self-mastery such endurance would require—Florence did not possess.

She didn't turn back to him until Mellish had disappeared into the dark hall above.

"Now," she whispered. "What's done is done. There's nothing to gain by bringing up—the mill. Higham told me he thinks the man went west. I think we should advertise. Print up broadsides about him, too. If he knows something, anything about what happened—"

"Advertise?" Hammond reared back, and she waved a furious hand to hush him. "You cannot be serious."

"How else are we to find him?"

"He's a phantom. If he was here, if he did know her, he's long gone. The more attention we draw to him the more likely someone might realize or remember that they saw Bertha with him—"

"That's what we want!"

"That's what *you* want," he retorted. "That's what Higham wants, apparently. I want to protect her from this circus of newspaper nonsense."

"What does it matter?" Florence whispered. "If she's dead, what does it matter anymore? You see how my father is now. It can't shame him."

"The letter says she is still alive," he said, just as urgent. "What if she won't come back, now that the story has been published?"

"Do you believe it? That she's alive?"

He jerked back in consternation, almost disgust. "I have to. Don't you?"

But Florence didn't answer. She just looked at him, her worn face a faded echo of Bertha's. He stood for a minute watching her. "I'll have a word with Higham about this foolishness," he said finally. "Keep him on if you will, but I won't be paying for him."

She blinked at him in shock, then lurched forward to grab his arm just as her father had. Had Bertha ever touched his arm? He thought she must have, but he could not imagine when. Not when they had walked, with feet of space between them, around the ponds on campus. Not when they sat, exchanging polite talk, in the parlor of this house. "But what will we do?" Florence asked in anguish.

"I will find the letter writer," Hammond said. "You can count on that."

28

*E*va Bissell caught her on the icy front steps of Porter that afternoon. Agnes was in a rush—she'd forgotten to take her biology book to zoology, which she never did, and had only a few minutes to fetch it between classes. She turned on Eva with a vicious frown when the girl clutched her coat sleeve, but Eva didn't seem to notice.

"Have you seen it? You must have seen it." Short of breath, Eva swiped at her dripping nose. Half her hair was down from her bun in a frizzy mess, her pale cheeks reddened, as if she'd been running across the snowy campus.

"I don't know what you're talking about," Agnes said. "I have to get my book before class."

"There's a story of Bertha's in the paper." Eva squinted and bit her lip. She looked for all the world as if she expected a blow to the face. "I thought you must know about it already."

"What?" Agnes said blankly.

Florence Mellish had said nothing about Bertha's story. She'd sent Agnes an appallingly kind letter apologizing for not having written sooner about the dead girl who wasn't Bertha and asking: *Did Bertha have a friend in the Sayles mill, a man named Joseph or Paul, who could have knowledge of her disappearance? Are you certain that she never mentioned either of those names? I know you would have told us if she had.* And Agnes had just written back a short, disingenuous note: *I am so sorry to say that I know nothing of this Joseph or Paul—*

Eva was staring. Agnes tried to sound calm. "Oh, yes, the story. Her sister told me about it. I didn't know it was to be printed."

"Oh, thank goodness. I was afraid—if you didn't know—because there's a death in it, you know—but of course you know. I mean, I didn't want you to be surprised by it. If you weren't expecting that."

"Thank you," Agnes said, "that's very kind."

Eva looked startled. "Well, it would be so terrible to read—Anyway, I wanted to tell you."

"What paper?"

"The *Willimantic Journal.* That's what Mollie said."

Agnes nodded through a pang of nausea. She couldn't look at those words in print.

"I could try to find you a copy? One of the girls must have it."

"No. I'd rather not." Agnes tried to gather herself. She'd needed something—her book. She drew back from Eva, up the stairs, wishing that she knew how to get away without being rude.

"Of course," Eva said. "Of course. But there's good news, too."

"Oh?" She would be late for her very last biology class. She was never late.

"The doctor is back. The Mellishes' doctor. He's at Mrs. Goren's again, Mollie says."

"Oh."

"It must be good, don't you think, that he's come back here? That he hasn't given up?"

"Yes, it must be good," Agnes echoed. It wasn't good. It wasn't good at all.

"I just keep thinking," Eva blurted, "how wonderful it would be if they found her now, just before Christmas, and she was fine and healthy and could go back to her family and everyone could be happy, the way it ought to be at Christmas. Imagine!"

Agnes tried not to imagine it, but Eva's words were too

compelling to resist. She didn't think of the scene Eva meant to describe—a happy family standing together in front of a hearth all ablaze, a goose on the table, a holly wreath on the door. She thought instead of herself in her room in Porter. She thought of the door creaking open in the silence as she worked and of Bertha's beloved little face appearing around its edge, relieved of all the anguish Agnes had last seen her wearing. Relieved of all distractions. Returned at her best and dearest. *I am home, Agnes,* Bertha would say and reach out for her hands. *You will be with me, won't you, to do our work?*

As if that fantasy could block out the real memory: Bertha prostrate on the floor of Agnes's room in the night, telling Agnes about the assignment she had turned in to Neilson. Agnes had hissed, *How could you write that, you stupid girl!* and then put her hand to Bertha's cheek in horrified apology.

Everything she had done, everything she had tried to do, to lead Hammond away from Joseph and the mill, for nothing. She had lied just as Bertha told her to, for nothing. Bertha's own words would see to that—and it was Hammond's fault for letting the paper publish. She would never feel a speck of pity for him again.

"When do you leave for the holiday?" Eva asked.

"I'm not leaving. I don't have the money."

"For the train? Well, I'm sure—I'm sure we could find it for you. Have you told Mrs. Mead?"

"I stay over Christmas every year," Agnes said.

"But—"

Agnes turned to look at her. "It's not just the train. If I stay here, I can eat and my family can eat. That won't happen if I go home."

"I understand," Eva whispered. "My mother—"

"I have to get my book," Agnes repeated and fled.

THAT NIGHT, AS AGNES was writing the paper about her completed cat skeleton, she flipped through one of the pamphlets she'd gathered on the cat fancy: *Cats and Catteries in America.*

Near the end of the pamphlet, in a section on "High-Bred Cats in America," she saw Hammond's name.

It *was* the same Hammond. He was a cat fancier—a breeder. Had Bertha ever told her so? She thought not, which was strange. Everything else about Hammond had been fair game for Bertha's mockery when he had first begun writing her letters. *My life is yours, my love is yours, if you will but ask it. I would give my life to know that I had made you a happy woman*—how they had savaged him. Bertha had known that Agnes was reading up on the cat fancy; they'd discussed its relevance to her debate speech. But that had been in September, before everything went wrong.

Agnes tried to focus on the pamphlet. *Dr. H. L. Hammond, of Killingly, Ct., makes a speciality of the rare Australian cats, and has taken numerous prizes with them at every cat show in this country . . . Dr. and Mrs. Hammond are extremely fond of their unusual and valuable cat family, and tell the most interesting tales of their antics and habits. They have spells of sleeping when nothing has power to disturb them, but when they do wake up they have a "high time," running and playing. They are affectionate, being very fond of their owner, but rather shy with strangers. They are uncommonly intelligent, too, and are very teachable when young.*

In the blurry, badly printed photograph accompanying the text stood a striped creature more delicate than the stocky tabby Agnes had killed with chloroform, awkwardly posed, its head turned back as if to look at something behind its flanks. Every muscle and ligament stood out in the cat's slim forelegs, but its ringed tail drooped. Around the cat's neck sat a thick leather collar with a leash clipped to a heavy metal ring. The leash extended out of the photograph's frame, but Agnes saw Hammond as clearly as if he were pictured, with the other end of the leash wrapped around his knuckles and his face folded in an indulgent smile. *Felis catus domesticus*: the creature tamed and kept.

Uncommonly intelligent and very teachable when young.

Agnes closed the pamphlet and pushed her zoology work aside. She had written the first letter to Hammond because she could not believe that her silence would be sufficient to keep him from learning the truth. A man like that needed another story to follow.

She'd used her old looping schoolgirl scrawl rather than the copperplate draughtsman's script she wrote in now. (Bertha in her head, in their first year, teasing her about her high school notes as Agnes glowered and demanded them back: *What is this, your self-nomination for class president? So earnest, so sweet. Look at those big-bellied A's! I rather like it. But I suppose it's not a doctor's hand-writing, is it? Not even a lady doctor's. Too much lady, too little doctor.*) It had been terribly hard to write the letter. She'd reduced her first attempts to a mound of ragged little triangles to be swept into her chamber pot, all the imploring words she'd written scrambled to form new sentences. *You must save The child I miss her Secretly she escaped.*

The letter was deceptive, and yet it was not. She didn't believe that Hammond was the only one who had faith in Bertha. Agnes knew he could not save Bertha. No one could. But for a few moments she'd been able to pretend. Even a false Bertha, present in the world, improved it. Writing her into life made Agnes's own life more bearable.

So she'd thought.

That was over now.

Her hands clenched. Her fingers remembered wrapping around the soft anterior side of Bertha's arm, where the brachial artery throbbed. "You must keep calm," she'd said to Bertha as she pulled her in so close their foreheads nearly touched. "You must. I'll take care of you. I'll fix it."

Dear Dr. Hammond,

I had thought to begin this letter with a plea to forgive my long silence—now I wonder that I thought it wise to write to you at all. You have betrayed my trust, and Miss Mellish's!

Though my situation remains precarious, I had made up my mind that I would tell you all I knew. I have labored to protect

Miss Mellish's reputation—to protect you from learning the worst tribulations she suffered. I have told you that she sought an escape and did not want to involve her friends in her troubles. But it was not only the College she intended to abandon.

She fled because of a man. The name she gave to me was Joseph. He is not from South Hadley, though he followed her to the College. Miss Mellish fell in love with him. She was blind to his origins and his crudeness for a time, but his treatment of her became intolerable. I am afraid to say that she needed to escape this Joseph for the reasons you may expect—for the worst and deadliest reasons. I have told you that she loved him. But there is more.

He had discovered a ramshackle cabin in the woods, near where they often walked together. He showed her to the little structure and said it would be their home; he would rebuild it and they would wed and live there, humble but happy. He knew enough of her to promise her plenty of time with her books in the evenings. He said he would wait for her to finish her studies. He told her—lie of lies!—that he admired her mind.

In that cabin Miss Mellish gave herself to that unworthy young man; I tell you this only because she told me so, for I would never otherwise have believed it. But she was deceived by him; she loved and trusted him, unworthy as he was! He first grew distant, then demanding and cruel, as men do when they have gotten what they want and have no real care for it after. He wanted her to leave the College at once and to lock herself away in that cottage as his mistress. The more he demanded, however, the more Miss Mellish began to draw back. Though she suffered greatly, though it distressed her mind, she resisted and conceived a plan to escape his power.

I am sure Miss Mellish must still be alive. This disappearance was a part of her plan, but it was never, I believe, meant to endure so long. She meant to make him think her dead and gone and then to return home to safety. Yet I have still heard nothing from her. I cannot understand it.

Surely you see now why I kept this secret, which she begged me to carry to my grave. Surely you know why I feared her father's response.

But it seems that all I fear will come to pass. I see that a story under Miss Mellish's name has been published in the newspapers. Now the name of Joseph will be on everyone's lips, tied to her eternally, sure as if they had been wed. I no longer know how to advise you. I had decided to break my silence in the hope that if you could find him, all might be remedied—but now I fear that to look for him too publicly will reveal Miss Mellish's weakness to the world. Since you have chosen to publish this story, I surmise that you must already know of Joseph. But you have done nothing with this knowledge.

I am no longer sure you are the one equipped to rescue her—I cannot imagine what possessed you to put that story in the papers! She will be judged, Dr. Hammond, she will be judged and abandoned, and the fault for that rests at your door. For who else could have saved her but you? And yet you have not.

I have told you all I can. I will wait in hope, praying that Miss Mellish will seek me out, driven by her heart's knowledge that I am her true friend and would give my life to secure her safety. Should she find me, I will urge her to reunite with her family—but I will not write again.

Some of it was even true.

Agnes put the letter in its envelope unsigned.

THE TELEGRAM ARRIVED AT six-thirty the morning after the story was printed. Higham was awake.

REV MELLISH NO LONGER ABLE TO RETAIN YOU STOP SUGGEST YOU RETURN TO BOSTON STOP SEND EXPENSE STATEMENT STOP PAYMENT WILL FOLLOW DIRECTLY STOP HAMMOND

Higham tipped the bellboy extravagantly. Hammond's fury was satisfying, though it was a pity to be sent away before he'd had the chance to determine if Bertha was really dead. But months more of tracking the mysterious Joseph might not have led to any revelations and, after all, Higham was fairly certain that she'd died within days of her disappearance, if not the same day. They usually did.

He had a theory of the case. The French-Canadian had clearly gotten up Bertha's skirts, but perhaps he'd found somebody else there first. Not Hammond, much though the fellow evidently wished it. Maybe Agnes Sullivan, though, for all her cold restraint. He knew a few Sapphic ladies in Boston—the town was proverbial for it—and Agnes could have fit right in with them. Do-gooders, public speakers, reform-minded women. In fact he knew a female doctor who reminded him of her: a medical lady monk of sorts with stern eyes and weathered cheeks, a campaigner for modern birth control. A worthy enough cause. Look at Florence Mellish and her troubles—there was a life that could have been made easier with Dr. Taylor's little sponges and creams.

He packed up his case and sent it ahead to the station. He could catch the earlier boat train, but if he took the three-twenty he could make one more visit to the mill workers he had cultivated, to ensure their continued service as informants, and still be back in Boston in time for a good supper near the Square.

Before he left the hotel he telegraphed a message back to Hammond.

DISMISSAL RECEIVED STOP GIVE MY REGARDS TO FLORENCE MELLISH STOP HIGHAM

29

Hammond had an appointment with Mrs. Mead at eight. He was the first to open the rooming house door that morning, and when he did a familiar cream-colored envelope toppled onto the stoop.

Elation, as he read, then fury. He composed and discarded replies in his head. *My dear lady: How could you possibly justify keeping this information from Miss Mellish's friends? We have discovered her connection with the real Joseph, as it happens, but your delay could have cost Miss Mellish her life. I pray that it has not—*

Yet he fell quickly from rage into a gray despondence. For all Higham's perfidy, Hammond wanted nothing more than to show the man this new letter. His own belief that the letter writer must be an intimate of Bertha's—must be Mabel Cunningham or Agnes Sullivan—had been proven correct. But now that he had fired Higham he could tell no one about it, seek no counsel. He didn't know what to do without the detective. He was ashamed to admit it, even to himself.

He went back into the rooming house, back to his dratted familiar room, and sat upon the bed with his head in his hands and his hat beside him on the bedspread. He met his own gaze in the small gilt-edged mirror propped upon the dresser. He looked old and gouty, and the brim of his hat had pressed a red mark into his forehead. He was late for

his appointment with the college president. He stood and slipped the letter back into the envelope, then tucked it into the same inner jacket pocket where he carried the other, over his heart.

MRS. MEAD WAS NOT inclined to share examples of her best students' handwriting, especially with no provable connection between the letter writer and Mabel Cunningham or Agnes Sullivan. "Your perseverance is commendable," she told Hammond, "and I fervently hope it will result in Miss Mellish's safe recovery. But I will not disturb my students in the last days of term with baseless requests." If Agnes or Mabel were willing to speak to him, she said, he could seek them out.

But in the midst of their exams, that was easier said than done. Mabel Cunningham had finished her essays and was spending the afternoon off campus with a cousin. Nobody seemed to know where Agnes Sullivan was, though the slim nervous sprite of a girl who answered the door at Porter promised to tell her she was sought after, if she turned up.

At one in the afternoon, Hammond retreated in frustration to the canteen across from the campus and chose a table by the back wall. The place was emptier than he'd seen it, and the cheerful serving woman stood chatting idly with one of the cooks as if that were her job. He had just tucked into his delayed meal when Agnes Sullivan appeared at his table like a terrible visitation. Hammond found himself staring up at her, undignified, with half a bite of sandwich still in his mouth.

"I'm told you want to see me." Her voice was flat. He swiped ineffectively at his mustache with the napkin and pointedly did not stand. Let her sit if she wanted to; she was interrupting his dinner. "But I'm told, too, that there's no news about Bertha. What is this about, please?"

"Miss Sullivan." He gave her a bare nod. "Yes. Have you been writing any letters lately?"

He found her impossible to read: Was it real surprise that

widened her eyes, or was she playacting confusion? "I've been writing exams. Unless you mean—I did write a note to Florence Mellish."

Florence hadn't said a word about it. This world of women—it was like standing in quicksand. "And why did you do that?"

"She wrote to tell me about seeing the body. I wrote back to thank her." She shifted her weight from one hip to the other. Unusually, she was not carrying books, and her long arms hung by her sides as if she didn't know where to put them. He noticed once again her worn wide leather belt and faded black jacquard skirt, the mismatched button on a sleeve too short to cover her bony wrist. He'd never considered the effort Florence must have expended to be sure Bertha didn't bear similar evidence of her family's humble status—the hems she must have let out, the alterations done at night after her teaching.

"I am not speaking of letters to the family," he said, dragging himself from those thoughts. "There have been others, delivered to me. Letters written by somebody who knew Miss Mellish, or so it seems, with information about her private life."

"I don't understand. If I knew anything private about Bertha, anything at all I thought could help find her, why would I write it in a letter to you instead of telling Mrs. Mead?"

"The letters are anonymous. Meant to be secret, judging by their delivery. If you knew a secret about Miss Mellish—"

"But I don't," she said. "Not that she has many secrets, once you published that story of hers."

He imagined tightening his hands around her throat, thumbs across the voice box. Strangle her, strangle the letter writer. Anything to be up and doing, rather than playing what felt like an endless game of verbal checkers. "I had nothing to do with that. That was—I did not want it published. But that's not at issue here, Miss Sullivan. I am asking what you know about these letters."

Agnes was silent for a moment. He thought he saw uncertainty flash in her eyes. "I know they mentioned a Frenchman," she said, more tentative than usual.

"How in God's name do you know that if you didn't write them?" he exploded.

"Florence Mellish told me. She asked me if I knew any secrets of Bertha's, too. I already told her I didn't."

"Why didn't you—No." Hammond let his hands fall heavily upon the table. The rattle of silverware made the other man in the canteen glance over. "Never mind. Listen to me, Miss Sullivan. I want you to stay away from the Mellish family, do you understand me? You're to have no contact with them. No more letters to Florence Mellish."

"Why?" Another girl would have crossed her arms defiantly or cocked her hands on her hips. Agnes Sullivan stared down at him until he began to regret not standing or asking her to sit.

He put his elbows on the table and leaned toward her. "Never mind why. You go home for the holiday and pray for Bertha as you have been and stay out of this unless you have something new to tell them. They deserve as much peace as they can find this Christmas. They have enough nonsensical letters arriving daily without having to sort through more."

"I am not returning home," said Agnes.

He watched as she stalked off. His soup had gone cold.

30

gnes crept past Mrs. Abbott's room and up the stairs with her boots in hand. Since the building was new, few of the boards creaked, but she knew the placement of each. She could hear girls snoring behind their closed doors—*the sleep of the righteous*, mocked Bertha in her mind. She had sat her last exam at two, after facing down Hammond at the café. A quarter of the girls had already left campus; the rest would go tomorrow and had spent the supper hour pinching mistletoe sprigs above each other's heads and landing enthusiastic kisses on each other's cheeks, or elsewhere. The laughter and hooting had driven Agnes to the library. She had no more work for the term, but the mistletoe had reminded her of a book on parasitical diseases she had meant to track down before the library closed. Once there she'd not been eager to suffer the revelry in Porter or to mute the girls with her presence. An *Engaged* sign was hardly the neutral signal it had once been on their third-floor hallway.

She eased open her door and slipped inside, letting the latch spring as quietly as she could. Her wet boots she put beside the closet, her books—

"Agnes," someone whispered, and her heart kicked in her chest. She stumbled toward the shadow on her bed with arms outstretched and then stopped short—the loose curls, the perfume. Not Bertha alive or dead. Mabel Cunningham, sitting in the dark, her face a gray blur. Mabel whispered her name again.

"What are you doing here?" Agnes whispered back.

"I have to talk to you."

"Why are you in my room?"

"I have to *talk* to you!" Mabel touched the blanket. "Come here, would you?"

Agnes went reluctantly to the bed and sat beside her. "Abbott's drunk again. She won't check rooms." She was still whispering, because Mabel was there. Why was Mabel there? It had to be something to do with Bertha. With Hammond? Her heart was skittering.

"Listen." Mabel sounded calmer. She was wearing a fancy nightgown with ribbons and lace around the collar, and she smoothed it over her knees now as if she were in a flounced skirt. "Dr. Hammond was here, earlier—"

"I know. I saw him."

Mabel exhaled. "Yes, well, he was asking about us both. I haven't the faintest idea why, but it's very bothersome. Did you— What did he want?"

Agnes could see well enough in the dark room to measure Mabel's expression. She looked—frightened. Which made no sense at all. Mabel had nothing to be frightened of. "Something about tip letters he's been getting. With the reward. They keep coming in."

"But he was asking for me, too."

Agnes shrugged. "I don't know. He didn't say anything about that."

Mabel sat in silence for a moment, clearly upset. Agnes watched the beautiful planes of her face shift. She didn't think Mabel was there for sympathy. Not only for sympathy, at least. Mabel had barely noticed Agnes's presence before Bertha disappeared. Then that strange conversation in the lab, and now this.

Mabel grabbed for Agnes's hand. Her fingers were sticky-hot against Agnes's chilled palm. "Can I trust you, Agnes?"

"I suppose so," Agnes said, not at all happily.

"I'm sick," Mabel whispered, and Agnes was struck by a terrible memory of sitting with Bertha in the night and crying, both of them crying.

"Don't tell me." It came out like a plea. "I can't—"

"I have a sickness, a mania. I steal things and I can't stop. I don't mean to. I saw a doctor once, when I was in high school, he said it was hysteria. That's just ridiculous, I know it is, but I really can't stop. And I can't tell anyone. I can't. You understand."

"You're the thief."

Mabel winced, truly winced, as if she'd been cut.

"I never mean to do it. It's an awful habit, like drinking or—or gambling—and I always tell myself I'll never do it again, but I just find myself in other girls' rooms, just to look, and then I have to take something. Just something small." Her voice dwindled to a yearning whisper.

Agnes sat in confusion. "I'm not a doctor," she said finally. They were both staring at their joined hands now, speaking to their laps. "I don't know. I don't know what you want me to do."

Mabel straightened up, as if her good bearing were its own moral proof. "You were there, when they found the money. In the laboratory."

Agnes nodded. "After."

"I left it there on purpose. I don't want it! When I see it I feel sick. But I couldn't just give it back. They'd know. I brought yours, though," Mabel whispered, "your money," and she fumbled for Agnes's hand again, her hot fingers thrusting a dollar coin into the webbing of Agnes's thumb as if giving it back would rid her of her shame.

Agnes's fingers closed around the coin. "Mabel. What do you want me to do?"

Mabel flinched. Then she said, "There's something I should

tell Dr. Hammond," tense snapped words, and Agnes jerked her head up and stared at the tight way Mabel's mouth was working. "Or Mrs. Mead. I saw Bertha out late one night. In September. She was coming back from the woods by the pond and she was all mussed. She didn't see me."

"I think you were mistaken." Her voice sounded hollow. She felt hollow.

"No, I wasn't," Mabel said stubbornly. "I may not know Bertha like you do, but I know what she looks like. It was her. And she was a dreadful mess, her clothes. I'm not a fool, Agnes. I know what she'd been doing. But I didn't tell anyone. Why would I? I know what it's like to be in love. I'm lucky nobody ever caught me and William. I was surprised, though. You know why. She's not the kind—Well, I never said a word."

"No," Agnes echoed.

"I saw something else, too. When I was in your room."

Agnes couldn't speak. She looked at Mabel and Mabel looked back. The room seemed to hum with their breath.

"In your trunk. When I took the money and the ribbon. There was a letter from Dr. Hammond to Bertha. You had it."

The letters of his she'd kept. Tucked so carefully away—

Mabel squeezed her hands tight. "I know you didn't hurt her. I know it."

"What do you want?" Agnes croaked.

"Agnes, I'm not—I don't want to know what—"

Agnes pulled her hands from Mabel's. "Don't lie."

"I'm not lying!" Mabel cried, and they both shrunk back as if they could hide from the volume of her voice. But no one came to the door; no one else in the house was awake. "I'm not a liar," she whispered. "Don't tell me where Bertha has gone. Don't tell me about the letter. You must be trying to help her. You see how I trust *you*."

"What do you want, Mabel?"

"Nothing dire," Mabel said, with a hasty, pathetic murmur of a laugh. "Just promise you won't tell them. Don't tell Mrs. Mead.

If she says anything, about the things that went missing, you have to tell her it wasn't me."

"What good would that do?"

Mabel pulled back a little, frowning. "I know you loved her."

Agnes wanted to bend her head, to hide her face in the darkness, but forced herself not to.

"You don't see." Mabel tilted her head to study Agnes the way Clapp did when she wanted to point out a particularly fine example of some biological feature. "Everyone believes you," the girl went on, almost wistfully. "They'll believe anything you say."

A creak on the stairs; they both caught their breath, but it was nothing.

"And if they don't," Mabel said, her voice lower, "I'll say you're the one stealing."

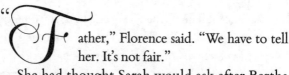

31

"Father," Florence said. "We have to tell her. It's not fair."

She had thought Sarah would ask after Bertha when carolers came timidly to the door and candles appeared in the windows of the houses opposite. Out of habit, if nothing else. Sarah usually seemed pleased enough to see Bertha on her Christmas holiday breaks, perhaps because of the celebratory trappings that accompanied Bertha's return.

Sarah did not ask. She probed around the edges of Bertha's absence; she asked Florence if they had a large enough turkey for their dinner and if there were to be any guests this season, as if, in their decades living in that house, they had ever willingly welcomed guests. But she did not seem to miss Bertha. She drank mulled cider with Maggie in the kitchen and hummed "Good King Wenceslas" after the carolers left. For her there was no howling lack, no ceaseless stomach-caving fear. She could watch the snow drift in the street without imagining it feathering over the frozen lines of Bertha's body.

Now Sarah was in the sitting room, helping Maggie decorate the tree delivered by one of John's most loyal former congregants. They were just completing the cranberry garlands, Maggie doing the needlework while the finished strands draped between Sarah's hands like strange organs. Under the evergreen scent, the house smelled of mulling spices and the sweet pyramid of oranges on the sideboard.

Florence turned back to her father. Against the tall back of his chair at the dining table he looked small as a boy on a throne. He had torn his sweet bun into pieces to make it look as though he'd eaten more of it—just like a boy, too.

"I cannot tell her," the Reverend said, staring down at the table.

Florence would have expected to relish the sight of her father bereft of the words that had always been his power. She had tried to usurp that territory when she was younger and discovering the bitter limits of her role as Bertha's spinster sister-mother. To be known as a poetess would have been a salve; to sell her poetry might have offered her freedom. Once when she'd sold two poems in as many weeks she'd dared to hope that she could support herself and Bertha by writing. But she had sold no more poems that year. She'd put the small amount of money she'd earned toward a deadbolt for her bedroom door and a second for Bertha's, and the sound of the bolt shooting home with Bertha safe behind it had been a poem in itself.

Though Florence had still listened, every night. To be sure Bertha was safe—to try to be sure.

Since Bertha disappeared Florence had written nothing but letters. So very many letters, in answer to kindly meant cards from neighbors and commiseration from distant families whose daughters had also been lost.

What could she say to Sarah, who didn't know of Bertha's loss at all? No words could disentangle the rotting vines of feeling that connected them all.

She said, "I will, then. After she has finished with the tree."

THE REVEREND DID NOT quite approve of exchanging gifts, though he had allowed that children should receive something on the holiday. Florence and Bertha had generally traded presents in one of their rooms, whispering and giggling. On Christmas Eve everyone got an orange, and on Christmas Day they had the traditional dinner, after services on both days. They would go to church this year, too, even Sarah. But Bertha would not fidget or page through the hymnal in casual boredom. Bertha would not be there to kick Florence's ankle if she fell asleep. Instead Florence would have to face the scrutiny of the congregation, knowing that the town's opinion on the likelihood of Bertha's survival had turned as the holidays approached. No one spoke to her these days—all unsure what to say—but she could guess their reasoning: a girl who doesn't come home for Christmas is either dead or in such serious trouble that she might as well be.

Sarah came toward her now, finished with her decorations, smiling. "Florence, look." She pointed at the tree.

Sarah's decorating had been energetic enough that fallen pine needles mazed the red flannel skirt around the tree's base. Her ornaments were haphazardly arranged and her strings of fruit draped at diagonals. Bertha's trees had been precise: even spaces between cranberry strings, popcorn baubles fixed at regular intervals, the yellow wax angel atop the tree upright as a soldier. When she was small Bertha had begged in vain for candles—the Reverend did not approve of excessive ornamentation and Florence hadn't wanted her mother near so many flames. But this year Sarah had found the golden cardboard stars from Germany, the ones Bertha called ugly, and hung them in odd clusters. It was surprisingly, stingingly beautiful.

"It's right pretty, ma'am," Maggie said with a sideways smile at Florence as she gathered up the half-empty sacks. "I'll just put these in the pantry."

Sarah nodded absently at her. "Do you like it?" she asked Florence, shy and prompting. She wore a dark green velvet skirt and jacket, as if she were ready for an outing. Maggie dressed her in whatever she liked, no matter how difficult it would be to clean.

Florence took Sarah's thin hand in hers and pulled her unresisting mother toward the sofa. "Let's sit a moment." Sarah folded down onto the cushion, eyes intent on Florence's face. She looked disconcertingly well. Maggie had labored over her braids, and her hair was smooth today, a translucent white-gold scrim over her pale scalp.

"What is it, dear?" She sounded so much like the mother Florence remembered from her earliest days that Florence felt tears start at the corners of her eyes.

"It's Bertha."

Sarah waited for her to continue. A little smile of anticipation started around her eyebrows.

"She's gone away," Florence began. "Some time ago, she left the College, and we don't know where she went. We're trying everything to find her, Mother. There was a detective, and—" She remembered in time not to mention Hammond. "The police are working hard, and the College, too. There's a reward. We'll bring her home. We just don't know how long it may take."

"Bertha went away," Sarah echoed, slowly. Then she said: "Why?" It wasn't her usual spiraling girlish question.

"What do you mean?"

"Why are you looking for her?" Sarah's eyes met Florence's. The dilute blue of watercolors, of pale cornflowers. The only blue eyes in the family.

"Because she's *missing*, Mama." She hadn't called Sarah "Mama" in years. "She could be hurt. We don't know—she could be—"

Sarah sat waiting for her to finish. It seemed clear that she didn't understand what Florence could not bring herself to say.

Florence sat beside her mother and breathed in the stillness of the house, Maggie's rustlings in the kitchen pantry, the Reverend's dazed silence, her mother's green guttering spark. Atop the tree the wax angel lay sideways, propped by two branches like cradling arms. *When the bough breaks, the cradle will fall.* So many times Florence had watched Sarah holding Bertha in public—Bertha squirming unhappily in Sarah's arms or, worse, sitting calm and unnervingly quiet—and tasted envy sour at the back of her throat. But Sarah's arms did not ache with emptiness now.

"Isn't the tree lovely?" asked Sarah.

And Florence, exhausted, agreed that it was.

OVER THE CHRISTMAS HOLIDAY they remained in Porter: Agnes and Hide Yegashira, the Japanese girl, and a French girl from Brigham Hall called Antoinette, both of whom had been received warmly at local family Thanksgivings but were not invited by the same families for the longer winter break. Some years more students stayed, but this year the three were alone with Mrs. Abbott, who took advantage of seasonal administrative laxity to indulge her habit. The housemistress stumbled red-eyed around Porter, smelling of juniper berries.

The two girls wintering over with her were of no concern. Quiet Hide stayed in her temporary room writing letters, perhaps relieved by the absence of the girls who treated her like a fascinating pet, and Antoinette slept, as far as Agnes could discern. The French girl sat drowsily through meals and then climbed the stairs to the second floor as slowly as if she'd been dosed with laudanum, one languid hand skimming the banister. Agnes walked behind her. Before, she would have been impatient. Now she made her own heavy way up to her room on the third floor and closed her door and pulled her chair away from her desk and stood looking at it in bewilderment.

She'd sat in that chair for thousands of hours in perfect concentration. She had ignored the complaints of her body, lived in her thoughts, suppressed any feeling that threatened her mind's supremacy. For twenty years she'd lived that way, and now that state, that safety, was as unreachable as the halls of Harvard.

Agnes's body jangled constantly with tension. The chair was newly uncomfortable. She could hardly sit still. A furnace of fear in her abdomen, alarm blazing along the branching conduits of her nerves. Mabel might tell—Hammond might find her out.

She had to go to the furnace again. But not yet. Tonight. After midnight. Four hours?

Unendurable. Intolerable.

Not to be borne.

"Not to be born," Agnes whispered to her quiet room. To the spot on the bed where Bertha always sat cross-legged, creasing her skirts.

She pushed the chair back under the desk and yanked open the bottom drawer of her dresser, shoved her hand between lace petticoat hems. There—the tubular black leather case. A tool she kept close, would always keep close, unlike the gun she'd taken from Bertha, still hidden in its knothole, or Mollie's knife.

Agnes opened the case and drew out her scalpel. She slipped off its paper sleeve, turned it in the candlelight. She couldn't seem to unclench her jaw.

Slowly Agnes pulled her skirt and petticoats above her sharp knees, her ribbed stockings and garters, and tugged back her loose cotton drawers to expose the tender skin of her thighs. Sparse downy hair. She pinched the meat of her left leg, then thrust her fingers under the rucked-up cotton to feel for the strong beat of her femoral pulse in the hollow between pubic bone and iliac crest.

Two shallow, dangerous slices, which she would bandage herself.

SHE WAITED UNTIL TWELVE-THIRTY, to be sure. The other girls were rooming on the second floor, and Abbott was drunkenly quiet in her room, not a streak of light under her door as Agnes slipped by on her way to the back stairs and the cellar.

The cellar held the laundry room as well as the furnace, and the machinery inside loomed against the weak light of Agnes's candle. Sinks, two large vats and a small stack of aluminum tubs for washing-water, wooden crates filled with cakes of rough soap, scrubbing boards piled like slates or tombstones, a silent mangle for pressing clothes, spindly racks built from dowels and cord. There was even a row of new electric Seeley irons that could be plugged in to heat up. Agnes had been on laundry circle as a freshman, before the main building burnt, and the scent of soap and bluing was the same.

Yet this place was entirely changed. Changed by what had happened here—and how Agnes had tried to sear the memories from her mind.

Three drains were set into the floor in a triangle. Agnes had washed Bertha's blood down those drains.

She put the packet she was carrying on a white-painted table along one wall, where the girls assigned to laundry circle folded sheets and undergarments. Inside were Hammond's letters to Bertha. She'd once thought the letters might be useful as leverage against him, but she couldn't keep them any longer, not after Mabel's threats. She was the only person the letters could damage now.

Agnes had thought she'd gotten used to the workings of the furnace, the heavy door and the insulated handle, the tremendous burst of heat. She could be efficient and quick about it; she could pretend not to remember. But this time tears swelled in her eyes and dripped down her cheeks.

She had carried Bertha's body to the basement. She'd stripped off her clothes and underthings, wiped her as clean as she could with a cloth and water, and dressed Bertha again in one of her own nightgowns. The cap sleeves had hung down over Bertha's shoulders and the hem had trailed over the white arches of her feet. Agnes had bent to touch those feet, and they had been cold. Bertha had always quoted a phrase from Shakespeare. *Cold as any stone.*

A fresh well of tears rose in her eyes, and the gnawing, hectic feeling grew in her chest. It was done! It could not be changed, it was the past.

So why cry now? she asked herself—not fiercely, as she would have bare months ago, but in unmoored fright. Compared to what she had already done for Bertha this was nothing. She hadn't cried for Bertha before, not once, not even when the pinkish water swirled around the drains beneath her feet, not even when she lifted Bertha's body in her arms one final time and felt how light she had become. How easily borne up and folded and how difficult to let go.

Back in her room, Hammond's letters burnt, her tears dried, Agnes began writing once more. But this letter she would never send.

32

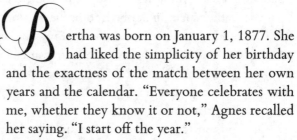ertha was born on January 1, 1877. She had liked the simplicity of her birthday and the exactness of the match between her own years and the calendar. "Everyone celebrates with me, whether they know it or not," Agnes recalled her saying. "I start off the year."

She would have been twenty-one. She had looked forward to being twenty-one.

TWENTY-ONE YEARS TO THE day since Florence had given birth. She sat in the bath and looked down at the white mass of her body through the water, at the mounds of her breasts, her thighs. She had never been a thin girl, but bearing a child had added weight to her sturdy bones and streaked her body with silvery lines. Those striations had long since faded, and she had been glad of it—she'd looked on them for so long as evidence of her degradation—but with Bertha gone the marks seemed the sole proof of her motherhood.

Later, she would hardly remember these months of her life, as she hardly remembered her pregnancy. Most of her own twentieth year came back to her as a long smudge of guilt and misery, then an iris of light opening in the months after: Bertha's dear infant face, round as the moon.

Twenty-one years ago she had been standing in this very tub, about to climb over its rim, when her waters broke. She had felt the hot rush course down her thighs and calves into the bathwater. She had thought for a moment that if she could just catch that spreading liquid in her hands and force it back inside of her everything would stop: the labor to come, the dark hours her father spent in her bedroom, the world's very motion. But she couldn't seem to move. She'd sat for long minutes in the cooling bath, and before she'd been able to rouse herself she'd felt the first clench deep in her back. Nothing had stopped. The world spun on and propelled her to this New Year's Day—propelled Bertha ever further away from her.

"Oh God, oh *God*," Florence said and clutched at her knees, which ached as they always did. It was not a prayer.

BY THE FIRST OF the year, grades were released at the College. Agnes, still on campus, had just received her record for the fall term. She had earned high marks in all her courses, even zoology—Dr. Clapp was notoriously stingy with As. Clapp wrote on the grading card in her angular script: *Miss Sullivan has the finest appreciation of anatomical science I have seen.* She remarked especially on the delicacy and precision of Agnes's reconstructed feline skeleton and of her careful, calm dispatching of the animal in question. *Miss Sullivan,* Clapp wrote, *understands the suffering of other creatures and always treats them with profound respect.*

Agnes's drawing portfolio earned praise for her fine shading. Her Livy translations were a tad workmanlike but precise, and she had progressed well in Latin. She had written the best biology exam paper. Her Elocution mark was her lowest, a B+, but Wilmot had written beside it: *Honestly earned. Miss Sullivan is not a performer, but I do not doubt her deep feeling.*

This was what Bertha had saved her for, was it not? To excel, and to escape.

She had received no letters back from Boston, but she never did. Bertha's mailbox, halfway across the room from hers, sat empty, too. Evidence of the small measure of equilibrium that Agnes had recovered: she could suppress the bizarre impulse to place the letter she had written to Florence Mellish in Bertha's empty mailbox, as if some metaphysical postal service might deliver it, and her.

She'd thought once, upon waking, of Bertha's birthday and had chased the thought away by washing her face briskly, angrily, with chill water from the pitcher she'd left on her windowsill, as if the chill might sink from skin to bones, from skin to heart.

33

*H*ammond had been told he'd find Mabel Cunningham on the basketball court in the gymnasium, practicing with the team she captained. She was on the sidelines, facing away from him, laughing with a group of younger girls who drew together when they saw him enter the gymnasium. They ought to be embarrassed, he thought. They were wearing the most ridiculous, immodest uniforms he had ever seen: light blue bloomers and loose white blouses and sweaters, their hair pinned under kerchiefs as if they were washerwomen.

His determination to track the letter writer had only grown. He had written again to Mrs. Mead, now that the girls were back on campus, and had received samples of the handwriting of Agnes Sullivan, Mabel Cunningham, and four other Porter girls he'd chosen at random. Mabel wrote in a looping script very like the anonymous woman's. Very like, indeed.

"Miss Cunningham?" She looked over in pretty surprise as he approached. "May I speak to you a moment?"

"We're just getting started with practice," she said with reluctance as the other girls hung back behind her. Brave Mabel, speaking to the intruding male. What would they do, he wondered, if he accused her here—denounced her and revealed her secret?

He advanced. "I really must speak with you. Concerning Miss Mellish, of course."

Her cheeks flushed. "Of course." She turned back to her group of shrinking violets and clapped her hands like a Sunday-school teacher. "Ladies, drills, please! Caroline, you run them. I'll just be a minute."

Her blithe confidence, her brazen cheer, grated. "Miss Cunningham, I must ask you about some letters."

She nodded encouragingly. Above the collar of her sweater her throat was creamy pink. He thought of the cameo fastened with black velvet that Bertha sometimes wore around her ivory neck and how much he'd wanted to trace it with his lips.

"First I must request that you keep this conversation between us." He waited for her nod. "Letters have been sent to me anonymously, purporting to explain Miss Mellish's disappearance. These letters suggest that the writer was close enough to Miss Mellish to have spoken with her about personal concerns. I am not here to discuss those reasons; they are private to the family. I want to ask about the letters themselves."

"What about them?" Mabel drew back and her luminous eyes swept over him. He felt suddenly aware of his wrinkled jacket and the stale tang in his mouth.

"In a moment. Your handwriting—" he began, but she cut him off in bewilderment, her voice edged with what sounded like relief.

"My handwriting? Oh dear, it's horrible. But what in the world could my penmanship have to do with anything?"

"Mrs. Mead was kind enough to turn over to me samples of writing from the students in your dormitory house. Yours, Miss Cunningham, was the closest in form to the handwriting of the anonymous author of these letters."

"How very strange!" the girl breathed. "But what does that mean? I'm afraid I don't understand."

Hammond crossed his arms. She was nearly as tall as he was;

unsettling, to look directly into a woman's eyes. "You have no knowledge of the letters sent to me, then?"

Mabel shook her head and frowned. "No, of course not. What an odd question, Dr. Hammond. Why would I be sending secret letters? I would go right to Mrs. Mead."

Agnes Sullivan had said almost precisely the same thing. Hammond blinked and withdrew a little. Was it really possible that neither girl had anything to do with the letters?

But Mabel Cunningham also did theatricals, he remembered. She was the campus star. He steeled himself to go on, to share the information he had meant to hold back as long as possible. "Those are not the only letters in the case, Miss Cunningham."

Again that encouraging nod, as if he needed her encouragement. A vein began to pulse in his left temple.

"I had written to Miss Mellish, and I believe the letter writer to be aware of that correspondence. This is another reason to think that the letter writer knows her well and may likely be a student here or live nearby."

"Oh, I see," said Mabel, her words encompassing a world of discreet feeling. "I'm sorry, I'm afraid I can't tell you a thing about that."

Nothing for it but to bluster ahead. "But you knew Bertha well enough, you said. You were her senior—is that not the right term?" He watched her as he spoke, but she betrayed no discomfort.

"Well, that's simply not the sort of thing girls tell their seniors," she said, earnest, her large eyes limpid. "It's like I said. We talked about school and William and sometimes basketball—or class events; I do so many. Bertha would only have come to me with a matter of the heart if it were crucially important. Girls just don't bother their seniors with every little detail of their lives. It isn't done."

"What do you mean, isn't done?" The disapproval in her tone struck him.

"There's hardly any sense in having a crush if all you do with your senior is rattle on about yourself, is there? I mean to say— Bertha was always a bit half-hearted, you know. I never got the sense that she cared a great deal about crushes or dances or any of the other things we do. But she was still very proper and sweet about it. Just never terribly intimate with me, not that she had to be for a senior crush, you know. Agnes Sullivan is the only girl I ever saw her in intimate conversation with, and that was no crush, to my eyes, even if it was a rather queer pairing. They were more like a couple of old birds, not even a bit romantic. But I've told you this already."

Hammond stared at the beautiful girl before him, who stood comfortably in her awkward garb, the basketball still balanced between her hip and forearm.

The matter-of-fact way she spoke—what on earth was she describing? She said the word "crush" as he might say "wife," as if it were a recognized social role that required no further explanation.

He had known that the junior girls were each responsible for a senior every year, but he'd assumed that responsibility to be similar to his own fresher-year memories of playing man-servant, cleaning boots, fetching breakfast and beer. Of course, there were boys whose friendships seemed particularly deep, but he'd known nothing like this foreign world into which Mabel's words had cast him, where college girls spoke casually of their intimacy with other women, where they participated eagerly in some system of codified loves. He thought dizzily of that book of Krafft-Ebing's—he'd struggled through the German, thinking it worthwhile to keep up with the frontier of medicine. All the while the frontier had been here, hidden in this institution meant to produce educated wives and mothers.

"Do I understand that there is a rulebook of sorts governing this behavior?"

"Oh, you make it sound so dull and formal!" Mabel laughed and let the basketball roll down her forearm into her joined hands. "Hardly a rulebook. It's a school tradition—like Founder's Day.

The juniors never feel left out, the old girls get a bit of attention in their dying days. It keeps us going, you see. First you have someone to look up to and then you are looked up to. There's so much a girl can learn from her senior."

Hammond stared again. He knew he must look ridiculous, goggling at her. Probably the other girls in their bloomers would laugh. Probably they were already laughing behind their hands, bumping one another in the ribs with their pretty round elbows. "Is that so," he said finally.

"Why, yes," Mabel said, her eyes serious again. "How to be a good woman. That's what we're here to learn."

HAMMOND STRODE TO PORTER Hall.

He went right for the stairs and marched up them, right-left right-left, as if he were back in uniform. He breached the third-floor hallway and walked to Agnes Sullivan's room. The *Engaged* sign hanging on her door swung a little from the force of his palm against the wood.

Footsteps within, slow and shuffling. After a moment the girl opened the door. She looked pale as a wraith, and she held a pencil in one hand, her fingers grubby with lead, a dark smudge above one eyebrow.

"What is it, Doctor?"

He stepped closer, but she didn't move and he found himself inches away from her. She smelled faintly of something sharp and chemical. "You wrote those letters," he said. "I know it."

She simply stared at him, unblinking. She said not a word: no denial, no protestation of confusion, no plea for mercy.

Agnes was a different sort of alien creature, not like Mabel and the other jolly college girls with their bizarre intimate society, not like anything he had seen before. In that moment Hammond felt absolutely certain that she knew where Bertha was—and that she would never tell him.

His hands were around her throat, and they stumbled back into her room as a linked unit.

He had never choked anyone. Always before he had palpated and pressed. His thumbs crossed over her larynx, and he felt the jump and struggle of cartilage beneath his fingers and the surprising dense muscle along each side of her neck. The act was like nothing else. He had pushed together torn flesh, but he had never compressed life in the circle of his fingers. Her eyes were hot golden green, reddening, rounding. Defiant. "Damn you," he said hoarsely, "damn you!" Her body made wet sounds, but he could see in her eyes that the noises were involuntary, that she would not speak even if she could. That she would not give in to him.

He let her go, and Agnes reeled away, her own hand to her throat, that ungovernable impulse to reach for damage—how many times had he seen it, how many limbs lost or holes in the body found? The marks of his fingers clotted her white neck. They were both panting, but her breath came in a horrid rasp. The hall seemed utterly quiet outside her room; no one had heard what he had done. No one had come to see.

There was nothing to see, he told himself fiercely. She still breathed. They stood now about three feet apart in the small room, but the air between them carried a charge and her eyes were still hard and angry on his face. She had put her hands down by her sides now, and he watched them tremble. His own hands felt hot and used.

He had no proof. Agnes's handwriting looked nothing like that of the letters. They had not found a shred of Bertha's clothing or even the imprint of her lovely small body: only that damned manuscript and those footprints on the road by the river, long ago.

"You go to Hell," Hammond said bitterly and turned away.

When Agnes vomited into her wash basin, he was too far down the stairs to hear it. Nor did he hear her laugh.

34

The frothy vomit gave off a hot tangy smell. Agnes wiped her mouth with the back of one shaking hand and put the basin on the floor, startled by the painful burst of laughter that had overtaken her. It seemed born from a bubble below her diaphragm—not a bubble, no; a spiked expansion like the tropical fish she'd seen in a museum in Boston that could blow up to thrice its size. A kind of dreadful—joy.

It had felt as though he would pop her head right off. Not the most scientific of descriptions. But she was glad to know how it felt! She was glad for her rocky throat and the bruises rising there that told her he was as dangerous as she had always believed.

On top of her dresser sat a note from Dr. Clapp instructing her to visit Mrs. Mead to take her pick of some donated anatomy textbooks, news that would once have thrilled her. She'd received the note a week before and still she had not gone to see Mead. She had not sent the letter she had written to Florence Mellish, nor had she been able to make herself destroy it; if anyone searched her room again, all would be known, and yet she could not do the simplest thing to prevent discovery. She'd barely been able to rouse herself to attend classes and complete her work.

Agnes hauled herself up and leaned on the dresser, breath sharp in her burning throat. *Was* it joy? Or the sick relief of seeing the shape blurred behind the trees resolve itself into a single predator and knowing exactly what is hunting you?

He had stopped short of killing her, this time. He would have been a fool to do it on campus where he had surely been seen. Yet his fury had been too powerful to resist—because he could not prove she had written the letters. For now, he could not prove it.

Considering events rationally, she was more endangered than ever before. But she was smiling. She could not help it. She was alive.

AGNES SPENT THE NEXT week in a vibratory state— concealing the bruises with her highest-necked blouse and dodging her fellow students, in case anyone had seen Hammond approach her door. She had not managed to avoid a strange run-in with a sweaty, white-faced Eva Bissell, who blurted out on the stairs that she'd overheard outside the president's office that Mollie Marks was failing her classes and had been credibly accused of stealing and would be leaving the College at once. Mollie Marks—a likely candidate for valedictorian, the worst instigator of the thievery rumors, an interfering prig, and, Agnes knew, not the Porter thief.

She did not know what to do about Mabel.

Mabel could change her mind at any time; she could go to Mrs. Mead or to Hammond. The Christmas break had worn on her, too. Already she was doing stupid, dangerous things; two days before, she'd dropped a note in Agnes's lap at supper, where anyone could have seen, telling her to meet at the gazebo. There, in the snowy dark, they'd gone over the same ground: *I could tell, you mustn't tell, swear neither of us will tell a thing*. They had parted silently as spies, Mabel back to Porter and Agnes to huddle in Clapp's lab and pretend to concentrate on her Latin.

She couldn't let Mollie Marks take the blame for Mabel's thefts—could she?

IT WAS GOOD LUCK that Mabel had the privilege of a single room, as Agnes did. It was better luck that Agnes had, as a child, lived next to a girl named Sally who'd taught her how to pick a simple lock with a hairpin and a knife. Sally was a dark-haired, narrow-faced single young woman with frequent male visitors; even Agnes's generous mother had looked askance at her on the stairs. Sally had liked Agnes because Agnes would listen to her talk while she picked at her fingernails or darned her stockings or worried at a wrinkle forming by her eye. Sally's tiny apartment had been safer for Agnes than the street outside, though Sally liked to tease her for what she called Agnes's "ny-efty." The room had smelled of cigarettes and a yeastiness that owed something, but not everything, to the beer she drank. It had always been dimly lit, with filthy purple curtains hanging stiffly over the two windows. So Agnes had learned not only how to pick a lock but how to pick one in the dark.

At dinner Mabel told her table of friends with forced giddiness about her plans to stay with her cousin overnight in Springfield so she could meet her William for an anniversary dinner. Agnes took a second helping of grainy corn pudding so that she could listen to Mabel spin out the evening in advance—how she and her chaperone would take a private carriage to the train, how grandly she expected William to squire her about. Agnes wondered how Mabel's friends could miss the strain in her voice. More evidence that Agnes had to act.

Abbott made a real effort that night, knocking on doors at ten, even ordering Nan Miller out of Daisy and Eva's room and back to her own. Agnes put out her little lamp and lay awake in the gloom. The thump of her pulse echoed between ear and pillow. When she was sure Abbott had retreated, she lit the lamp again to try to soothe herself with studying. She had not needed to resort to the scalpel since that bad night at Christmas. It was time for a different blade.

At two she put away her books and got out Mollie Marks's pearl-handled knife, the one Bertha had stolen months before.

Mabel lived at the opposite end of the third floor. In the hallway Agnes crouched to slide the knife into the keyhole and tried to breathe quietly, regularly, to steady her hands as Sally had shown her. She felt the plate lift—pressed in the bent hairpin, each twist and scrape unbearably loud—heard the lever swing aside to pull back the bolt. She eased the door open.

Moonlight on framed photographs, on the gilt-backed uncracked spines of a full set of Dickens's novels. Moonlight on clothing strewn on the bed earlier that day when Mabel dressed for her man. Moonlight blurred by smudges of powder on the mirror, shining from a silver-plated hairbrush. Two perfume bottles and a bushy black wig from Mabel's winning stroll at the cakewalk party the Rockefeller Hall girls had hosted in September. Girls' faces on the posters; in the photographs, Mabel swarmed by girls, laughing, or the soft faces of female relatives. Girls kicking up their heels to show their ankles. A basketball, a kitten-ball mitt, a fencing foil—Mabel's very own fencing foil.

Agnes stood at the center of the room, clutching the knife. At first she'd thought it wouldn't matter where she hid it; she'd write another letter to Mrs. Mead, and Mabel's room would be searched and Mollie's knife found, proof positive. But Mabel would know she had done it. Mabel would tell. Agnes could drop it in a jacket pocket in hopes that it would tumble out during some scramble. Yet if Mabel felt the weight of it when she dressed, or if it fell unnoticed—Agnes surveyed the room again. She had to leave the knife here; she couldn't keep it.

Then she saw the wicker picnic basket behind the armchair. It was large and sturdy enough to carry the kind of spreads a girl like Mabel Cunningham would pack; each side of the basket closed securely with a wooden flap and toggle. She worked one side open, and within the basket she found tin plates and cups and napkins rolled around a sheaf of silverware, tied with a dark ribbon.

Her fingers trembled as she loosened the knot, trembled more as the silverware clanked when she unbound it. She snapped Mollie's knife closed and laid it at the center of the pile, then rolled the napkins tight again and tied the ribbon badly—tied it again—then it was done. Agnes ran her tongue over the dent her teeth had left in her lower lip. She replaced the bundle of silverware in the basket and stood looking over the room, the moonlight, the turquoise faces in the snapshots tacked to the fishnet grayed by the night.

Forgive me, she thought and didn't know if she meant to address Mabel, who would soon be blamed for taking the knife, or Bertha, who had stolen it from Mollie with the intention of cutting her own wrists.

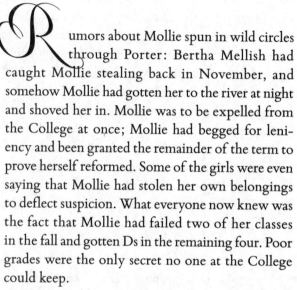

3 5

Rumors about Mollie spun in wild circles through Porter: Bertha Mellish had caught Mollie stealing back in November, and somehow Mollie had gotten her to the river at night and shoved her in. Mollie was to be expelled from the College at once; Mollie had begged for leniency and been granted the remainder of the term to prove herself reformed. Some of the girls were even saying that Mollie had stolen her own belongings to deflect suspicion. What everyone now knew was the fact that Mollie had failed two of her classes in the fall and gotten Ds in the remaining four. Poor grades were the only secret no one at the College could keep.

Agnes could not avoid overhearing this storm of gossip, especially in the dining room.

She was on supper dish-washing circle this term.

Ida Burney was, too, but she was a terrible worker, always dashing off for a break with Nan or one of the others. This evening was no different. Agnes had gotten three-quarters of the way through a towering stack of plates by the time Ida came back from her "little sneak-away" and she returned trailing Nan and Daisy, all of them still chatting excitedly about something.

"—Mead even apologized!"

Agnes lifted her head from the dishes, but they were too caught up in their talk to notice her. It seemed that the case of the Porter thefts had been up-ended that afternoon. Mollie had been cleared and sent home. Her elder brother, the one who had given her that pearl-handled knife she'd made such a fuss about, was quite sick—that was why she'd failed her classes, nothing to do with thievery. Mollie had kept mum about the whole business until summoned home to say her farewells, and learning of her unaccustomed reserve left the other Porter girls disposed to excuse her obnoxious campaign to catch the larcenist. Daisy said that it was a dreadful pity, losing a brother like that—it might sour any girl's spirits—and Nan and Ida agreed solemnly enough.

Not my fault, Agnes thought on a rush of relief. *Not Bertha's fault*.

But then the girls were newly astir: now that this mysterious revelation had absolved Mollie, the thief was presumably still on the loose in Porter. Ida, who had yet to pick up a rag or brush and was still leaning against the half window through which the girls passed their dirty dishes, said, "Maybe we ought to toss everything we own in our trunks and keep them locked. It would be tedious in the mornings, though. Need a hairbrush, unlock your trunk—"

"Oh, Ida, how preposterous," Nan said in a teasing way. "Nobody wants your nasty hairbrush. I doubt anyone would dare touch the thing."

"I'll have you know—"

"Are you sure?" Agnes said. The girls turned to her, and Ida, suddenly remembering her work, hastened into the kitchen to stand beside Agnes at the sinks.

"About Ida's hairbrush?" Nan asked. "Oh, certainly."

Agnes stared at her. "About Mollie's brother. That she left because he's ill."

Ida's hands stilled in the soapy water. Everyone looked to Daisy, for some reason, who nodded. "Quite sure," she said. "A wasting disease of some sort, I heard."

A fraction of Agnes's mind began at once to catalog possible diagnoses. "Thank you," she told Daisy, but she must have said it too seriously—the girl's smile faltered.

Nan shot Agnes a look she could not read before lifting her chin in mock challenge at Ida. "So, Miss Burney," she said. "When you're done pickling your fingers in dishwater we will await your presence."

"My room?" Ida asked, and Nan agreed and slung her arm around Daisy's waist.

"Ow," said Daisy. She kept complaining as the two girls wandered through the dining room toward the rest of the house. "Lord, I am sore. Kitten ball will be the death of me. Put it right on my tombstone: here lies Daisy McFarlane, done in by pitching practice, requiescat—"

Beside Agnes Ida was silent as her fingertips played against the surface of the scummy water. Then she cleared her throat. "Agnes, why don't you—you should go." She looked down at the dishes. "I can finish up. I know I'm an awful shirker sometimes."

Agnes felt an unwelcome clench in the muscles of her throat. "All right," she said hoarsely. "Thank you." She dried her hands and untied her damp apron. But as she hung it on its peg for the next day's work, she caught the edge of Ida's glance as the girl bent to the dishes in front of her and had a strong and sudden sense, undercutting that bolus of sentiment, that Ida did not want to be alone with her in the kitchen.

THE SAME DAY AGNES learned of Mollie Marks's exoneration, Henry Hammond found himself dissatisfied with a local cat show in Newburgh, NY.

The show itself was pleasant enough. It was the rare event not overrun with Maine Coons and a writer for *Fur & Feather* stopped to interview him briefly about his Australians. He always found it satisfying to be recognized among the crowd of women in their ivory cat-silhouette brooches and gaudy shawls. Knowing that Newburgh's guesthouses would be full of such fanciers, he'd chosen instead to stay in the Palatine Hotel. It was new and grand and tortuously expensive. He meant to ensconce himself in his splendid room with its electric lights, have tea and soup to stave off the streets' slushy chill, read his medical journals. He would not think about Bertha or about how close he had come to murder.

It had been more than a week since the terrible day when he'd nearly throttled Agnes Sullivan. The feeling of her hot throat under his fingers returned when he did not expect it. When dressing that morning he'd hovered motionless in the memory of it, sweat rising under his mustache. This trip, the distraction of the cat show, had seemed like an opportunity to put on his old self again: trustworthy medical man, veteran, expert breeder. But all he could think about was Agnes Sullivan.

He would have to outwit her. Come at her indirectly. He sensed, though he did not think it consciously, that the world would always take his side against Agnes—if only he could restrain himself from killing her.

He could not relax alone in the rich quiet room. By eight o'clock he was sitting in the hotel's dining room, three whiskeys drained. The steak with béarnaise had been unexciting, the Black Forest cake a regrettable indulgence. The finely appointed room had filled slowly with couples and a few families—he'd forgotten it was Friday night—and he had amused himself for a while by distinguishing the New York City visitors from the upstaters. That game exhausted, he felt melancholy rise again.

A blond woman, perhaps the age his Emma would have been, smiled at him from a table near one of the broad windows. He hadn't noticed her arrival and wasn't sure how to categorize her. The style of her navy-blue dress suggested the city, but she was alone, at a table that could seat four but was set only for one. Against the dark wet glass, under the shimmering light cast by the rows of chandeliers, she looked quite beautiful.

Her hair was the color women called ash blond, he thought. Perhaps she was younger than he'd assumed.

She was drinking white wine. He sent her a glass. Within

fifteen minutes he'd taken the seat across from her at her table. Conversationally they had established that he was a doctor, not traveling for business, exactly; that he bred cats, had once done so with his wife, before she died; that they both took the New York City papers largely to read the *Yellow Kid* comics; that the Palatine was of course the best hotel Newburgh had to offer, better than many in Manhattan, but the town's theatres were even more appealing, in her opinion. Her name was Hope Delano and she was a musician, she said—a pianist and occasional harpist. The backs of the dining room chairs, he noticed, were carved to look like lyres. He found himself watching her long neat fingers as she toyed with the stem of her wineglass. No ring upon her hand.

"Have you met the hotel's mascot?" she asked him, laughter in her voice. She had blue eyes, as his Emma had. Prettier and larger than Emma's, if he was honest. "Or are you so partial to cats that you ignore the canine race entirely?"

He assured her that he found dogs perfectly amiable creatures. "Though that pit bull terrier they call a mascot looks as though it's fed by every member of the staff, and most guests as well."

"Not a bad life." Miss Delano had a fetching dimple in her chin and a way of leaning forward so that he could see how well the beaded collar of her bodice lay upon her breast. "And he seems a dear animal. Still, it's a man's beast, a dog like that. That massive chest. Cats are more feminine creatures, don't you agree?"

Hammond agreed wholeheartedly. He had not been in such a good mood for ages. He'd told Miss Delano nothing about Bertha; in conversation with her, he was not the man whose hands had closed around Agnes Sullivan's throat. He found the momentary freedom from that reality so intoxicating that he began to consider how soon he might return to Newburgh.

Her gloved fingers brushed his knuckles. "You must have a great deal on your mind, Doctor."

He tried to laugh, embarrassed by his wandering attention, but her gentle smile transmitted a sort of miraculous calm interest. *You fascinate me*, said the crinkling of her eyes, the apple of her cheek. "I suppose I do," he admitted. "Nothing that makes for pleasant dinner conversation, though. Tell me, how did you first learn to play the harp?"

Rather improbably, the story involved a childhood trip to Paris, a bohemian uncle, and her observation of a fight between two organ-grinders in a public park. She told it in a practiced manner—she seemed, he thought, a bit more like an actress than a musician. But her voice was pleasing and well-trained, a soft contralto, and when she stopped to laugh at the memory of the two monkeys clinging to the shoulders of the organ-grinders the patter of her mirth played happily upon his insides.

She bore little resemblance to Bertha and only reminded him of Emma in the way that a particular wisp of hair seemed determined to curl forward and touch her eyebrow.

Someone new, he thought. That was what he needed.

They each ordered another drink from the elegant colored waiter and sipped them. Finally the clock caught his eye—it was nearly eleven. He turned in his chair and saw only a few couples lingering. He hadn't noticed the hush of the place.

He turned back with a smile, considering how he might ask her for the honor of another evening like this one. Thinking again of how pleasant it would be to have something, anything, to anticipate with happiness rather than with dread.

Miss Delano leaned forward again, and Hammond found himself listing toward her.

"Would you like to conduct a bit more business on this trip of yours, Doctor?" she asked in an undertone, looking at him from beneath lowered lids.

Hammond's stomach tightened. He drew back, thinking he must have misheard. "Pardon me?"

A precise pause. "Oh, dear," she said with a wry smile. Her eyes still crinkled at him, her lips still looked inviting. She had even managed a blush. "Are we not in agreement, then, as I thought?"

"In agreement?"

"I thought we might make an arrangement for the evening," she murmured, and her gray-gloved hand curved around his: firm and warm, surprising in its strength.

He pulled his hands from the table to his lap, where he felt the evidence of her success. "I'm not seeking any such arrangement." He sounded like a prig, but by God, he felt like one. A prig and a fool, an old fool. The constant dupe of women.

Miss Delano tilted her head to regard him. "Are you quite sure? I suspect, dear Doctor, that it would do you a world of good." Those eyes, warm and fond, as if she knew him. "I'm very rarely mistaken."

Hammond huffed a laugh. "I imagine it might, for a short while. But I'm afraid you can't provide what I'm seeking, Miss Delano." He dropped his napkin on the table and stood, adjusting his jacket.

She canted her chin up at him, bold as brass. "And what's that?" she asked lightly.

"I'd tell you if I knew," he said.

36

It was February and the world had not ended. Mabel had not buckled under the strain of her secrets, Mollie Marks had not returned to school. Hammond had not swept down upon Agnes with policemen at his back.

Agnes should have felt safer at the College, but she did not. Nothing in the world felt safe. It was February and Bertha had been dead for nearly three months.

Agnes still had two full months to endure before the spring term's end and another year to follow.

The weather was unseasonably warm, near fifty-five degrees. The girls spread themselves over the green-brown lawn south of Mary Lyon Hall on blankets that looked like rafts on a sea. They would be washing mud from those blankets and complaining for the next week, but it was a Saturday and for now they seemed content to eat apples and cheese and drink tea in the sunshine. Agnes envied their comfort more than she ever had before.

Agnes sat on her folded jacket a few feet away from the other girls, close to the gravel lane that separated the lawn from Mary Lyon Hall. She told herself she was keeping an eye on her classmates, but loneliness drove her, too; she could admit that. Today she didn't mind their occasional bursts of laughter or endless ribbing of a sophomore who'd just gotten engaged, though her Logic text was dense—Lindsay's translation of Ueberweg—and deserved her full attention.

She squinted against the glare of the page until her eyes almost closed in the sun. She had never slept outside; it wasn't safe in her neighborhood in Boston. But on campus, where all appeared safe, it was a common practice once the weather warmed. Girls napped in the Pepper Box gazebo or by the ponds. A freshman had broken her arm last year by falling from a tree branch in her sleep. "Down will come baby, cradle and all," Bertha had laughed, and for once a joke they'd shared had been general among the students, who still called the girl Baby.

A cry among the sprawled girls jerked Agnes from her reverie. She peered into the sun for its origin. Faces turned, bright faces, many eyes narrowed against the sun or shaded by the brims of wide hats.

"That's—that's Mollie's!"

Someone bolted up on a blanket perhaps fifteen feet away: Eugenie, that sophomore devotee of Mabel's. She was pointing at Mabel with one hand to her mouth like a theatrical heroine.

Pointing at something Mabel was holding.

Mabel went brick red. "It's not—" she said, and then: "It's mine. It came with the basket!"

In her hand was Mollie's knife, and as the sun lanced off its blade Agnes felt a rush of relief that seemed to loosen the cartilage between her ribs. It was happening, the discovery she'd invented. Whatever must come would come. She put down her textbook. No one was looking at her. They were all staring at Mabel.

"Mabel, how could you?" cried Eugenie, her shoulders rising in pure revulsion. "It *is* Mollie's, I know it is. She made such a fuss. And you took it."

"But I didn't," Mabel insisted. "I told you, it isn't hers."

Eugenie was still pointing at Mabel's hands. She looked as stunned as if she'd been hit. Most of these girls never had been. "She went home because of *you*, Mabel."

Mabel tried for scorn. "Don't be daft. Her brother's ill, that's why she went home."

"Why would you keep that even if you found it?" Tears dripped onto Eugenie's cheeks. "Mabel. Why?"

Mabel scrambled to her feet, boots marking her pink blanket. "I wouldn't, you know I wouldn't."

"You wouldn't what, Mabel?"

Nan Miller stood behind Eugenie. Her belligerence, the bullish thrust of her head shifted the air around them. She crossed her arms over her wide chest. "Were you going to let poor Mollie take the fall, then?"

Mabel's laugh edged into harshness. "'Poor Mollie,' Nan, really? That's a bit rich coming from you, isn't it?"

Agnes heard gasps from the girls around them. More of them rose to their feet.

Nan gave Mabel a grim smile. "I'll poor-Mollie her all I like, old girl. I'm a junior, I can make up my own mind. But it's these girls you ought to be apologizing to. They looked up to you. You know how much they did."

"That's absurd," Mabel cried, her beautiful face knotted up in confusion. "I told you, this knife is part of my picnicking kit. If Mollie had one like it, that's news to me. I won't stand for these accusations."

Agnes watched in disbelief. Mabel honestly seemed to believe the knife was her own. Could she really have forgotten what she'd taken and what she hadn't? Had she stolen—did she possess—so many things?

A rough half circle of girls began to array themselves around Mabel, herding her north toward Agnes. Agnes remembered that loose cohesion from the gangs of children she'd evaded on the streets around her school, the sense that any member of the group might separate and dive at you. She half expected to see broken bottles or lengths of chain appear in their hands. Agnes pressed her book against her chest and rose to a crouch.

Mabel held the knife tremblingly before her. "I'm going inside," she said, her voice rising. She nearly tripped on the blanket as she backed away. "I'm going to see Mrs. Mead right now."

Nan was glaring at Mabel, focusing the wrath of that phalanx of girls behind her. "It's Saturday." Nan lifted her chin. "You think Mrs. Mead's there?"

"If she's not I'll find someone else."

Nan stepped forward. Mabel faltered back, and Agnes retreated farther. She ought to go now, she knew, but she was too absorbed.

"You don't scare me, Nan," Mabel said, trying for her easy, lofty old ways. But her voice shook and even in profile her face was distorted.

"I don't mean to scare you," said Nan, raising her dark eyebrows. "I mean to tell you what a horror you are, Mabel Cunningham, if you did this. I know you deserve forgiveness same as anyone else, but after what we've already suffered this fall, I say you won't get it from me, not yet. So you go tell your sad story to Mrs. Mead and then you go right to that chapel and ask God to forgive you, you stuck-up, selfish *bitch*."

Mabel gasped and wheeled and dropped the knife. It flashed in the sun—and Agnes choked as Mabel crashed into her and gripped her arms. Their heels crunched on the gravel lane and between their bodies Agnes's book jammed into her ribs.

"Agnes—" Mabel said, half breath, "Agnes, please come with me, please—"

Mabel pulled her across the lane to Mary Lyon Hall and up its stone steps toward the arched door. Agnes's shoulder slammed against the doorframe. She dropped her book and heard it slap on the stone. She felt herself swallowed up by Mabel's fear, and she tried to struggle free but the girl's fingers clamped hard above her elbows. They stumbled through the door into the vestibule of Mary Lyon Hall—Agnes caught a glimpse of the girls on the lawn standing motionless and captivated—and then Mabel yanked the door shut as if she expected the girls of Porter to surge forward at any moment and tear her to pieces. Agnes could have told her how unlikely that was. They would want a slow, polite disarticulation.

Mabel's panting breath echoed in the vestibule. They fell apart from one another now as Mabel sagged back, drained of defiance. The hectic flush had faded from her cheeks and left her white as bone.

"They can't be serious," Mabel whispered. "They can't really believe that I'd steal from Mollie, could they? I mean—how ridiculous—how idiotic—even if I had taken Mollie's stupid knife, why would I ever put it to use in front of half of Porter? I'm not a fool. I'm not—"

Her bright blue eyes snapped up to Agnes's face. Mabel was not crying. She looked desperate and canny. She looked like Bertha had as she'd explained to Agnes what they would need to do, and Agnes wanted, for just a moment, to slap her lovely face.

"You have to help me. Tell them I didn't take anything. Tell them it must have been someone else."

Agnes shook her head fiercely. "It won't do any good."

"Yes, it will!" Mabel cried. "You promised! You said you would!" Now tears were forming, color seeping back into her cheeks. She crowded Agnes out of the vestibule and over to the stairs, so close that Agnes smelled her frightened sweat.

"I can't." Agnes inched back against the banister. "I'm sorry, Mabel."

"I'll tell them what I saw." The toes of their boots bumped, and Mabel's arms trapped her against the rail. Agnes tried to battle the instinctive rise of fear, the memory of brick scraping against her skull, but her breath sped between her open lips.

"Mabel, it won't matter what—"

"I'll tell them about Bertha. I'll say you're the one stealing."

Agnes felt a drop of Mabel's saliva land at the corner of her mouth. She pulled her arm up tight against her body to swipe it away with her thumb.

"I know you will," she said, low.

The other girl sank back. "But they'll hate you, then, and everybody will know, about her and that man. You can't want— you helped her—" She was shaking her head while she spoke, unaware of it. Then she cut herself off. She was staring at Agnes, through Agnes: staring at a new future. "William," she said and paled again.

Agnes watched her warily.

"You have to help me. You helped her run away. You have to help me, too."

Agnes closed her eyes for a moment. She heard Mabel breathing and a strange lack of other sounds. The stairway was walled in stone and the doors were heavy. Nobody was coming to interrupt them—not one of the girls outside, not any of Mrs. Mead's staff.

She opened her eyes.

"You don't want my help."

"But you said—"

"Mabel," Agnes said. "You can tell them what you want to. Nobody is going to believe you."

The truth of it struck the girl. Mabel's mouth fell open as if she might scream, and her shaking hands came up from the railing. Agnes raised her hands, too, thinking to defend her face. Mabel had lost the knife, but she could scratch or bite—the girls Agnes had grown up with would have. But not this girl. She collapsed and pressed her hot face against Agnes's ear. "Why?" Mabel groaned, clinging to Agnes's back. "Why didn't anybody stop me?"

Agnes knew that lament.

There were no answers for Mabel, as there had been none for Agnes.

Mabel's breath steamed into the tunnel of her ear, her lips brushed the shell of cartilage around it. Agnes raised her arms and enfolded Mabel awkwardly within them. The line of her corset pressed into the inside of Agnes's elbows. She radiated heat.

Agnes wished, not for the first time, that she were still a believing Catholic—that she could pray without feeling fraudulent. She had said Hail Marys over Bertha's body anyway. As Mabel sobbed into her shoulder, she said another. The girl would need all the female intercession she could stand.

Mabel finally drew back and scrubbed at her eyes with the heels of her hands. "I have to go upstairs." She laughed, brokenly. "Oh, I must look a fright."

Agnes watched her wipe mucus from her nose and lips, tuck strands of hair back into her bun, and straighten her collar as if she could revert to the Mabel of that morning, the one who had not yet been found out.

"They're going to hate me," she said, matter-of-fact. She met Agnes's eyes.

"They might."

"I suppose they should." Mabel floated her hands once more over her hair and her cheeks, dabbed at the bruised flesh beneath her eyes. She tried a smile, and she was beautiful again, though red-eyed and miserable. "Farewell, Agnes."

"I'm sorry," Agnes found herself saying, but Mabel just shrugged and shook her head.

"*C'est de ma faute,*" she said with mock cheer and gathered herself with visible effort to walk up the stairs. Her steps were slow and her boots left mud on the treads. After a few moments she disappeared onto the floor above and then Agnes heard the door to the second floor hallway open and thunk closed.

Agnes stood in the stairwell for a few minutes, braced against the banister. Then she went to face the Porter girls. By the door she kicked something—her fallen Ueberweg, which she'd forgotten entirely. Agnes smoothed the book's bent pages.

She pushed open the door and blinked at the sunshine. It felt as though the world should have darkened, as if she'd spent hours in Mary Lyon, but of course everything looked the same. The girls had not gathered up their blankets. They sat upon them still, some with arms around each other's shoulders, some slumped alone. When she emerged they looked up at her in mute expectation. Agnes stared back. Anger surged in her throat. All this over Mabel, who had accepted their adoration and then taken their money, too.

"Go home," she said to the waiting girls. "It's over."

They didn't move.

Her hands were clenching by her sides. "Go *home*. Mrs. Mead will sort it out."

Nan Miller lumbered to her feet then, eyeing Agnes with a kind of distant respect. "Come on, all of you," she said roughly. "We don't need old Mabel anyway, do we?" She picked up an edge of the blanket she'd been sitting on and flapped it. "Back to Porter with us all."

A few girls—Ida, Ruthie, some of the other faces Agnes associated with Eva—scrambled to their feet. All at once there was a mess of activity, blankets being folded, books piled together in waiting arms. Some of the girls cried as they cleaned up. Nan relinquished the edge of the blanket she'd been holding and thrust her hands into her pockets.

"You coming?" she asked Agnes.

Agnes shook her head, and Nan nodded. She took her hands out of her pockets. In her right hand was the folded pearl-handled knife. Nan tossed it once, twice as she watched the rest of the girls begin to walk toward Porter, then shot Agnes another half-friendly look and turned to follow.

MABEL LEFT THE COLLEGE on Monday morning. She would receive no degree, though she could reapply for admission in three years if Mrs. Mead felt confident that she had addressed the personal defect that had required her removal from the school.

Just as she'd threatened, Mabel had spilled her secrets to the president when she was caught. Agnes had given her the knife and must be the thief herself, she'd insisted; Agnes was hiding letters from Dr. Hammond; worst of all, she'd seen Bertha out late at night, meeting a man in the woods. Agnes must have helped Bertha run away with him.

But Mrs. Mead had believed none of it. "You must accept blame, Miss Cunningham, if you truly intend to return," she'd told the crying girl. "It's cruel to target Miss Sullivan and beyond propriety to slander Miss Mellish in order to deflect attention from yourself. I expected better of you."

Mrs. Mead wrote to the Mellishes and to Hammond with the news of Mabel's crimes, leaving out the accusations levied against Bertha and Agnes. Instead, she included a brief note she thought might reassure Florence Mellish, as it spoke well to the character of Bertha's only friend: *Miss Sullivan showed kindness to Miss Cunningham and calmed her Porter classmates when Miss Cunningham's thefts were discovered.*

A hired carriage arrived to collect Mabel before the breakfast bell—not quite under the cover of darkness but in the pale dawn light, which fell strikingly on her drawn cheeks. A few students came out with her, the stubbornest and most loyal, who were already beginning to insist at meals that "it surely wasn't her fault, it wasn't as if she'd *wanted* to steal those things." But the crowd was smaller than the group that had seen off Florence and Reverend Mellish in November. February was a hard time for sympathy, especially before breakfast.

Florence read about Mabel's expulsion at her desk at home. She had Maggie deliver the mail directly to her bedroom now and keep her door locked; the week before, the Reverend had found one of many foul and poorly spelled letters she'd received from the public and raged about the house threatening to kill the pseudonymous ingrate who dared call his daughter a "low deseeving girl."

She had come to her desk thinking she might try to write a poem. But the letter from Mrs. Mead scoured that self-indulgent impulse from her mind.

Miss Cunningham has confessed to a most unfortunate habit of stealing,

Mrs. Mead had written. Such gentility. Florence remembered sitting in Mabel's room and watching the girl wring at the ruffle on that pillow as if she could squeeze the truth from the satiny fabric.

Bertha gone, the all-around girl fallen. What had happened to the College?

There was a single leavening fact in the letter—the bit about Agnes having been kind to Mabel. Florence tried to imagine what that meant. She could not picture reserved Agnes Sullivan offering a handkerchief or a supporting arm. But she could imagine Agnes serving as a stalwart, quiet wall between Mabel and the sharp tongues of former admirers. She was quite sure Agnes's stolidity had stifled the spread of rumors about Bertha. And in recompense, the girl had been subjected to Hammond's suspicions, Higham's questioning, and Florence's neglect.

She would have to try to thank Agnes adequately. Florence turned it over in her mind, what that might mean—over and over like a wheel spinning helplessly in a deepening rut.

37

The queen had been dead for less than a day, Dr. Clapp's note said, and remained a perfectly good specimen. Agnes was cordially invited to participate in the dissection if she was free at four o'clock, which, of course, she was.

Agnes had thought to get through the month of March with head-down determination. She read for so many hours that a ghost of the small type in her Latin book hovered stereoscopically above its original on the page. She'd fetched those anatomy books from Mrs. Mead's office—an awkward errand, now that Mrs. Mead seemed to see her through a sentimental wash: brave Agnes, kind despite her loss. The girls of Porter smiled at her.

It left Agnes unsettled, waiting. She did not trust this quiet. But all she could do was continue to work. She'd sent her mother a few dollars earned by drawing careful figures for other girls' lab reports and received back a terse dictated note assuring her that *All is well here my girl and I hope the Lord keeps you well. We will see you in the summer I suppose as usual? Thank you for the money it is most welcome. Your loving mother Nora*—and Nora's mark, a spiraling scribble, by her name. Agnes had to read it twice to believe it. *All is well?*

She opened the laboratory door that afternoon to find only Clapp, smiling at her over the dissection table, garbed for surgery in her stiff canvas apron and half sleeves. Her stomach unknotted. She never knew

whom Clapp might favor in a given week; she might have suffered the presence of some freshman newly deemed promising. Instead they were alone.

"Dropped off this morning by one of my usual farmers," Clapp said in greeting and continued setting out her instruments. The bright laboratory light shone off her black hair, raked back into its usual tight knot. "Dogs got her kittens, more's the pity. There were two born before this one that's stuck. Get your apron on and assist."

Agnes fumbled with the apron ties. The cat on the dissection table might have been a sibling of the female Clapp had chloroformed days after Bertha died. Black with white markings, underfed despite its swollen belly, the sternum like a wish-bone beneath the fur of its chest. Rigor had stiffened its body, yet its tail hung soft and flexible over the side of the table, and beneath the tail a lump of flesh covered in wrinkled amniotic sac protruded like a damp knuckle. The cat's tongue lolled dry between its pale gums. The tiny barbs along the tongue's center looked like white mold.

Clapp leaned over to thumb open one of the cat's cloudy, bloodshot eyes. "What happened here, Miss Sullivan?"

"Dystocia," said Agnes at once.

"Yes, indeed. How would you discern if the incomplete kittening is a symptom or a cause?" The professor rolled the cat onto its back and propped the limp body in place with wooden blocks. There was a strange feminine smell in the air, beneath the urine-and-hay-barn must the cat's fur exuded. Blood and wetness. Clapp lifted one of the cat's forepaws and looped a length of cord around it, then bound the cord to a hook at the edge of the operating table. When she was done, the cat's limbs bent awkwardly back so that its paws tucked down on either side of its upturned chin, as if it were peering over an invisible barrier. Clapp looked up at Agnes in expectation.

She tried to gather herself. She had not experienced a bit

of distress when she had chloroformed her own cat in the fall. "Examine the uterus for signs of infection—for rupture or—"

"Or?"

"Cancer. Torsion." Agnes was sweating, though the sun was low through the basement laboratory windows. "Look for other pelvic malformations or scarring."

"The Caesarean section. Tell me what you know of its current practice."

"In cats?"

Clapp gave her a droll look. "In women." She left the table for a moment. Agnes stood by the cat, feeling most unlike herself. The animal's paw pads looked as though they had a leathery texture; or perhaps they were hard, like small dried beans. Clapp returned with a bowl of water, a bar of soap, and a folding razor. She wetted the cat's distended belly and set about working the soap to a lather.

"High mortality," Agnes began, "but improved in the last decade by the new style of incision."

"Which is?" Clapp scraped black fur from the cat's stomach in short strokes.

"Transverse rather than midline."

"Performed with what cause?"

"To—prevent bleeding?" Her own uncertainty startled her. She had read journal articles about the surgery's success, translated from the German.

"To reduce bleeding," Clapp corrected her. "In addition to suturing the uterine incision after delivery. It's too late for this old girl, I'm afraid. And the anatomy is, of course, quite different in a litter-bearing quadruped. But let's see what we can see, shall we?"

The cat's belly was bare and white now, the teats milk-swollen around each dot of a nipple. Clapp cut a horizontal line across it, and the laboratory swam around Agnes in an unfamiliar way. The abdominal cavity's stink was not so bad yet—it wasn't that. It was the motion of the scalpel in Clapp's hand and the lips of flesh that opened under the knife. The shapes, other kittens, beneath the queen's skin, the yawning of her abdomen, the trickle of blackening blood that Clapp wiped away—

"Will you widen the incision?"

There was a strange silence as Agnes stared at the windows set high in the wall behind Clapp's head. She had not thought before about why the lab had been situated in a basement, with its strip of windows at ground level—to insulate the room, perhaps, against South Hadley's extremes of weather. To keep the instruments inside, the specimens, from degrading. But the placement meant that greening grass and dirt hunched just below the window frame, as if she and Clapp were operating in a massive grave. Her heart thundered in her ears.

"Miss Sullivan," Clapp said, precisely.

"Yes," Agnes said after a moment. "I'm sorry. I feel—unwell."

The scalpel clinked against the table. Clapp regarded her, head tilted. Bertha had always said that Clapp reminded her of a stork. A falcon, Agnes thought.

"There's a Boston woman who's been bothering Mead for a summer companion, you know. I've thought of recommending you."

The implication was clear: she must perform as expected.

The professor held out the scalpel to Agnes, handle first, and Agnes took it and spread the skin of the cat's stomach with her left hand and cut from the center of the wound down toward the cat's tail, toward the sac-enveloped kitten, where she did not want to look.

"Observe the uterus." Clapp put her hand over Agnes's fingers, pushing down before Agnes could pull away—as she had, without knowing it, begun to do.

38

Clapp called Agnes in again on a Wednesday afternoon in early April.

On her way to the lab, she saw three men in dark coats too thick for the weather entering Mary Lyon Hall. Their faces weren't familiar, but she knew their look; impossible to grow up impoverished in South Boston and not recognize policemen. She forced herself not to stare after them. If there was news, if the local police had developed suspicions, Mrs. Mead would have summoned her, not Dr. Clapp.

Clapp kept her waiting for some interminable minutes. Agnes leaned against the wall beside the laboratory door and drummed her fingertips silently against the painted plaster. Perhaps Hammond had taken the letters to the police. Perhaps the three men were, at that precise moment, asking Mrs. Mead for her whereabouts and would descend upon her in the lab hallway to drag her bodily away under Clapp's severe and disappointed gaze.

Agnes was almost certain that Mabel had said nothing to Mrs. Mead. They would not have waited so long to come for her.

She could not anticipate what Hammond might do.

Her stomach quivered when Clapp opened the door and said her name. No apron over her brown gabardine today, so no surprise surgery, at least.

"Excuse me, Professor," Agnes said. "There were men—"

"Men?"

"Going to Mrs. Mead's office. Police."

Clapp brushed a dark strand of hair impatiently away from her eyes. "Yes?"

"Were they—is there—"

"Sullivan, I assure you, if there were news of Miss Mellish, you would know at once. The sheriff visits on occasion. Largely a formality, I'm afraid. You will forgive my speaking plainly. I wish it were otherwise."

Agnes inclined her head, trying to quiet her thundering heart.

"In other words, why don't you come in and forget about those men." Clapp stepped back from the door. Agnes went past her into the room, looking at the empty lab tables, uncertain why she had been summoned. Clapp rummaged in her desk drawer and came up with an envelope that bore Agnes's name in bold print.

She smiled and handed Agnes the envelope. "Your ticket, Miss Sullivan."

The envelope was not sealed, just tucked shut. Agnes pulled up the flap and touched a red paper ticket. She looked up at Clapp in confusion.

"Amherst will be hosting a special dissection demonstration next Saturday. I have secured ten seats for my most promising students with an interest in the medical profession. I assume you would like to come."

"Yes, Professor." The words came out rough with pleasure and relief. "I would. Thank you." A thought struck her: "But the cost—"

"The cost will be covered by the College." Clapp lifted her pointed chin and smiled. "Being the chief show pony for wealthy donors does have some benefits. Tell no one I said that."

"Yes, Professor," Agnes repeated, clutching the envelope between sweaty fingers.

Clapp laughed, the sound sharp but not unsympathetic. "Yes,

go on, no need to strain yourself, Sullivan. I expect you in front of the chapel at eight A.M. The demonstration begins at eleven."

"Yes—" Agnes closed her mouth on the rest. She nodded and backed out of the room and not until she was safely in the hallway did she allow herself to slip the ticket out of the envelope and examine it in such minute detail that anyone passing would have assumed her to be studying a living creature.

On the morning of the demonstration Clapp was dressed in a great swooping purple shawl, presumably to frighten the Amherst men into submission. She stood outside the chapel like a bright tall bird and checked off the girls' names on a list as they arrived. Agnes was first. "Good morning, Sullivan," Clapp said. She even had a bit of carmine paint dabbed on her thin lips. "You look alert and ready."

Agnes nodded. No one had come to arrest her. She was beginning to think that she might last out the remainder of the semester after all.

"I expected no less." Clapp turned away from her then to mark down Amy Roberts, one of the girls who'd sent her parents breathless updates about Bertha's disappearance, who was yawning and breathing a perfume of coffee into the air around them.

Clapp had hired a large open wagon to bear them to Amherst rather than carriages, despite the strong breeze. "If you get cold, sit closer together," she said as they climbed on.

Agnes sat facing west, toward the river and Batchelder Brook, with the mountain at her back and the sun on her shoulders. Since Clapp had given her the ticket, since she'd understood herself to be among the chosen students who might progress to medical school, the world possessed a new depth and shine. Clapp's acknowledgment draped over her warm as the sun on her jacket. But as they traveled parallel to the brook that had been dragged for Bertha's body and passed the mountain where Bertha had chosen to set her mill-girl's final leap, even this small joy crumbled to gilded ashes.

I do not have to be happy, Agnes thought. *I only have to prove my worth.*

Agnes had never been to Amherst College before. Its campus was flatter than Mount Holyoke's, buildings of lighter-colored brick, spaces more open and spare and Augustan: land thoroughly tamed. Agnes liked it very much, though she had grown used to tangled ponds and Gothic arches. The broad quiet lawns pleased her. She was glad to be walking in this male preserve.

The dissection demonstration was to be held in a theatre in the science building. Clapp knew precisely where she was going. The girls followed her through double doors and down a tiled hallway, stepping lightly to quiet the strikes of their boot heels. Midway down the hall a door sat propped open. A boy ripped Agnes's ticket in half and handed her one ragged end. She dropped it into a jacket pocket and pressed it against her side. Agnes did not make scrapbooks, but she would keep that ticket for years.

She followed Clapp into the demonstration theatre and slowed to look up in wonder at the room's rising ceiling. Amy Roberts trod on her heel by accident but Agnes hardly noticed it. The theatre felt like a church, and at its head lay a dead man, not spread upon a cross but lying on a steel table equipped with funnels and drains.

Clapp took the aisle seat in the row cordoned off for female observers—four rows back, apparently a decorous distance from the corpse—and Agnes claimed the seat beside her, which required her to stand and glare at two of Clapp's other favorites who expected her to move aside. Amy Roberts had passed by Agnes without a word and was now flicking smiles at the nearby Amherst men as she fussed with her gloves and hat. Even the more studious girls ducked their chins and blushed under masculine scrutiny. Agnes removed her hat and held her head straight. She waited until the other girls had settled before she folded down her own seat. She wanted the best possible view of the operating table.

She cared not at all about the boys and men in the viewing seats, only about the man on the table. He had been portly in life, and now his white-purple flesh looked solid as marble. She wanted to prod that flesh and test its density. She wanted to know its every quality. If she could not do it herself, not yet, at least she was here to watch it done.

Beside the body, a shining constellation of tools sat arrayed upon black velvet: bone saws with their triangle teeth; drills, tweezers, tongs, clamps, and pins; long-handled hawk-beaked shears. The demonstrating physician adjusted the placement of each object. He bent over the table with a hand to the front of his coat to prevent it from brushing the clean tools.

Someone was speaking as Agnes watched the physician arrange the instruments, informing the audience of the doctor's name and the sponsors of that day's demonstration. The court and the coroner had organized the event, apparently, to show the Amherst students how a medical inquest functioned. There were names, titles. Agnes knew she ought to commit those details to memory, but the metal and the body drew all her attention.

Finally the speaker was gone and the physician was ready. He held up one hand, a scalpel glinting like an extension of his finger, and the audience hushed. The power of the knife, Agnes thought. Even when it wasn't aimed at your viscera, it commanded silence.

"We will begin with the cranium." The physician dipped the scalpel to the man's hairline. As he cut evenly across the forehead, he went on: "This man was a laborer. He worked in a furniture factory, where he operated machinery and carried heavy items." He sliced arcing lines along each side of the man's head. "He died on the job, suddenly. Cause of death has been tentatively established by the testimony of witnesses, and this likely verdict supports the factory's claim that the man's death was not brought on by any hazard of his working conditions. However, the court wishes to confirm this suspected cause of death through physical examination. This demonstration serves, therefore"—he paused to peel back the scalp like a cap—"to display the best practices of examination and to assist the court."

Agnes could hear the whistling breath of the boy sitting behind her. She shifted forward on the wooden chair and hoped he would not vomit.

"Though we do not necessarily suspect that the man suffered illness of the brain, in all cases of sudden death one must rule out bleeding there." The physician put down his scalpel and lifted the smaller bone saw. The sound of it rasped in Agnes's throat. Finally the doctor lifted away the cup of the skull to expose the pale gray runneled slope of the brain. He curved his hands around it and it slipped free of the body with a faint sucking pop. The boy behind Agnes gasped. The physician set the brain in a steel dish beside the dead man's head. He wiped his hands on a pristine white cloth, smudging it brown with old blood. "There are no obvious marks of bleeding on the external surfaces of the brain," he said before separating the halves of the brain. "None between the hemispheres. In some cases, more thorough dissection would be required. In the interest of time, we will proceed to the remainder of the body."

Quiet inhabited the theatre.

"Next, the thorax," said the physician, and a few moments later the scalpel scored a rough Y over the man's chest and mound of belly.

Agnes remembered sliding her fingers into Bertha's still belly, pressing into her flesh, lukewarm blood slicking up to her wrists. In the interstices between organs Agnes had touched black blood, some of it jellied, some hardened. She had probed the tight swells and felt the perforation that had killed Bertha, and though she had been crying before she cut into the body her tears had ceased when she forced her fingers into Bertha's fading warmth. In wonder, in marveling, at what Bertha had given her even in the misery of her death.

Bertha had given her this, too. Her presence in this room,

among the dissection's observers, honored Bertha. The yellow, blood-streaked fat of the man's abdomen honored Bertha. The crunch as shears crushed rib, the creaking jaws of the spreader used to pry the man apart so he lay split upon the table. A butterfly; an insect; a specimen. The man's face, still intact below his truncated cranium, looked calm. He bore a slight resemblance to Agnes's father, despite his darker coloring. She had not noticed until now.

"May I have a volunteer to hold the heart?" the doctor asked. "And to recite the known diseases of the heart and their symptoms. If you can observe evidence of disease in this man's heart, we will inform the court of our opinion accordingly."

Agnes raised her hand. In the corner of her vision she could see Clapp smiling.

"A question, young lady?" The physician's eyes darted to Clapp, then back to Agnes.

"A volunteer," said Agnes.

The room rumbled, but the doctor cut his eyes at the Amherst men and they subsided. "Very well, miss. You may come forward."

Agnes stepped over Clapp's booted feet. Clapp reached up as if to steady her and gripped her hip through her skirt. "Bravo, Sullivan," Clapp whispered. "Be careful and true." Then she let go and Agnes descended the stairs to meet the physician beside the operating table. She stripped off her gloves as she walked and tucked them into her waistband.

He shook her bare hand gravely. "Your name, please, miss?"

"Agnes Sullivan."

"Thank you, Miss Sullivan. Now, if you will be so good as to stand beside me." He drew her around behind the table, behind the dead laborer, and lifted her hands into the air between them. "Like this." Then he returned to the body and made several quick incisions; his moving arm blocked her view. In a moment he lifted the heart, studded with stumps of vessels like sliced roots, and turned to place it in her hands.

Agnes felt the heft of the heart, its sticky solidity, its chill. She lifted it a little, just to feel the effort needed. Anatomy texts often spoke of the ancient Egyptian myth of weighing the deceased's heart against a feather in a scale of moral judgment. Now she was this man's arbiter, she supposed. She would judge the story of his heart.

"Diseases of the heart, young miss?"

She began to speak.

39

Where was Bertha then—in those last months when only Agnes knew that she was a mound of ash at the bottom of the Porter Hall furnace?

She was everywhere and nowhere. A web of girls spread out across the towns near South Hadley, spread out through time. Each girl moved through her individual scene like a figure in a miniature; each possessed a slightly different profile, a different cadence to her steps, a different world of worries enveloping her. One wore a black jacket and one a tam-o'-shanter. One had Bertha's dark eyes and another her small bowed mouth.

These supposed sightings of Bertha continued to torment Florence and Hammond, but neither acted, nor did they communicate often. They passed these reports to the police. They wished, with longing darkened by different resentments, for Higham's expertise.

Then, in early summer, rumor found Bertha elsewhere.

Florence came home on a Saturday afternoon from doing the week's dry-goods shopping with Maggie to find her father on the front steps in his dressing gown and a weedy black-haired boy standing in front of him, scribbling something down in pencil on a stack of note cards.

"Where was this?" the Reverend was saying. "Where, again?"

"In New York, sir. A hospital. I don't know for certain which one." The boy had a smirking mouth and a shocking voice, deep and blatty as a tuba. "We were hoping you might know that, you see—"

"George—" her father began to say just as Florence burst up onto the step beside him. Maggie trailed behind her with her arms full of grocery sacks.

"What exactly do you think you're doing?" Florence said to the boy.

"Who's George, ma'am?" the boy countered, tapping the pad with his pencil. She had taught his type—the miasma of cologne, the obvious and inflated sense of his own cleverness. "Tell me that."

"Who are you?"

"Samuel Stroslev, Associated Press. And you are?"

"That's none of your concern." Florence put her arm around her father, intending to guide him inside, but he shrugged her off in anger.

"Florence, this young man says Bertha is in a hospital in New York," John Mellish said. "Why have I not heard of this?"

Florence had grown so accustomed to the flare that lit her nerves at any suggestion of Bertha that she needed merely to breathe for a moment, to shake her head, in order to tamp down hope. *A hospital in New York*, she scoffed to herself and turned that hope to scorn for the wretched boy who'd stirred it. "Because it's not true. It's been most of a year. If she'd been found now, I think we would have learned of it before the papers did."

"Well, I said the same. I said it couldn't be. But he says he doesn't even know which one. Which hospital." John turned pleading eyes on Stroslev.

"This story just came to me, sir. I'm only starting to look into it. That's why I thought I would see you first—go right to the source, find out the real story. You don't want unverified rumors in the papers, do you?"

Florence pushed John behind her and beckoned Maggie forward.

Stroslev gave no ground, forcing Maggie to inch past him with her burden, and Florence lifted one of the sacks from her arms. "Maggie, will you take the Reverend inside, please." She kept her eyes on Stroslev's narrow face. His cheeks were speckled with black stubble and his bare upper lip sparkled with perspiration. It was a warm day in early June, and Florence became suddenly conscious of the sweat dampening the band of her hat and slicking her armpits and the insides of her thighs. She drew herself up and glared at the reporter. "There's nothing for you here. Bertha is not in any hospital. Coming here, stirring my father up, is unconscionable. Take your rumor-mongering somewhere else."

"So you're, what, the sister?" Stroslev flexed the hand holding the pencil until his knuckles cracked. "I'll take a quote from you, too."

"No, you certainly will not. You will turn yourself around and march down that walk, or I'll send Maggie for the constable."

Stroslev lifted both hands as if to ward her off. That was another gesture her least favorite students abused: the look of mock-dismayed innocence, *what did I do, not a thing, not me!* "All right, all right. I see you don't want to give me a story. I understand."

"You don't understand a thing, you parasite." Florence turned and shouldered the front door open—Maggie, bless her, had left it just ajar. She slammed the door shut and dropped her head back against it until her hat pressed against the nape of her neck. She let her arms go lax, forgetting the paper sack. It tumbled to the floor and split, and the bag of flour within it split, too. Flour puffed into the air, across the carpet, onto the hem of Florence's dress.

A sudden series of knocks vibrated the door against her shoulders. Flour settled in the sunlight. Florence heard herself make an odd sound, a laugh and a sigh together.

She yanked the door open. "What in Hell do you want now?"

It was Stroslev, smirking. "Pardon me, Miss Mellish, but can you least tell me who George is. Your father—"

"My father's brother," Florence said. "He lives in New York. If we want to look into this nonsense, rest assured we shall speak to him, not to you or any other member of the Associated Press."

"You got his address?" His pencil hovered, waiting. He shot her a look, self-absorbed, self-confident. The swelling vetiver cloud of his cologne reached her, and she stepped back from the door. Stroslev looked down at her dress. "What's that on your skirt, ma'am?"

Florence sprang forward and slapped him over his left ear. It was extremely satisfying.

"Ow, Christ!" He dropped his pencil and grabbed at the glowing rim of his ear. "What the fuck—"

"Say one more word and I'll do the other one."

"What—I just asked—"

"You asked for a hiding. Now leave us alone."

"You can't—"

"I told you I would call the constables," Florence repeated over his attempt to interrupt her. "Tell them I hit you. Go ahead. This is a small town, Mr. Stroslev. Do you think they'll care if I did? A woman being persecuted by a journalist with some false report of her missing sister?"

He still had a hand cupped over the afflicted ear, as if she might hit him again, and Lord, did she want to. But she'd been foolish to do it once. He could publish whatever he wanted, and she saw the knowledge of that in his muddy brown eyes as he glared at her. She thought of trying to apologize, but she saw, too, that it would be useless. So she shut her mouth and crossed her arms and held tight to her dignity, instead.

"Look for your name in the papers," Stroslev said and turned on his heel.

He was, unfortunately, true to his word. The next day, the following headline appeared in the papers.

IS MISS MELLISH ALIVE?

Her Father Does Not Credit Story That She Has Been Found

KILLINGLY, June 6—Rev. John Mellish, father of Miss Bertha Mellish, the young student at Mount Holyoke Seminary who disappeared during Thanksgiving week, 1897, was seen to-day by a representative of the Associated Press at his residence in Dayville and asked as to the truth of the report that his daughter has been located in a New York hospital. Mr. Mellish stated that he knew nothing of it, and believed it hardly possible. He has written, however, to a brother in New York, who will investigate.

The story that Miss Mellish is in New York comes from South Hadley, Mass. It is said that Miss Mellish could not explain her disappearance satisfactorily, but is in a dazed and half-demented condition. Her friends are now keeping the young woman out of the way of publicity.

Some color is given the story because while everything indicated that Miss Mellish had drowned herself her friends have been persistent in searching for her, traveling to distant parts of the country in their quest. Moreover, although the river was watched very closely for months, the body was not recovered. The only trace of the missing girl was footsteps in the snow, thought to be hers, that led to Titan's Pier, a rocky promontory from which she is thought to have drowned herself.

Miss Mellish was a pale, silent girl, and seemed to be devoted to her studies.

"Damn the boy to Hell," said Florence as she read it. Hammond had sent her the newspaper, no note enclosed. She could imagine the conversational pleasures she might anticipate upon his next visit to the house.

Florence had written to her uncle George at once after Stroslev left. They had not corresponded much since the visit to Auburn. She didn't believe Stroslev, of course, but Hammond had received those absurd letters claiming that Bertha had run off on her own. Several days later, she received the apologetic response she'd expected. George had brought a photograph of

Bertha to Bellevue, Wards Island, and a few other small private New York hospitals, and not a single patient resembled her closely enough to explain the rumor. *I wish I had better news*, he wrote, *but I am afraid, dear niece, that this report is entirely false. It is dastardly of the press to spread such chatter with no verification. If this harassment continues, you must allow me to obtain legal advice. I will soon be in Boston for work, and I hope you will come to visit me there for a brief respite from this awful business.*

That snide boy and his insinuations! The sneer that Bertha "seemed to be devoted to her studies." Seemed, *seemed*—Florence had come to hate that word for its poisonous mildness, its slippery invocation of hidden truth. Sometimes, she knew now, there was no secret to discover, nothing held back from the hungry public but a wretched trembling uncertainty that never ceased.

Those who read this report would think their family had hidden Bertha away in a madhouse, would wonder—was Florence the sort of sister who could consent to see Bertha confined? Bertha "dazed and half-demented" in a bare and dirty room.

Florence folded the newspaper in two and replaced it in the envelope from Hammond. He could not think her capable of abandoning Bertha; he would have been hammering down their door if he had. The sole benefit of having revealed the truth of what John had done to her: Hammond knew exactly how much she loved Bertha. Perhaps he was the only one who did.

Hourly, the Reverend asked Florence why she had not told him Bertha was in a hospital. Was she sick? Was that why she never came home any longer? Florence said, "No, she is still missing. You remember. She is gone," but he didn't seem to understand. Once, horribly, she heard him ask Sarah where she thought Bertha was. She didn't stay to hear Sarah's reply.

40

The Mellish case wasn't like an itch he couldn't scratch. It was more like a splinter just under the skin, where you could see it but couldn't dig it free and after a time it rose to the surface of your body or became part of it. Higham had known plenty on the force who wore tattoos of dead faces or mysterious words in memoriam, but he was not a tattooing man. The cases he would never unravel cracked in his joints and ached in his muscles. Sat irritant beneath the wrinkles time built on his body.

Higham had left Killingly largely untroubled, thinking he'd sorted the case in his mind, if not in the world. But he found himself ticking through its possibilities at surprising times. Overhearing the chatter of college boys on a Cambridge street and wondering how Agnes Sullivan was getting along in her studies. Considering where Joseph-Paul might currently be chasing skirt as he himself strolled the wooded paths of the Public Garden.

Then Samuel Stroslev's piece suggesting that Bertha Mellish had been hidden away in a madhouse was syndicated in the *Daily Globe*. Being a habitual reader of newspapers as well as novels, Higham discovered it at once. He'd been thinking for some time of a move to New York. Stroslev's article encouraged him to visit.

First he found a room on East 2nd Street, close to the cemetery; second he visited the Everard

bathhouse on 28th, which he found satisfactory; and third he
began a survey of the city's asylums in search of Bertha Mellish,
broadside in hand.

His first stop at Bellevue was unproductive. His second stop
was the city asylum at Wards Island.

The boat to the asylum left from an Italian neighborhood in
East Harlem, out and back every hour. Higham stood with his face
to the stinking river air as the boat rocked and slapped across the
small channel. He didn't feel the fear most visitors to the asylum
possessed, of being the single clear mind in a madhouse: *If I set foot
upon this island I may never leave.* That bold reporter Annie Green's
exposé of the old city asylum on Blackwell's Island had magnified
this fear for many—she'd gotten herself admitted and been trapped
with an assortment of poor, generally sane working women and
pitiful mad inmates until the *World* had come to break her out.
She'd written rousingly of beatings perpetrated by coarse nurses,
rotten food, and patients "blue with cold" in flannel slips. A fine
horror story if you thought an asylum was the only hole a person
could be trapped in, if your work did not require delivering people
to and from other oubliettes.

A thick burnt breeze swept the shore as they landed at the
dock and the other passengers walked toward the hospital gates.
Higham turned to survey the city stretched out across the East
River, the long, low blocks of brown tenements spreading across
the upper half of the island and the gray thrusting towers farther
south. Brick and wood in the north, and stone at the city center.
He listened to the water and the wind and the hoot of a steam-
ship downriver, the cries of birds, the muttering of the boat crew
as they sat smoking their stubby cigarettes at the end of the pier.

The dark spires of the hospital building, its maroon towers
and Gothic flourishes, resembled the main Mount Holyoke hall.
Higham inquired at the visitors' desk about whether he might be
able to see the female residents in hopes of identifying a Bertha
Mellish.

The heavily freckled middle-aged matron signing in visitors laughed and fanned herself with a piece of paper. "Lord almighty, what is it with this Bertha girl?"

"What do you mean?"

"That newspaper fellow shouted at me for five minutes about her the other day. I told him, I can't magic a girl up out of thin air if she ain't here." She raised a saucy reddish eyebrow at Higham. "I coulda told him, you got to rub a genie right before she grants your wishes."

"I don't shout." Higham cracked a grin at her that sent her off in search of the supervisor of the women's section while he waited in the stale room.

Fifteen minutes later, a stubby, balding doctor assured Higham that, as he had told the boy reporter and the girl's uncle, there was not a single girl in the institution who resembled Bertha Mellish in more than generalities. The doctor had already accompanied the uncle as they visited every female detained in the hospital; he could not spare more time to tour around another inquirer. The girl was not present and Higham was kindly invited to leave.

A bit disappointing, Higham acknowledged, standing outside the building again, under the gray sky. When he'd read the report about the asylum he'd felt an inner catch and flare like an engine starting up. He had been spinning his wheels in Boston. With his pension he could pick and choose what work he took, and he'd turned down two new cases for reasons that seemed practical at the time: tedious surveillance work with one, likelihood of getting in the middle of some Irish-Italian tussles with the other. But really he had been waiting for excitement to kindle again.

He looked across the river to Manhattan and weighed what he ought to do. Hammond could go hang, of course—but Florence Mellish deserved to know what had happened to her child.

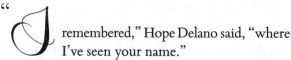 remembered," Hope Delano said, "where I've seen your name."

She looked so lovely in the light of the bedside lamp that Hammond nearly missed what she'd said. Her voice was nice enough, but the curves and shadows of her hips, the soft crinkly brown of the hair between her legs, the dimpling of her thighs—those were better. When she lay upon her back with her knees up and together, the soft flesh at the very tops of her thighs folded over her mons as neatly as the corners of Christmas presents. He was fascinated. Emma had not been fond of lazing about in the nude.

"Mmm?"

She opened her knees a little, teasing, then clapped them together. A poor rebuke for his inattention. "My dear Dr. Hammond. I *said* that I recalled where I'd seen your name before."

"I didn't know you had seen my name before."

"I told you I had," she said, frowning. "The second time you visited."

Hammond gave her an apologetic roll of the shoulders and reached out to card his fingers through her tangled hair. "Oh? Do you read many medical journals, then? I had a fine article in the *New England Journal of Medicine* about afflictions of the lung, but that was some years ago."

She propped herself on one elbow among the disarrayed pillows at the head of the bed. Her small breasts slid charmingly to the side. "No, not exactly. This was a newspaper story."

Hammond was under a sheet; he'd been considering throwing it off and rolling her over once more, for the room was hot and already smelled of their bodies and their exertion. But he went cold at her words. He knew instantly what she had read.

"Was it," he said and pulled the sheet higher.

"Don't come over all stony," Hope said. She put a hand on his waist and leaned in with a serious expression. "You know I had to say something, or you'd just be wondering—does she know about the Mellish girl?"

But he hadn't been wondering. He had gloried in not wondering, in treating the Palatine Hotel as if it were another planet far outside the circulation of the New York dailies he knew very well that she followed.

"I don't want to discuss it."

She lifted the hand from his waist in surrender. "All right. Of course. I just—she must be important to you. I thought perhaps—perhaps you might need a person to talk with about it."

"Talking," Hammond said deliberately, "is not what I pay you for."

Instead of blushing or crying or slapping him, Hope gave the little laugh he still found beguiling. "Why, of course it is." She smiled at him, and he searched that smile for pity or a professional chill and found nothing but warmth. "Not the only thing, but an important one."

He huffed an attempt at an answering laugh.

"I won't ask you about her, if you don't like." Hope traced a spiral over his hipbone as she spoke. "You see, it's just that—if you were in love with her, there are other things I could do for you."

Hammond watched her for a moment. His heart beat in his ears and in his belly. There was a thick white roaring behind it as if the bed, the room, the whole building would momentarily be engulfed by a tidal wave. But he was the wave; the wave was his fury.

If he stayed in the bed with Hope he was going to kill her. It was a perfectly calm thought. That was what frightened him most.

"Get off me," he said, pushing her hand from his side. He stripped back the sheet and sat on the edge of the mattress for a moment, gathering himself.

Hope scrambled up, startled. "Henry, I'm sorry!"

"No." He put an arm out as she reached for him and shoved at her breastbone—not hard—he thought—but she fell onto her rump with a wild little grunt.

He got to his feet. He didn't look at her. In her eyes he would see mixed outrage and disbelief at this treatment or he would not, which might be worse, to see her so flattened under his swell. But he shook off that disquiet. Told himself that a woman like her, society's wreckage, didn't merit his concern.

"I'd like you to leave, Miss Delano."

"Henry, please." She sank back to the bed. "I shouldn't have said a word. I'm sorry. There's no reason we can't still have a good time. Don't we have a good time together?"

"Oh, yes." He took his trousers from the back of the chair, his shirt from the table. Cold motions. "A very good time."

"Then you must let me make it up to you."

He turned. He thought she would look less stunning now that he had remembered she was mere flotsam, but she didn't. She'd thrown her slim arms out on the bed in front of her as if to pull him back with an imaginary rope, and this pushed her little breasts together. A red flush covered her throat and made her blue eyes more striking.

She couldn't have looked like Bertha if she tried.

"Take what you want and get out." He stalked to the bathroom and locked the door behind him.

It was appointed in ridiculous luxury, with a flushing toilet and gold-plated fixtures. He leaned on the marble counter and studied himself in the mirror. His eyes looked like a bulldog's, the skin beneath them bagged and swollen. The low light made it difficult to tell for sure but he thought his mustache had gone entirely gray.

He would not be made a fool of by women any longer. Not by Hope Delano or Florence Mellish, and not by Agnes Sullivan.

Where his fury receded he felt cleansed. Honed. Hope had touched a nerve—his desire to protect Bertha—and given him a vital reminder. Everyone had such a nerve, such a place of weakness.

He had felt Agnes's pulse under his thumb, and even then he had not realized what he must do to shatter her self-containment.

No one lived without ties or responsibilities, not even a cold shrew like Agnes. He would come at her sideways. Trace her Boston connections. Set a watch upon her, if need be. She couldn't hide on that campus forever.

She would not buckle?

She had kin who might.

When he emerged from the bathroom Hope was gone. She'd taken from his wallet precisely the amount they had agreed upon and clipped together the remaining bills with a rhinestone-topped hairpin—a final reproof, a further invitation, Hammond wasn't sure. He threw it in the wicker rubbish basket and went to catch a train home to Killingly.

42

"Strange," said Florence's uncle George, "that we have both been called to identify her now, mistakenly, and found nothing."

George, not particularly religious, had invited Florence to meet him late Sunday morning for a midday meal in the sunny dining room of his waterfront Boston hotel before he concluded his business trip. She'd felt obliged to accept. Now, as the afternoon began, the room echoed with the happy babble of families arriving for a fancy lunch after church.

They'd been talking for more than an hour: the first memorable conversation Florence had had with her uncle. In the past he'd asked her perfunctory questions, half listened to the answers, and genially said "Good, good" in response as some men do when young women speak. Today he paid careful attention as she summarized the journey to Auburn. He had already described his survey of the hospitals of New York in detail, reassuring her that he had been thorough.

They did not speak of why his wife had not joined them for watercress salad and oysters, lobster and lemon ices. Florence kept thinking of the quiet of the emptied house in Auburn and the three babies' funerals.

"Not nothing," she said. "Other people's children."

George looked out to the water. "You're certain you don't want to sue that reporter?"

254 • Katharine Beutner

She shook her head. "It wouldn't be worth it," she said, meaning, *It wouldn't unwrite his story, it wouldn't bring her back.*

"I'd pay the fees gladly," her uncle said, and he meant, *Money is for salving losses*, and Florence knew then that they had come to the end of what they could discuss. She thanked him and they rose.

"Tell John I'll come to see him soon," George said when they parted in the hotel lobby—he wouldn't, nor would she tell John to expect him. But they smiled and shook hands, and Florence walked out into the summer air and the strangeness of an afternoon unconstrained by work or family duty.

She had decided to visit Agnes Sullivan, who was home in Boston for the summer. She wanted to see how Agnes was faring—to find out if she could help the girl.

SHE'D FOUND AGNES'S BOSTON address on an old letter in one of Bertha's desk drawers, tumbled amid pencil stubs and bits of ribbon, buttons, intricately folded notes from junior high school, a single rosebud dried to the color of Florence's skin.

Bertha had kept her drawers neat, but Florence and later Higham had searched them after she disappeared. After that, Florence had not been able to steel herself to tidy the ephemera of Bertha's childish life—as if the mess might draw Bertha back to fume about the breach of her privacy. But when George invited Florence to Boston, she'd eased the largest drawer free and set it upon her lap where its edges bit at her thighs through her skirts. She'd flipped through crisping papers and clinking buttons.

Strangely, Bertha had saved just one letter from Agnes, dated August 21, 1897. It said:

Dear Bertha,
You know that I will be with you. The work is all.
I cannot say I felt as you did after the fire. I do remember seeing
Mrs. Mead, and I am glad that her hopes for the College have
been answered and that we go back to something greater than we

knew before. If the school has been cleansed by fire, perhaps that is for the best. But I hope that our new house will greatly resemble the old. Change for its own sake is no virtue.

I am happy that your sister is well again. Are you sure you will not think of following me into the medical profession?

Until we meet, I remain,
Your Agnes

It wasn't so strange that Bertha had written of the fire in the week before they prepared to return to the new-built campus. The letter itself was queer, though. The way Agnes wrote of the fire sounded almost reverent—and what had Bertha said to prompt Agnes's opening assurance? *The work is all.*

All Florence knew about Agnes's family was that there was an incapacitated sister, younger than Agnes. Bertha had let that slip once after her first year at college and had forced Florence to swear she would never tell anyone else about the girl. "Agnes does not talk about it," Bertha had said, and that was all. Agnes's silences were to be respected.

The Sullivans lived in southern Boston—not South Boston, but just across the rail yard from it, on Thayer Street, far enough from George's hotel that Florence was glad she hadn't allowed her pride to reject his offer of carriage fare for the afternoon.

Their tenement block was indistinguishable from the others surrounding it. In the alley beside the building a knot of children hooted and kicked at something; Florence was almost certain it was a bottle and not an unfortunate animal. A few older men stood by the building's front stoop smoking pipes. They nodded respectfully enough at Florence and stumbled back to let her pass through their beery midst. The building's front door opened under her hands before she had even turned the knob.

There was no front lobby, just a dirty entryway with a wall of locked cubbies for mail delivery. The sideboards of the stairs had been smeared sticky black with soot, smudged by bootsole edges, and scraped by descending furniture. In a few places children—or adults—had carved names and phrases along the upper rim of the sideboards, as they did to the high school desks. *Mikey + Sarah. Lamh ladir an uachtar. Southie Bastards Go to Hell.* The density of the inscriptions suggested generations of carvers had hunched on these sad stairs.

Florence climbed to the third floor and knocked on the door to number thirty-three. For a long time, nothing but shuffling from inside and a few thumps from the apartment next door. Then, "Right with you!" someone called and a woman opened the door, her face all bright confusion. She had Agnes's square build on a smaller scale and her arms were round with muscle. Tired blue eyes.

"Mrs. Sullivan?" Florence asked. "Agnes's mother? I'm a friend, from the College. Agnes went to school with my sister."

"Your sister? Oh, do come in, then. It's a horrible mess in here, pardon me, so sorry. I'm just back from church, you see, no time to tidy up yet today, and they do keep us busy down at that factory." Agnes's mother backed into the room, almost bowing in her eagerness to usher Florence in. "What can I offer you, Miss—or is it Missus—?"

"Miss Mellish. Florence, please, Mrs. Sullivan." First she noticed the apartment's darkness: it faced south and they'd tacked up sheets over the few windows to keep out the worst of the June sun while letting the weak moist breeze move through. A garbagey stink rose up from the alley and swelled in the room, but the floorboards were scrubbed clean. The place consisted of two rooms separated by a worn rug tacked in the doorway. Through the gap between carpet and doorframe Florence saw two beds, two trunks, and a pair of worn boots set upon the nearest trunk—far too small for Agnes's feet.

On the wall above the chairs hung a crucifix.

"Oh dear, oh dear, yes," Mrs. Sullivan said. "You'll be *her* sister, then. Agnes talked so much about your Bertha. I am so sorry, so very sorry that you've lost her. And you must call me Nora, of course. Won't you sit?"

Florence had trouble imagining Agnes talking so much about anything, even Bertha, but she knew how a mother's love could deceive.

"They were such great friends. Agnes was lost without her, I know. Even when she was home last, I thought she still looked a little down, now that—it's been how long? Not a year yet, I know."

"Agnes isn't living with you here this summer?" Florence leaned in, as if she might spot Agnes in a spider-shadowed corner.

Nora shook her head. "No, no. She brought some of her things home, but she's got a place for the summer with a woman that needed a companion. It brings in a little money, you know. The house is down close to the Garden, the other side of the university. She comes by on Sundays when she can. Oh, bless me, I've forgotten—" as a teakettle whistled weakly from the tiny stove. "Will you have some tea?" she asked over her shoulder as she went to fetch it, and Florence, helpless, said she would.

She wondered if Agnes stayed long enough for a cup of tea when she came by on Sundays. If she would come by today. Now that she was sitting in Nora's apartment, drinking tea from Nora's chipped stoneware cup, she felt less certain that she wanted to see Agnes. What if her presence angered the girl? Bertha had never been anxious to bring friends home.

"You must be quite proud of Agnes," she ventured. "She works very hard, I know."

"Oh, sure, she's a good girl. Always quiet. Always studying. You know she's sore burdened by what happened," she finished, dropping to a whisper for the last two words. "But we need more girls like her, smart girls. The factory's no place for a girl like Agnes. Of course, I do wish she were home more. I miss her, for all she's so quiet. She writes to Adelaide sometimes from her College, and that's a kindness. We get Miss Helen upstairs to go through the letters for us. We've such a stack now, though! She's been unwell this last year and some—I do hate to pester the poor old lady. And Agnes makes no bother about it."

"Would you like me to read you anything?" Florence asked, then immediately regretted it. That Bertha would never have forgiven—to read a friend's correspondence.

Nora's smile folded her eyes. "So kind of you, Miss Florence. But I couldn't ask it, not now. They're Adelaide's letters, really. She may not be home till a half hour yet. Takes her four times as long to do a wee errand now, I dare say. Yet it's a blessing she's here at all, and I praise the Lord himself for that."

"What do you mean?"

Nora told her about the feckless boy who'd gotten her daughter in trouble and of Adelaide's near-suicide. It seemed that every family, every woman, had a story that began with a man who took what he wanted.

Agnes sent them money from college when she could, Nora said, her smile fond. "She thinks she's got to keep us safe. There's no keeping anybody safe in this life, I told her, that's for God to do. You just pray to God and Our Lady, you pray to the saints, and you ask for health and happiness, and the rest is out of your hands right enough. But Agnes never thinks a thing is out of her hands. Such big hands she has, after all."

Someone kicked at the door and Florence started and spilled tea down the side of her leg. "Oh, I'm sorry—" she said, but Nora didn't hear, already bustling to the door to relieve the girl of the packages in her arms. The girl was not Agnes but her younger sister—Adelaide—the girl cut down from a noose of ragged sheets. She looked at Florence with mild friendly curiosity as her mother collected her parcels from her. She was smaller and prettier and finer-boned than Agnes—prettier, too, than Bertha, her brown hair thicker and her cheeks alive with pink roses. Blue eyes like her mother's, not hazel. "Hello, Mama," Adelaide said. "Who's this lady, then?"

"This is Miss Florence Mellish, Adelaide." Nora looked up from the cabinet where she was storing the fruits of the girl's harvest: goods from a charitable pantry, it looked like. "Go and shake hands like a lady yourself, why don't you. Say you're very pleased—"

"I *know*," Adelaide huffed. She approached Florence with an outstretched arm, white hand hanging diffidently from her wrist, and waited for Florence to put down her half-empty tea cup and dry her hands on her skirt. "How-do-you-do, very pleased to meet you." She smiled.

Florence took the girl's hand and pressed the sweat-damp palm against her own. "I am pleased to meet you, too, Adelaide, and I am quite well, thank you."

Adelaide looked to her mother—Florence remembered that look—the combination of pride and restlessness children displayed when they had behaved well and wanted to be freed to play.

Jars knocked together as Nora replenished the family's stores. "Adelaide, child, Miss Florence can read you a letter from Agnes if you like. She's offered, isn't that kind?"

"That's very kind," said Adelaide. "There are so many."

"Well, I think just one, dear heart," Nora said. "Miss Mellish hasn't got all day." Adelaide eeled out of her mother's grasp and trotted awkwardly to the bedroom. Florence had not noticed her limp before. In a moment she returned clutching a slim envelope, and the glee on her face hurt Florence's heart.

"What's that one, love?" Nora asked absently. "Is it new? Isn't there a longer one, in that big envelope? From your birthday, you know."

Adelaide shrugged and held out the envelope for Florence to take. "I want this one. I found it. In her trunk, silly goose." Florence pried out three little sheets of paper, almost onionskin-thin. As she stroked the pages open, she felt the tentative weight of Adelaide's hand on her knee. The girl looked at her with hope.

"Can I sit?" she asked, nodding toward Florence's lap.

"Adelaide——" Nora reproached.

"No, it's quite all right." Florence shuffled the papers to her left hand. "If the chair will bear it, I can, too."

"If you're sure," Nora said. "Do you mind if I get to that sewing, then? I'll leave you to it. Adelaide can tell me what her sister wrote. I'm afraid I used up my listening ears at Mass today."

Adelaide lowered herself gingerly to Florence's right knee, the bad knee, with one hand braced against the arm of the chair. She was as bony as an old woman and her hips pressed sharp against Florence's thigh. Florence bit the inside of her lower lip and tasted blood.

"Of course," she told Nora, when she could speak easily. "We'll be all right."

Her arm had gone around Adelaide's waist without conscious direction. Agnes's sister hummed a little as she leaned closer. She smelled of talcum powder and lye and cinnamon.

On the first page, Florence saw her own name.

You were very dear to Bertha, dearer than anything—

43

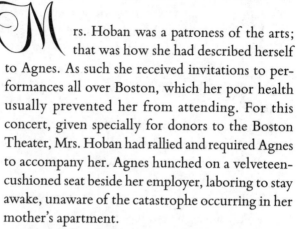rs. Hoban was a patroness of the arts; that was how she had described herself to Agnes. As such she received invitations to performances all over Boston, which her poor health usually prevented her from attending. For this concert, given specially for donors to the Boston Theater, Mrs. Hoban had rallied and required Agnes to accompany her. Agnes hunched on a velveteen-cushioned seat beside her employer, laboring to stay awake, unaware of the catastrophe occurring in her mother's apartment.

Mrs. Hoban had bought Agnes a nicer dress— red-and-gray checked cotton, to complement her own coal-colored silk—for outings like these. She believed people could be reupholstered like arm-chairs. She hated bright colors, popular music, and prissy femininity and liked Agnes very much, in her brusque way.

All the decisions made in the house were Mrs. Hoban's alone. She was preposterously wealthy, eleven years widowed, her two sons lost in the war. She'd already been speaking of hiring Agnes again after she graduated from Mount Holyoke, before she started medical school. Agnes should have been delighted by the prospect. Mrs. Mead and Clapp would be, she was sure.

In Mrs. Hoban's circle, social consensus rendered Agnes invisible in the same manner as the old woman's wheelchair—acknowledged when necessary but never spoken of and certainly never spoken to. She didn't mind. Mrs. Hoban's largesse had secured them a box to the left of the stage, which they'd reached by rolling the wheelchair up a ramp laid over the carpeted stairs. By now Agnes had grown accustomed to the way the world accommodated itself to the rich, but she couldn't help remembering all the old women in her neighborhood who hauled themselves up the stairs one step at a time. How they panted and cursed.

Mrs. Hoban had lent her a pair of opera glasses, and she spent most of the performance examining the faces of the audience. The stage lights shone on their jewelry, their white and blond and dark hair. Mostly they were old and rich, but some were young and rich. They stared back at Agnes with their own opera glasses, swiveling to see who had been seated where, whispering to one another during the singing. Sometimes the chatter swelled to a clear hum beneath the music. These people talked whenever they wanted to. They had paid enough to be here, and the evidence of their generosity glittered down upon them from the cherub-painted ceiling and the electric lights gleaming under every polished balcony rail.

Mrs. Hoban tried to educate her by telling her what the music was about—love, death, or both, tangled in ridiculous plots. Opera featured a surprising number of shepherds and soldiers. The first singer in this recital was an older man with thick white sideburns and thinning black hair. As he sang he thumped his chest with a fist, twice, a third time. Agnes thought about how the sternum he was pounding would look if split on the dissection table.

Finally the man finished his series of songs and with much bowing ceded his place onstage to the last performer, a younger woman in a dramatic red dress and a great deal of rouge. The chatterers in the audience quieted.

"Ah, Delilah," Mrs. Hoban whispered to Agnes. "I saw her do this at its première. She's singing to Samson, trying to get him to tell his secret."

Agnes knew some French but found it difficult to follow the

round opera pronunciation. That hardly mattered—Mrs. Hoban followed each line with a whispered translation. Her breath smelled of peppermint candy.

"My heart opens to your voice," the old woman repeated, "like the flowers open to the kisses of the dawn."

Agnes let her eyes drift over the crowd.

"But, O my beloved, to dry my tears the best, let your voice speak again! Tell me that to Delilah you will return forever. Repeat to my tenderness the oaths of other times, the oaths that I loved."

You will be with me, won't you, to do our work?

Bertha's voice, clear as if she sat in the box with them.

The lights of the theatre blurred.

Agnes remembered Bertha's eyes in the dark morning of Founder's Day, pain-dimmed and desperate. Bertha's eyelids closing under her fingertips after she drew the chloroform-soaked cloth away.

This was why Agnes could not enjoy her comfortable position with Mrs. Hoban, why she struggled to dredge up a smile for Adelaide when she visited their tenement apartment.

Bertha's death touched everything. It traveled in spreading circles like a ripple in water or the singer's voice in the air. It rang through Agnes's body and through the grand gilded space of the theatre, it sank into the plush seat covers and the silk-draped corseted shapes of the rich who sat upon them. They lived in a world changed, though none of them knew it, by Bertha's absence.

Around them the audience had burst into applause, and the singer bowed her head over her clasped hands to accept their praise.

"Remarkable, isn't it?" Mrs. Hoban murmured after the applause faded. She had noticed nothing of Agnes's distress. "Even a ruthless whore sounds beautiful in French. Now take me to the ladies' room before the rush begins, child, I'm bursting."

Agnes swiped at her eyes—blessedly dry—and stood to pull her employer's wheelchair back from the edge of the box.

44

lorence read the first few sentences of the letter aloud before she realized that she held in her hands a confession, addressed to her. "You were very dear to Bertha, dearer than anything, but it would be shameful in me to call you dear. I should not write to you at all. Yet I wake in the morning, I lie sleepless at night—"

Her voice failed, and Adelaide, confused, squirmed in her lap to ask what was wrong.

"Nothing," Florence said. "Nothing, my dear." She lifted the letter again. The words blurred on the page and her eyelids stung. Oh, she ought to have known as soon as she saw her name on the page . . . *with my head full of words I must say to you, to tell you the truth.*

"But what is it about?" Adelaide pressed.

"Nothing," Florence said again, mechanically, then, in a wild grasp for composure: "Just a story." She couldn't make her eyes focus properly but still she tried to skim the letter and gulp down as much of it as she could in case Adelaide changed her mind and took it back.

I think you know what Bertha was to me and I to her. I loved and admired her, I cannot say how much. She made this college my home, my mind's home, and she gloried in my achievements as I did in hers. She valued my work almost more than her own. Even at the end she kissed my fingers and told me that I would be a fine doctor—

"What kind of story?" Adelaide interrupted, and

Florence nearly gasped at the sound of the girl's voice so close to her ear. The touch of her breath against Florence's cheek.

"A story for—for a class. At college."

Miss Mellish, I swore to her that I'd tell you nothing so that you could maintain hope, but I cannot keep my word. You must not be angry with Bertha for making me swear.

Oh, she must not be angry, Agnes thought? Florence expected a suffusion of rage as she read that sentence. Yet oddly she was not angry. She felt instead as if she were floating again in a great void, tethered to life by Adelaide's weight on her lap.

"Are there drawings? Sometimes she makes me drawings."

Florence made a quick show of shuffling through the papers. "No, no drawings."

She wanted to spare you pain. I don't think she knew how much pain exists in the world, waiting to be apportioned to those who must carry it.

"I want to hear the story," Adelaide said with a younger child's directness. "Agnes never tells me stories."

"Oh." Florence swallowed. "Does she not? Well, you are—you are a lucky girl today, then."

I entertain no hope that writing to you will change my own feelings. My sentiments are neither expressible nor capable of relief. But I can no longer add to your burden of suffering, not when I can tell you the single thing you are most desperate to know.

Her heart was pounding so hard she could feel it in her teeth. She heard Nora in the bedroom humming a snatch of song over and over as she sewed. Some rhyming confection she recognized: *Oh, what a lovely day!* And still she was reading, flipping to the second page: *I know what happened to Bertha. She is gone, she is dead. Her French Joseph is responsible, but I am to blame—I did not watch over her as I should have, I did not see what was happening until she was already endangered.*

Adelaide shifted again. "You a'right, miss?"

"Oh, yes," Florence said automatically. She is gone, she is dead. She is gone, she is dead.

She is gone. She is dead.

Adelaide slipped from her lap, took Florence's empty teacup, and went to the water pitcher. She brought back the cup of water and pressed it into Florence's hands, then pushed her hand toward her lips. The water tasted like pewter, but she drank it all. Adelaide took away the cup and settled back onto Florence's lap, and Florence held the girl helplessly. She wanted to shove Agnes's sister from her lap again and flee with the letter—and she wanted never to have to read it, never to know of it, to slip backward in time before this day, this fateful visit.

And yet the letter continued. There was more to say after reporting Bertha's death. How could there be more? What else could matter?

She was close-mouthed about Joseph—all she spoke of was his name and that she had met him at the mill. She never wrote of him in her letters over the summer.

"Story," Adelaide said. "Please."

Florence took a deep shuddery breath. "All right. Agnes writes—she says—it's a story about two girls."

When we first returned to college and she told me of him, I thought he would divert her while she was in Killingly, perhaps enliven a college break or two; you will understand that hope. It seemed harmless enough.

"Like me and Agnes!" Adelaide burst out, then quieted. "Sorry."

"Not sisters." Florence tried to keep her voice even. Trying not to remember what it had felt like to hold Bertha on her lap, to read to her from picture books and fairy tales. "Let me see. Here. There are two girls who work in the mill together in a small town. These girls are hard workers, always doing their best. They are the dearest of friends. They are—they are wise and clever girls."

Thank God the girl could not read. Florence focused her eyes for a moment on the crease between her thumb and forefinger, the rough and folded skin there. Her sweat was crimping the edge of the letter.

On a night early in November she came to my room. Her eyelids and nose were red as if she had been crying. You know she never cried. She shut the door and made me sit on the edge of the bed with her and held my hands. How tightly she gripped my fingers. She told me that she had been persuaded to give herself to him.

"They work in the mill, but they dream of a different life. One of the girls meets a young man"—she choked on the words—"and falls in love with him. She is late to work because she is so happy, and the man who runs the mill thinks she is not a good worker anymore. So she has to leave the mill and leave her friend. She goes to live with the man she loves, and she has—a baby." As she said it she nearly caught herself—talking of babies to this poor child, what was she doing? But the words came out anyway.

Adelaide made a querulous little noise. Florence tore her eyes from the paper—the girl was frowning.

"This is a dull story," Florence said. "I should tell a different one."

"I want to hear *Agnes's* story." As resolute as Bertha had ever been.

"So do I," said Florence grimly.

She is your sister. You must know how I felt to hear her say that. I wanted to slap her, I imagined her head snapping to the side, but at the same time I wanted to cradle her in my lap the way I held my own sister. I had never thought to worry for Bertha, not even when she told me about Joseph the first time. She was good and bright. I thought she would be safe, but I should have known better. None of us are safe.

"Her friend is very worried," Florence continued. She gulped in Agnes's writing with her eyes, while another part of her, the writer, remote and distant, chose each word of the story she was telling deliberately. "She does not see the other girl for a long time. Finally she can go to visit the house in the woods, where her friend lives now."

The sad rows of brick houses near the mill. The trees behind their house, behind Hammond's. How the trees pressed so close to the roads and grew dense as fur. She drew another ragged breath.

"But her friend is too sad to see her. Her friend runs away. Into the forest. She follows after. She is afraid—"

There she stumbled. Who was afraid? She was describing the narrator in Bertha's story—or herself? Or Bertha. Or Agnes. All of them, in the woods, afraid.

Adelaide peered at Florence from under her lashes, looking concerned.

Florence tried to gather herself. "She's afraid, afraid that her friend is too sad. They run and run through the woods until they're near a mountain, and they scramble up it, and her friend is standing by a cliff. She tells her friend to come back down. She is so—so scared. She tries to pull her friend back from the cliff."

She wanted to forget what she had done, to return to her work as if nothing had happened, but she could not. I swear to you now that I tried to save her. But my efforts came to nothing and now Bertha is nothing, too.

Florence couldn't go on speaking. Her head dropped forward as if the tendons at the back of her neck had been cut. She wasn't crying. Simply—disintegrating. Becoming nothing, like Bertha.

Adelaide twisted on her lap and she felt a warm hand cup the puff of hair at the base of her skull. "Miss Florence?" Adelaide whispered. "She catches her, right? She catches her friend?"

Florence shuddered and lifted her head. Adelaide's blue eyes were wide with worry.

"She tries very hard to catch her," Florence said. "But they both fall."

"Not the little baby," Adelaide said, pulling her hand back from Florence's hair, affronted.

Some spurt of noise escaped Florence's throat. She coughed to clear it, wishing for another sip of that tainted water. "No," she said, "no, the girl finds her friend's child later and takes her in and raises her as her own and loves her very, very much."

I cannot bear to continue writing this. I will honor my promise to her as I can. Miss Mellish, they are saying black things about her in the world, but she cared only for your opinion of her. She would not thank me for telling you even as much as I have, and I will say nothing more, not if the police arrest me, not if you beg me. I hope you will not beg me. She was my dearest friend.

"But where did the other girl go after she fell?" Adelaide asked when Florence went silent. "What about that?"

Florence put the crumpled papers down upon the small kitchen table. She felt perfectly blank. "She went to Heaven, Adelaide. She went right to Heaven."

And the letter's signature, clear as anything. *Agnes Sullivan.*

Adelaide sighed and bent her head against Florence's, just for a moment. The pins in their hair bumped and dragged together. Then Agnes's sister lifted her head away.

"That wasn't a very long story, and it was sad, Miss Florence," she said, frowning again. "It would have been better with pictures. I like it when Agnes puts in drawings."

"Well, I—she says she's sorry for that." Florence looked down at the letter, swallowing a sob. "She says—the story was very hard to write. She talks about that, how hard it was."

"Sometimes Agnes is boring," Adelaide said matter-of-factly and hopped off Florence's lap as if nothing had happened. She went to the counter again to pour herself a cup of water. Florence watched her in numb amazement, feeling the ghost weight of a girl on her lap, the presence of Bertha in the room with them. She could imagine Bertha smiling at her desperate guile; she could imagine Bertha raging. But it didn't matter what Bertha would have wanted, now.

Even at the end she kissed my fingers—

"I must go," Florence said. "May—may I keep this letter? I write stories, too, and I would—I want very much to talk to Agnes about this story of hers."

Adelaide agreed and went to fetch her mother.

Florence left the Sullivans' apartment in a blur of nodding and thanks. "Sure you don't want to wait, in case Agnes comes to see us in a bit?" Nora asked as she pinched a piece of darning between her fingers. "Or I can give you her address at the lady's house."

"No, no," Florence said, lost in the hollow shell of her body, and let Nora embrace her. She floated down the building's dirty stairs and out onto the dirty street. The rubbled bricks of the sidewalk spun under her feet and tears ran unheeded down her cheeks. The quickening breeze touched the dampness along the line of her jaw, under her collar. No one approached her to ask what was wrong, which was just as well. Florence was inconsolable. She would be inconsolable for the rest of her life.

I hope you will not beg me, Agnes had written. Well, Florence would not beg. She would do better than that.

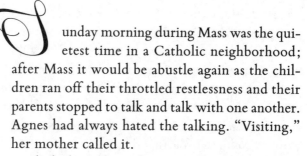

45

unday morning during Mass was the quietest time in a Catholic neighborhood; after Mass it would be abustle again as the children ran off their throttled restlessness and their parents stopped to talk and talk with one another. Agnes had always hated the talking. "Visiting," her mother called it.

She let herself into the apartment, which smelled of burnt porridge. Nora had not washed the breakfast dishes. Usually she labored to clean the kitchen before Mass, as if God might sense the residue of cooking oil in a pan when she knelt to listen. Agnes put down the picture book she had brought, another loan from Mrs. Hoban's library, and tied Nora's thin gray apron over her dress.

By the time her mother and sister returned from the parish church Agnes had washed the dishes and scrubbed the top of the stove and was just untying the damp apron from her waist.

"Agnes!" Adelaide galloped across the room with Nora behind her, shushing. She was wearing the blue calico dress Agnes had bought for her after starting work with Mrs. Hoban, and the pattern brought out hints of cornflower in the gray of her irises. "I missed you."

"I missed you, too." Agnes let Adelaide wriggle under her arm and press the warm length of her body against Agnes's. Adelaide was breathing hard from the climb up the stairs, and Agnes listened to the rhythm of her breath for any changes. Once she had a stethoscope she would check Adelaide's lungs every time she came home, she promised herself.

"You're here early," Nora said as she took off her hat, then lifted Adelaide's from danger before it could be crushed.

Agnes swung her other arm around Adelaide and linked her hands. "Mrs. Hoban's keeping to her bed today, but she didn't want me near. Her head, you know."

"I don't know what that lady needs a companion for if she doesn't want to be kept company." Nora flipped open the book and thumbed through its opening pages, smiling at the lithographed children frolicking there.

"I know. But I won't be the one to tell her so."

"Well, it's for the rich to be so strange. And to have so many books. My." Which meant that when Agnes read the story aloud to Adelaide, Nora would find a way to sit close enough to look and listen.

But the book would wait. First they had to sit together for a while.

Adelaide led Agnes by the hand into the bedroom. She pressed Agnes down upon her own bed, the bed where she'd been born, and slid down to sit at her feet. Agnes let Adelaide arrange her. She had always served as a kind of giant doll for Adelaide, even before the hanging. Adelaide was the only person other than Bertha whose touch did not discomfit Agnes much. They both liked it best when Adelaide sat by Agnes's feet so that Agnes could stroke her hair and speak to her without looking constantly into her eyes.

"Did that nice woman find you last week?" Adelaide leaned her head against Agnes's knee. She picked up Agnes's hand and placed it upon her head, where it curved around her braids, her skull, the heat of her muddled mind. Agnes imagined the dense lobes of Adelaide's brain beneath her hand—imagined that she could cut into Adelaide's skull and mend the damage inside. Someday the techniques for such a surgery would be determined, she had faith. But not in time to help Adelaide.

"What nice woman?" she asked, tucking frizzed strands of hair back into Adelaide's braids. "Mrs. Hoban isn't exactly nice."

"Not Mrs. Hoban." Adelaide pushed Agnes's hand away. She enjoyed being petted but had little use for grooming; Nora often had to swat her with the hairbrush to keep her still when she braided Adelaide's hair each morning. "That college lady."

When the human body freezes, water within each cell expands and bursts cell walls—demolishes the minute structures of life. That was what Agnes felt when Adelaide spoke.

That college lady. Mrs. Mead, she thought, but why, and how— why now, when Mrs. Mead had shown her nothing but favor for months? All over she was ice, unsure if she'd been found out. But she said with apparent calm, "What college lady, Adelaide?"

From the kitchen, Nora said, "Miss Mellish, the sister of your friend that's gone, dear. She came to see us here, a week ago it was, Sunday. She was looking to see you, but she wouldn't stay. She was so kind, wasn't she, Addie? Reading you that letter. Agnes, what a tale that was, sure! I'd no idea you could think up things like that. Addie told me all about it after."

"Very kind," said Adelaide, obedient. She had turned at the waist to peer up at Agnes's face.

"I don't—" Agnes had to stop for lack of breath. "I'm not sure what tale—"

"All about the two mill girls." Nora stuck her head in the door and frowned. "Agnes, are you all right now, dear?"

It was as if Nora had begun speaking Latin. Florence Mellish had come here to find her, read her sister a story about mill girls, and left. A week ago. And nothing had happened since. "Fine," said Agnes, still breathless. "I forgot about that story. Was this— from a letter, you said, Adelaide?"

"I found it." Adelaide watched Agnes with round worried eyes. "It was just a little one. Was it wrong?"

"No, no. You found it? The letter? Hidden in my trunk?" There wasn't enough air in the room or enough blood in Agnes's body. Her head felt light and strange.

"*Yes*," said Adelaide, with a bit of an exasperated squirm.

"All right, Addie, that's enough of that," said Nora, though her eyes were on Agnes. "Let me have a word with your sister, now."

Adelaide shoved herself up from the floor and sulked into the other room. "Not too long," she called as she went.

Agnes blinked, but the world did not alter. "Florence Mellish," she said and did not even startle when Nora sat down beside her on the bed and laid a hand upon her knee.

"Aye, it was, I said. The sister. She did seem to want to speak to you, but she wouldn't even take Mrs. Hoban's address when she left. Is something wrong, Agnes?"

The room smelled as it always did: dust and linens and the accumulated aroma of human bodies. The mattress below her felt as it always did. If she stripped off the sheet she would find that stain, that pair of bloody wings. Her mother's hand tightened on her leg.

"Agnes?"

46

She wasn't coming. Was she coming?

Florence drummed her fingers on the sticky table, trying not to chew her fingernails.

She'd sent Agnes a card, care of her employer Mrs. Hoban, that listed the address of this dingy restaurant and a date and time and said simply: *Agnes, we must speak in person. Florence Mellish.*

Florence had found the restaurant after she left the Sullivan apartment on that last horrible visit—it was walking distance from Mrs. Hoban's mansion but in a far seedier neighborhood. In this jumbled warren staffed by one overworked waitress, they might reasonably hope for some privacy. She'd arrived around four, let the woman know to watch out for a tall girl asking for her, and given her a substantial tip right then. For the first hour or so the waitress kept swinging by hopefully with a jug of iced lemonade and a menu in hand. But finally Florence held her hand out to cover the full glass, and her hand was shaking visibly, they both saw it—and the waitress's face crumpled a little, as if she knew what it felt to tremble so, and she'd whispered, "Sorry, sorry," and backed away. She hadn't returned again, which was better and also worse, for Florence was alone with her thoughts, waiting.

What would she do when she saw Agnes? She didn't trust herself. She'd been thinking—on the train ride to Boston, in the lobby of the ramshackle hotel where she'd rented a room for the night, on the slow hot walk to the restaurant—of all the moments when Agnes might have told her the truth before. All the suffering she could have averted.

What if the girl didn't come?

The appointed minute had not yet arrived. She was half expecting a wild blare of firehouse bells and trumpets at any moment: here she is, the girl who knows the truth of Bertha's demise! But all she heard was clinking glassware and muttering voices, an occasional eruption of laughter or complaint from one of the other small rooms. The place had filled as the afternoon stretched into evening, despite the heat.

Would she track Agnes back to that fancy house? Bang her fists on the ornate front door and wail? Cry out to the whole neighborhood what Agnes had done—

Agnes stumbled through the doorway and stood there blinking.

Florence was struck by how wan she looked, the skin below her eyes purple again. Clutched against her chest Agnes held two thick books; a bag hung from one shoulder. Better clothed now than she'd ever been at Mount Holyoke, in a checked cotton day dress that fit her long limbs and broad body. Around her hung the haze of her future adult self, almost handsome, had she not looked so ill.

"Miss Mellish," Agnes said.

"Agnes. Come sit down." To her own ears she sounded frighteningly calm.

"Miss Mellish, you didn't say—you said we had to speak—"

She'd never seen Agnes flustered. "Sit down," she said again. "We have a great deal to discuss."

"I don't know what you mean." But it was obvious that Agnes did know. She edged awkwardly around the table, still clinging to those books like a shield. When she pulled back a chair it made an absurdly loud scraping sound. She sat and put the books down in front of her. Florence could see the girl's chest rising and falling, rising and falling.

She set the envelope containing Agnes's letter on the table. "I want you to tell me what happened."

"I don't know what you mean." Agnes wouldn't quite meet Florence's gaze. She had a trick of looking instead at your forehead or your eyebrows that Florence had missed before.

"Why didn't you tell me what happened? Why didn't you send this letter?"

Now Agnes's hazel eyes met hers. "If you read it, you know why." Her voice quavered. "Bertha made me promise."

"No. No. I read what you wrote, Agnes, but I cannot believe it. You must tell me what happened. Now."

Agnes was silent, clench-jawed. Her cheeks had gone the sort of white that speaks of nausea.

"If you don't," Florence said, "I'll take this letter to Mrs. Mead."

"Bertha never wanted that," Agnes burst out. "She did all this, all this, so no one else would be hurt."

"All this?" Then, on a surge of vicious feeling: "She died for your sins?"

Agnes's spine seemed to snap into alignment a bone at a time. The white of her cheeks flooded red. "You don't know *anything*," she said furiously, grabbing at the books as if she meant to flee. "I don't know why I even—"

"I know that she is dead."

The room froze for a moment, like a living photograph. Then the waitress's high call of greeting to some favorite patron rang in through the doorway, and Agnes's hand fell open on the books.

"You said you didn't believe me," she whispered.

Florence leaned forward and pinned the envelope to the table's tacky surface with one finger. "Bertha," she said, "was no coward."

"I never said she was." Agnes's mouth twisted. "People do idiotic things for love."

"Not her! Not Bertha. Agnes, don't you understand." The

words wrenched from her gut. "It's killing me. It's killing me. I have to know."

"I can't tell you. She made me swear I wouldn't tell anyone, not ever."

"Because you were to blame." Not quite a question.

"Because she couldn't bear to see me lose my place," Agnes retorted. "You saw where I come from. I'm not meant to be at that college. I was born a *Papist*. I'm the devil to them. They'd never let me graduate, much less go to medical school, if they knew."

Rage bloomed in her heart. "I don't care a whit about your faith. Is that what you've been thinking, I was going to turn you over to the church for burning?" Agnes tried to interrupt, but she wasn't done. "Is that the whole of it? I go back and forth, you know, since I read that letter. I think it must be all this Joseph's doing, then I think it must be your doing. I think you must have killed her. Or sometimes I think you were the innocent and Bertha—"

"She loved *you*," Agnes said, leaning over the table, righteous pose abandoned. "She didn't want—she was afraid to disappoint you. She thought you would be angry. Because of what she did. Because she let that man, and, and, because of—"

"How did she die?" Florence demanded, each word distinct.

She could almost see the phrase above Agnes's head, like the caption of a newspaper drawing: *I did it*. But what came out of Agnes's mouth was not an admission of murder.

"She was pregnant," Agnes said. "He got her pregnant."

"You're lying." Florence's ears were ringing as if they had just been boxed. Pregnant? Bertha? It was not possible.

"I'm not. She only let him do it a few times, but it was enough."

"But then how—what hap—"

"You know how." Agnes leaned back. She had gone chalk white again.

Still Florence couldn't make it fit in her head. "I don't—" She stopped, her heart thundering, and fumbled for a long swallow of the lemonade. Of course she had thought about it, too, when she realized she was carrying her father's child. There were many tall and unforgiving staircases in Old Main. There were pills, elixirs, offering safety and discretion. Rumors of agreeable doctors. But she'd had no money and no trustworthy friends, and John's power had smothered her will. Years of sermons and lectures had fixed his teachings in her. She had just—gone through with it, borne the baby and the pain and the shame. But Bertha hadn't.

"Joseph didn't kill her," Florence said. "Did he?"

Agnes shook her head. In the next room, someone shouted a line of raucous song and was hastily quieted.

"Did he threaten her? Is that why?"

A short, mean laugh. "Oh, no. He was having a lovely time. He was quite happy. She ran him off. She swore she needed a gun, so I got her one—"

"A gun?" Florence snapped.

"It doesn't matter. She never used it. I took it away from her, after she got—when I saw what was happening."

"Did you find her—an abortionist?"

Agnes shook her head fiercely, *no*, her eyes on the books in front of her. "She made me. She was taking these stupid powders—and she kept thinking they'd worked, but nothing did. I told her she ought to go to you. I did. But she wouldn't. She thought you would hate her—and Hammond—"

"What about Hammond?" Florence asked sharply, clutching at his name.

"He wrote her letters. He wanted her to marry him, too. She didn't like him at all, but she wouldn't just tell him so. I don't understand it."

And what would Hammond have done, if he learned that Bertha was pregnant with another man's child? Florence remembered with brutal precision the expression he'd worn when he crouched down to examine her where she lay on the bathroom floor and realized she was in labor. The thin film of sympathy laid over revulsion, disgust, anger.

What would he have done? Nothing good.

"How did you find the woman?" It felt vital that she understand each step of the process that had taken Bertha away from her—as if, when she comprehended the pattern of events fully, she might be able to run it in reverse. She was sure that Bertha would not have gone to a male doctor. Not with Hammond in her mind.

"What woman?" Agnes, confused, looked up at her.

"The midwife."

"You don't understand," Agnes said. That straight spine, those vibrant golden-green eyes. "I am the woman."

In the silence that followed, Florence reached across the table and turned the two books so that she could read their spines. *The Principles and Practice of Surgery*, said one; the second, *A Manual of Surgery for Students and Practitioners*. Florence stared at Agnes, and suddenly the girl broke helplessly into words, almost under her breath, so no one but Florence would hear.

"Bertha stole a knife from another girl on the hall. After I hid the gun. She said she'd kill herself if I didn't help her. She wasn't lying, either. She started to cut her wrist and I hit her. But I knew she'd do it. She was so stubborn, she wouldn't—There was no stopping her. So I told her I would do it. I promised."

"Do what?" Florence asked, full of dread.

"The procedure," Agnes said in a flat tone that sounded as if she were reading from a textbook, "is known as dilation and curettage. It requires an implement of some kind that can be threaded through the cervix—"

"Enough," she said, but Agnes couldn't seem to stop. The girl was staring down at the table as she spoke.

"I took tubing from the zoology lab for a catheter. I was so careful. I disinfected everything. We did it at night, and I gave her a little ether so it wouldn't hurt too badly, and she seemed fine. I swear. She bled, but not too much. She was so happy. For a few days she was fine. But there was—a perforation. Sepsis—she had gotten an infection, systemic. It came on so fast. She was so ill when she came to me. She—she waited too long. Just like she did with the baby."

"Why?" Florence whispered. "Why?"

She wasn't exactly talking to Agnes, but the girl shook her head fiercely. "I don't know! I told her she had to do it while the fetus was small, but she just kept saying it would be all right, she would figure it out. She wouldn't let me talk about it. She was so—She went somewhere, in her head. I could see it in her eyes." Agnes looked up and her red-rimmed eyes locked on to Florence's own. "Then she made me swear, when she was dying. That I wouldn't tell you. I am sorry. I believe she thought you might—have hope. Not knowing."

Florence barely heard the last sentence. She was thinking of Bertha dying, just as she had been after she read Agnes's letter. But now it was real. It was the truth of what had happened to her daughter. Dead for nothing.

"You were with her when she died." Agnes gave a jerky nod. "Her body—" But Agnes was shaking her head, and the true horror of it struck her then, the horror of what Agnes had done.

"She's gone," Agnes said, just as she had written it in the letter. "I—The furnace."

"Oh God," said Florence. "Oh my God."

They stared at each other. Her eyes fell to Agnes's hands. Such capable hands, large but nimble, long fingers and clean-scrubbed nails, where her daughter's blood must have lingered.

"A doctor," she choked out. "If she had gone, right away—with the infection—could a doctor have saved her?"

"I don't know. Perhaps. I don't know," and then Agnes said in a low rush, "I hate her! She had no right!"

"I know." Florence had the shocking distant feeling that, despite what she knew, she wanted to take Agnes in her arms and comfort her as she would have done for Bertha. *Oh, the poor child,* she thought dazedly. *Poor child.*

"You don't know. You can't."

The gun seemed to come from nowhere, though she realized later that Agnes must have had it in her handbag. It looked tiny in Agnes's big hand. She tucked the snub nose of the pistol against the underside of her chin. Above it, her mouth was a straight hard line.

Florence's mouth went dry, her innards frozen. "Is that it? That's the gun you gave her."

"Oh, yes." Agnes, bitter. "A lot of good it did. I wish she had shot him. I wish she had shot me," and her face closed and her fingers moved on the stubby handle of the gun.

"Agnes," she said quickly. "This is senseless. You can't mean—"

"But I can," Agnes said. Her eyes popped wide and fiery. "There's nothing else I can do. If you found out, Hammond will. My mother—I'll never be a doctor. That was it, you see. That was what she died for. To protect me." The last words rasped in her throat.

"And you tried to protect *her*," Florence said, desperate. "Just like you did Mabel Cunningham. Mrs. Mead said you were kind, that you helped her. That's what you do, Agnes, you help."

Agnes barked a laugh. "No, I wasn't kind to Mabel at all."

"I think you were. Whether you know it or not."

"She saw Bertha coming back from meeting him. She saw the letter I wrote. She would've ruined it, so I ruined her. And now it doesn't even matter—everything's ruined anyway." Agnes closed her eyes, but before she could gather the nerve to shoot herself, Florence dove across the table and wrenched the little pistol from her hand.

She fumbled the gun, trying to hold Agnes off, and heard a squeak from the doorway—the waitress, vanishing again—but got it into her hands, finally, and held it close as she stood and stumbled back against the wall behind the little table.

After a moment Agnes subsided, panting. Her books were on

the floor. She bent down to pick them up and straightened slowly, looking a challenge at Florence while she put them on the table.

"You do it, then." Her eyes flickered between the derringer and Florence's face.

"No," Florence said. "No, I don't think so."

here were several things Higham might have expected to find slipped under the door of his rented room—a bill, a noise complaint, a solicitation—but a letter from Henry Hammond was not one of them.

Higham had found himself disinclined to return to Boston. When you spend a lifetime in one city, it's easy not to feel how much the city itself has shaped your operation in the world. In Manhattan, in the Bowery, he shed a primness of spirit that no observer could have identified but *he* felt. To work as a detective here, to reestablish himself, would require real exertion—and he would be equal to it, energized by the city and its pleasures. He enjoyed Manhattan's novelty, he enjoyed its parks, and he very much enjoyed the dark active back room of the Excise Exchange, fortuitously located only two blocks from where he stood in the sparsely furnished bedsit, reading Hammond's short letter.

> *Det. Higham:*
> *I have been attempting to contact you for several weeks now. I understand that you are not currently in Boston. Presumably, wherever you have gone, the US mail, telephones, and telegraphs exist. Please contact me in Killingly at your earliest convenience. I wish to employ you again, briefly, on the Mellish case.*
>
> *Respectfully,*
> *Dr. Henry Hammond*

In his line of work, Higham had received many disgruntled letters but never one requesting his services in such a teeth-grittingly frustrated tone. This letter had been forwarded in a discreet cover by his landlords in Boston, whom he had paid for several months in advance.

It couldn't be the asylum rumors driving Hammond now; something else must have changed in the case. It would be pleasurable to deny the man. Hammond hated to be ignored. But Higham could not suppress thoughts of Florence Mellish alone in her sad classroom. A real disadvantage to feel tied, however loosely, to the figures in an investigation—it gave him an itchy unsatisfied feeling. For now, he would respond. If the doctor had stumbled onto something real, Higham had to know.

Higham's rooming house had no telephone, but he'd learned that you could pay to use the one in the Helvetia Hotel on 4th. He wired Hammond the number and a time the next afternoon and waited on the sidewalk outside, smoking a cigarette and peering up at the grand building's odd fire escape, enclosed behind in a half-circular woven metal screen—an excellent hideaway for surveillance.

Soon enough the pimply young attendant came to lead him to the candlestick telephone at the desk. Higham lifted the base from the counter gingerly so he wouldn't have to stoop. The connection crackled and spat in the earpiece.

"Hammond. This is Higham. What do you want now?" No sense in pleasantries.

"Agnes Sullivan," Hammond said after a short pause. "She's lying. I want to make her tell the truth."

"You have new information? About her involvement?"

A longer pause. "She's been—resistant."

"You tried to interrogate her." Higham gloried in the scene he imagined: a stone-faced Agnes Sullivan and Hammond apoplectic. "What are you hoping for here, Hammond? You want her expelled from the College?"

"I want her arrested."

Higham huffed, amused. "On what grounds? Being too Irish?"

"She knows what happened to Bertha. She wrote those letters."

"You want the police to take you seriously now, you'll need a confession, clear written evidence of guilt, or a body. You have none of those. Am I correct?"

The attendant had stopped writing in the ledger before him and hovered behind the desk as if he could broaden out his ears like trumpet bells.

"I can make her confess," Hammond said. "With the right pressure applied. I want to know about her family. How they get by. I've been watching her. Having her watched. I need you to dig deeper."

"And what will you do with that information."

"That's not your concern. I'll pay you for the work, of course. Half again your previous rate, since you'll have to go back to Boston. What are you doing in New York City, for that matter?"

"Enjoying myself." Higham handed the telephone back to the attendant, who nearly fumbled it in his effort to pretend he hadn't been listening. "I'm done," he told the boy. "End the call." He took out his cigarette case and tucked another behind his ear as he waited to be sure the line had disconnected, in case Hammond could still hear. "You send wires as well?"

48

Florence sat in the desk chair, Agnes on the edge of one twin bed. The hotel room was stiflingly warm even with the window sashes raised. Late as it was, the clatter of wheels and hooves on brick still rose from the street below, and a faint breeze fluttered the slip of paper in Agnes's hand. The front desk clerk had given it to Florence, who'd glanced down in surprise, then shoved the paper into her handbag and hauled Agnes to this room and bolted the door behind them.

"We need a plan," Florence said now. She was clutching the handbag on her lap; there was no chance of getting at the gun, if Agnes had wanted to. The fever that had seized her in the bar, the certainty that she must die, had waned slightly. Now she felt drained and overstrung. Florence was still talking. "I never thought—I told Maggie where I'd stay. He must've gotten the hotel name from her—through the Killingly office. If she told the telegraph operator—"

Agnes didn't know what she was talking about. Her mind was skittering over the short message in the telegram, again and again. It was from the detective, Higham.

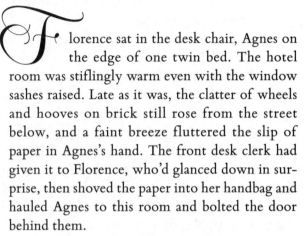

**TAKE CARE & WARN SULLIVAN STOP
HAMMOND SEEKING HER FAMILY STOP
TRIED TO HIRE ME AGAIN STOP**

Agnes cleared her throat and said, as steadily as she could, "He won't stop. Hammond. He came to campus in January. He was—very angry. About some letters."

The words sat in the stagnant air for a moment. She'd seen so many variations of dawning horror on Florence Mellish's face in the past few hours; this one was flavored with disbelief. "The letters that said she had run away—that talked about Joseph? Did you—Was he right? Did you send those?"

Agnes nodded and told her, haltingly. How desperate she had been to direct the doctor elsewhere; how she'd claimed that Joseph meant to entrap Bertha into marriage, which was a lie; and how infuriated Hammond had become at his inability to prove her authorship of the letters. How he'd nearly strangled her. The crease between Florence's eyebrows deepened as she spoke.

When she stopped, Florence leaned forward, frowning. "But what do you truly know of this Joseph? Did he treat her kindly?"

Agnes shrugged. What did it matter if he had? Bertha was still dead, like so many other girls, whether their men had adored or brutalized them. "She said he did. She said he was gentle. But I needed a reason. To tell Hammond why she'd run."

"Did Joseph know? About the child?"

"Oh, no, never. He might have tried to make her carry it. To marry her. She didn't want to marry him, not at all."

"Then why did she ever take up with him?"

It felt as though she had to break past a logjam in her throat each time to answer—and then the words spilled out. She couldn't look at Florence while she talked, so she studied the room's rough floorboards. "I don't know. Bertha never bothered herself a bit over a man before, besides putting up with Hammond. She wanted to be a philologist or study law. We were going to live in Boston while I went to medical school. But when she came back, last fall, something was wrong." That first prick of worry Agnes had felt when she'd asked Bertha about her summer research on applause and gotten a dismissive, *It no longer interests me much.* Bertha had still prepared for the debate, completed her assignments, done what was necessary, kept up a good public face. But she no longer seemed excited to talk over their plans.

Agnes went on, "After the operation, when she was ill, she said it didn't matter what she did, now or ever. She said she could never have children. It makes no sense. She was having one right then. That was the entire problem."

Florence asked in a shaky voice: "Did she say why? Why she couldn't have children?"

Agnes shook her head.

"Did she know—did she find out—" Florence fell silent, and after a moment Agnes looked up to see her throat visibly working, as if she were struggling to swallow something down—words, or bile, or a scream. Last year she'd read a medical journal article about Chevalier Jackson's laryngoscope, a new tool to examine the esophagus. Jackson used it to pull objects from the throats of hapless children. But Agnes had no tools, medical or verbal, to coax out whatever obstructed Florence's speech. She just waited.

Finally Florence drew a shuddering breath.

"Did she know who her parents were? Did she know I was her mother?"

"What?" Agnes said. And then again: "*What?*"

For eight years the Reverend Mellish had raped his elder daughter. That was not the word Florence used, but it was the word Agnes felt reverberate in the room. Bertha was the child John Mellish had gotten on Florence, and Hammond had delivered her, as he was so proud to note. He had known all along that Bertha was Florence's daughter. Yet when Florence had tried to tell the doctor recently about what her father had done, Hammond had refused to believe her.

Florence recounted this stonily at first but began to sob quietly as she tried to describe Hammond's reaction. Agnes went to her and curved a hand around her stout shoulder. What had happened to Florence didn't shock her. Terrible things happened to children everywhere, and in tenement quarters those terrible things were harder to conceal.

Yet it explained so much about Bertha. If Bertha had learnt of her parentage—

And *Hammond*.

He hated them, Agnes thought suddenly. Women. His fingers hot around her throat.

Agnes let Florence cry into a handkerchief for a few minutes, and then she sat down on the bed again. Her stomach was tight and trembling.

"I have to tell him."

Florence, sniffling, shook her head in confusion. "What do you mean?"

"Hammond will never quit. He thinks I killed her," Agnes said through her horror. "And he's right. So I'll confess. Before he can hurt my mother and Adelaide."

"You didn't—" Florence said. "He wouldn't—"

But then she stopped because she knew that Agnes *had* and Hammond *would*, and she could say nothing to alter those truths. She was looking at Agnes in the most despairing way. She saw what Agnes really meant. What would happen if she confessed to Hammond.

Agnes had seen only one path: to go on to medical school, credentialed and safe, achieving her dearest dream and penance for Bertha and protection for her mother and sister, all at once. She'd been working toward it since childhood.

She could not simply leave Mount Holyoke for one of the irregular doctoring schools. If Hammond learned what she had done, she would likely face prosecution—and even if she did not, the stain would be severe enough to block any alternative strategy.

And if the dream was gone—if that single path had closed to her—

She wouldn't need the gun to end her life, and Florence Mellish knew it.

"No," Florence said, her miserable confusion gone, and came up off the bed with a fearsome expression. Nemesis, Bertha might have called her. Bertha had always loved the fact that the Furies were also known as the Kindly Ones.

"He can't have you, Agnes. You don't tell him a thing."

AGNES SLEPT UNEASILY IN the plush armchair and fled as early as she thought the streets would be safe, to escape the discomforting intimacy of waking in a room with a near-stranger. She'd thought to take the gun with her, but Florence was too clever—it was gone from the handbag. Agnes gathered her books and stood by the other twin bed, watching Florence sleep: deep shadows under the woman's closed eyes, her mouth open against the pillow under which she had probably hidden the gun while Agnes was in the washroom the night before.

She had to get back to Mrs. Hoban's in time for her employer's nine o'clock appointment at the Jordan Marsh department store. Reluctantly, she found a hansom cab and let the driver take her down the narrow, quiet streets. It was Friday morning; it had rained in the night, she remembered suddenly, a brief burst of storm. The streets felt scoured by an unseen force. Agnes felt scoured. Not cleansed but worn down.

Alive, despite having admitted to performing the procedure that killed Bertha and cutting her body up to hide the death.

Alive, because Florence Mellish did not want her to die.

All this was baffling. Agnes had told Mrs. Hoban she was visiting her mother, the night before, half expecting not to return at all. But here she was: counting out fare for the cabbie, letting herself in through the back garden, accepting a plate of buttered toast from the cook as if she deserved it. Everything going on as it had before.

Hammond was still coming.

Agnes devoured the toast, surprised at her own hunger. She washed, changed her dress, and met Mrs. Hoban in the foyer at eight-fifteen precisely, as ordered, to take over duties from the maid who had wheeled her out of her sumptuous bedroom.

"You look tired, child," the old woman said, peering back over her shoulder as Agnes levered her chair across the threshold.

"The storm kept me awake," said Agnes.

At the grand department store, Mrs. Hoban bought three more dresses for herself and ordered another pair of custom-sewn summer gloves for Agnes, whose hands did not fit the ready-made variety. Agnes tried to object, as she always did when Mrs. Hoban spent money on her.

These women who were helping her—their care made her want to crawl out of her skin. Agnes hated feeling so beholden. But from the first, from Miss Kelly recommending her to the College, she had been pulled up a ladder of women as surely as if she had stepped from one cupped bridge of hands to another. They assisted her though she was not sociable or pleasant. She was no Mabel Cunningham, to smile in their faces and boost their spirits with her chatter, and still they smoothed her way. They believed in her future, as Bertha had, yet their attention to her felt threatening. Helping Agnes fulfilled some need for each of them, and she rarely felt certain what it was. Why did Florence look on her with such—love?

She could not say she liked these women, Miss Kelly or Mrs. Hoban, not the way she liked Clapp, whose interests aligned neatly with hers. Not the way she'd loved Bertha. She could not even say if she liked Florence Mellish, whose stricken looks pained her.

But she owed them. She owed protection to her mother and sister. And she owed Bertha.

If Hammond came, she would face him.

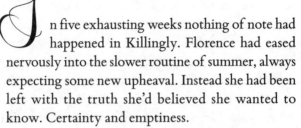

49

In five exhausting weeks nothing of note had happened in Killingly. Florence had eased nervously into the slower routine of summer, always expecting some new upheaval. Instead she had been left with the truth she'd believed she wanted to know. Certainty and emptiness.

At night, when her parents were asleep or at least quiet in their rooms, Florence would unlock her desk drawer and pull out the relics of her confrontation with Agnes. The telegram from Higham she'd scrutinized desperately, as if it might contain secret instructions, hashmarks, lemon-juice letters transparent against the light. And the gun.

She'd tried to bend her thoughts away from all of it. Ruminating on the danger that still faced Agnes felt like tempting fate, and if she let herself consider the realities of what Bertha had experienced, her mind stuck and spun like a gear clogged with grit. She imagined all the details Agnes had kept back from her that would color in the story's grotesque outlines. It was so difficult not to stew in loathing. Hating herself, Hammond, Agnes, the mill worker Joseph.

It had been a bad night and she was still groggy when a hard knocking sounded at the door around eight in the morning. Maggie had not yet arrived and her parents were still asleep. Florence rushed from the kitchen to fling open the door, ready to chide the telegram boy.

A man she had never seen before stood a respectful

distance from the door. He was startlingly handsome, slight, clean-shaven and red-cheeked, with dark wavy hair pushed back from bright blue eyes. Decent clothes, a bit worn but stylishly put together. He held several books against one cocked hip, a knapsack slung over his opposite shoulder—all angles, contrapposto, like a classical statue. Florence stared at him without speaking.

"Pardon me, madame," he said in a strong Québécois accent. "You are, I think, Missus Florence Mellish? You are—the sister?"

Florence nodded. She still had her bag in one hand, clutched tight.

"Oh, I hoped this. Sorry, madame, I don't want to disturb. I want to say, I am very sorry. About Miss Bertha Mellish."

She looked down at his shoes to stop herself from staring helplessly at his beautiful face or from saying something unforgivable. So many people had told her they were sorry about Bertha's disappearance, and she hadn't known what to say to a single one of them. Each time the interaction felt newly impossible.

But his shoes did not make sense. They were much worse than the trousers and jacket: creased and battered, multiply mended. The footwear of a man who walked because he was too poor for other transportation. Florence's eyes flashed back up to his. Her whole body prickled with suspicion.

"You see," the man said, "I just today have learned that she is gone. I would have come before to give you my sympathy. And I bring these for you." He held out the books. "These were hers."

Florence snatched the books from his hands. There was a hissing in her head, a voice saying *how could you* and *did you love her at all* and *was she happy* and *I should gut you*—but all she said to him was, "You're Joseph."

A flicker of surprise. "*Oui*, yes, madame."

He overtopped her in height only by a few inches. The "French Joe" in Bertha's story was described as "six feet three and well proportioned." How like Bertha to refract the truth so slyly, a joke on him and herself at once.

"You didn't know about her disappearance."

"The papers, in English, I do not read," he said with an explanatory shrug.

"Then why did you leave?"

He was watching her closely, wariness rising—he must be wondering how she knew his movements, how she knew of him at all. But he answered readily enough.

"Ah, I knew, she was no more my friend? But gone, no, I knew nothing. I went out west for the work. I return, to work *comme avant*. I am truly so sorry, madame." With the corners of his mouth turned down and his strong dark brows drawn together he looked like an engraving of a sorrowing angel. "Miss Mellish, she is, I want to say, she has a sweet heart. *Doux et formidable*. I hope very much that she comes back to you."

At this bold expression of tenderness Florence made a startled sound. Agnes had admitted that Bertha thought well of Joseph even at the end, that she'd called him gentle. To Florence he did not seem gentle. His charm was electric, his beauty so loud one could hardly absorb it. He radiated an attractive force.

Since Agnes had recounted the miseries of Bertha's last months Florence had thought compulsively of the anguish her daughter had suffered in mind and body. Now she was faced with a strange possibility: Had Bertha also been touched with desire? Had she known delight?

Seeing him made nothing better. It made nothing worse. She didn't know what she had expected.

"Christ," Florence said. "You have to go now."

"Pardon, have I—"

"Listen," she said fiercely, and his eyes snapped to hers. "You have to leave Killingly. There's a man—he will be furious if he finds you. He thinks you may be responsible. For Bertha."

His eyes went to the house behind her, imagining a father.

"*No*. Dr. Hammond. Do you know him?"

"The doctor? He is—*impérieux*?" She was nodding. "But why—he thinks I—" For the first time he looked frightened.

"It doesn't matter." She put the books down and glanced back at the house. The remaining money from the sale of Bertha's story was locked in her desk, too—but if she let him out of her sight before she'd convinced him he must leave town—"Can you go to Canada? Far away. You shouldn't come back here, not for a while."

An acid distaste in his expression. "If you think I will say, make gossip, about Miss Mellish—"

"I think you will hang if the mood strikes him."

His head turned sharply as if she'd struck him, the way she'd fantasized about doing when he was only a blurred and faceless villain in her mind. But then she saw what he had already heard— men on horses rounding the street corner and a carriage close behind them, Hammond at the front of the pack with one arm flung out toward the house as if he were leading a charge in the War. They halted in a storm of hoofbeats and jangling tack and hauled themselves down and marched into the yard. The other men were town constables Florence recognized, some fathers of her students: Merrick Holt, John Deane, two others whose names escaped her. One stayed with the carriage and horses, and the others converged on the house, following Hammond.

Joseph was still standing there stricken before her, clutching at the strap of his knapsack, his cheeks white marble.

"Joseph Poirier, also known as Paul Beaulieu?" Hammond was flushed and breathing hard, his eyes hostile on Joseph's face. Florence could see that he, too, was startled by Joseph's prettiness and that it fueled his rage.

Joseph said, "I don't—"

"It's him," Hammond said to Holt the constable. "Why else would he be here?"

Holt told Joseph, "You must come with us to answer some questions."

"What questions? I don't understand." Joseph looked to Florence helplessly. "Madame?"

"Questions about the disappearance and probable murder of Miss Bertha Mellish," said Hammond, puffed up with anger.

"What is the meaning of this?" Florence pressed forward as if to get between them. "What murder? This young man says he was a friend of Bertha's. He came to pay his respects, having just returned to town. We don't know that she has been murdered. Is there evidence that this man harmed my sister?"

"Is there evidence—" Hammond's cheeks were brick red. "Miss Mellish, I know you will hear nothing against your sister, but it is well known among the mill employees that this fellow pursued her. She has been missing for eight months now—and he for longer—and now he returns, as if nothing has happened? He must answer for his actions. Where has he been? What did he do to her?"

"I don't want to go nowhere with you." Joseph tried to wrench his arm free from Deane's grip. "I never hurt Miss Mellish. I never knew she was gone."

"If you won't come willingly, you'll be under arrest," Holt said.

"For what?" Florence said. Hammond was still scowling at her with an edge of confusion, uncertain why she, too, was not braying for Joseph's blood.

"He is under suspicion for the murder of your sister, and we can arrest him on that account." Holt and his son had the same calm plodding manner. He was talking placidly of murder, while Florence's mind raced.

"I did nothing!" Joseph flailed out against Deane. "*Je ne suis pas un meurtrier!*"

After that it seemed to take mere seconds. One of the constables pulled Joseph's knapsack roughly from his shoulder, and they chained his wrists and loaded him into the carriage and all the while he protested, now mostly in French, that he had never harmed Bertha, would never harm Bertha, that he had just come back to work at the mill again. The constables argued about where best to take him, Hammond insisting on the jail in nearby Danielson, all of them ignoring her now that they had Joseph in custody. Florence could see his ashen face through the carriage window. His pleading eyes locked with her own.

A connection sprang up between them, a glowing rope of fear stretching from the steps to the carriage. Florence's own sweet heart turned, as it had for Agnes. For months she had denied his existence; then she'd seen him as the man who'd precipitated Bertha's ruin. She had hated him in a cold, clear, abstract way. But she knew he had not done what they accused him of.

He was little more than a boy, barely older than her students. He was petrified.

Sweet and formidable, he'd called Bertha. At least one more person in the world had admired her rightly.

In the carriage, Joseph had already cycled through panic about his old charges: the fight with the vicious boss in New Hampshire, delinquency for a drunken mishap, theft for borrowing a battered wheel when he was late for a shift. They knew both his names, they would lock him away. They might hang him like Bertha's old sister said. But he had fixed now on one other thought, trying to relay it to her sister just with his eyes, so she would know he had not done it:

Tout ce que je voulais c'était lui plaire—all I wanted was to please her.

The link broke as Hammond stepped between them, ruddy and fervent, frowning at Florence. "It may be some time before they finish interrogating him. I'd have thought you'd be overjoyed. This is the first movement in so long. Now we'll find out the truth of it."

"Overjoyed," Florence said faintly. Behind him the carriage jostled into motion, Joseph a smudge in the window.

"You needn't worry. I'll ensure Holt is discreet. We don't know how it was between them. It could be that she rejected him and sent him into a rage. I think it's likely. We don't know his depravity. Coming back here, to gloat."

"But the letters—" Then she cursed herself silently for reminding him.

"Spurious," Hammond said, a base glitter in his eye. "You'll see." He clapped her on the shoulder as he might a fellow soldier and hurried down the walk to mount his horse, where Deane was holding it. They went after the carriage at a canter and then the street grew quiet, expansively still.

Someone had kicked the books Joseph brought onto the grass beside the stone walk. Florence bent to retrieve them and stroked them smooth with a quivering hand.

Three slim volumes cheaply bound, Anne Dacier's *Odyssey* in French and two books by Jules Verne: *Voyage au centre de la Terre*, she read, and *Le tour du monde en quatre-vingts jours*. Surely purchased with Bertha's money from the mill, carefully chosen with the desire to open new worlds for her uneducated lover—a generous, loving, patronizing gift. Their spines were tight, as if they'd never been read.

Florence stared down the empty street again. A neighbor's dog trotted out in a loose semicircle to chase a mourning dove and back to its yard.

If they were set on blaming Joseph, could Agnes be free? Would Hammond cease to think of her?

Or would the men surmise, as they questioned him, that a college girl with a lover might find herself in trouble—and turn to Agnes with renewed suspicion?

That was what Agnes would think. Florence knew it, sickly, in her gut. And then the worst struck her—that it would never go so far. Joseph's arrest alone would be enough.

In her guilt, Agnes would not stand by silently and allow Joseph to be condemned. She would confess, as she had already threatened to.

50

*H*ammond had expected the constables to confine Joseph Poirier to a cell immediately upon their arrival at the Danielson jail. They did lock him in a small plain room—but then, mystifyingly, they stood outside its door and conferred about where the sheriff had gone and when he was likely to return. Deane set about making coffee, as if to prepare for a long delay. Another fellow was rolling a cigarette. The place smelled of mildew, tobacco, and fetid wool.

He thought he might burst with impatience. They had the man! He'd already told them what they needed to know to interrogate Joseph: that the mill man had been linked to Miss Mellish by some of the workers, including good Mr. Fortin, who'd notified Hammond of Joseph's return and stated intention to visit the Mellish home. Hammond had informed the constables, too, that he doubted very much that Miss Mellish had returned the fellow's attentions. People of that sort were likely to regard any conviviality between a handsome young man and a pretty girl as romance. Fortin had said that Joseph was known to pursue the mill girls more generally, and no real evidence had yet come to light of any intimate connection between him and Miss Mellish.

All this Hammond said calmly, as if it didn't torment him to think of the sort of connection Bertha had probably enjoyed with this vulgar peacock. As if he hadn't burned with contempt at the sight of the man: contempt and a terrible hollowness he tried not to probe.

The letters he had left out, for good reason. He would point the police to Agnes Sullivan later if it served him. Once he knew what this Joseph had done to Bertha. What she had let him do.

"Holt, you can't mean to wait, my good man," he said to the lead constable, trying to sound amiable. He'd always thought Holt was something of a ninny, and this episode was not controverting that opinion. "He's here. We have him. If you must first discuss strategy, I understand, but surely we can begin questioning him posthaste."

Holt shook his head. "Dr. Hammond, could you write down your statement of the facts, sir? As you told us just now, before we went to fetch him. Your understanding of the man's importance to the case and his connection to Miss Mellish."

"My statement? Isn't his statement more vital at this juncture?"

"The sheriff will need it, Doctor. The court may as well."

"I will be happy to testify at any trial," Hammond said, his eyes on the door behind which Joseph languished. "And I will write your statement now—if you will redouble your efforts to get the sheriff here immediately."

Holt collected pen and paper for him and cleared off the sole desk in the outer chamber where they waited. The other constables were still just standing around. Hammond waved off an offered cup of coffee and tried to settle his mind to write. Stimulation he did not lack. Marshaling his concentration was the challenge, while the man who had usurped his place with Bertha sat in the next room.

The news of Joseph's return had discomposed Hammond in the extreme. For months now he had been directing his wrath at Agnes Sullivan, plotting how he might corner her again and succeed where he had failed before. First he'd tried Higham, then he'd pressed the Boston chief of police to recommend another private detective; no luck, surely due to Higham warning others off.

Finally he had determined to sort the girl himself, though trips to Boston had reduced his practicing hours considerably. He'd been away so often that Mrs. McDowell had been first to notice when Tricksey went off her food and had to be tempted back to eating with canned fish and pumpkin.

He'd spent the last weeks doing things he would never have imagined: buttonholing priests after Mass to ask about their parishioners, cultivating Boston social connections among the factory-owning class, paying street children to watch the mansion where Agnes Sullivan currently lived as a companion to an elderly widow. Often, as he performed these grim transactions, he saw himself as if through a looking glass: an increasingly unfamiliar figure with a hardened, tarnished glow. The shadow self that had come so close to killing the girl had not been extinguished, only adopted a new form and tactics.

So far it had come to naught—Agnes barely left the fine house except as the Hoban woman's attendant, and he wouldn't approach her on the street in that neighborhood, where she might appeal to a passerby and pretend he was a masher threatening her virtue. But he was getting closer. He had learned where her mother lived and was seeking, through Cambridge friends, an introduction to the fellow who owned the factory that employed Nora Sullivan. He meant to destroy Agnes, but he wanted to do it all so subtly that nothing could be traced back to him, and his status in the communities that mattered to him would be unchanged.

None of this subterfuge was necessary. The Sullivans were exquisitely vulnerable people. The slow prologue had two purposes: to torture Agnes and to bolster Hammond's confidence. He could not admit to himself how much she scared him, still. How he saw her eyes, incandescent, implacable, in the dim hours near sleep. This time, he had to be ready.

Then this news, as if the world had paused in its rotation and begun to spin backward: Joseph, returned to Killingly.

He'd given up the mill man for gone, especially now that he

knew how difficult it was to track a person who operated outside polite society, whose name was on no property records, no boards of benevolent organizations. If Higham couldn't find him, he was not to be found. But the fool had come back of his own accord.

Holt had gone off somewhere to get another message to the sheriff, finally. Hammond had gotten down a few sentences laying out the preliminaries—*Joseph Poirier, who was hired at the Sayles mill under an assumed name, is known as a scofflaw who considers flirtation a chief amusement of life*—when the doors to the jail swung open and Florence Mellish marched in with his neighbor Darling, of all people, trailing behind her. Hammond stood to meet them.

"Dr. Hammond," Florence said. "Where is the man? What have they done with him?"

"Very little, Miss Mellish. What is he doing here?" He nodded at Darling.

As always, the surgeon seemed incapable of taking affront. He smiled as if Hammond had greeted him politely. "Miss Mellish needed transportation here, and I was glad to offer it."

"I met Dr. Darling on the Pike." Florence peered over Hammond's shoulder distractedly; looking for Joseph, he assumed. She seemed to have gathered her wits from the shock of his appearance.

"You would know the best way to the jail, I suppose," Hammond said to Darling, whose brother's yearlong imprisonment in Worcester had been the talk of the town a while back. But Darling only smiled again, and Florence pushed past him, not listening.

"Where's Holt? I must speak with him at once."

She had three books tucked under one arm, as if she'd brought her school work or some light reading for the prisoner. Hammond revised his estimate of her mental acuity. He touched her shoulder gently to settle her, and she dragged her gaze to meet his.

"Miss Mellish, what is it that you need? They are waiting for the sheriff, to interview him, I understand. I'm writing down for Holt—"

304 • Katharine Beutner

"There's a note," she broke in. "From Bertha. In the book he brought."

She had a paper in her hand.

"The book?"

"She gave him books. One of them had a note in it. It's—it says—"

"She gave him *books*?"

Florence turned to face him. "Dr. Hammond," she said, "the note says she has killed herself."

Hammond hovered in that moment between impact and pain, hearing and comprehending.

He'd known that Bertha was likely dead. For months he'd known it. He had tried not to know it as he met with the South Hadley police and Mrs. Mead and Higham. He had tried not to know it as he tracked the writer of the anonymous letters. He had tried not to know it in Hope Delano's bed.

That was the emptiness he'd felt when seeing the honest confusion on the young man's face at talk of Bertha murdered. If she hadn't run away with Joseph, if he knew nothing of her whereabouts—

"I don't believe it," he said now. "Let me see it."

Deane and Holt were there, crowding close, and Darling right behind her. They had heard what she said. They were all eager.

"I'll read it." Florence's voice had gone gravelly. She put the books down on the desk and held the small sheet of paper close. She would need spectacles soon, he thought helplessly.

"Dear Joseph—my apologies for concluding our friendship so abruptly. Do not wonder at my withdrawal." She took a long breath and let it out slowly, then continued. "I must write quickly. I am here and then I am gone. Cannot trust my mind any longer. My sole glory. My one distinction. All wrong. I fear what will come. I know how my uncle shattered. I can't bear it, I won't."

There her voice cracked. Darling put a paternal hand on her shoulder. Everyone in the room was holding his breath.

"Please give this to my sister and my friends so they will not suffer overmuch. I know my death will trouble them. Yet I would have them see it as an escape. I must end my agony. Can't face them in this state. They would stop me. I'll choose the coward's way."

Florence lifted her eyes from the paper.

"It's signed with her initial. That's all."

A thick silence. Holt said, "It is her handwriting?"

Florence nodded.

"Why would he have kept it? Why not deliver it as she asked?" Hammond exploded. He couldn't fathom it. How could anyone keep the knowledge of a child's death from her family?

"He doesn't read English." Florence would've seemed composed were it not for the tremor in her voice. "He wouldn't have known what it said."

"She speaks French!"

"She was losing her faculties," Darling said quietly, as if he knew the first thing about Bertha. Hammond wanted to hit him.

Holt took the paper from Florence to look it over, handling it delicately. "Miss Mellish, do you believe this document to be genuine?"

"I do," said Florence.

Their faces were all somber and set. Hammond felt as if he were the one losing his mind. They were simply going to give up, to turn away, when Joseph was right there, terrified, awaiting the force of their inquiries.

He held out his hand for the note, and Holt gave it over. The handwriting did look like Bertha's, it was true. Her letters back to him had always been short, perfunctory, like the note.

"We must ask him about this," Hammond insisted. "We must hear his version."

"When the sheriff—" Holt began to say, but Florence laid a hand on his forearm.

"Pardon me, Constable Holt, but—what can this fellow have to say that is worth hearing? He will claim he knew nothing about the note or any misery she suffered. He won't want to be blamed. Either he will distance himself from her entirely or he will say that my sister was merely a plaything. Perhaps an attachment did exist between them. If that is true, surely it is because her judgment was already compromised by the effects of this—familial inheritance." Florence swallowed audibly and lifted her hand from Holt's sleeve.

So that was it, Hammond thought, livid. That was why Florence was so eager to buy this patent nonsense. If Bertha had cracked up like her uncle and Sarah Mellish—was no longer responsible for her actions—then she could not be blamed for giving in to a man like Joseph. And Florence, whose weak morals had produced Bertha, could absolve herself of guilt, too.

Florence continued, "I know you must complete your investigation. But as she died by her own hand—I wish—I ask—will you take care, with what is known? My sister has been the subject of much talk already. It has broken my parents' hearts. You've seen it, Doctor. I have no desire to pursue this matter further. She accuses this Joseph of nothing in this letter. She addresses him as a friend. I would have it end here."

All the constables were nodding now, not just Holt, with a sympathy that sickened Hammond. "He might have driven her to it." He gestured at the room that held Joseph. "Did you consider that, in your eagerness to acquit the man?"

Florence turned her dark eyes upon him. "Think, Dr. Hammond. You knew her well." He flushed at that. "You know how difficult it was to make her do what she did not wish. Do you believe a man could drive Bertha to harm herself?"

Once he would have agreed with her. Once things had seemed vastly simpler—his belief in Bertha unshakeable. No longer.

Hammond saw pity in the faces of the constables; they knew that the commonest cause of self-destruction in young women was abandonment or mistreatment by a man. But they would not say this to Florence, and their eyes urged him not to say it, either. He subsided, simmering.

Holt told Florence that the sheriff would have to sign off on releasing Joseph, that they would still need to interview him, but that they would do everything in their power to keep the business quiet and to resolve matters quickly. There was no need to make public the knowledge of Bertha's rash act. They wanted no more distress for her family.

"I am awfully sorry, Miss Mellish," Holt added, "that you have learned of your sister's passing in this way."

Florence acknowledged that with a nod. She looked toward the room with Joseph in it. No doubt he was agonizing over what would become of him, with no idea that his paramour's sister had become his defender.

"He wants to go back to Quebec, he said. When you are done with him. Dr. Darling, I will take a moment, if you don't mind," and she turned, pushed open the front doors, and fled.

Hammond followed her. He couldn't help it. Darling reached out for him, but he pulled free and shoved through the closing doors into the sunlit day. Outside the church bells were just tolling eleven o'clock.

Florence had her face in her hands, her shoulders shaking.

He didn't care.

"You should have brought that note to me first," he said coldly.

It took a long moment for her to lower her hands and meet his eyes. She had not been crying, as he'd thought, though splotches of color marked her cheeks. "All I could think was to bring it here. The police know best how to handle these matters."

"They seem to take your direction admirably."

"My direction? My direction is that she is dead." Her shoulders dropped, pushing her chest toward him—a shift that would have been menacing, in a man. "My direction is that I would not have Bertha dragged through the mud to punish some foolish boy for being taken with her."

"Being taken with her," he scoffed. He heard the doors open behind them. "You won't admit that she lowered herself to consort with such a—"

"She was losing her mind," Florence said. "She was—in torment." Her face crumpled as she spoke.

"Control yourself, man," Darling growled. He had come up behind Hammond and now clapped a weighty hand on his shoulder, swung him away from Florence with his surgeon's strength. "Leave the poor woman alone."

The poor woman, Hammond thought bitterly, glancing back at Florence as he allowed himself to be guided to his horse. Well, she would be alone. And so would he.

51

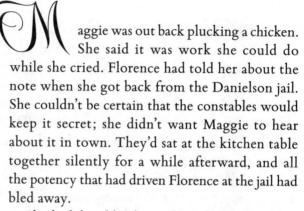aggie was out back plucking a chicken. She said it was work she could do while she cried. Florence had told her about the note when she got back from the Danielson jail. She couldn't be certain that the constables would keep it secret; she didn't want Maggie to hear about it in town. They'd sat at the kitchen table together silently for a while afterward, and all the potency that had driven Florence at the jail had bled away.

She hadn't told John and Sarah yet. Dr. Darling had offered to help explain to them, but she couldn't imagine watching that decent man repeat the story she'd constructed. Florence was so new to subterfuge that her mind was still scrambling for the means to explain this experience, to accustom herself to how it felt to deliver so massive a lie. Now she had to explain it to Agnes as well. If Agnes heard that Joseph was detained and didn't know what Florence had done to clear him all this lying would be for naught. She had to write at once. But at her desk, with paper and pen ready, she just sat and pressed the heels of her hands against her closed eyelids until lights burst in the darkness.

How in God's name was she meant to summarize the day's events?

A heavy pounding at the front door. She startled like a rabbit and barked her knee against the underside of the desk.

Florence's room was in the back of the house; she had no way to check who it might be. But she knew anyway. She'd been certain he would come.

Another resounding series of blows against the door.

FLORENCE STOOD AND UNLOCKED her desk drawer and took out Agnes's derringer. She didn't really know how to shoot it. You had to bend back the hammer—she tried it, then reversed it. Since she had taken the pistol from Agnes it had come into her mind at moments that it would feel good to aim at something, someone. It did not feel good to hold the thing now. She sucked in air and crooked her arm to tuck the pistol into the back of her waistband like a fist against her spine.

She could smell the alcohol on Hammond when she opened the door. A keen, angry stench. His gray eyes were red and watery, the top buttons of his waistcoat unfastened and a tendril of shirttail escaping at his belt. She'd never seen him like this. Her stomach dropped, but she spoke to him in a civil, guarded tone. "Dr. Hammond. What is it? Why have you come?"

"A fine greeting." He squinted over her shoulder. "Will you not invite me in? Are you harboring more fugitives?"

Just then Maggie called, distant, clearly having stuck her head in the back door when she heard the knocking: "All right, Miss Florence?"

"Yes, just fine, Maggie," she answered, eyes on Hammond as the back door slammed. He was swaying slightly in place like a tree with a great heavy crown. "Of course, come in." She stepped back from his whiskey emanations as he crossed the threshold. He drifted into the parlor. She watched him there amid the furniture so familiar she hardly ever noticed it: the ugly walnut hutch, the straight-backed tufted navy armchairs. The plates on the walls, the hand-knotted pink-and-blue oval rag rug on the floor, the small grandfather clock notching time with its ticks. He seemed to be looking it all over with faint distaste, his manners drowned in drink.

"Here to apologize." Hammond turned to face her. "As a gentleman must do. Shouldn't have spoken so harshly."

"I need no apology," she stammered. Something was wrong. A mismatch between what he was saying and what her body could tell of his anger. A thrumming note of peril beneath his polite words.

"No, you don't, do you?" He regarded her, discontented. "You don't need anything from me. A man appears, a man who wronged you, so you decide, on your own authority—he'll have mercy. Whether he deserves it or not."

"He didn't wrong me," she said, trying to believe it.

It was hard to tell what was wrong any longer. Had she been right to engineer Joseph's release so Hammond could not martyr him? To let Bertha bear the stain of self-murder, even though she had never completed the act? Was it right to keep the real events of Bertha's death from Hammond, to protect Agnes? She detested this man. Why did she feel so guilty for deceiving him?

"Don't lie," Hammond said sharply. "You don't want to know if he wronged you. You'd rather let him go than face what your precious Bertha got up to."

What she got up to. A lightskirt like her older sister. The baby on the bathroom floor, succumbing to her destiny.

"I don't care. I don't care what she did. I would never love her any less. If she took up with this Joseph, if she died by her own hand"—each time she said this, it felt more real—"I forgive her all of it. What would it help to hang an innocent man?"

He listed toward her, and she edged behind one of the armchairs to keep some barrier between them. He was breathing heavily, his mouth loose. "That fellow was never innocent. Not the day he was born."

"Dr. Hammond, you are acting in the strangest manner."

He laughed abruptly. "Am I? I can't judge. I think you"—he pointed at her—"*you* are acting quite strangely. I know you'd skin any man who touched her. But my suit was honorable. I would've married her. Next year—she'd be a wife. But this Joseph, him you wish good fortune—"

His certainty. His presumption. Her fingers clenched on the back of the armchair. "I wonder that you wanted to marry her, when you think so ill of her now."

"I would have cared for her." Hammond thrust a finger at her again. "If she'd declined. She'd have wanted for nothing with me. And who's to say"—the finger wavered—"outside that nest of vipers—did you no good, either, that college—"

"What?"

He straightened up and tried to smooth his waistcoat. "No," he said, "no matter." He turned away, moved urgently to the mantel as if it was vital that he examine the few trinkets displayed there. He touched the rim of a porcelain bowl, picked up a small ceramic lamb. Florence watched each movement as carefully as she had watched Bertha's infant chest rise and fall. Over his shoulder, he said, "Now what, then, Miss Mellish? You are resigned? We'll never find her body. Never know how she did it. Hold no one to account."

That was why she felt she must tell him what had truly happened. Because he believed he was entitled to know. His belief was so immense, so heavy with the world's support, that it had half pressed her into believing, too.

Bertha had gotten away from him, had broken a compact he alone had created, and he burned to discover how. He wanted the knowledge of her body—if not in marriage, in death. How it had failed and why. The same alarming hunger she'd seen when he stared at the dead girl in the Auburn tomb.

When she remained silent, Hammond turned back, eyebrows raised. He was still holding the lamb in a loose grip. The clock sounded unreasonably loud.

"What would you have me say?" Florence stammered.

He lifted his chin as if he scented her resistance and put down the lamb on the table beside the armchair closest to him, so gently that it didn't rock on its uneven clay feet.

"If she went mad," he said, slowly, sounding clearer than he had yet, "Agnes Sullivan must have known."

"No." A reaction she couldn't suppress.

"No? Living in each other's pockets, and she didn't know?"

"Stop this, Hammond," she said.

His eyes were steady on her face. He took three steps closer to her, and her chest heaved.

He said, "I've been meaning to pay the girl a visit in Boston. If she lied, she will answer for it."

He had found Agnes at Mrs. Hoban's, then. Her mother, too? He was too close. Too close to Agnes, too close to Florence. The whiskey smell again, rank on his breath. The height and bulk of him.

She reached back and jerked the derringer free. The *tock* of the hammer was so much louder than it had seemed in her bedroom. Hammond's bloodshot eyes widened. He stumbled back a step and lifted his hands. Lightning shot through her belly—terror and power at once.

"Damn you, you leave me alone," she told him. "Leave Agnes Sullivan alone. It's over. Bertha is dead."

He rushed her, and she tripped on the rug and nearly went down. His left hand came to her waist like they were dancing. She clutched at the gun's small stock, trying not to drop it, and he wrenched it from her hand effortlessly.

Florence cringed back. Her parents would hear the shot. Maggie. Someone would come.

But Hammond frowned down at the gun and thumbed the hammer up, then shoved it in his right trouser pocket. "No, no," he said, in a tone of sudden, eerie calm, "none of that, Florence."

It had all happened in an instant. They were both panting, his other hand still hot at her waist. The whole world smelled of sweat and liquor, and the grandfather clock ticked on relentlessly.

Hammond took her face in his sweaty hands and kissed her, bristly, sour, awful. Open-mouthed. Beseeching.

She got her hands up to shove him away, but he lurched back, covering his wet lips. He wasn't looking at her. She couldn't stop watching him. The handkerchief in his waistcoat pocket had been crushed by their bodies. The chain of his pocket watch hung askew.

Hammond ran a trembling hand over his face, straightened his collar. Then he turned and left. He didn't say one more word. His steps were still uneven, but he shut the front door quietly.

Florence scrubbed at her mouth with the back of her hand, suddenly weeping a little. Maggie came rushing in from the kitchen, crying out, "Miss Florence, oh, did he hurt you?" Her kind hands fluttered around Florence's face and body like delicate fearful sparrows. She dove forward and gathered Florence to her, and Florence's hands, empty now, came up to press against her warm back, then balled into fists.

"It's nothing," she whispered into Maggie's shoulder. "He's nothing."

52

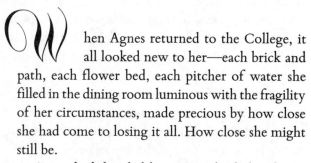hen Agnes returned to the College, it all looked new to her—each brick and path, each flower bed, each pitcher of water she filled in the dining room luminous with the fragility of her circumstances, made precious by how close she had come to losing it all. How close she might still be.

Agnes had dreaded how it might feel to begin a new school year without Bertha, without the vitalizing power of their fall reunion. Of course, this was foolish. Bertha had been just as dead in July as she was in August—the loss the same whether Agnes was in South Hadley or Mrs. Hoban's mansion. But each new marker of time that passed without her ached.

She came back a week before classes began. Mrs. Hoban had left to take the waters at Ballston Spa and had declared that Agnes, too, should get out of the dreadful city heat. "Nobody stays in town in August, child," she'd said, counting out the fare for a first-class train ticket as if she wasn't perfectly aware that Agnes would travel third-class and save the rest.

To escape the heat she took to reading in the Pepper Box after breakfast circle, when the air still hung cool over the dewy grass. Few girls were back yet, so she was not likely to be disturbed. But on the third morning she was startled from her zoology text by the sound of her name—startled again to see that the speaker was Mrs. Mead.

"Miss Sullivan, good morning," the president said as she approached the gazebo. "You're looking well. I trust your time with Mrs. Hoban has been satisfactory." She looked well herself. Better rested, her shirtwaist starched crisp against the humid air. She nodded at the bench beside Agnes, who hurried to clear her books away and to tamp down a flare of that constant, ambient fear.

"Most satisfactory, Mrs. Mead, thank you. I am grateful to you and Dr. Clapp for the reference."

Mrs. Mead sat with a sigh. It felt distinctly strange to sit next to her in the gazebo as if they were peers dillydallying before a class. "I'm glad you have returned. I know it must be difficult."

"Yes."

"We would be disappointed to lose you, Miss Sullivan." She could feel Mrs. Mead giving her a long, considering look. Another sigh gusted over Agnes's hands where they lay folded on her lap. "Let me be direct. I understand that Miss Mellish's family has good reason to believe that she did end her life. I expect that you have already been informed of this."

"I have." Florence had written her about Joseph's reappearance, the "discovery" of the note, and Hammond's wrath. Once more she'd forbidden Agnes to consider giving herself up. Then more letters, as the summer progressed—Hammond *had* left her alone, Florence wrote, her bafflement clear, and the scuttlebutt from her housekeeper was that he was drinking habitually. *He has become quite unpredictable. You must remain cautious, Agnes.*

"I am very sorry," Mrs. Mead said with unusual feeling.

"They have not found her remains." Agnes spoke steadily. "Nothing is certain."

"Of course." They both stared out over the quiet campus for a moment. "We will make no announcement to the student body. But rumor is difficult to contain. I will inform the faculty of this development so that they can be alert to any whispers. They will be circumspect, Miss Sullivan, you may trust in that."

"Thank you," she whispered. Mrs. Mead's hand gripped her own for just a moment, a squeeze of her knuckles, then retreated.

"A sad event indeed." The president pushed up from the bench and looked down on Agnes with a warm, reserved expression. "You will let me know, Miss Sullivan, if you encounter any difficulties this year. I am sure you will make her proud."

Agnes sat in the Pepper Box for another thirty minutes that morning without ever touching her textbook—simply working to breathe without the stabbing spasm near her breastbone that periodically afflicted her, as if ghostly fingers scrabbled at the cartilage there.

HER OWN INCLINATION WOULD have been to skip the senior traditions, but Florence had told her she ought to do the minimum expected. *Don't make waves,* Florence had written, and Agnes pictured herself, a solitary boat, wakeless in a quiet channel. She submitted herself to occasional interactions with the junior girl Ida Burney chose for her, an unobjectionable blond Mainer named Rosamond, whom Agnes had never noticed before, who at least had an interest in chemistry.

She knew at once when Rosamond learned about Bertha. The juniors were supposed to bring their seniors breakfast in bed on the second Sunday of term, but Agnes, uncomfortable with the servitude that required, had requested that they meet by Lower Lake to eat instead. The day dawned gray and glaring. Rosamond had spread a blanket on the grassy bank and set out a tray with hard-boiled eggs and toast and another small jar of the blueberry preserves she'd brought from home. "No use hoarding, it's made to be eaten," she'd said stoutly when delivering the first jar. Agnes had already gathered, with appreciation, that Rosamond was not one for frivolity, either. So she was surprised to see that her place at the picnic was marked with a fat bouquet of white flowers—chrysanthemums and Queen Anne's lace—and that Rosamond would not quite look at her as she picked it up.

"What's this?"

Rosamond shrugged and pushed a reddish-blond curl behind her ear. "You're my senior, aren't you?" She was blushing a little, on the apples of her round cheeks.

Of course Rosamond would have heard by now. Bertha's absence was no longer such a sensation, and the other girls were careful not to gossip where they knew Agnes could hear. But she listened from the kitchen, from her library carrel, from behind her cracked-open door, and she knew they were inviting even the freshmen into the mystery. *You'll never believe what happened on Founder's Day last year*—

The students knew the search had ended, though they were unsure why. Some had guessed that evidence of suicide had come to light while others, having read Stroslev's article or a similar report, believed that Bertha must be confined by her family. Agnes had even heard a girl whisper that Bertha had converted to Mormonism and run off to the new state of Utah to find a husband there.

They watched Agnes, distantly. They were not unkind. Alone and ignored or alone and pitied—it didn't make much difference. But it pricked her unexpectedly to see what she read as pity in Rosamond's candid blue eyes.

Agnes lifted the bouquet to her nose, breathing in the acrid herbal tang of the chrysanthemums and the carroty greenness of the Queen Anne's lace.

Queen Anne's lace had once been widely used as a contraceptive. A woman could chew the seeds or make a tea of the dried flowers, which was said to be more pleasant. Agnes had been in the library often since she'd returned to campus. In its silent stacks she'd read of yarrow and rue and a mysterious herb called silphium that had once flowered in the Mediterranean. She'd recorded abstracts of this information—for what purpose, she did not exactly know, even as she wrote. Because the knowledge had been preserved for a reason. Because even lore might save a woman someday.

After that breakfast, Agnes tried to distance herself further. But Rosamond remained diligent and respectful in her role. On Mountain Day, when classes were canceled and the rest of the campus wandered about in the woods and orchards and Agnes studied, Rosamond dropped an apple at Agnes's carrel. She saved a seat for Agnes at assemblies, delivered plates of fudge and crackers from the other girls' parties, even offered to carry Agnes's armful of books to the lab.

Agnes dried the round sprays of Queen Anne's lace and crumbled the flower heads into an envelope along with a few relevant lines of information about its use as a tea. She handed the envelope to Rosamond one morning and did not comprehend—would never comprehend—the way the gift seemed to spark a disappointed confusion in the girl rather than the gratitude she'd anticipated. She liked Rosamond; she wanted to protect her. Still, the withdrawal she sensed there was a relief. It was a little tedious to have somebody paying attention to her comings and goings, trying do her favors, and asking about her work—somebody who wasn't Bertha.

IN THE MIDST OF the blizzard of 1898, Agnes wrote her applications for medical school. She submitted the finished essays for Dr. Clapp's approval, as there was no one else she wished to ask to read her work.

When graduation time came, after a long cool spring, she was still waiting to hear back from several schools—but she'd received an acceptance to the medical school of Tufts College. It was not Harvard Medical School, but it would do. She mailed letters to two addresses to notify them: to the little apartment on Thayer Street and to Florence in Killingly.

Mrs. Mead had decided their class ought to commemorate

Bertha with a short service in the chapel the afternoon before Commencement. Like all the College's attempts to honor Bertha, the kindness of the impulse was alloyed by its complete mismatch with what she would have wanted. A marathon reading from the Neoplatonic philosophers—that Bertha would've considered an excellent tribute. But Agnes would go. She would do this one last thing.

The Porter girls were there: Rosamond, chatting attentively with a younger girl Agnes didn't recognize, and Eva, Ida, Eugenie, and Daisy.

So was Florence Mellish, seated in the front row beside Clapp and Dr. Neilson. She nodded to Agnes when their eyes met but did not call her over.

The pastor began with a prayer. Then Eva Bissell, blushing, stood and sang a hymn about trusting in God, the Father, whose love shall never fail. *In Thy arms I rest forever, safe within the second veil.*

Mrs. Mead gave a short speech praising Bertha's accomplishments at the College and expressing the great sadness they all felt at her absence on this day of celebration, never venturing into distasteful specificity about the reason for that absence. The girls did look sad, Agnes saw, but composed. The fever of their fear had passed months ago. They'd committed Bertha to memory, lacquered her rough edges with sentiment. After the service concluded they filed out hastily, eager to spend their last golden evening on campus with their friends. Eva pressed Agnes's hand as she passed, Rosamond nodded to her, and Mrs. Mead and the professors paused to congratulate her on the awards she had already been given.

Their footsteps echoed among the wooden pews and the grand stone arches. Just Agnes standing in the aisle then, and Florence, both dressed in black. The two who knew the most.

"Magna cum laude." Florence's brown eyes were steady and warm on Agnes's face, as Bertha's would have been. "Well done."

"It would have been summa," said Agnes, "except, you know."

She had won Best Science Student, a commendation for her Latin translations, another for her anatomical drawing. She felt that she ought not be proud but she was.

Florence smiled.

"I couldn't have," Agnes began, and faltered. "Without you."

"I know."

"You won't stay for the ceremony." She wasn't sure what answer she would prefer—Florence in the audience as she accepted her diploma, or not.

Florence shook her head. "They won't read her name. Mrs. Mead asked, but I'd rather not."

A long pause. Agnes didn't know what to say. Florence touched the back of the pew beside them.

"You'll write to me, Agnes." It wasn't a request. "When you earn your medical degree. When you find a residency. Any accomplishment, I would like to know about it."

Agnes gave a fierce nod. "Yes."

"Look forward." Florence's voice dropped low. "Not back to this time. You've done well here. But you must—you must try to put it away now, everything that happened."

Agnes nodded again, patiently, at this instruction she did not need. Florence couldn't see, even now, the structure of her mind. Agnes Sullivan, all enclosure.

"What will you do?" It occurred to her suddenly that Florence would have no such triumphant alteration to sever her from these memories, no awards, no promise of the scalpel and the saw.

Florence looked up into the remote elevations of the chapel. "I imagine I'll care for my parents until they die," she said calmly. "Eventually I'll retire from teaching, though not as soon as I would like, and not long after I'll grow infirm myself, and someone else will have to care for me. I'll have a small pension."

"You'll be safe." That was the important thing.

Florence laughed a little. "Yes. I'll be safe."

THE TWO WHO KNEW the most.

The two who built the story. Agnes, who tried to save Bertha, and Florence, who did save Agnes.

Even their shared knowledge had one terrible omission. A lacuna: the word that can mean a missing section of a manuscript or a hole in bone.

They had come so close to the truth. Bertha had in fact written a note, when she was at her lowest.

It was, like the note Florence crafted, addressed to Joseph. But that was the chief similarity. This real note was not brief and functional. It was a cry, not a resolute dispatch.

Bertha burnt this note herself, in the furnace that would become her grave.

This is what she wrote:

Joseph—I cannot call you by your summer name in this cold season.

I must part from you—I am sorry—you asked for none of this. I will try to remember you light of heart, light-fingered, juggling lunch-pail apples, your only requests my body & my good humor. You said, What are you reading, never mind, I will fall right to sleep, no, please, keep on, your voice is pleasant, I will just doze ici—your head in my lap, where you like it. I hold to that. The dregs of pleasure in a sour cup.

When I told you of my father, this summer, you did not want to believe it, either. Mais non, you said, over & over—it cannot be true—such beauty from such sin! You examined my hands, & lips, as evidence, or distraction.

But it is true, you see.

He loved your mother too much, Sarah Mellish said to me one day last May. Merely that & I knew, I KNEW that she did not speak of herself. I could see a scream in her eyes, locked away. I have always seen it. But I didn't know why.

I thought my home safe enough—as hapless children do. It was what I knew. I thought it usual to follow nighttime prayers with bolting the bedroom door—not once did I consider what or WHOM the lock barred. I, queer solitary bird as the girls love to call me, rarely stayed in others' houses. My mother—once-my-mother—was of little use, but I could look to Florence for everything.

She screwed the bolt to the jamb. She lifted me from Father's lap as from a precipice. Before Agnes, Florence was my happiness—yet I did not value her properly. I thought less of her for leaving college. But she did not warn me! She did not tell me. I did not KNOW.

I watched them, this summer, after I learnt my origins. In his dotage he becomes like her child. I thought I, too, would scream to see it.

You made me scream. I thank you for it, but no longer.

Agnes is all I have, you see. All I will have. Work, & Agnes.

I told you because I cannot tell her—I had to purge that knowledge. I could not bear to see a change upon her face: disgust or even a kind discomfort like your own. She would assure me of her love, I know. She would swear to it, & I would disbelieve her.

She is why I came to you—I thought you would guess it, scent it out—something burnt at my heart. A hunger, hollow. After the fire, we were always together, & striking off each other—sparks.

I can't tell her what I feel. At times I have considered it, but there is something in her face, well though I love it, that repels confidences—a line of judgment to the mouth—& now too many secrets stoppered up in me.

You diverted me—like a river from its banks. I should have denied you. & yet—by whose morality? I would walk into Old Main aflame before I would walk into Heaven to join the God my father preaches of—so it is well—that there IS no Heaven, & that I would be cast from it.

Tu reviendras, you told me—but I will not.

B

Later, the note's ashes mixed with Bertha's in the furnace chamber. Nobody read it. It changed nothing. Bertha went to Agnes and confessed the one secret she could bear to impart. Agnes went to the lab to steal a catheter.

But we can read it now. We can listen. We can know.

gnes was cutting—what was she cutting today? She had grown used to the dreaming haze of surgical work, the smudges in the corners of her vision, the odd brightness the world took on when she had to emerge from the hospital to return to the two-room apartment where she lived alone or to visit Mrs. Hoban.

On the worst and longest days she sometimes shook herself alert mid-motion to find her knife embedded in someone's skin. But today she was awake and ready, though it was day only because her shift at Boston City Hospital had already passed through a long night; today she was cutting a man's thigh to remove a tumor growing close to the femoral artery, to shave away at it, to peel the fine threads of blood vessel from its surface like stringy pith from an orange. Her specialties were general and emergency surgery; Florence Mellish had tried to insist that she work in gynecology or obstetrics. It was the only stipulation of their agreement that Agnes defied.

Mrs. Hoban hated the nurse Agnes had secured for her. "I need a doctor here, child, not some hopped-up nursemaid," she'd complained on their last visit, still angry that Agnes no longer lived with her in the huge house. On the night before Agnes had moved to her apartment, though, the old woman had directed one of the servant girls to shove a paper under Agnes's bedroom door—a formal-looking Last Will and Testament, naming Agnes as her sole beneficiary. They'd never spoken of it, before or since.

While Agnes cut, alert in the early hours of that morning in 1902, Higham lay awake in the darkness of a Lower East Side single-room-occupancy hotel, present, quiet, listening to a different sort of incantation as the couple in the room beside him fought about the man's fondness for a bar girl. "I din' fuck her," the man replied in answer to each piece of evidence offered by his shrieking lover, and Higham smiled at his tenacity and smiled again, truly delighted, when the man's blunt repetition finally won the day and the bed began to creak and thump as if the row had never occurred. The behavior of men and women together would keep private eyes like himself gainfully employed in perpetuity.

And Florence—like Higham, awake, alone. She had not been wrong when she imagined her last years, our Florence. She had always been clear-eyed. For the next twenty years her life stretched on much as she had predicted.

On February 20, 1919, Florence wrote the following note from Melrose, Massachusetts. Her parents had been dead for a number of years, and she was sitting up in the guest-room bed in a friend's home—another former teacher from the high school who had moved north, a woman lucky enough not to be alone. She had received an inquiry from the College about how Bertha ought to be listed in its catalogue of alumnae.

By then, with the false suicide note buried in the memories of the Killingly constables, Florence could be delicately vague with anyone who inquired about Bertha. It was one of the few kindnesses time afforded her.

> Dear Miss Cremell,
> You will pardon the delay in answering your kind note which has been forwarded me from Killingly.
> I think I can suggest it might be best to omit my sister's name

from the address book and later to place after her name in the general catalogue—died in 1897. I have had the date engraved in the family monument under her name.

I have no knowledge of my dear sister except what I could gather at the College some time after her disappearance, but I always think of her as dead. Her loss, as you can understand, was a terrible tragedy in our family life and is to me a perpetual sorrow. My usual address is Killingly, Ct., but I am spending the winter in Melrose.

Yours very sincerely,
Florence Mellish

The College sent Florence alumnae update cards, too: little squares of paper lined with aggressively cheerful questions about their graduates' accomplishments. At first she filled them out dutifully: *Date entered College: 1874. Date left College: 1875.*

She wrote that she was teaching in Rhode Island and Connecticut, but under *Your Work or Position (specify exactly)*, she wrote *Housekeeping*. The rest remained blank. No family, husband, children.

On a questionnaire dated December 1920, she wrote: *I am a cripple boarding in an institution called "The Old People's Home."* Those quotation marks, sharpened at the edges, cut indiscriminately. The College and the "Home" and Florence herself: all sliced to shreds. Nonetheless, she still completed the section marked *Publications*, noting some *Fugitive poems and stories in* Independent, Springfield Republican, Boston Post, *etc.* But by 1924, when the next questionnaire arrived, she did not mention her writing at all. In the space after *My occupation is:*, she wrote in a shakier hand: *Invalid.*

On New Year's Day in 1931, aged seventy-five, she died—on Bertha's birthday.

Henry Hammond did not live so long. He died in Saratoga Springs, though it was reported in the Yale medical journal that he had died instead in California after moving there in 1903 in an attempt to restore his failing health. The next decade obliterated him, then erased him. By 1912 he was dead. The journal reported no specific cause, but that was typical for cases of his sort, in which it was difficult to determine whether the deceased had simply been cleaning a gun or had meant to fire it. Even a little derringer needed careful handling.

Agnes did read the Yale medical journal on occasion, but she did not read the issue that noted Hammond's death. She had just been promoted to visiting physician, and she slept some nights, some afternoons in a closet in the surgery ward with a cot jammed into it. Once it had been the mop-drying closet, and during Agnes's tenure at the hospital it still smelled of foul damp. The cot reminded her of her bed in the apartment where her mother and sister still lived. Sometimes she read while lying on the cot, if she was too jittery from an operation to sleep. Sometimes she fell into dreams and in those dreams she heard from behind a closed door the cry of a woman in pain.

We can see behind the door now, with Agnes.

Behind the door it was always Bertha.

It wasn't the surgery Agnes dreamed about, the failed D&C, but the aftermath. Bertha on the floor beside her bed, curled in on herself, wearing her wrapper and nightgown as if she had meant to go to sleep, though it was midmorning. Sweating and white, her hair fallen over her face. In the dream Agnes knelt beside her. She knew she shouldn't move Bertha, but she pulled her into her lap anyway and Bertha whimpered. *What is wrong?* Agnes asked, every time, as if the answer would differ, and every time Bertha told her that it hurt, which she knew already, and then she began to cry and Agnes began to cry. Agnes remembered holding Adelaide that way when her sister was little and remembered Nora holding Adelaide after her troubles. Agnes and Bertha sitting on the floor crying and crying until Bertha took a sharp breath and pushed herself off Agnes's knee and said, *Shut the door.* So Agnes did, and Bertha lay down upon the floor again, on her side like a fetal animal, and talked with her eyes closed against the pain and delirium. *You have to understand*, she said, but Agnes never understood, and as Bertha talked tears pooled in the tiny divot beside her left eye, the medial canthus, and dripped across the bridge of her nose.

The terrible flashes. Bertha's teeth clenched as she talked, her damp forehead. *No one will know what has happened to me. No one will find out. You have to lie.* Bertha's face set and awful in the dining room on Founder's Day as she asked Mabel to go for a walk, and Mabel, cheery, distracted, did not notice how sick she looked already. *The furnace is new. But be sure—you must be sure—*

Be strong—

Bertha's breath, shallow and whispery, falling down upon Agnes from the height of her bed where Agnes lay on the floor. The sun moving across the wall of Bertha's room. How slowly and how quickly it went. And outside the girls singing to Mary Lyon's grave, not a care in their hearts, as Bertha died. Agnes's sobs under their music.

Agnes's own cry muffled in the little hospital closet as she woke.

The surgery ward was never quiet, but in the smallest hours of the morning it was as quiet as a hospital can be. The patients from the day's surgeries had been moved elsewhere for care, and the only operations ongoing were of the direst sort, true emergencies that could not be put off even for hours. Their noise remained concentrated behind doors pulled shut. In the main hallway, the hall onto which the sleeping closet opened, something close to silence settled in. If Agnes opened the door in those quieter hours and slipped down the hallway with her white coat rustling around her thighs, if she walked past the porthole windows in the doors of the operating theatres and saw her colleagues—all of them male—not in need of her assistance, she might exit the surgery ward and turn to the stairway at the end of the building. There her footsteps echoed on concrete and metal. There she could descend to the belching heat of the furnace room beneath the wards. In the winter, the nurses and the orderlies sometimes snuck down to laze in its heat, so Agnes looked about her as she entered to be certain she was alone.

Of course, Agnes was always alone.

In the furnace room she took off her doctor's coat and unfastened the topmost button of her blouse. Step by slow step she walked deeper into the room, and when she stopped she stood so close to the contained fire that droplets of sweat formed at her hairline and ran down the length of her jaw like tears. Perhaps mixing with tears.

Or perhaps not.

54

Poem written by Florence Mellish and published along with her obituary in the Windham County Transcript, *January 8, 1931.*

The boatman pierced the shrouding mist
    That hides the farther shore
And pushed across the dark, still stream
    With strong and silent oar.

A gaunt, gray form, he stood erect
    And raised a beckoning hand.
They answered one by one; the boat
    Was gliding from the strand.

I reached lame arms, my eyes were wet,
    For I was left behind.
Beneath his stern and shaggy brows,
    The boatman's eyes were kind.

Again he crossed the stream. His course
    Was neither slow nor swift;
But arrow-straight through those gray mists
    And clouds that never lift.

I linger on the sunlit side
    With eyes no longer wet;
The boatman tarries for a while,
    But he will not forget.

END.

MARY DEAR, AT LAST you have asked me
to tell you the whole story of your mother. Why
did you wait until you had gone away to school that
I must write it to you? If your mother's life had been
a fortunate, a happy one, you should have known her
story long before you had reached your nineteenth
year. But now wait a little longer. I shall see you soon.

You say I have not told you enough about my
own life, either. I am not after writing, Mary, for I
think the education that came so late fits clumsily
upon me, like gloves on work-worn hands. Still I
will tell you a story now of that long-ago mill-life
of mine. It shall be a sequel to our hearth stories of
my girlhood on the Massachusetts farm.

It was June of the second year that I worked in
the finishing room of Mattawaugan woolen mill
where Boss Darley set a new hand to burl with me.
Not over skilful myself, tho' I had worked so long,
I crossly obeyed him. "Show 'er how, an' look after
the knots on her side the cut." The new hand wrote
her name for the boss, Marie Racine—a pretty
name, I thought, as apt for her trim prettiness as was
Maggie Klemm for my clumsy strength.

She was a dainty, tiny thing, quite French from
the heels of her brown leather shoes to the little
aigrette on her straw hat. It rained that first morning
Marie worked in the finishing room, and the rain-
drops had made little white streaks down her pink
cheeks. The girls were murmuring, "The little
one's washed her rouge off crying for mamma;"
but Marie's bright hazel eyes shed no tears. She

radiated cheerfully in the damp room. "What a jolly, big dance hall," she said, "and there is my partner!" As French Joe, six feet three and well proportioned, came lumbering up with a load of cuts. Another thing I shouldn't have noticed if the hands hadn't been murmuring about "that deformed girl"—one of the new girl's shoulders was a trifle higher than the other.

Teaching Marie to burl was not hard. Her little hands had felt all over her side and cut and taken out every knot and running long before I was ready to pull over. She used to burl half my side, too, when the boss wasn't by those summer days, and I could turn about and look across the street with its swarming children, sweet even in their rags and dirt. Out on the walk that led to the wall in front of the mill they had a rendezvous. I can see now the towheaded lad from across the way hopping along on his bare toes, astride the imaginary support of a decrepit velocipede, whose two remaining wheels, fastened together with rope, parted company at every jolt and set off independent, and his chubby neighbor keeping time to the ceremony with solemn and extreme contortions of face and limbs. How Marie laughed! She reached a penny to the towheaded urchin out of the window, but she threw the chubby one's penny at him; he was so grimy. Past the little brown mill tenement across the way, with its rainbow of clotheslines in the rear, I looked, to the hillside beyond with twinkling birches, sedate oaks and grim pines on its crown, and farther yet to the low, green craggy mountain range outlined against the northern sky. Beyond these mountains flowed the wild Moswansicutt River, to which our placid little mill stream was taking its way. Those were happy days for me that summer, when Marie made the work no longer hard. The sunshine preceded us in the morning and waited upon us home at night. All out-of-doors looked in at our open windows. The girl beside me sang softly at her work, and the mill was even a cheerful place. I pacified my conscience with the thought that if Marie did most of the burling, I did all the lifting and pulling.

She proved very popular with the French girls, who, with French aptness, called her "La Petite." Not counting the two or three English and Americans and myself, half the hands in the finishing room were of French descent or birth, and half of them Irish. I was the only German. There was bad blood between the French and the Irish. The gaunt leader of the Irish faction, Lily Galooly, one of the sewers-in, took a great liking for La Petite, and it came about that in gathering around her to hear her chatter or sing at noon, the two parties mingled on neutral ground in friendliness, and the feud was healed.

Marie and I were good friends. She told me how she had left her home, "because Papa isn't steady, you see." Ah yes! I saw, too, why the child was so slender and small, and how the slight deformity was caused. Marie had never known her mother.

Do you think I am long in telling my story, Mary? I linger over those bright days. Darkness and sorrow came too soon.

One August morning Marie was to come to the Mill an hour late, for she had gone the night before to visit friends in the adjoining town, where her home had been. Boss Darley gave her leave of absence rather gruffly, for the work was pressing. The southbound train came in at seven-thirty and Marie did not arrive. Boss Darley waited an hour longer, then sent for someone to take her place. He was just and stern. "She'll be shelved sure," Lily Galooly said, when I went down to her place with the cut. "What'll she do now?" I could not bear the Irish woman's excited interest. "Marie is the best burler in the room," I answered. "Boss Darley will be glad enough to excuse her and get her back."

Not many minutes after that, as I looked out, Marie coming hastily up the street, already blinding with dust and glare, stopped in front of the mill to speak to French Joe, bent under a heavy cut he was bringing around. Boss Darley was looking out too. His stern eyes grew sterner as he saw the child stop. She came in and, nodding to me, passed to the boss's desk to speak to him. He was writing a note. The girl waited. It was her dismissal. Her face did not change as she walked firmly out between the rows of piled up cuts and the shearing machines on one side, and the burlers' boards and sewers' frames on the other, speaking or signing a kind good-bye to the sympathetic, excited hands.

Work was very hard to get for a skilled, strong hand just then; it proved impossible to get for Marie. She had made many friends, but they were poor. I loved her as I love you, my little girl. I had no home then to which to bring Marie.

French Joe took Marie to his cottage over the hill. She could not be his wife. In Canada years before he had parted from his wife. Ah, how my heart sickened the day that news went out as I passed the group of French girls shrugging pitying shoulders over "La Petite qui s'est revenue tard." No more to try to get work for Marie! Yet once I went to that house to see her. If only I might bring her away. Surely some place could be found.

It was a lonely little house standing at the end of a green lane. Marie was bending over some bright asters in the yard as I came in sight of it. The tears blinded my eyes as I saw the familiar little figure. When I went round a clump of arbor vitae it disappeared, and the house was locked and still when I stood at the door.

There was a darker contrast for me in those winter days than the mere noisy loneliness of the mill room, now shut in by its glazed windows from all the world outside. The arrival of good fortune in the portly person of Uncle Fritz broke only the outward monotony of my life, leaving the inner grief unchanging. The good God spare me such another sorrow! None but you could give it to me, Mary, and you are good and true, I know, and never will.

Staying in Mattawaugan till I should go to school the succeeding fall, once more I tried to see my poor girl, in May, five weeks after her baby was born. She seemed to have no friends now. The little house looked desolate and uncared for, unlike anything which could belong to Marie. There was no one in the yard, no visible life in the house. I sat down by the step, to wait even till French Joe came home. I must see Marie, help her, comfort her.

I do not know just how long I had sat by the step, in the warm sunshine, quite still, thinking sadly of happy days that had been and of the sad days that were and were to be, when something made me look around. There was no sound, I think. Just at the turn of the wall behind the house, I saw a little figure that I knew, stealthily disappear. Instantly I called Marie, and followed. She knew without looking back that she was pursued. Surely I was mad to pursue her. A rumor that I had heard had made me so persistent to see her. It was that which made me follow now. They said in the village that La Petite à Joseph was not herself, that French Joe had twice brought her back from the river road. Had the sight of me, stirring bitter memories, recalled that dreadful purpose?

She had not turned to the road now. She could not without passing in front of me as I sat. On the east the road skirted round the mountains; she was going straight toward them. Down a hill we ran, across a stream at its foot, and up a slight incline through a narrow belt of hemlock trees that skirted the foothills of Mount Holly. Then there were rough woodcutters' paths winding among broken ledges and boulders. On she went, ever the same undiminishable distance before me. The paths stopped. Surely she could not, would not go further. In despair I called to her. She paid no heed, lightly scaling the scarred faces of the crags. But I knew the mountain better than Marie, and I saw the way she went, straight as death to the river on the other side. Near the spot where I stopped a deep gorge cleft the heart of the mountain, and down it flowed a little stream. I ran with all my might up the stream's bed, climbed the precipice at its head, clinging to the clefts in the rocks, and reached the west summit, to find Marie skimming along the ledge that walled it before me. Unless that strange endurance should fail there was hardly a hope of catching her now. A fresh danger was added. The north side of the mountain was a precipitous mass of trap rock. Between the crumbling cliffs, steep slopes covered with square-edged loose stones, large and small, broken from their faces, ready to be dislodged at a touch. If I followed Marie, clinging by the hands to the same roots and branches, at every movement I should start stones that might fall upon her in their downward course. I waited in agonized suspense at the top. Without a glance back, always looking for a bush or tree to cling to, now sitting and sliding with the sliding stones, now staying the doubtful support of some dead branch by a yet more doubtful foothold, every moment escaping the danger which seemed unescapable, she reached the belt of trees that clothed the steep base of the mountain just above the river, and disappeared in them.

She would hear no sound and know that no one followed her over the rocks. The time was endless, yet unrealizable. Suddenly I heard the sound that warned me that the river had its own. Then I flung myself down those rocks, lost my hold, and fell. They found us both that night; Marie at rest, it seemed, with none of the death agony in her still face; me bruised, half covered with a mass of small stones, at the foot of the low cliff.

In my long illness afterward I felt happier about Marie than I had for many months. Heaven's mercy had let her out from her shamed, stifled life to a guiltless death.

There is only a word more of the story, Mary. Marie's baby was left to me by the dead mother and the living father, and I loved her as Marie's self. That was eighteen years ago. Yes, darling, that was you.

Bertha Lane Mellish.
South Hadley, Mass.

Author's Note

HISTORICAL FICTION READERS
JUSTLY wonder what's real and what a writer has
created. This novel is based on real historical events
and incorporates many real figures, documents,
and newspaper stories, but the story it constructs
is deeply fictionalized. Bertha Mellish was never
found, nor does it seem that a suicide note, or other
clear evidence of her fate, was ever discovered.

I stumbled across an account of Bertha's mysterious unsolved disappearance from the Mount
Holyoke campus while working as a graduate
research intern at the Harry Ransom Center, the
rare books and manuscript archive at the University
of Texas at Austin, in 2009. My internship duties
included answering patron queries; someone had
written in with an exceptionally broad genealogical
question related to the Spanish-American War that
sent me skimming through microfilm copies of
the *New York Journal-American* from the late 1890s,
feeling increasingly motion sick. I paused at a story
from 1900 headlined LED TO DEATH BY HER CHILD OF
FANCY—an account of Bertha's disappearance and
supposed death as explained by Henry Hammond,
the family doctor. Hammond suggested that Bertha
had gotten so caught up in her own fiction that she'd
died by suicide, like the character Marie in her short
story. (The manuscript is indeed real and was published at the time.) I was struck by the headline, by
Hammond's evident obsessiveness, and by the lithographed illustration of Bertha's serious face, drawn
from the broadside image included in this book.

Having graduated from Smith College, I found the women's college setting and the historical differences between Smith and Mount Holyoke simultaneously familiar, strange, and tremendously compelling. As a PhD student, my first impulse was to dive into the archives—as a novelist, my second impulse was to make a lot of things up.

Agnes is entirely fictional, as is Higham (though the Mellishes did employ detectives). Because I was interested in exploring the aftermath of Bertha's disappearance, I needed her to have a closer friend at college than she appeared to in life. Very early in the process of conceiving the book, I thought that Agnes might be Bertha's personal maid—some current Smith students live in tiny single rooms still known as "maids' quarters"—but discovered that Mount Holyoke required all students to contribute to the College's domestic work. So Agnes became a student, an equally driven fellow outsider with a lot to lose; while nativist discrimination against the Irish in particular had receded from its peak in the 1850s–60s, anti-Catholic sentiment still animated many Americans.

Mount Holyoke did not officially admit Catholic students until 1899. Its founder, Mary Lyon, disapproved of Catholicism and saw Catholic schools as a nefarious means of expanding the Roman church's "dominion" in the United States. As late as 1846, an alumna reported back with horror that a fellow alum had converted to Catholicism: "She is a person of fine talents and a good scholar . . . It is a mystery to me how any enlightened person can become a Catholic." After a battle for approval through the 1920s, a Newman Club for Catholic students was finally formed on campus by 1934.

The college girls are nearly all fictional, though a student was sent home for stealing in 1900—"a very pretty stylish girl—unusually attractive and very fascinating," who was taking money from her housemates in Rockefeller, according to Amy Roberts's letters home. I've excerpted letters written by Amy and Helen Calder, which are preserved in Mount Holyoke's Special

340 • Katharine Beutner

Collections, and borrowed their personas. The girls' passionate friendships, crushes, frequent cross-dressing in theatrical productions, and "dear baby" letters are all drawn from the archives. The question of how thoroughly the romance of these relationships would overlap with contemporary understandings of queer love between women is complicated—understandings of identity in relation to sexuality were quite different (the Foucauldian take), romantic friendships between women were celebrated (as Lillian Faderman has documented), the existence of sexual connections between women was often obscured (cf. the Woods-Pirie case, which Faderman addresses in *The Scotch Verdict*), and the pathologization of queer sex was just beginning. I do feel confident that a man like Henry Hammond would've been mystified by the ways the girls related to one another, ways that certainly could read as queer to modern eyes. For example, Helen Calder wrote to her parents:

> Marie Nelles took me to the Junior entertainment Tuesday night, and [Toby?] Bellam was up visiting then and went with us. I had a very nice time, especially or since I didn't have to pay for anything. I see how nice it must be to have some one to pay the bills, though I should rather go with a nice girl like Marie Nelles than a *man*. (Emphasis hers)

Yet the potentially subversive elements of the campus community at the time were thoroughly intertwined with oppression. Because the letters and scrapbooks preserved in Mount Holyoke's Special Collections document the everyday lives of the students in the late 1890s, these materials reveal not just their hard scholarly work and devotion to one another but their casual racism. As Hilary Mantel wrote about historical fiction: "A relation of past events brings you up against events and mentalities that, should you choose to describe them, would bring you to the borders of what your readers could bear. The danger you have to negotiate is not the dimpled coyness of the past—it is its obscenity."

In the archives, I found a hand-colored invitation to a cake-walk party, pink and green and black, shaped like a slice of watermelon. At this party the white students performed for one another in blackface. A girl named Edith Packard wrote to her parents: "You would have laughed I am sure to see a great roomful of ordinarily fairly pretty girls transformed into a company of darkies . . . There is nothing that takes away one's self-respect so much as blacking up, but I don't believe it hurts one to act like a goose for one evening." Afterward, she wrote, she felt "morally heroic" for being bold enough to parade in blackface and wrote of the "great satisfaction" of being chosen, with her cross-dressed partner, to compete for the cake at the party's end. In the novel, Agnes briefly sees the wig Mabel wore for her winning cakewalk when she sneaks into Mabel's room to plant the knife. As this moment indicates, the segregated society in which Agnes, Florence, Higham, and Hammond move is foundational to their experiences. They interact with comparatively few Black and brown characters and live largely in ignorance of the lives of their contemporaries of color. This reflects the segregation I observed in the documents I drew on as well as my desire to avoid tokenizing characters of color or including historically accurate scenes of racist behavior in ways that might feel subordinated to the disappearance of a missing white college girl.

Though she would not think of it, the intense pressure Agnes herself feels to defend her position at Mount Holyoke and prove her "worth" has its roots in 1890s white America's sense of precarity and racist paranoia. As white reactionaries of this time fretted about the social changes that were creating the "New Woman"—bold, educated, independent, participating in the public sphere—they also developed Jim Crow laws, enshrined "separate but equal" in Supreme Court precedent, and, in Wilmington, NC, in 1898, conducted a white-supremacist coup. The coexistence of these fears was (and is) not coincidental.

Some coincidences in the book *are* real: Hammond was a cat fancier, and the girls did dissect cats and reassemble their skeletons in Dr. Clapp's zoology class, as described enthusiastically by Amy Roberts. Before she disappeared, Bertha was scheduled to debate the affirmative position on vivisection—her speech is fictional but borrows heavily from a contemporary pamphlet arguing the same position. She did grow up in the wonderfully named town of Killingly, Connecticut, and spend summers working in the mill there.

I have no direct evidence that Florence Mellish was Bertha's mother. Florence left Mount Holyoke Seminary after one year, in 1875, and Bertha was born in January 1877. The notion that John and Florence were Bertha's parents, rather than John and Sarah, is entirely speculation. Contemporary reports do note John's and Sarah's advanced ages and Sarah's fragile mental state. Bertha's uncle David Mellish did indeed suffer a psychological breakdown while speaking in Congress and die soon after in an institution. And though Henry Hammond clearly remained deeply interested in Bertha's whereabouts, to the extent that he was giving dramatic interviews to national newspapers three years after she vanished, the report of his death being caused by a "gun accident" is totally fictional—and of course, he never harassed the nonexistent Agnes or Mabel. He was a Union soldier, a supporter of abolition, and apparently a respected member of the Killingly community. I find the real Hammond's intense commitment to Bertha's case unsettling, but my portrayal of him here is pure invention.

I've massaged some details of the investigation. While Hammond and Florence were called away to identify a girl who might have been Bertha, they traveled to Florida, not Auburn, MA—and the girl in question was alive. The papers did report rumors that Bertha had been spotted in a mental institution in New York City, but as Florence Mellish's note to the College makes clear, these rumors were unsupported and the family found no definitive answers. The material concluding the book—Florence's responses to alumnae questionnaires, the documentation of her death, her poem, and the fact that she died on Bertha's birthday—is real.

My answers for what happened to Bertha are fabricated—I certainly don't know if she was ever pregnant or procured an abortion. For research in this area, I'm deeply indebted to Leslie J. Reagan's phenomenal, clear history *When Abortion Was a Crime*. The landscape of social attitudes toward abortion in the 1890s differed vastly from what we might imagine, looking back in our fragile post-Roe days. Despite the Comstock Laws and a dramatic newspaper exposé series on "abortionists" published in Chicago in 1888, many doctors and midwives continued to offer their services, and newspaper ads for pharmaceutical abortion aids were widespread. Ending a pregnancy before quickening was largely normalized, seen more as a process of restoring menstruation. As Reagan notes, "One physician observed in 1891 that leading ladies of the community 'not only . . . commit this crime, but talk about it very unconcernedly, or engage in disseminating a knowledge of the work among friends as earnestly as they would work for a supper for the benefit of a hospital, kindergarten, or the far-distant heathen'" (25-26). Furthermore, in the 1890s and in other eras, most women did *not* die after having abortions, despite prevailing stereotypes. Reagan writes:

Most of the women who had abortions at the turn of the century were married. Tracking changes in the demographic characteristics of those who had illegal abortions is difficult, but evidence shows that abortion continued to be a practice of mostly married women until after World War II. Yet the image of the seduced and abandoned unmarried woman dominated turn-of-the-century newspapers and popular thinking. The image of the victimized single woman spoke to fears of the city and the changing roles of women in the same way that visions of married women aborting had expressed mid-nineteenth-century

anxieties. Newspapers, physicians, and prosecutors high-
lighted the abortion-related deaths of unwed women.
(Reagan 23)

From one perspective, Bertha's death perpetuates this stereo-
type—though she is not a "seduced and abandoned" single woman
betrayed by a man who refused to marry her, she does die as a result
of infection caused by a surreptitiously performed abortion. I don't
want to contribute to a misunderstanding of the dangers of abortion in this time period, however, any more than I want Bertha
to be perceived as yet another dead fictional queer woman. I see
my fictional Bertha as a casualty of reproductive injustice, twice
over—first through the damage caused to the family by John's abuse
and control of Florence, and then through Bertha's own inability
to access medical care that would have saved her life, allowed her to
pursue her academic ambitions, and perhaps enabled her to grapple
with her own sexuality (and to understand what I see as Agnes's
asexuality).

Bertha Mellish lived in a profoundly unequal society, a Gilded
Age marked by panic over the enfranchisement of Black voters,
uproar about immigration, exorbitant displays of wealth, violent
suppression of labor activism, and distress about the overthrow
of so-called "traditional" ideas about gender roles. Some of the
constraints that constituted her particular cultural moment will
feel unfamiliar to us—others won't. In fictionalizing the aftermath of her disappearance, I've tried to consider what it might
take for a woman of Bertha's time to free herself from those
constraints and what constraints she might not even be capable
of seeing, much less resisting. In our own Gilded Age, those
questions feel pressing.

Acknowledgments

This book has been a ridiculously long time in the making, which means an equally long list of people to thank. First, my marvelous agent, Elisabeth Weed—thank you for your tireless work on behalf of this book and my career. I can't express how lucky I feel to have found you. Huge thanks as well to DJ Kim, Jenny Lopez, and everyone at The Book Group!

I'm thrilled to be back at Soho with my once and future editor Juliet Grames, and to work with Taz Urnov, Paul Oliver, and Rachel Kowal, among others there—and just as thrilled to be working with Sarah de Souza and the staff at Corvus. My sincere thanks to you all for your care, dedication, and enthusiasm.

I so appreciate the kind research assistance of: the staff of Mount Holyoke College's Archives & Special Collections, including Leslie Fields and Deborah Richards; Sari Bitticks, President of the Auburn Historical Museum and Society; and the volunteers of the Killingly Historical Center, especially Marilyn Labbe and her granddaughter. And many thanks to Donna Albino for the beautiful image of Bertha!

During this book's long gestation, I moved through a series of home departments and benefited from more mentorship than I can describe here. At UT Austin, my most profound thanks to Lance Bertelsen for endless moral support, recommendation letters, and cover mock-ups. Michael Adams, Beth Hedrick, and Elizabeth Harris were stalwart advisers; Richard Workman cheered on my research. Dissertation fellowships from the

American Association of University Women and PEO indirectly supported this project, too. The Harry Ransom Center and UT English supported my first trip to Mt. Holyoke and to the now-defunct Norman Mailer Writers Colony, where I was so lucky to befriend Chrissy Kolaya, Jasmin Darznik, Ben Healy, and Jesse McCarthy. Several years later, at Sycamore Hill, Catherynne Valente, Meghan McCarron, Derek Nikitas, Richard Butner, Dale Bailey, Ted Chiang, Christopher Brown, Christopher Rowe, Alice Sola Kim, and Delia Sherman gave generous feedback that helped shape this novel in its early stages.

At the University of Hawai'i at Mānoa, Anna Feuerstein, Jack Taylor, Laura Lyons, Craig Howes, Shawna Yang Ryan, Frank Stewart, Cristina Bacchilega, John Rieder, Rodney Morales, Cynthia Franklin, John Zuern, Susan Schultz, S. Shankar, Gary Pak, Kristine Kotecki, Gaye Chan, Nandita Sharma, Caroline Sinavaiana Gabbard, Alice Te Punga Somerville, and Sarah Allen shared aloha. Friend and neighbor Maya Hoover kindly assisted with opera research; Ray Madigan gave support and the best dragon fruit I've ever eaten. Particular thanks to Charles R. Lawrence III and the other members of the 2013-14 Hawai'inuiākea Interdisciplinary Faculty Seminar on Race, Gender, and Culture.

The College of Wooster granted me a much-needed research leave in 2021 that allowed me to finish revising this novel, and has been a wonderful intellectual home, not least due to the support and friendship of the following folks: Kathie Clyde, Nat McCoy, Tom Prendergast, Leslie Wingard, Jennifer Hayward, Deb Shostak, Travis Foster, Craig Willse, Claire Eager, John Barnard, Anthony Tognazzini, Robin Beth Schaer, Michele Leiby, Iemanja Brown, Susanna Sacks, Christopher Kang, Bryan Alkemeyer, Elizabeth Schiltz, and of course Dan Bourne. Thanks also to my students, especially Dana Smith, Katie Markovich, Nell Gram, Margy Adams, Chann Twyman, Rocko Foltz, Carolyn Thornton, Lillie Soukup, Hannah Keough, and Deena Williams, the best research assistant in the world.

Finally, deepest thanks to: Katie Williams, trusted friend and first reader; Andrea Lawlor, stalwart supporter; Amy Boutell for query letter assistance; Jessica Kilgore for thoughtful suggestions; Tobin Anderson, whose enthusiasm buoyed me; Carmen Machado, always generous; Tricia Perry, the very best college roommate; Rachel Dalton, extraordinary friend; Liz Newbury, Aija Simpson, and Theo, who give me hope; Miriam Bird Greenberg, Rajiv Mohabir, Hilary Plum, and Benoit Denizet-Lewis for writerly support and care; Christabel Devadoss, always reaching out; Jean Lee, full of love; Alex Cox, who always believes in me; and my mother Betsy Beyer, without whom I could not have made it through a very difficult year. My love and gratitude to you all, to anyone whose help I've inadvertently neglected to acknowledge here, and to all readers, everywhere. Thank you.

About the Author

KATHARINE BEUTNER is an associate professor of English at the University of Wisconsin-Milwaukee; previously, she taught in Ohio and Hawai`i. She earned a BA in Classical Studies at Smith College and an MA in English (creative writing) and a PhD in English literature at the University of Texas at Austin. Her first novel, *Alcestis*, won the Edmund White Debut Fiction Award and was a finalist for other awards, including the Lambda Literary Association's Lesbian Debut Fiction Award. Her writing has appeared in *Tinfish*, *The Los Angeles Review of Books*, *Public Books*, The Toast, *TriQuarterly*, *Humanities*, and other publications. Recently, she received an Ohio Arts Council Individual Excellence Award. She is the editor in chief of The Dodge, a magazine of eco-writing and translation.